A Maiden's Misadventures with the Starless Sorcerer

Soul Selection 1

EmC Lorenzo

Bisellar Media

Cover book design by Santiago Latorre

ISBN 978-1-7636706-0-0 [paperback]

ISBN 978-1-7636706-1-7 [ebook]

Published by Bisellar Media

www.emclorenzo.com

To Bienvenido:
Sorry, it took forever for me to show you this.
But this is me, and I hope you're okay with that.

Chapter 1

Keri, Aberkyz

Keri, princess of the land, lay on her luxurious bed while the prince of the elven kingdom massaged her neck and back.

"My dear," he said in a sultry voice.

She purred in delight.

"Your skin is as fair as the goddesses of beauty. So delicate and soft. Your lips are as red as the blood of the high dragons themselves. How is it that every time I touch you, you seem to grow even more beautiful than before?"

That's right, keep touching me there, she thought. "You overpraise me, your highness," she snickered. "I am but a woman who has drawn a lucky card from birth in the aspects of beauty."

"Lucky as it may be, you always take my breath away whenever I see you," he whispered at the back of her ear.

She turned around and faced him, beet red. "Then I shall take your breath away as many times you want."

His face tensed from lust. "Forgive me, my dear. This conversation, touching you, arouses me."

Oh my gosh, oh my gosh, here it comes, she thought.

"I am unable to hold myself back any longer. I want to be one with you." He disrobed himself, revealing his well-sculpted torso and legs.

"Prince, are you certain of this?" she asked, unsure, even as her eyes could not tear themselves away from his growing penis.

He grabbed hold of her hand and ran it down his chest to his abs, before guiding it even lower. "I am certain. Love me, Princess."

Her lips quivered as her whole body trembled. "Oh Prince, take me, I am yours—"

"Hey, *lady*," a voice cut in. "Don't you work here?"

Keri glanced up from her handheld device, a *glassy*. It was a rectangular computer made most entirely out of glass, projecting graphics and user interfaces. The interruption forced her to pause the game and place the glassy down. Her day job had the worst timing ever. She was in the middle of conquering (and by that, she meant fucking) the elven prince in her game. And now she had to deal with this. A delivery guy stood behind the counter she manned with a sour face, disheveled hair, an unruly uniform, and—she crinkled her nose. The stench of the man was unbearable, like rotting fish soup.

The figure in front of her was a far cry from the handsome elven prince, with dreamy eyes and six-packed abs she'd love to slobber her tongue on. She yanked herself out of her daydream and asked the living disappointment in front of her, "Yes. How can I help you, sir?" Her willpower pushed her to crack a well-rehearsed, forced smile.

He slammed his own glassy on the counter. It projected multiple codes, presumably for the boxes and crates behind him. Keri stared at it. It was time to fulfil the responsibilities of a checkout lady at Padala Courier Services. She entered the codes from the tablet into the warehouse system and instructed the delivery guy where to place the packages. After she was rewarded by ungrateful expressions and a stinking breath, she moved onto the next—a man whose face rivalled the moon's surface with his acne and blemishes. Then after, another man who appeared to be mostly made of hair, came up with his unkempt beard, bushy brows and forest hair on his head. Was her job where the ugly went to work? As the hours went by, the number of packages increased alongside her overwhelming need to escape her dreary daytime job.

The clock struck four as she departed with a click-off on her work computer and cubicle lights and a jiggle in her step. Outside, she traversed busy crowds and narrow side streets with blazing neon billboards and holographic advertisements. Though everything was colorful and bright, she had her head down and eyes glued to her glassy—unperturbed by traffic noises, the buzz of passersby and the deafening music and celebration blaring from the plaza. She only looked up every now and then to make sure a car didn't run her over, nor cross paths with drugged partiers celebrating their nation's Founding Day.

All holograms and displays projected advertisements on how Founding Day came to be: more than a century ago, the whole planet plummeted into a war against monsters from another world. They invaded from rifts in space and terrorized the lands, reigning over the skies and claiming the seas. Countries militarized and fought back, but the poor and small nations tumbled and folded against the might of the alien beasts.

The extant nations drafted various treaties, remaking and unifying countries and strongholds from the survivors and untouched territories. The masses migrated to humanity's few safe havens and rebuilt anew, leaving abandoned areas of carnage and ruins that were dubbed as the lawless lands. One of the safe havens that grew their military might withstanding monsters was Keri's own country; Zuobic. Today was a celebration of that day—to remember the strength of humanity and the continued threat of rifts and monsters in their world.

That was then. There was once a cause for celebration for all the hard work that had gone into remaking the lands. *But now it's 'let's all get shitfaced, drunk and spend credits as much as you can.'* No one here ever did that type of dangerous work. The only ones who really did the dangerous work still were the military, who Keri assumed to be out there doing their job—at least that's what the media said.

Today was an excuse for federates to party, but it wasn't her style. *I'd rather spend my time playing* Love Me, Princess. But at the back of her mind, she desired to mingle and party; she just never entertained the thought for more than a second. She was content with her game, her prince and other virtual men.

As Keri entered her favorite pharmacy-convenience store, WalkBy, a drunk man with a rabbit mask over his head pushed ahead of her. She stumbled forward and fell on all fours. Her spectacles and glassy slid on the floor, sliding in different directions. As she reached for her glasses, she heard someone say, "Is this *Love Me, Princess?*"

Keri wiped the lenses with her shirt. "It's the remastered game of the year edition. All the love scenes are uncensored. It was only released recently for beta testers—" She stopped mid-sentence when she put her glasses on. The lady in front of her was curvy in all the right places. Her eyes were like heavy paintbrush strokes—alluring and captivating. Her mini gold dress revealed mountains that made Keri's own body feel insufficient. Keri gasped as she looked at the woman's beautiful face. If she had been at a gaming convention, she could swear she was cosplaying the duchess in *Love Me, Princess*, the sister of the female lead, a villain in the story.

The beautiful woman rose from the floor with her hand clutching the game. "I didn't know it came in this edition. I haven't played this in years," she said.

Keri gulped as she stood. The woman's proportions were even more spectacular up close, with a bum that was like car air bags. "Yeah, I'm a beta tester," she said as an excuse. She'd usually say that in a more confident and condescending tone, but looking at the person she was speaking to, she dismissed all that.

"Jella, come over here," a man yelled from the corner of the store.

The duchess—no, Jella—handed the glassy back to Keri. "I better go before my boyfriend picks out tequila—you know what that's like."

"Ye-head," Keri blurted out, a mix of 'yeah' and 'go ahead,' though she had no idea what Jella was referring to.

The duchess gave her a weirded-out look but smiled at her before she went away.

Alone, Keri skulked away into the empty aisles of the store. Her hand grabbed a basket, putting in a variety of junk food that she usually bought. Even after the tenth item, the body of the duchess still lingered in her mind. She squeezed her bulging side belly, then groped her semi-flat tits and saggy butt. Catching sight of a mirror on the wall, a woman in her thirties looked back at her with cat spectacles. She combed her hands through her dyed green and pink hair and tugged at her oversized blouse. How did it feel to be hot like that? Would she actually have a chance with men?

She pushed the thought away and settled for her 'real' men—the targets of her sim-dating game. In particular, she was very fond of the elven prince, and for Keri, he was enough. When she turned to the next aisle, she backtracked and exchanged two potato chip bags for veggie chips. No time like now to start a diet. Seeing the duchess in real life somehow inspired her. Deciding that was enough, she walked up to the counter with a smile but quickly stopped when she arrived next to Jella in queue. Keri was about to strike up another conversation with her but stopped, looking ahead. The rabbit masked man swung a pistol back and forth to Jella and the pharmacist.

"Robbing a pharmacy is not appropriate," admonished Jella in a strong, clear voice.

"Bitch, shut up," the masked man barked.

"Do you have eyes under that mask? There's a bank right next door." She flailed her manicured hand to the left. "Who even uses cash these days? Everything is in credits."

From the corner of Keri's vision, movement stirred. A man snuck closer to where the robber was. His square frame and slender yet vascular arms rippled as he made his way toward the robber. Though Keri felt alarmed by the implications of what the man was going to do, something about the stranger calmed her. The man bore an uncanny likeness to the elven prince from her virtual game. From his chiseled jawline, and the abnormality of his cleft chin and dimples that added to his attractiveness, it was as if he had crossed over to her reality to save the day. What was going on today? Two people resembling characters in her game, and a robbery at WalkBy? Were they filming a live-action version of the game?

"Hey," the robber muttered, waving the gun at Jella like a wagging finger. "I'm not here to be judged by some—"

The elven prince lunged at the robber, catching him by surprise. The two sprawled onto the floor, engaged in a messy wrestle. Each one tried to outdo the other, both fighting for control of the gun. Keri stood rooted, not knowing what to do, except cheer silently for the elven prince. If she had a snack and some soda, this would've been so—wait, she did have some in her basket. She grabbed one of the veggie chips and—

BANG BANG BANG BANG!

The pistol fired multiple shots.

The two men froze, their eyes bulging.

Two other customers slumped to the floor, bleeding out. Keri's heart raced at the sight, beating even faster when she saw the open wound in Jella's stomach and a graze on the side of her head.

The elven prince rushed to catch the duchess as she lost balance and fell. "Jella!"

"I gave you all the money and meds we have! Please don't kill me," the pharmacist behind the register screamed.

"I didn't...You forced me to," hounded the robber.

Keri was on the floor with blood on her glassy and chips. Her heart pounded and screamed for her to leave, but her body was frozen in place. She followed the trail of blood by sight and smell. The two customers seemed dead while Jella twitched in the arms of the elven prince.

A sudden piercing headache overrode all of Keri's senses.

The reality of her situation shifted. She envisioned an even more chaotic scene. On the floor, instead of Jella, was Keri's mother bleeding to death. The robber was replaced by her father, who held a gun and had shot Keri's mother. The elven prince was replaced by a glowing child.

The two scenes superimposed each other as if she was experiencing high doses of hallucinogenic drugs. But Keri had never been a druggy nor taken any dangerous medications in her life. She didn't even take vitamins—her money was well spent on games, plushies and posters. As the pain in her head reached unbearable levels, her jaw dropped. She took a sharp breath and screamed.

A sign, like a computer prompt, appeared before Keri's vision. But with the pain overtaking her, it disappeared without her notice:

Prima Candidate's soul is at below average health. Traces of damage are still present.

Candidate has forcibly reawakened soul fragments due to stress and trauma. Current environment under high level of threat. Scanning potential candidates, reading...status.

Complete.

Nearby souls are viable for selection.

Initiating candidacy selection.

All the hallucinations suddenly stopped. Her vision was clear, and she was back in WalkBy with the same customers as before. Two people were dead. The duchess, Jella, was dying next to the elven prince. Everyone else was on the ground with the robber still pointing his gun.

A sudden earthquake rocked the store, adding to the chaos. When it stopped, the environment outside the store had changed.

From the cool night air, heat surged as morning instantly arrived by the appearance of a large sun and two fading moons. Daylight pierced through the windows as the buildings that would have blocked the small shop ceased to exist. Unrecognizable mountains and floating rocks replaced the scenery of airships and drones with their half-off specials and late-night news.

Keri's breathing slowed. The changes around her caused her anxiety and confusion. Was this another hallucination? As her eyes darted around, she noticed everyone else's shock and distress. Some pointed at the oddity of the sun and moons, while others screamed at the floating rocks. No longer could they hear the cacophony of loud music, cars honking, random street chatter, the rushing footsteps of passersby, nor the stream of dull advertisements at each corner from holographic screens. Rather, the whooshing of the winds against the leaves and plants nearby resounded.

"Oh my god, he's dead."

"Is this a new advertising gimmick? Another linko plugin?"

"It's an outlier!"

"Shit, he's getting away."

Keri couldn't distinguish between the voices. She couldn't feel the glassy in her hand, but then she heard someone call out, "Help!"

The elven prince begged under his breath as he applied pressure to the woman's wound. "Someone, call an ambulance. Please." Jella now lay motionless, soaking in her own blood.

Keri ignored the ferric smell in the air as if she was used to it and used the linko that was attached to her left ear. "Call cannot connect. Service not found," the linko automated system jingled.

"Anyone?" the prince asked in a guttural voice.

"There's no service," answered Keri. This had never happened before.

Her focus returned to the woman bleeding in front of her. Was this actually real? She told herself that it was just another hallucination. Was it possible that staying up late last night playing games had impacted her? This was a game—a very real game.

Right. The villainous duchess was dying, and the elven prince could not save her. Wait. But that wasn't the plot of *Love Me, Princess*. Was this not a game?

As people in the store cackled and ran around like headless chickens, the pharmacist brought out a first-aid kit and helped the prince before checking on the other two people lying on the floor. The few customers still alive either ran out of the store, called for help or hid in the back. The minutes flew by as panic turned to arguments and heated discussions.

"This is an outlier, I tell you. We're all doomed!"

"If it's an outlier, the army will rescue us, I'm sure."

"Monsters are going to eat us!"

"I don't want to die like them..."

Jella had stopped bleeding, but she was still deathly pale when the elven prince finished with the first aid. "Don't panic. The army will come soon if this is a new outlier," he declared out loud.

"Who the fuck are you?" someone shouted at the back.

"He looks much braver than you," another retorted.

The elven prince caught them talking and sighed. He rose to his feet and flashed a badge just enough for everybody to catch a glimpse of it before returning it to his pocket. "I'm Lake Deskenn, a member of the Zuobic army. I can't wait for a rescue to arrive because of the state of my colleague. I'm heading outside to look for help. Can anyone please watch her while I'm away?" He addressed the whole room, where everyone was in the midst of their own crisis and turmoil.

The customers shut their mouths and avoided his gaze.

"I'll watch her," the pharmacist volunteered, who was still sitting by the dead.

"Thank you," he answered.

Keri filtered out the ugly faces of the customers and homed in on Lake's angelic face. When he had started talking, she interpreted it as, "Do you want to come with me?"

She nodded quietly in her own little space against a shelf. So she sat there for quite a while, waiting, while Lake said his farewell to Jella and prepared. Then, when the elven prince was ready, he left. After a few moments, she followed him.

Questions flung in the air, asking her where she was going, what she was doing and so on. But she paid them no mind and kept following her dream man's trail. The elven prince had asked for her, and as the princess, it was her duty to oblige.

<u>Outliers.</u> It was a term coined by the surviving nations of the new world for all of the strange occurrences after the first rift's appearance. The military used these as labels to categorise the proper approach in dealing with them and educating the population.

Some popular ones are:

- Outlier #1 or alien beasts or monsters from another world.
- Outlier #2 are called rifts or portals, where all the monsters ome from.
- Outlier #3 is the environment and the name of the new world inside rifts.
- Outlier #7 are the artefacts, items and treasures found inside the new worlds.

The most popular world that seem to appear regularly within the rifts is called Bisenti—this is only known to the armies and guilds. It is a very different world from ours, which is Silaw.

—page 4, Lake's online notes from OUT01 - Basics in Outlier

Chapter 2

Lake, Aberkyz

The pop-rock song "Breaking Hearts and Breaking Cores" boomed over the speakers in one of the hangars at Zuobic's army base in Aberkyz. A silver mech, 15-metres-tall, rested in one of the bays, its engine humming softly underneath the song's bombastic beats. Next to it was a slightly bigger red mech with a gigantic sword attached to its back. While their systems ran, Lake was analyzing the engine's performance on a wide multi-panel monitor on a scaffolding, which was at the level of the mechs' heads.

A young man in his twenties with short red hair and freckles walked from behind him, wearing the standard combat suit of the army—dark grey cargo pants, a vest and a full-body skin suit underneath. He spoke to him, but his words were drowned out by the songs. Lake continued reading the screens while bobbing his head.

The young man grunted and waved a hand over the glassy on one of the tables. The music suddenly stopped. "Is it done yet?" he asked, the irritation in his voice obvious.

Lake whipped back in surprise. "Hey, Tony. Almost there. I just need to do a final check, then you can do a test run."

Tony crossed his arms. "You sure? I didn't score highest from the last mission, and trade all my hard-earned merits for top of the line cores, just for you to blow it up."

"Come on, Tony, I wouldn't recommend this if I couldn't do it."

He stared hard at him. "That doesn't give me much confidence coming from you, Starless."

Lake stretched his neck out of reflex. He hated hearing that nickname. "See, it's working fine." After running another scan, he showed the screens to him.

Tony watched the screens closely as the tensed muscles on his face relaxed. "So it is. Ready for a test drive?"

Before Lake could say yes, a voice shouted from below, "Careful, Tony. You might get the starless disease." Another man in a matching combat suit was on the ground floor with a bunch of guys. Lake recognized them all from Tony's squad.

"You might not rank up to Captain," said another.

"Or worse, get demoted," responded the first, then they all laughed.

Tony snickered and shouted back, "Hey, hey, you know nothing's gonna beat the ace grad of the training program. Not even starless disease. Who closed their first rift on their first mission?"

"You, Tony, you're awesome," said one of the guys as the rest clapped their hands and chanted Tony's name.

Lake was about to leave, but Tony pulled him back. "Hey, where you going? Haven't paid you yet. We still have to see if the test drive's okay."

He looked at him with a deadpan face. "You know I'm good for my work, Tony. That's why you come to me." He touched his linko on his left ear and reached his right hand out.

After staring at the hand, Tony smirked. "For someone who sucks at spell casting, you're a real robot nerd." He reached for his linko and shook Lake's right hand.

A small screen that only Lake could see appeared before him. It said: *[3500 credits transferred]*. After confirming his money was in, he descended from the scaffolding through an escalator, passing the guys who kept cheering on Tony and chiding him. At the door, Jella stood there in her combat outfit, with a scowl on her face.

Lake continued to walk away from the mech wing with Jella in tow. "I can feel you breathing on me. What?"

"Why do you let them treat you that way? Is it because we're all soldiers now and you're a still a trainee?" she asked.

Tony, Jella and Lake all started at the training program of the Zuobic army in the same year. Both regular soldiers and sorcerers attended classes that were similar, but Lake had courses specific to sorcerers. Due to his inability to pass them, he was stuck repeating them, unable to graduate.

Yes, of course, yes. They're doing what I want to do! How do you think that makes me feel? he thought. "No, definitely not. Tony's an ass but he pays well. You know I need the money." He earned a salary as a trainee for basic living expenses, but it wasn't enough to pay for his needs and interests, especially mechs.

"You know I can always get you that part time job in my family's mech business," said Jella. "You won't have to worry about money anymore."

He shook his head. "I want to be a sorcerer, you know that. I want to save people. I don't want to just keep tuning up mechs and embedding systems. I want to be where the action is."

Her face was crestfallen. "So it's a man-thing? Are you insecure about Tony? That's why you let him treat you that way? Because he might be really good, but you have some strengths that can't compare—"

"Please don't go there," he interrupted her. "We both know that's not really true. We're both soldiers—at least he has the spades to prove it."

She closed the distance between them. "Sorry, I'm just stressing about another assignment coming up. I won't bring it up again." She reached out and clasped for both of his hands.

"I'm sorry too." He exhaled a big breath.

"Come, on, it's Founding Day. We should be out there partying." She squeezed his hands.

"Like this?" He pointed to his greasy overalls and her combat suit.

"No, silly. We'll change of course," she said. "I wanna see the parade."

He smiled and let her drag him away.

***

On the train heading to Aberkyz Plaza, Lake stood in the aisle wearing soft jeans and a buttoned-up violet shirt that Jella had gifted him before. It showed off his arms and a bit of his chest. When he found out how much it cost, it didn't sit right with him. He could buy a rare-grade monster core for just what the clothes cost. He wasn't sure how to wear such luxuries.

Jella sat in a seat right next to him, wearing a gold minidress with slits at the sides. "Stop fidgeting. It looks nice. It shows off your shoulders and arms. Don't worry about how much it is."

"What if I rip it? Or I spill drinks on it?"

"If it happens while you're having fun, that's fine. Get out of your head." She clasped his hand and squeezed it.

Lake's attention turned outside the windows. The sun cast a golden hue at the bottom of the sky, giving skyscrapers a golden glow and adding a picturesque view with the lights on each window. The train they rode connected to rails that were twenty meters above ground and went around and through most of the buildings in Aberkyz and the other zones. It gave the passengers a majestic view of the ground.

The streets below lit up with holographic billboards, advertisements, and images of lifelike plants, trees, and flowers. People bustled along the streets, shopping in the stores or crossing through the escalators and moving walkways linked through the top floors of various buildings. The roads themselves had lanes and signs that lit up with directions for both cars and pedestrians. Lake remembered his textbooks informing him that road lights changed upon an attack or an emergency, guiding people and cars to safe places. If a rift were to appear inside a building, the building itself would be lit up red and mark itself as dangerous. All of the building's doors, windows and walkways would shut off and block entry with titanium walls, caging the danger inside. Trapped people would be made aware of escape routes through holographic marks on walls, ceilings and floors. These led to underground panic rooms and living areas blocked by multiple automated gates. But ever since the invention of ward generators, this had happened less and less within Zuobic. They prevented rifts from appearing within zone walls, but it did not stop the occasional monster from drifting by from rifts opened in nearby lands. That was why the army was still vigilant and active.

"For my next mission, I'm heading to Kermoz," Jella said softly, her eyes on the floor.

Upon hearing the zone, Lake felt a sting in his heart for both of them. "Is that why Maggie wanted to see you?"

Her face confirmed it. "She is the doctor assigned to check on the mission participants."

The memories of the past started dredging up in his mind, but he suppressed them and told himself that it'd be all right this time. The abandoned zone was already free from monsters, and Jella belonged to a capable squad. He was about to ask why they had to go there after it had been blocked off from everyone for so long, but said, "I can't ask why you're going in there, right?"

"Not unless you have a major-level clearance."

His brow rose. "That high?"

"Apparently."

"So Maggie knows all about it?"

"Only where I'm going," she said. "She also couldn't stop herself from telling me that I should break up with you. An ace mech pilot should not mess around with a trainee and repeater. She said you'll only drag me down."

There it was—the breakup conversation. He wasn't surprised that Jella's best friend would tell her that. She was right, after all; he was dragging her down. For all the reasons in the world, he still couldn't understand why she wanted to be with him. She was the best mech pilot in their graduating class. Though Tony was the overall ace with his superb fighting, no one outclassed Jella inside a mech. She was smart and beautiful, too. She could have any guy in their class or even in the army. But she chose him: the Starless Sorcerer.

"I told her what I always say," continued Jella. "To mind her own business. She's a great friend, but she is not the best person to be giving relationship advice."

He smiled at her comment. When it came to her life, no one could really make her do something she didn't want to.

The train's broadcast chimed in with an upbeat leitmotif. "You have arrived at Platform 80, Zone Aberkyz. Thank you for riding ECCENTRY—the only outlier core powered monorail system in the world. An outlier train for an outlier world. Until next time."

Jella dragged Lake over to the doors. "No more of this negativity, time to party." The train cruised to a stop and the doors slid open. They could hear the music and beats from the plaza and the lights shooting up in the air.

For the next two hours, as the sun slowly disappeared and gave way to the night sky, the two lovers danced and drank. The stress about their relationship, his precarious position in the army and other issues were all forgotten thanks to strong drinks, dancing to fast-paced songs and make-out sessions with his girlfriend. He could worry about all of these things next week. Today was all about fun. *Jella was right. She was always right,* he thought.

When both were sweaty and smiles painted their faces, the hunger in their bellies made itself known. They decided to grab a quick bite from a nearby WalkBy for something easy to digest, and maybe more drinks. Lake made a beeline over the cold section where all the drinks were, while Jella hovered over the food. The choices of juice, alcohol and carbonated drinks swirled in his vision. He lost track of what he wanted and tried to concentrate on why he was there. Maybe it was best to have water or coffee. He didn't feel like getting even more wasted, and wondered if Jella felt the same. "Jella? Jella, come over here," he shouted.

After a short while, Jella came back with a basket full of rice cakes, cured meat and cheese. "I ran into someone who plays *Love Me, Princess*," she said.

"The porn game for women?" he asked.

She slapped him lightly on the shoulder. "It's not porn. It's a reverse harem dating sim game, okay? It only looks that way with all the sex scenes. But in real life, dating is kinda like that, if you're a bit promiscuous."

"Whatever." He proceeded to grab a coffee bottle from the shelf.

Jella stared hard at him. "You know what, you kinda look like one of the target men in the game."

"Target men?"

Her head tilted. "Mhmmm, that's what you call the men the main character tries to hook up with. Was it the knight or the prince? Maybe the duke?"

His eyes squinted. "Is that code for role playing sex?"

The teasing look on Jella's face quickly disappeared and her body turned rigid. Lake was about to ask what was happening when he turned and saw a masked man draw a pistol and threaten the pharmacist up at the counter. His hand swiftly reached for his linko. "I've sent out an emergency signal for our location. ETA: 5 minutes. Until they get here, I can tackle him from behind while you distract him," Lake suggested in a low, stern voice.

"I should be tackling him, you're the trainee," countered Jella, matching his volume.

"In that dress?"

They both looked at her heels and mini dress. Her face seemed to consider his words for a moment and then defended, "If I had a weapon, this would be different." Jella marched over at the counter. She erupted with specific observations to confuse and draw the robber's ire.

Meanwhile, Lake crouched and stalked behind the robber, getting into his blindside. At the peak of the robber's fury, Lake jumped up behind him and pushed him to the ground. Lake stole the gun from him, but the robber caught his arm and tried to get it back. They rolled over the ground with Lake wrapping his legs around his enemy, trying to gain dominance over the struggle. His training kicked in, and he tried to pin the man down, but the massive man was strong enough to resist. Lake was unable to execute his moves fully as they continued to roll around. The robber head-butted him in the nose, which momentarily made him loosen his hold. The man grabbed hold of the gun again and was about to shoot him in the face when Lake kicked the robber's arm. The gun took off with multiple shots.

The sound of the gunshots arrested Lake's senses. He quickly looked around and saw two customers on the floor. He briefly thought about attending to them, but stopped when he noticed Jella was unbalanced and about to fall. The wound on her stomach and head alarmed him. "Jella!" He let go of the robber, rushed to her side and caught her as she fell to the floor.

Screams and shouts echoed in the background, but Lake tuned them out. Jella twitched in his arms, her eyes glazed. After quickly scanning around, he found diapers on a nearby shelf and put it over her wound. At that, her body calmed, but her skin paled.

"Help," he begged as he searched his memory for anything that could help his girlfriend. Healing runes came to mind, but he quickly pushed that aside. He couldn't even cast basic attack spells, so healing was out of the question.

Lake thought back on his medical training, then cursed at himself. He had failed those classes in his first year, but he tried to at least remember anything that could help. Something that was related. "Someone, call an ambulance," he pleaded again.

Maybe if he wasn't such a useless trainee, he would actually be able to help. Maybe if he wasn't the Starless Sorcerer, he could easily cast a healing spell. Maybe his father was right. "Anyone?" Was it going to be like this again? Was he going to lose someone in his life again because he couldn't help?

"There's no service," said a little voice close by.

No service? We're in the most technologically advanced zone in the world. How can that be?

The pharmacist came to his view with a first-aid kit. "Here. Do you know how to use it?" He took out a medgun from the kit and passed it to Lake.

He nodded. Finally something he knew how to use. With quick movements, he put the pieces of the gun together, locking a canister filled with green liquid. He pressed the nozzle over Jella's open wound and slowly pressed the trigger. Green liquid oozed from it and solidified over her stomach area. He kept at it until the whole wound was covered with the ooze and the bleeding stopped. Then, he covered the wound on Jella's head as well.

The pharmacist had slid a watch-like device around Jella's wrist and reached for his linko. "She's stable for now, but she needs a doctor to check if there's damage internally."

Those words gave Lake a bit of perspective. His pumping heart quieted a bit, though his mind still raced. Jella would need a doctor, but if there was no service, he could run for help and—his eyes widened. The whole world outside was changed: open skies, a large sun, two moons, floating rocks and various plant life that clearly didn't exist in the vicinity of Aberkyz or Zuobic, for that matter.

Everyone's cries and curses finally made sense as he heard them. He scanned WalkBy for the remaining people. There were around eight of them in the store, including him. Where was the robber? Someone said something about him, then he understood he had gotten away and left two people dead.

No rifts should be able to open in Zuobic. The army had made sure of that. So the only explanation was that this was a new outlier. Something that warps a whole place into somewhere else? What kind of surprise was the world throwing at them this time? "Do not panic. The army will soon come if this is a new outlier," he declared out loud.

"Who the fuck are you?" Someone shouted at the back.

"He is much braver looking than you," retorted another person.

Lake sighed. These people were civilians caught in a new outlier. He had better gain control over the situation and then—and then what? Was he going to play squad leader to a shop full of civilians without weapons or backup? If only he had spells. *Stop. Jella needs me.* He forced himself to calm down.

He rose to his feet and produced his army badge briefly for everyone to see. "I'm Lake Deskenn, a member of the Zuobic army." Technically, he was still a trainee, and the starless badge he had shown proved that further. Real soldiers had to have at least three stars on their badges to signify they had graduated from the training program. But none of the civilians knew that, so he kept it as that.

"I can't wait for a rescue to arrive because of the state of my colleague," he continued. "I'm heading outside to look for help. Can anyone please watch her while I'm away?"

The customers shut their mouths and avoided his gaze.

"I'll watch her," volunteered the pharmacist.

"Thank you," he answered.

Lake scanned the shop for the items they had. He picked out some cleaning materials, bottles of alcoholic drinks, tape, matches, a lighter and other items. He went to the toilet and made molotov cocktails. After that, he placed them all in the bag from one of the dead customers, after emptying out their personal items. Then he added some food and water.

Packed and ready, he bent down to Jella. "I know you'll probably hate me for going out, but we don't have options. Hang in there, okay? I'll find help," he whispered, then kissed her.

After putting some fabric over the heads of the deceased, the pharmacist moved next to Jella. "I'll take care of her," he said.

Lake nodded and left.

<u>Ward Generators</u> are under the outlier #30 category or any technology that uses outlier cores or items that are integrated in society. Mechs and military weapons are common examples when this is discussed. Less popular ones, like the ECCENTRY train and energy companies that use cores, are usually overlooked but play a very important part of modern federate life.

Ward generators are powered by cores, these house-sized devices send electronic waves into the ether, disrupting high concentrations of source and pushing them out to nearby areas. Source levels are never high or compressed inside the wards therefore eliminating the danger of rifts ever being created.

—page 8 Lake's online notes from OUT01 - Basics in Outlier

Chapter 3
Keri, Somewhere not in Silaw

The fresh breeze, vast open space, lush greenery and tall trees relaxed Keri for a bit, though her stomach was in knots. Despite having no idea where she was nor where she was heading to, the atmosphere had a pleasant feel, far different from the hustle and bustle she would have encountered in the noisy city streets of her home zone in Zuobic.

The surroundings weren't the only factor that tickled her senses. The scents of citrus and spices filled her nostrils as she stalked behind and out of earshot of the elven prince. She admitted that she had little to no concern over the condition of the dying woman back at the pharmacy. What mattered to her was the man before her; Lake. Now was her chance to take him.

Options on how to do that blanked in her head. All she wanted to do was smell him. *Gosh, he smells so nice, even from this far*, she thought. *Can I lick him? Or maybe accidentally put my thigh onto the middle of his legs?* This wasn't the time for daydreams, but what could she do? Her reality and fantasies had collided when she saw the living version of the crown prince of *Love Me, Princess*.

A shadow moved behind her. Taking by her surprise, she immediately turned about and fell on her butt. Something was touching her foot. *Is it a bug? A snake? I hate snakes!* She screamed. Lake came running to her rescue. Hope swelled in her heart. *I'm saved,* she thought. "There's something clawing my foot. Help. I want to walk again," she pleaded, almost too dramatic.

Instead of helping, Lake just stared blankly.

She wondered why he wasn't helping, so she cried out louder, "I don't wanna die here."

He raised a brow and said, "A bamboo fell on you."

Her screeches halted. "Huh?"

"It's a very light tree."

She looked down at her feet and saw one yellowish bamboo on her foot. It was not even a complete tree due to its decaying state. "Oops." She broke an embarrassed smile and moved away from it on her own.

"Please turn back. It's not safe here. More bamboos might fall on you," he said, then turned away and continued on his journey.

After getting back up, Keri kept following him, a little closer than before. They did not talk as they walked. But after a few incidents, like Keri almost falling in a pit full of bones and blades, and almost eating an odd-looking spiked fruit out of curiosity, Lake had to save her. He had pulled her back from the pit and smacked the fruit away from her hand.

"Seriously, you need to go back," chided Lake.

"I won't. You need help," she said with confidence.

"From you?"

She looked unsure. What could she possibly do to help? Manual labor was not her thing. "Uh, yeah. I mean, I don't look good for lifting heavy things, but you can't be alone out here in the middle of nowhere. Like you said, it might be a new outlier. Someone with you isn't really a big deal."

Lake considered it for a moment, then grumbled, "Fine. Do what you want." He continued walking.

Keri followed while her stomach kept growling. At this hour, she would normally be eating dinner in front of the TV. Then she remembered the veggie chips she got from the store. "So what kind of outlier is this? Did the ward generator not work?" Her hands rummaged inside her backpack.

"The ward generator only prevents rifts from opening in our zones, not whatever this thing is," answered Lake.

She opened her chips and munched on them. "I heard the freezones and colonies are having a tough time maintaining the older generators. They were asking for more help from us. Either help with repair or buying the newer version we have. It was on the news."

"Quiet. We're not sure what's around," he hissed. He gestured at her chewing mouth.

She pouted and put the chips back in her bag. Was eating so wrong? She was hungry, and she was trying her best to appear worldly and current—not at all like her usual shut-in self—so he would take more interest. Did that not help?

As they emerged from the forest, they had unknowingly stepped into a dance hall, inside the ruins of what might have been a mansion or castle. The missing ceilings and broken arches let the daylight straight in, driving away the shadows formed by the tall, dilapidated posts and crumbling walls. Rusty armor, moldy statues, faded artwork and grassy floors suggested a high-class of grandeur before decades transformed them into wreckage.

Keri rushed up a large, cracked staircase leading to a balcony. She squeezed through a split door and gasped.

"Wait," Lake screamed as he leaped over the dents and fractures on the floor.

When he reached her, he let out an amazed breath as well.

A whole view of a city in shambles gazed back at them. The mansion, the roofs and ceilings of the houses were all open and light freely went through. Mold and plant life grew through the cracks in the streets. Tall towers and buildings remained in half of what they used to be.

"A different world," she breathed out.

"Yeah," agreed Lake.

"Wait. If this is a world like the ones inside the rift, who is supposed to help us now?" Keri turned to him with a blank stare.

He ran a hand across the ageing statues. "I was hoping an army squad would be here. We were transported in Zuobic territory, so they might've scanned for anomalies and tried something already. Zone surveillance runs every hour."

"How would they get in?" she asked.

He shrugged. "They've been experimenting with rifts. I'm sure they have something that can help."

Keri liked the idea of this new world. Breath-taking, untouched, historical, but at the end of the day, there were no food deliveries, showers or online shopping. She wasn't built to be stuck in a place like this. "And if not?"

"Closers, maybe?"

She never really met any closers before. Those types of people rarely existed in Zuobic, since they had the army to protect them, and she rarely left her home zone. "Have you ever met—"

Lake grabbed Keri and yanked her under the cover of a half wall. "Quiet," he mouthed and peered at the side.

Right below them on the street, a wolf the size of a trailer landed with a bloody harpy in its mouth. Its eyes glowed red as it chewed on the half woman, half bird monster. Above, three more harpies flapped their winged arms and scratched with their talons at the end of their human legs, desperate to save their ally. But the attempts proved futile as the wolf's blue and grey fur defended itself from sharp attacks, shining like metal in the sunlight.

Keri's eyes were glued to the fight. The incoming breeze brought the mixed scents of blood, feces and urine. She gagged. "Are those—"

"—monsters from another world, outlier #1," Lake cut in. "We better go."

"I-I can't," pleaded Keri in a hushed tone.

"I get it. You're tired, but you have to—"

A rainbow-colored snake, twice the length of Keri's height, slithered up her ankles and coiled on her thighs. Its forked tongue slid in and out, taking in the scent of chips and fabric softener. Every centimeter it climbed, the more an icy chill spread through her body. She gulped. The quarrel of the monsters and the attempts of the princely man to calm her seemed to not enter her ears. Silence reigned instead. All she was able to worry about was the long, fat snake. Its face levelled with hers, opened its mouth and threatened her with golden fangs.

She screamed.

Keri swiped her arms in a flurry, by reflex, and managed to knock the snake back. It rebounded and lunged again. Before it hooked on her flesh, a rock smashed the head. Guts and blue blood splattered over her.

Adding more pressure to the rock, Lake heaved, "Are you okay?"

With eyes locked at the dead snake, she stammered, "Uh-ea."

A harpy cried from above as it caught Keri's scream and started searching for her.

"We have to leave." He pulled her for a run.

They dashed to a staircase that led to a cobbled, broken road. They weaved against fallen posts and narrow streets and hopped over pits and debris—all to flee from the harpy's view. But the monster's agility and keen perception detected them whenever they tried to lose it, hiding under covered architecture.

He scouted for a place to hide, dragging her by the arm and checking on her. Keri's hyperventilating and rolling perspiration signified her heightened distress. A dark, tiny entrance to a collapsed building captured his attention.

"We're almost there," he said.

Inches from the entrance, the harpy dove down, grazed her and flew back up. The steel-like talons claimed a chunk of her back muscle. Keri toppled forward and slammed against a huge rock. She cried out on impact. The flying monster swooped back in for the kill. As the talons loomed over her, a flaming bottle shattered across the harpy. Fire splashed across its wings as it narrowly missed Keri and fell beside her. Another bottle flew at the harpy. The fire blazed even further.

Lake sped to her side and pulled her up. Her weight sagged down, but he mustered the strength to carry her all the way to the entrance. The inside of the building had all caved in, leaving only enough room to crawl around. He put her down in the corner next to the fallen ceiling. He waited alongside her, peering at the opening.

The harpy staggered to climb off the debris, flapping clumsily. As it lifted into the air, the wolf from before pounced out of nowhere. Its jaws locked onto the harpy's neck. It struggled for a few moments, before its life pulsed away. Sensing death, the wolf laid its prey down and snacked on its feathery flesh.

Lake returned to Keri. "Are you okay?"

Despite her condition, she felt no pain nor feeling anywhere. "It doesn't hurt."

"We should be good now. The wolf ate the stupid bird."

Feeling the adrenaline rush through her, she asked, "What was that earlier? Was that magic?"

Glancing back and forth at the wolf eating, he propped himself on the ground. "Not magic, but sorcery. The art of using an alien alphabet and graphics known as runes to manipulate source. Ergo sorcery. But that wasn't sorcery, it was a regular molotov cocktail."

She frowned. "Aren't you from the army? Don't you do sorcery there?"

"I'm training to be a sorcerer. I'm not good at casting spells yet."

She tried to smile. Dots of perspiration appeared on her forehead and at the side of her neck. "That means you can kill more monsters, right? You can just blast them away. Your hands go *pew-pew.*"

Lake opened and closed his hands. "I doubt that. I've never really cast any combat spells before."

"Why not?"

"I... Combat spells require a lot of source, which I barely control, and can barely convert it around me for one," he explained. "I usually get tired, sweat, and break my concentration."

"You just gotta train, right? It'd be easy-peasy in no time."

He snickered. "I don't know about easy. I'm actually the worst in my class."

"So you start at the bottom, everybody's got to start somewhere," she said in a positive tone after coughing twice. "It's like being level 0."

He rested his arms over his knees as he sat. "Trust me, at the academy, everyone's great. Birds like that—they can take it down in a blink. They can cast spells of lightning and ice. Except me."

She tasted blood in her mouth before she said, "All I saw was a guy taking down a robber and blasting a monster all to help a damsel in distress. I'd say you're a hero." Something around her body caressed her, willing her to relax.

He shrugged. "All I'm good at is circuit boards, capacitors, transformers—machines. Not sure if that makes me a hero. And a damsel in distress won't sneak up on the hero and surprise him."

Though Keri's skin was already pale from the lack of sunlight due to her hermit-like ways, a deeper pallor set in. She smiled at the comment and said, "I like *Love Me, Princess.*" She wondered who turned the aircon on.

"The game?"

"Mmmm..." she answered with a groan. "I love games like that. I don't know why, but I always thought I was the princess. Being a princess with healing powers would be nice." Coolness still wrapped around her like claws, penetrating deep within her skin. She did pay her bills this month, so she wondered why they cut off her power.

His face relaxed. "Maybe in another life?" Lake gave her a thoughtful expression that turned grim. Blood continued to flow out of her, pooling where she sat.

"That'd be cool. Me attending balls and social gatherings. Trying on dresses..." Her eyes fluttered from opening and closing until it steadied to a close.

"Wait. Wake up. It's dangerous for you to fall asleep. Stay with me," Lake shouted loud enough to get her attention but not to alert the monsters outside.

"Huh, did you need something, Prince?" she asked, half-awake.

"Prince? Your name. Tell me your name."

"The prince was supposed to ask that first," she replied in a soft voice. "But that's okay, you were charming enough and saved the princess."

"Come on. Stay with me." He slapped her face a few times.

"But I'm not going anywhere..." Her words fell flat as her breath finished and life fled from her.

Chapter 4

Lake, Somewhere not in Silaw

Lake gaped, wanting to say something, anything. But no words formed. The academy had schooled him on how to deal with the loss of life—a part of his psychology classes. Yet now that death was right in front of him, his brain blanked. None of the lessons or steps presented itself.

He knelt for a few hours, staring at the lifeless body of the girl—who until a while ago was alive and well. Maybe if he had practiced sorcery more, he would have known how to cast healing spells, then he could have saved her. A strong self-loathing welled up within him for not taking any medical courses. Maybe if he was stricter and didn't let her leave, she would be alive and talking cheerily about inconsequential things. But that was not the case. He dallied for a while longer before nearby rumbles shook him from his distress.

Panic and fear restrained him again. He was reminded of where he was and the danger present. He was in another dimension where monsters reigned supreme.

Jella popped into his head. His mind nagged at him to return to the store and hole up in there until help arrived. But the thought of dragging the girl's corpse or abandoning it weighed on him. After an internal struggle, he piled rocks over her body as a type of burial.

A prayer or a farewell crossed his mind. But he knew nothing about her—not even her name. He settled for a proper salute and left.

Retracing his steps, he hurried back to WalkBy. Corners, large debris and shadowed pathways covered him from danger. Whenever he felt tingles on his skin or unknown sounds alerted him, he doubled back and sought another way.

Taking deep breaths, he reached the entrance to the convenience store. He had, at last, made it. Luck sided with him this time as he had no encounters with monsters or any other beings.

He pulled himself inside from the frame of the door. "I'm back. We have to lock the place down. Everything is crazy out there," he rambled as his drumming pulse eased. "Monsters are eating each other and—"

His foot stepped on something sticky. He looked down to find blood stained the sole of his shoes. A frown creased on his forehead as he followed the source. The red trail snaked up the back aisles and around the corner of the store. As he turned, he covered his mouth as bile and alcohol erupted from inside of him. Inside one of the fridges, next to the ice cream and desserts, butchered human body parts were carefully stacked and stocked neatly on the refrigerator's shelves. A sign on the glass door above it read, *Special: 10 credits per kg.*

Lake bent down and vomited as a wave of nausea enveloped him. This went on for minutes before he grabbed a water bottle and washed his face and mouth. Then he drank a whole bottle. When he recovered a bit of rationality, he hastily looked up and searched for Jella. His mind screamed for him to run and get out of the place, but he had to find her. He had to know. A quick, thorough scan told him she was not one of the heads. Quickly, he backtracked to the counter where he had left her.

She was still there, lying peacefully, still with a bit of color on her cheeks. Her chest slowly rose up and down. Joy and relief blossomed in him before he rushed and picked her up in a princess carry. As he stepped through the door, a soft flowery smell stopped his tracks. Before he could check where it was coming from, he felt blades stab him in the back. Once, twice, then multiple times. He felt the blade go through him over and over. Blood leaked from his lips. Strength left his arms as Jella fell to the ground outside. Then it disappeared from his knees as his face fell into the dirt. Footsteps sounded from behind the store and stopped right next to him. He craned to see who or what it was, but his consciousness slowly faded away.

Analyzing scenario... 8... 45....100%. Building Candidate profile.
Candidate profile built. Building system specifics for candidate.
System built. Scenario analyzed. Requirements completed.

Rewarding: Soul of Hero.

Re-initializing... 10... 64...100%

SOURCE

(aka. Outlier #10, mana, S-type, rift energy)

Source is a form of energy that presented itself after the first rift opened. It is invisible to the naked eye, but monster attacks and spells from sorcerers are able to show it just before they are executed. Sorcerers and other outlier items and man-made devices are the only things that can sense it.

It is present everywhere in the air, land and sea. Source is what powers the rifts and the worlds inside them. It is the air the monsters breathe. Particularly, monster cores (outlier #6) are the manifestation of pure, compressed source found inside of the monsters' bodies, making them highly valued loot for traders and closers.

One theory behind the source's existence is that it is a completely different element, existing on another dimension plane that has been superimposed onto Silaw.

—page 10, Sorcery and Rune Casting Theory

CHAPTER 5

LAKE, ARMY HEADQUARTERS, ABERKYZ

Inhaling a big mouthful of air, Lake jolted awake. Before him, bright noon sun hit the windows of the four cornered room, illuminating the various students rising from their seats. The instructor had turned off the digital screen in front of the room and walked out of the classroom talking to a student who had follow-up questions to the teacher's discussions. Sitting in the last row of seats, Lake released a long breath and sucked in air again. It felt like he was drowning. He patted his chest and stomach—no signs of pain or bruises. Only phantom pain haunted his body. Had it all been a dream? After a few more breaths, the smell of the wooden seats and lemon scented freshener blasting from the vents calmed him down. They were familiar. He was back in the sorcery academy building, which was in the compound of the Zuobic Federations Army.

Lake sat alone inside the classroom, staring at his glassy. Notes projected back at him about how cumin and curry could be used as poison against lizard-type monsters. Was he reading this? His head whirred. From WalkBy, to the monsters, to all the deaths, he recounted them—all felt real. The run of his thoughts hard braked at his girlfriend.

His linko dialed Jella's number upon voice command, but the answering recording played instead. He tried again. Successive failures made him stop. He tapped his linko three times until a round glass covered his right eye—a monocle. A digital screen came alive over his vision—this was the optic or video mode of the linko.

Connecting through the database of the army, he commanded, "Search Jella Saison, profile, status."

When her profile came up, he reached his linko with his right hand and tapped his left on his glassy. The contents of his search transferred over to the bigger screen. The screen detailed Jella's public profile and mentioned that she was out on a mission. He tried getting details of the mission, but a warning prompt appeared:

> Sergeant-level clearance needed.

Mission? He remembered something about Kermoz. *Is she in Kermoz?* He searched for Tony and his status. It showed his squad was doing prep work for drills. He quickly packed his things into his bag and left, arriving at the mech hangar soon after.

At one of the closest bays, Tony headed towards his mech with the rest of his squad. "Hey Starless, what you doing here?" he asked.

Lake spared him a nod, but he went straight to a muscular woman in her forties with long braids who was standing close to them, checking her glassy. Lake saluted, then asked, "Captain Falon, may I please speak with you?"

Falon was one of Lake's former instructors in the academy back when he started with Tony, Jella and Maggie. She got promoted after that and formed her own squad, taking Tony and some of his former classmates with her.

Her large brown eyes glanced briefly at him before crinkling her large nose. "Student Lake, I told you not to come in the mornings. You know the engineers get crabby when they see a student fiddling with the mechs. Makes them feel deficient and incompetent. I don't want another complaint. With that being said, nice job on Red Giant's upgrades. Tony's performance is a lot smoother," she said.

"Thank you, Captain. I came here for something else. Can you tell me where Jella is?"

"You know I'm not allowed to give students information on soldiers." She focus was on the glassy.

"Captain, please." He tried to look into her eyes.

Falon grumbled. "Kids these days. Did you two have a fight before she left? Did she not tell you anything?"

"Something like that."

She fiddled with her glassy, then read Jella's file. "Ah, I see. Says here she's on a mission from Major Cervantes to investigate Kermoz. Probably why she didn't tell you anything."

Lake breathed a bit easier. It seemed like she was alive and okay. Was the whole thing a dream? It seemed to be so real. His hand reached for his back where he had been stabbed.

"Yeah, no issues. She's fine. Says here deployed 19-Feb, Monday," continued Falon.

"19? Wasn't yesterday 14?" he spoke softly.

She narrowed his eyes at him. "Are you high? Listen, I know your grades are not in the best place, but keep trying. Maybe sorcery and the frontlines isn't really for you. There might be something else, you know?"

His eyes quickly darted to a screen on the walls displaying the available bays in the hangar. It showed both the time and date of today: 28-Feb. *Founding Day was the 14th. That was last night, wasn't it?* he thought. He murmured something unintelligible in response.

"Good. Have to run drills now. Good job on the mech again and get out before people see you." She patted his arm and left for her squad.

Fourteen days had passed since the incident or dream... His brain veered off to several possibilities: from new aliens to reality warps and many other inconceivable things. As anxiety and a touch of insanity gripped him, a violet icon obstructed his view. It appeared, not in the monocle of his linko, but right in front of him, like a holographic screen. Thinking a new update had arrived for his linko, he motioned his hand to confirm, but no download bars popped into view.

He wondered if it was broken. When his curiosity piqued at what the notification may say, something else intruded:

Selection completed. You have been rewarded with the Soul of Hero Profile.

Welcome Hero Candidate.

Please complete heroic deeds to earn Soul Points and grow the Hero Soul.

He skimmed through the blaring words on the screen: 10 coins. The strange writings were similar to the phrases in his death dream before he passed out. He closed the screen with a thought and figured it was a virus instead. A virus that allowed him to control his linko with thoughts instead of gestures and motions and had holographic screens. He wondered who had created this breakthrough tech. The situation called for a diagnostic check.

An event alerted in his linko. He popped up the monocle again and saw the details of his practical exam. He had an exam starting in thirty minutes? What was going on? His heart leapt. Distractions like the virus and the death-dream were for another time. His focus should be on getting his grades on track—or selling his abilities to slavers or black-market traders would be the most lucrative approach to making money for sorcerers like himself.

He cursed and banged a fist on his head, as if the gesture would make things clearer for him. Lake opened files in his linko while he made his way to the training rooms of the academy where he would take his practical exam.

The beginning pages of the file explained the steps in rune casting—a basic action in sorcery. Sorcery was the study and use of alien symbols and graphics that evoked supernatural phenomena to affect reality. These manifested as fireballs, lightning bolts, wind gusts and other acts of nature using the hands and fingers to direct them.

The advent of sorcery began around when outlier #2 arrived, portals or rifts in space which led to different dimensions.

More than a century ago, a rift had opened up in a now destroyed northern country. Various teams investigated the rifts, bringing all sorts of tools, scanners and more. They had found the frequency and energy patterns to be as strong as nuclear energy, but with minimal radiation. They focused on studying and harnessing this type of energy and named it source or S-type.

One day, a researcher accidentally tripped and entered the rift. When she returned, she reported monsters and strange domed towers inside. Seeing the researcher was alive and well, the northern country and its allies dispatched teams to investigate inside.

They used the latest in weapons technology: guns, cannons and mech suits clear and explore the dimension. Though they worked, some proved ineffective against other monsters. But still, they persisted.

Later on, the same researcher stumbled onto a library inside a dome-tower. The books depicted alien writing now known as runes. Through those texts, she became the first human to ever draw a rune from nothing and produce a spark of fire. The flames and strength within it reached heat levels similar to multiple grenade explosions. This phenomenon was dubbed sorcery, or outlier #16.

Since then, sorcery has been formalized and used in the academy to create sorcerer-soldiers for the Federation and other countries. The sorcerers, as they were called, were categorized as outlier #17.

Lake blinked rapidly to refresh his tired eyes. He had crammed as much knowledge as he could during his very slow walk to the training room. Once he reached the entrance, a violet notification chimed in his face:

> All heroes are skilled. Congratulations for unlocking the Soul Fragment:
> Storehouse - F.
> Description: The hero's body is familiar with the outlier energy called source.

His mouth dried up abruptly. Thinking it was another virus, he closed the notification with a swipe of his arm. He then placed his head right at the scanner. After scans read his corneas, the door opened and let him in.

The football-field-sized training room appeared empty except for fifty students patiently waiting their turn. They were either standing, sitting on the steel floors, or leaning on the cold titanium walls. Except for the doors, the only noticeable thing was a set of glass panels dividing the whole space from the control room.

Lake searched for familiar faces but didn't recognize anyone. All of the people he saw were new, even though he had been in the academy for more than three years. It was understandable since this was a class for first years.

A door across the room opened as a man in a burgundy blazer over a grey dress shirt and grey trousers entered—the standard uniform for officers. His knotted hair emphasized his wide forehead and crooked nose. Though his body was of average build, the mood and aura he exuded made him seem much bigger than he appeared. As he approached the cluster of students, their eyes gravitated to the patch of yellow stars on his left. Yellow symbolized the rank for majors. Whispers started around:

"Is that Major Cervantes? Where is Instructor Greyson?"

"Is he conducting the exam?"

"I heard she got fired for misconduct. Her scandal with a student was posted online."

"I saw that. Her tits were huge."

"I am so going to fail this exam."

"He is not that bad."

"What? Are you kidding me? He practically invented sorcery."

In the whole army, the man approaching them was the second most powerful man. He was only a step below the general of the army when it came to strength. In the whole nation, he was third, with the president taking the top rank. Still, it wasn't his near perfect grasp of sorcery nor his authority that was intimidating about him. What was frightening was his mind; it was what had given birth to linkos, ward generators, and other weaponry that they used to fight monsters. This made Zuobic the most livable and safest place in the world.

As the students continued to gawk and gossip, Lake noticed a red circle appear on the floor. The training room had top technologies that molded and changed the environment of the room to help train the students; it was capable of reenacting combat simulations. The circle numbered around fifty. As a repeater of this class, he acted quickly and stepped on the nearest one. Once the people around them saw him do that, some copied the act.

"5, 4, 3, 2 and 1," counted Cervantes at a slow pace. "For those of you standing on a red circle, stay. For the rest, please leave. You can re-take the exam after two weeks."

Everyone looked at one another, looking at the circle on the floor.

"What? What happened?" said the gossiping woman from earlier, who was not standing in the circle.

A fat man who only noticed the circle now hurriedly stepped on one.

"Too late," said Cervantes. "Please leave."

"Major, sir, I studied all day and night for this," pleaded the fat man. "I couldn't eat."

"The impromptu exercise helps weed out the potential sorcerers who are aware of the changes happening in their surroundings. If you aren't alert in the battle-field, you die. Or worse, you cause more deaths."

"This is unfair," shouted the gossiping woman once she had realized what was going on.

"I said leave," repeated Cervantes in a rougher tone.

The students who had not stepped on the red circle had anxious faces but kept their mouths shut and left quietly. All of them knew better than to argue with the major.

"Everyone else, do not celebrate yet, the test hasn't even started. That was attendance."

The students exchanged nervous glances. For Lake, he was calmer than the others. It wasn't his first time taking a Cervantes-led class. He was more than used to the improvised pre-exams, especially when he—

A spotlight appeared and focused on Lake.

"Ah, Student Deskenn, you are here, yet again. This is perhaps our third—no, fourth time meeting," said Cervantes. "Everyone, take a look at Student Lake Deskenn. This is what you do NOT want to be after three years. Still taking the same basic course, passing only in his dreams. If you have heard the rumors, yes, he is the one and only Starless Sorcerer."

Especially when he makes me an example, Lake finished his thought.

Murmurs rapidly fired across the training room. Citizens of Zuobic, or fed-erates as they were colloquially called, were bound by law to enlist as sorcerers as soon as they developed signs for sorcery—which was a feeling for source. For three to five years, they were supposed to learn to harness their potential. As stars were awarded for students' achievements, a trainee had to complete and earn the star in a basics class that utilized sorcery. It may be a basic sorcery course in medical, support, combat—any would do as a prerequisite, but sadly, Lake hadn't passed any of those.

"Omg, is that him? That's a shame. He's kinda cute," said a woman in a ponytail at the front of the row.

A man with pink hair beside her sneered at Lake. "Starless, though. He's only good for when you need a scratch."

"Girl, you've been scratching a lot of posts lately. You should rest and let me handle this," another woman chimed in.

"Not if I get him first," said the other, winking at Lake.

Cervantes looked over at the three. "I said observe. Not chat around like a noon time show. This is an exam. I see you three aren't in that mindset. You can leave."

The woman with the ponytail gasped. "But sir, the way we observe is through analyzing and chatting amongst ourselves. That's how we observe."

"Yeah," sounded the other woman. "We learn by talking."

"I find your voices irritating," replied Cervantes in a cold, indifferent tone. "Leave or I fail you in this class."

As the woman with the ponytail opened her mouth to speak, the pink-haired man put a hand over her mouth. The three looked at each other, glared at Lake, then left.

Lake smiled internally. Though this kind of thing happened all the time, it never ceased to amuse him. Cervantes was a strict teacher, yes. He would admonish anyone at fault and try to make them learn from their mistakes. But at the same time, he did not tolerate bullying or fraternization during his classes.

Cervantes inspected around the room for other complaints, but none spoke. "Let's begin."

A floating screen appeared before each student with details of what this exam will cover. To pass the exam, they had to execute any of the three spells they had learned in class: fireball, ice dagger and lightning bolt. On each side of the room, the floors slid open as a platform with a large equipment elevated into the room. It had a large glass circle more than five meters in diameter situated at its helm. The students were supposed to hit the glass with their spell for it to record its power. The higher the power, the higher the mark.

"I'll begin by calling your name, you have three tries," explained Cervantes. "Like any other tests, if this is the third time you get the excellent mark in a test, you get a star. Failure to do so, you repeat the course: Basics in Rune Casting. Understood?"

"Yes sir," sounded the students.

"Student Deskenn, you're up," announced Cervantes.

"Sir? I'm first?" squeaked Lake.

He stared at him with a deadpan face. "Don't tell me it's you're first time and you're afraid?"

A lump caught in his throat. "Uh-er-no sir."

"Good," he said. "Start basic rune casting test for Lake Deskenn."

The equipment to the north lit up as a screen with Lake's face appeared next to it. Right across was a large green circle on the floor. As Lake went to the circle, more screens flashed around him. The left ones indicated the rules of the test as well as sample videos of the three spells. To the right were choices of which spell he was going to perform.

All the notes he had taken before—the research and videos he had saved—appeared in his linko as he tried to mentally grasp what he was supposed to do. Like always, he followed the sequence in his head over and over—that was the easy part. Now for the hard part.

He summoned the strange invisible power called source. He gasped. The energy answered his beck and call without the need for him to struggle. Source was readily available in the atmosphere around him. His body needed only to absorb it for him to use it. At previous practices, half an hour flowed by before it ever touched his body. But now, he felt it the moment he called for it.

The next step was storing source in his body. Inside of him there was a metaphysical container to which source filled. Professional sorcerers, on average, could contain five spells-worth of source inside of their bodies, ready to be used at any time. For students like him, they could barely accommodate one, never mind maintaining it inside them for a whole day. But at this moment, as he filled himself with source, he felt different somehow. Usually after five minutes, he would be full and flustered, fearful of spilling source out of him or thinking it wasn't enough for a spell. But now, ten minutes had flown by and he was still absorbing source. He could feel his body hungry and thirsty for it. Like he had been starving for days and he suddenly found himself in an all-you-can-eat-buffet.

"I am a busy man, Student Deskenn. I don't have all day," spoke Cervantes. "If you can't do it just say so. Better to fail you now and move on to the others."

Though not as full as he thought, Lake knew it was more than enough for a spell. Source travelled from all over him and ended in his hands. A faint glow shined around his hands. He smirked. The process had all been second nature. He had never felt so close to the air he breathed, the power of electricity, or the solidness of earth as he did in that moment. Source, or mana, was the blood of the world—or at least that was what the alien nations believed.

The starting steps were done: source gathered and converted. Now, he had to draw. He doodled with his finger to create a snake-like pattern of orange light which condensed in front of him. This was rune one. Firsts always represented the type of nature, power or element needed by the sorcerer.

He drew a second pattern of a circle within a circle—this characterized the shape that the fire would take. If necessary, a ring, an arrow or a bird was possible. But the more complicated the shape, the harder or more runes it would require. As he composed the simplest, a ball, he maintained the presence of the snake pattern as well.

Source fueled the runes' power, and his mind kept them present. The stronger they were in the mind, the easier the release of the spell. In the past, at this point, Lake would be twisting his brows with a constipated face trying to concentrate on the two. But now, his mind retained the patterns with ease. Two incandescent runes now hovered before him.

"Isn't he the Starless Sorcerer?" asked one student.

"Yeah," whispered another.

"Why does it look like he knows what he's doing? I can barely keep three runes from disappearing."

"You're asking me? I can't even keep one alive."

The last step required the action runes. This needed one or multiple runes depending on how he desired the flame's motion to be. For now, Lake wrote the simplest house-like pattern, which meant straight ahead.

The three runes twinkled. They were complete. All that remained was setting them free.

With a swift hand movement, he grabbed and smashed them all in his palms. The light reddened in his grasp. A streak of blackness materialized through, mixing with reds.

Cervantes raised a brow. "Is that what I think it is? That can't be right," he said to no one in particular.

Lake aimed his fists at the glass of the reading equipment and opened it. Supposedly, a ball of fire would fly across the room and hit the glass. But instead, a ball of black-red fire coalesced in his palms. It grew in size by the second.

Cervantes howled, "Everyone, get back." His arms flung to the sides as his fingers rapidly wrote on air. Each finger scribed a rune over the other. When they finished, ten blue runes sparked to life. He clapped them all together and released it into the air.

A blue light snaked around Lake. When its ends connected into a circle, it flashed as a wall of water rose. When it connected to itself above and created a dome of liquid blue, the fire in Lake's grasp exploded. The impact caused the water wall to expand, but Cervantes fed the water more of his source as it doubled in thickness, containing the impact within its bounds. The explosion lasted a minute before it dissipated. Once gone, Cervantes ceased his spell.

Over the singed and glowing floor laid a flailing, injured Lake. The body-fit combat suit that he wore for practical exams was burned through, revealing his burnt and melted skin.

"Call for infirmary. Code blue," ordered Cervantes in his linko as he moved next to Lake. He cast a quick spell to heal him. The spell mended some of the melting skin but did little on the tiny embers.

"Did I...pass?" Lake managed to ask before darkness filled his vision.

He floated in and out of consciousness. He heard some chats and felt himself moving. He dozed off again and found himself in the operating room in the infirmary. On his back, he felt solid steel; it seemed like he was lying on an operating table with a glass chamber encasing him. Around him were doctors and nurses in scrub suits with hard faces and controlled, purposeful movements. A tall woman with downward-curved eyes was looking over the scans on a floating monitor along with a younger woman.

"We have much to discuss, Doctor Badez," said Cervantes, standing at the far corner of the room.

"You don't have to tell me. Now, be quiet and let me save his life," responded Doctor Badez, the tall woman with slanted eyes. "Maggie, diagnosis?"

He heard the two women discussing treatments to which Lake tried to follow, but all he heard was gibberish. Pain was absent in his state. What pressed on him was a phantom weight and exhaustion from nowhere. *What is happening? Did I pass the exam?* were the thoughts that ran in his head. He tried to vocalize them but found it hard to talk.

A white light smoke entered the glass chamber and completely engulfed the interior. The noises he heard drowned out as he fell asleep.

The **Zuobic Federation Army** has multiple bases in the country. A lot of them are in the frontlines which are the zones closest to the lawless lands, including one of their headquarters. Their second headquarter is located in Aberkyz.

Aberky is the designation of the zone which stood to be as the capital while the small z is taken from its origin—Zuobic. Most city and military affairs happened at the base in Aberkyz. It included cadet training for new soldiers and student training for sorcerers.

—*page 22, excerpt from Travel Guide to Zones*

Chapter 6

Jella, Hospital Room, Aberkyz

Jella did her business in the public toilets on the hospital floor in a hospital gown. It had been days since she was placed on this floor with nothing to do but wait. The hospital staff kept telling her that she was unwell and that she was unfit to be anywhere else. But physically, she felt fine. Her body felt so fit and healthy that she thought the nurses were insane to think otherwise. She wanted to smack them in the head every time they told her she couldn't leave. Well, it wasn't like there was anywhere for her to go to. Everything about what she was doing before this was hazy in her memory. It seemed like there was a block in her mind that she could not overcome no matter how hard she tried. To add to her confusion, a floating yellow screen kept appearing in front of her face. This had happened before, but like last time, she ignored it. The feeling of not being in control of her own mind was draining her.

She finished and flushed the toilet. When she washed her hands, she found herself staring at the mirror. Her hand brushed past her cheeks. Something was different about her. "I am me," she said to herself, feeling both doubt and certainty.

After a couple rounds of walking from the toilets and around the floor, she finally felt a bit tired to walk back to her room. The door was ajar and she could hear people talking inside.

"What are you going to do about Lake?" asked a woman's voice, who Jella recognized as Dr. Badez; her insufferable doctor who kept insisting she was suffering from an unknown condition.

"I won't lie, I thought this could be good for him. But it seems, the changes are more harmful than good. I will have to think more about what to do." Jella didn't recognize the other voice. It was low and domineering but had a certain eloquence to it.

"What about the other three?"

"I have not located them yet, but I have people looking," the stranger replied. "And the ones here?"

"In the same circumstances as Lake, they tried to use source, but their body or mind unfortunately did not make it, despite my team's efforts. They were not in control or even aware of what they were doing. Their cadavers might have some use. But you and I both know that dead sorcerers are useless in the lab. The source departs from them as soon as they die, leaving nothing to experiment on, truly tragic," she sighed. "But as for Mr. Deskenn, I believe his training may have given him an edge to be cognizant, so I advise to keep him alive and well, not dead. While Ms. Saison's abilities set her apart from the rest."

"Noted. You're the expert," he replied. "I should make the general and president aware of this new outlier. We have probable cause now that outlier #14 does exist, and is not just a theory."

Jella opened the door wide and came in. "Is that what I am? A new outlier?" she asked.

Badez and the stranger who seemed strangely familiar, looked at her in surprise. "You are here. This is Major Cervantes, you've met him before in the army. We'd like to talk to you about your condition." She gestured for her to sit on the bed.

Jella ignored the bed and sat on the couch next to it. "Are you actually going to answer? Or is this another test?" She had regularly questioned her about what she was doing here, but she kept on insisting she rest and that they would talk about it some other time.

The man with a wide forehead stepped up. "Sergeant Jella, I do not mind if you cannot remember me. The important thing is, has anything come back to you?"

"Do you think I would stay here if I knew where my home was?" retorted Jella.

"Sergeant Jella—"

"Stop with the sergeant thing, I don't like you calling me that," Jella snapped. Then she thought, *I'm not even sure that's my name.*

Cervantes clipped his lips shut. Then after a moment, he produced a glassy from his pockets. He faced the screen towards her. A video played, showing the inside of a WalkBy. A man with a rabbit mask threatened the customers, pointing his gun at them. They were all stunned still. A young man jumped out of the corner and wrestled with the masked man. Shots were fired, killing two and injuring one young woman—her.

"The night of the Foundation Day, about two weeks ago, between the hours of seven to nine in the evening, this happened, and you were there," informed Cervantes. "The odd thing about this is the next part."

The video blurred, seemingly wiping out all of the chaos that had just ensued. What remained was an empty store with all the products laid neatly on the shelves. No blood. No mess. It was as if nothing had ever happened.

"Passersby heard gunshots, but no witnesses could testify as to what had happened that night. Strange, since a massive crowd was on the streets. Then, this was recorded three days later. Same camera. Same store. No cuts or edits."

He plucked a new video file to play. It showed the same untouched, pristine store, then it blurred to a scene where everything was a mess. Products were on the floor, the drawers of the medicine cabinets and the registers were open, and blood stained the counter and walls. The customers were all on the floor unconscious, including her and the young man. The clip ended there.

"What is—what?" Jella had a hand over her mouth. Then she reached for her stomach, then the side of her head where she had been shot. Was that why her mind was blocked?

"Now you know why we want to know what happened."

Jella searched her memories. She could hear screams in her head, laughter, and something else. Her mouth quivered as she spoke, "There were a lot people. Panicked. Confused. I remember feeling scared and tired. And then there's this smell, something sweet, fragrant. Something...I can't."

Badez sat on the bed across from her. "Jella, your body has changed. Your body has high-cell regeneration without having a catalyst, a spell or drugs to help it whenever it is damaged. If you are harmed physically in any way, you heal much faster than anything known to man."

"Am I dying? Is it those things that make me brain dead? Like my body is okay but my brain isn't. Like you just said?"

She shook her head. "I have to be honest, we don't know what this is. Head trauma takes a long time to heal. Don't force yourself. Your ability may be external in nature, not internal. We want to run some tests, are you okay with that?"

Her mind felt like it was sinking, threatening to implode within her. But she managed a nod.

"Good, we'll get started. But before that, can you do something for us?" Badez turned to the door as a young woman with shiny long black hair and small facial features smiled.

The young woman waved at her. "Hi Jella, it's me, Maggie. Your best friend."

Jella stared at her then averted her gaze.

The corner of Maggie's mouth drew downwards, and her dark eyes threatened to water; but that was only for a moment. Her face quickly turned stoic. "That's okay. We'll get there. We'll chat about clothes and our moms soon. For now, is it okay if we record something?" She produced a half-palm-sized cube from her pocket. It was a cubex, a recording device usually paired with linkos.

She shrugged. "Whatever."

<u>Army Ranking.</u> Civilians who train to be soldiers are called cadets while sorcerers are students. Both are given badges with stars for sorcerers and spades for soldiers. Maximum stars and spades are 3 before the next rank

Cadet/Student: 3 white spades/stars
Private: 3 blue spades/stars
Sergeant: 3 green spades/stars
Captain: 3 purple spades/stars
Major: 3 yellow spades/stars
General: 3 orange spades/stars

—page 50, Lake's Notes from FORM1 - Squads and Formations 1

CHAPTER 7

LAKE, HOSPITAL ROOM, ABERKYZ

Lake breathed in the fresh air of the gardens outside and felt the morning sun warm his aching body. His arms were outstretched while he sat comfortably in his hoverchair. Patients and families chatted and laughed around him, the repeated chug of the sprinklers and the smell of flowers served to relax him. The time outside was much needed. He had holed himself in the past couple of days in his hospital room recovering from his wounds, being tested for his condition and watching videos of the incident from the training room.

Amazed, scared and excited were the emotions he had felt re-watching it. Had he really cast that spell? And in that short amount of time? Did he really almost blow up the training room? He was at a loss for what this meant for him. Was this finally the start to his career as a sorcerer? Or was this another block in his path? Either way, he couldn't help but feel positive about it.

He mentally created a list of things he'd like to try with his new abilities, that itemized safety precautions and increased control. Suddenly, Cervantes appeared from the hospital's back entrance and started towards him. "Sir, I—" He was about to stand when Cervantes waved a hand.

"Relax, Student Deskenn, you're injured. No formalities necessary," said the major. "How are you holding up?"

Lake was taken aback. It was rare for Cervantes to ask how his students were, but he took that in stride and felt a small joy well within him. "I'm well, sir," he said, trying not to appear too happy.

The major towered over him as he stood next to him and nodded. "Good, good. That means you can handle this."

"Sir?"

"There's no easy way to say this: The results from the tests came up. You have a rare condition we have not seen before. Your body is now so in tune with source it can easily absorb it. Very rare and very special."

He knotted his brows. "Sir, isn't that a good thing?" He recalled his past experiences and other slow sorcerers taking too much time casting their spells.

"It is for us sorcerers. But whenever you cast runes, an abnormality comes up. Your body seizes. Your heart rate and blood chemistry all shift to dangerous levels. It's like you're having a heart attack and being poisoned all at once. It is very unfortunate, but interesting, nonetheless." Cervantes produced his glassy and showed him the results of his tests.

Lake stared at the glassy with shock. "Sir? What do I need to do? Is there a cure?"

"Dr. Badez is working on something. I'm not an expert, but when it comes to medicine, I wouldn't rely on it that much since this is all new."

A bunch of questions ran through his head. Maybe he could help dissect the problem? Maybe he can make a device to help himself? There should be a way to be a sorcerer. "Sir, I don't understand."

He looked him straight in the eye. "I would rethink about your prospects of becoming a sorcerer if you want to continue living. You might have something better to offer the army instead."

The scent of the flowers, the chattering of people and the chug of the sprinklers seemed to all stop in Lake's head. Gloom and darkness overcame him despite the sun's bright morning light. He'd heard those lines from everyone—from his professors, his classmates, even Jella. But he'd never heard of it from the Major. A big part that kept him focused and determined was the father of sorcery and outlier technology himself, Major Christopher Cervantes. He had somehow convinced himself that if the godlike person that Cervantes was did not say anything about his dream of becoming a sorcerer, why should he listen to others? They were all beneath him. But now, even the sorcerer-major himself had said he was not worth it.

Lake managed a nod to something Cervantes said, before the major bade him goodbye and left. He honestly couldn't handle any more than that.

He exhaled a despairing breath. For each step he noticed himself taking towards his goal, he was always, always stopped in his tracks and pushed back down. When he got accepted to the academy when he was sixteen, his father refused to sign the waiver just because he didn't feel like it. Mr. Deskenn had said, "You have no business saving people when you can't even save your own god-damn family." Depression plagued him for a while. But after two years, when he was of legal age, he tried again, and he got in—without help or hindrance from his father.

The second time he felt like this was when he took his preliminary exams in the academy—he had shown an aptitude for sorcery only to discover he had meagre and pathetic talent. And now...Lake tapped the controls for his hoverchair, maneuvering himself away from the gardens and back inside the hospital building.

A tiny speck of excitement and hope had sparked in him when he cast the spell during his exam. Somehow, he knew, he knew that he could cast the spell. Source filling him up was like a desert welcoming the rain. But something had stopped him again, like always.

When he re-watched the recordings of his exam for the nth time, theories stemming from denial sprouted in his mind. He'd lost concentration; the equipment was faulty; there was too much or too little source in his hands. On and on, he kept thinking of what else could be the culprit of the explosion—not daring to think about his actual condition—his *illness,* as Maggie would put it. He mumbled to himself, "I should check my equipment again. Its status should be—"

A violet screen popped up in his vision, causing him to stop in the middle of the hallway on his way to the elevator. It showed his name with other confusing text.

> CANDIDATE STATUS:
> Name: Lake Deskenn | Profile: Hero | Coins: 10
> Activated Fragments: Storehouse – F , Hero's Retreat – F (innate),
> Available Fragments Left: 1

His immediate thought was that the virus affecting his linko was interrupting him again. But when his hands felt his ear, he froze. He wasn't wearing his linko. "What is this?" he asked himself, staring forward with wide eyes.

"An elevator," answered a soldier inside the elevator, holding it open.

The death-dream he'd had of WalkBy came to him. The exact font and graphic interface was the same as the one before he got stabbed. Why was it appearing here in his head? Was this the cause of his new condition?

"Yo, Starless, you coming, or you gonna stare out all day long?"

Lake snapped his attention to the soldier in the elevator. He only now recognized Tony. "Ten, please." He advanced his hoverchair until he was inside.

Lake kept his focus on the screen in front of him. He waved a hand over it, but it didn't disappear. Was there a new embedding technology for linkos that wired itself directly in his optic nerve? No, that's impossible—he would need surgery for that. He went to surgery recently, but that was for the spell incident, not this. Plus, the timing was off; he had already seen this screen even before that.

Once the elevator closed, Tony eyed him weirdly. "What's with you today, Starless? Heard you got blown-up. Did that mess up your brain? Well, it would, if there was something to mess with." He snickered.

Completely missing the question, Lake asked, "Has there been any linko updates lately that makes you see screens like Light Screen Technology?"

"Uh what now?" His face crumpled.

He forgot not everyone spoke mech-nerd like him. "L-screens. You know, holographic panels and floating displays?"

"You mean the ones we use in mechs and control rooms?"

"Like the ones in the training room," he concurred.

"Nah, I only see 'em in a mech. Think there's a head implant that makes you do that. But it ain't good for combat. I heard it made people woozy," he said. "It's not like I need them. I kick ass without them. Easy."

"Thanks." Lake continued to inspect the weird screen in front of him. His finger brushed over the text Storehouse.

Another screen appeared:

> Soul Fragment > Storehouse - F. Description: The hero's body is familiar with the outlier energy called source.

"What happened at training?" asked the soldier. "Was it a curse from a monster? Or you develop some kinda phobia? Or you a schizo?"

The elevator chimed as it arrived on the tenth floor and opened.

"A spell," said Lake, interpreting the question for the reason he was at the hospital. He waved bye and floated away on his hoverchair.

Was the Storehouse the reason for the ease in spellcasting? Then the blowing his face off part was a part of his condition? He touched the second fragment.

Another screen appeared:

> Soul Fragment > Hero's Retreat – F (innate).
>
> Description: A hero can live and fight another day. Open tears in space that allows the hero to escape. The current rank of this fragment has various limitations.
>
> Innate: This fragment is born from the candidate's soul. Not purchased or inherited.

"What's that face for?" asked Maggie, who stood waiting in his room. She was fiddling with her glassy.

Lake kept quiet as he hovered close to his bed.

"I know you don't want me to be here. I don't want to be here either. But I'm one of your doctors, so let's get it over with, okay?" she said, then proceeded to tell him his status. The staff would still need to check on him for one more day before his release. Then after a bit of physiotherapy and runotherapy to get back into fighting shape. It was a type of basics training and meditation through an instructor's help.

"You should count yourself lucky Major Cervantes asked for runotherapy for you," continued Maggie. "This is only available for *real* soldiers. Students have no business—"

"Does my condition make me see things?" Lake interrupted.

Her face morphed from irritated to confusion. "Hmm? No. At least not that we know of. Your body responds to source quite well, but to runes, the opposite. It almost seems like it doesn't want you to rune cast. To me, it seems like sorcery isn't right for you at all—not like it was. Maybe there's a correlation with illusions, but I think if you are experiencing this, I'd say it's stress."

"Stress?"

"Emotional, physical. I know you are under a lot of pressure. Jella told me some things." Her volume dipped low at the end of her words.

Lake whipped up to her and locked eyes with her. "She told you about me? I know you two are best friends, but we're—"

"—a couple? Are you sure about that?"

That caught him off guard. "What do you mean?"

Maggie bit the inside of her cheeks as she fiddled with her glassy. A jingle sounded in the room as Lake picked up his own glassy by the nightstand. Maggie had just sent him a video, so he played it.

Jella was in the video in a hospital gown just like him. Before Lake could ask where she was or how she was doing, she spoke, "Hi Lake, I'm sorry I have to do it this way, but we should stop seeing each other. I've thought about it long and hard. I want to do a lot more in my life, and I feel like we're going in different ways. I need to concentrate on my career, my missions, and being with you doesn't work with that. I'm sorry. I hope you have a good life." The video ended.

Lake was quiet as he stared at his own glassy. His head blanked.

"Jella and her team came back from their mission a day ago. They're in Jaz trying to recuperate," said Maggie, regarding him closely. "She asked me to deliver this to you. She said it's hard to send it directly."

She mentioned some other things, but Lake tuned her out. He remained quiet and slightly brooding. Just when he thought his shattered spirit was already too much to bear, his broken heart added to his despair. He hovered close to the window and looked out at the crowded streets, concrete jungle and colorful buildings of lights and advertisements. This was how he spent the rest of the day until night, staring, watching, breaking.

Chapter 8

Keri, Somewhere in J-Law

Out in the far north of the Federation, approaching the desert sands of the lawless lands, green, tall plant life dwindled with cacti sprouting in their stead. Grasses faded into dry rocks and hills of hard black and brown soil. In the middle of a dirt road, merchant trucks braked to camp. Drugs, firearms, mech pieces and monster parts filled each transport. Anything that had something to do with monsters, rifts and a way to kill them were precious cargo. At the rear, a large trailer-truck braked as a percussive banging inside it pervaded.

Inside the truck, in tattered pants and a dirty poncho, Keri slammed at the metal truck wall. "Please let me out. I am a citizen of the Federation. This is illegal!" she screamed.

After the weird death-dream she'd had, Keri awoke in a dark, stinky truck. A number of people rested and waited with her, having vacant, hopeless eyes, poverty-stricken appearances and malnourished bodies. No matter how she looked at it, she was being trafficked together with these people. The act was illegal in the Federation; but for the other nations, it's a less than favorable, but legal enterprise. With the decrease of inhabitable lands and an increase of monsters, black market trading opened their doors wide to any who had the money and resources for it.

She was dying to leave, figuratively and literally. Unattended buckets and bowls for excrement crowded and reeked in the corner. Human sweat and other odors hovered the air and stifled their breathing. Germs from runny noses and chest coughs rotated inside as the sick expelled them in a rhythmic pattern throughout the days and nights they had been imprisoned.

"I am Keri Bolo, a citizen of the Federation. Please let me out!" She felt a tug below her.

A boy with puffed cheeks, sunken round eyes from lack of sleep and tousled hair that covered his face, grabbed at her oversized poncho.

"I don't care, Chatterbox," said Keri. "I'm not going to stop."

"Would you pay attention to the boy?" said a dirty old woman. "They might beat us all again."

She momentarily stopped. Whenever they were noisy or rowdy, or whenever the captors wanted to, they entered and silenced them with large sticks and kicks. Some were even taken away, and never returned.

As she leaned against the wall, Keri huffed out in exhaustion and defeat. She guessed she'd been held prisoner in this truck for days. According to some of the people here, it had been a week since she had been picked up, unconscious. The smelly truck, the disgusting people, the asshole kidnappers—all of it had been a traumatizing event for her. She would've cried out in despair and confusion if not for one thing that kept her sane: the system.

A green window screen appeared before her. When she had awakened in the truck, it was waiting for her. Shock and confusion hit her upon first seeing it. But after some tinkering, staring and wondering, she believed she had won the lottery. The green system, which she had aptly named Soul System because of the various texts that had a lot of *soul* words in them, was the very system she saw in every game she had ever played in her life.

What did this mean? Could she have wound up inside a game? She had investigated and bombarded her fellow captives with weird questions:

"Are you an NPC?" asked Keri.

"An NP-what?" said a man with scars and bruises on his face.

"You know, a non-playable character? Am I inside an RPG? Or a strategy genre?" she rolled on with twinkly eyes. The man shook his head and went to sleep.

"Can you give me a quest?" Keri asked a woman in her twenties.

The woman gave her a wretched look. "Fuck off, weirdo." She moved to a different part of the truck.

After much prodding, and annoyed reactions, she had concluded that she was simply back in her own world, only a different part of it. Everyone around her, though not federates, were people of her world. And they knew well enough about the Zuobic that they'd laugh at her whenever she cried that she was from there. Nothing had changed—the way they spoke, the history, the culture—except now she was outside, probably around the lawless lands. Other theories came to mind, like the outliers the man in her dream had said. More than 80% of her was certain she was outside. The remaining 20% she thought of aliens? Either that or she was having a mental breakdown. But she didn't really care if it were outliers or if she was going crazy. This system had made her life so much more interesting.

Casually, she brushed her hair as another green window appeared. At first, the system felt very mysterious, but after a while, she found the data logs. They were a series of texts explaining the details of what had happened to her from the moment she got on the system. Going deeper, she realized it was the exact same system and interface *Love Me, Princess* used. It was basically a copy of it, which made it easy for her to navigate.

Apparently, she was a maiden candidate. She had not the slightest idea of what that meant, but she had an innate fragment that came with it. A fragment, she assumed to be a sort of skill, a power she possessed, much like it had been in the game. The skill, or fragment, was called Prima.

Soul Fragment > Prima – F.

Description: The maiden is the muse of the world. She has an affinity with Silaw, the world and his blessings.

CANDIDATE STATUS:

Name: Keri Bolo| Profile: Maiden | Coins: 50

Activated Fragments: Prima – F (innate)

Available Fragments Left: 2

Condition: Protected from harm*

The Prima skill or fragment didn't mean much to her. She felt like it was kinda useless. What she really focused on were the coins. The coins were the currency of the soul system. And if there was money, there had to be a place to spend them.

Keri cleared her throat as another green window displayed itself before her: *the soul shop*. Half of her expected swords, daggers, potions and armor to fill her view when she first saw the soul shop. She imagined rows of tabs filled with these items, much like the ones in regular RPGs. But there were only two sections that appeared before her: special items and growth. That was understandable since *Love Me, Princess* focused on the main character's growth and giving her special items to earn affinity with men and create special events.

The special items in the soul shop weren't really that special, since she couldn't understand what made them special even when she read their descriptions. They mostly mentioned something about gems and areas. What that meant—she didn't know. She focused on the second section instead; growth:

- Soul Growth - increases the soul's capacity for fragments and more.

- Body Growth - increases the body's overall physicality and physiology through fragments and more.

- Mind Growth - increases the mind's adaptability with source and fragments and more.

Like in *Love Me, Princess*, when she selected any of these, the main character changed. Body Growth could mean something simple to a fair and glowing skin; or something extreme, like the ability to turn their body into diamonds for protection, or the power to fly. A sort of randomness persisted when using it, making it a long, grindy experience. But the growth and changes mostly depended on the character's desires, needs and passions, so it did somehow always turn out to be something useful.

In any case, if she had any of these upgrades, she knew she could bust out of the truck and escape at any time. But the problem was that they cost coins. Right now, all of the upgrades cost 200 coins, and she only had 50. There had to be a way to earn some, but how?

Her head banged on the wall of the truck repeatedly, hoping the blows would knock some sense into her. She had been thinking about this same problem over and over again before she settled on two things. If this was a copy of *Love Me, Princess*, to earn coins, she had to interact with her lovers. But she didn't know who they were. Even if she did, she doubted one of them was in this truck. No dazzling eyes, knee-jerking smiles, nor ripped abs or broad shoulders. Not even any caring or affectionate personalities. No man in here was *Love Me, Princess* material.

So the next best guess was normal RPG games. In those types of games, how would she earn experience or money? *Kill monsters?*

"Grandma, I can't take it in here anymore. We will all catch a disease and die if we don't leave," complained Keri. "If they're going to keep us, they should prepare proper accommodations."

The old woman shook her head. "We're going to be sold as slaves. Nobody cares if we're sick or hungry. All they care about is money. And don't call me Grandma, I don't have an ugly granddaughter like you," she explained, a little too exhaustively. More than twice did she have to explain the situation after Keri's hysterical outbursts.

Chatterbox nodded his forehead with gusto.

"This is not okay," she countered. "Don't they know the quality of the merchandise equals the amount of money they can get? If we look and feel better, they'll get more than what was offered, right?"

"That seems interesting...looking and feeling better," a middle-aged woman agreed.

"Nobody cares about you, you ain't come close to bein' a whore," chimed a man from the back. "You look like my Uncle Sammy—big shoulders like you."

"Shut up. No one wants the opinion of a donkey butt-face like you," shrilled the middle-aged woman.

"Miss Federation lady looks like a man as well," another man hollered with a higher pitch. "Would be good if you had bigger titties so we can tell."

Holding her hands over her breasts, Keri tried to argue, but it was drowned out by a guy mouthing something crasser and more vulgar. A third voice yapped back. An older woman complained about how ugly men always wound up with beautiful women. A second lady argued about nice people having no luck. A man replied that she should put a bag over her head, and then he would nail her with his big pecker. Soon enough, the whole truck erupted with arguments and heated discussions. Each mouth tried to overlap with the other, believing in their truths and dismissing others'.

The doors rattled open as a burly guy popped his head in the entrance. "Shut the hell up, all of you," he shouted.

Everyone closed their mouths and shifted their attention. The dim light of the moon peeked over at the gaps of the door. Their hungry gazes lusted for freedom.

The burly guy selected three people. "You, you and you, get up."

Two men and a woman exited the truck.

"The kid and the forty-year-old nanny too." He picked Keri and Chatterbox.

"What? I'm thirty. I may smell bad and haven't bathed for a while but I'm definitely—"

"Shut up," he interjected.

The burly man cuffed and led them to the biggest tent in the area. A group of well-dressed people sat and enjoyed a table of lavish, colorful and sumptuous dishes inside.

As the handpicked five lined up in the front, the burly man stood before them. "Freshest catches, right here. Not much as fighters, but you can make 'em cleaners or bait. Whatever your fancy."

A stout man with plenty of golden accessories in his face and arms finished the food in his mouth and burped. "They look about to collapse with one flap from a harpy's wings. Are they at least skilled?" He chugged a mouthful of wine.

The burly man gestured at the two men and the girl. "These two were sold by their families. They work at a textile factory. This bitch used to be a cook."

"And the remaining ones?"

"Stray. Found them passed out in the wilderness," he answered. "The bitch seems to be from the Zuosh."

The stout man brightened and his triple chin jiggled. "I've heard better."

"You're tellin' me."

"I'm not crazy," sounded Keri. "I really am Zoush—"

The burly man slapped her. "You have a use for a barking dog?"

The stout man chuckled. "I can see that, or a night alarm."

"Yeah, well ya gotta teach her manners. Don't think it knows what it means to be a slave."

He laughed. "Oh, I sure will. I'll take the men as well."

The guards forced Keri and Chatterbox towards the exit, separating them from the slaver.

"You-you can't do this," shouted Keri. "I-I'm a federate—I have rights. I'm not a slave."

The burly man crossed the room and was about to slap her again, but an alarm sounded. "Now what?"

A guard entered the tent. "Bad news, boss. We're being attacked."

"Attacked? Who the hell would be attacking us in the middle of nowhere?"

Before the guard could reply, storms of bullets landed in his back as blood spilled from the holes and his mouth. He fell to the ground, dead.

"Defend the camp," howled the burly man.

Gunshots and explosions fired off outside as the invaders and smugglers battled one another. The unarmed civilians inside the tent fled to the entrance while some tore the fabric to make their own exits. From the incessant pushing and panic, Keri was forced out of the tent and onto the dirt. She rolled around as people kicked and stepped on her. After the weight cleared from her back, she hobbled away, trying to find a good place to hide.

At the corner, near a parked car, Chatterbox and a slave had their faces over soil and grass. A smuggler pointed his gun at the woman and shot her dead. He then aimed his rifle at Chatterbox. As he pulled the trigger, Keri jumped in between and shielded the boy. The bullets fired and vanished upon reaching Keri, as if nothing had happened all along.

The smuggler's brows met. He pointed his weapon at them again and fired. The bullets left the rifle, but somehow dematerialized once they reached the targets. A perturbed expression surfaced on his face. Upon checking the nozzle of his rifle, it misfired and shot through his head. He fell to the ground, dead.

As Keri hugged the boy, she peeked and gasped at the dead body of the assailant. Her body took control over her movements as she led the boy away. Finding a dark corner in between some large crates, they hid, sealing their lips and keeping their eyes out.

In the middle of the carnage, the burly man howled as he ripped his shirt off. A page-long text of green runes was tattooed over his torso with a green gem embedded in his chest. As it glowed brightly, a tremendous pressure vibrated around him. After inhaling a deep breath, he jumped high into the air and landed with a thump on the line of invaders. He grabbed the necks of two men, crushed them and tossed them aside. Then, he punched a hole through the gut of a third.

Bullets rained on him from all directions, yet they flattened themselves on his skin upon impact and fell away. He howled again, found the closest enemy and dashed to him. But before they made contact, a motorbike accelerated and smashed into him. He tumbled and crashed over a few tents.

From the motorbike on the ground, a man in a black battle suit and helmet rose to his feet. His body was strapped with knives, guns, magazines and a katana on his back. He drew the sword as he made his way closer to the enemy.

The burly man roared as he got back to his feet. His eyes blazed with fury and his body grew even bigger. He jumped high again and descended with all his weight, like a meteor crashing to the ground. The biker dodged back before impact. A big hole was left where he'd stood.

The burly man followed him with extreme agility. In the next second, he appeared right next to him. He jabbed and punched, which the biker avoided with swift precision. This continued for a couple of seconds—him striking while the other was evading. After a few exchanges, the burly man's speed noticeably slowed. His breathing grew labored and his punches were sluggish.

Taking it as a cue, the biker drew a knife from his body straps and whipped it at his opponent. A shadowy-grey aura covered the throwing weapon as it sliced the air and hit the burly man. Instead of bouncing off like the bullets had, the knife sank deep into flesh. The big man cried out but continued his assault, swinging his arms, albeit more slowly.

The biker drew two more knives wrapped in a shadowy aura and released them. Both hit the legs of the target, causing him to trip and fall to his knees. The biker quickly shifted from backing up to rushing forward. Seeing him charge, the burly man punched ahead. The biker swung down his sword, wrapped in a shadowy aura like his knives. The blade and fist met. A rebounding force caused the biker to step back, but a shallow cut was made in between the burly man's knuckles. The biker quickly drew a rifle wrapped in his shadowy aura and fired.

Bullets and shadows sprayed the big man as multiple surface wounds decorated his body. The force made him stagger as he fell to the ground on all fours as his breathing elevated.

When the rifle clicked empty, the biker tossed it aside and held his sword with both hands. Quickly, he attacked with a downward slash. He followed the strike up with two more at the sides as he made his way around the burly man. Each cut was shallow at first, but they continued to grow deeper and deeper with each strike. After a few minutes, the burly man was on the ground, painted red as his blood poured out; his flesh split open, dead.

The biker flicked the excess blood off of his blade. "Clean it up," he ordered through his linko as it blinked in the inside of his helmet.

From the stacks of crates, Keri was hugging Chatterbox with wide eyes. The battle of the two men was unbelievable, sure, but what made her jaw drop were the words of the system blaring before her. There it was—a way to earn soul coins.

Target lover #2 discovered. Earned 100 coins.

Chapter 9

Keri, Tent, Somewhere in J-Law

The invaders and saviors introduced themselves as closers. They were mostly hired mercenaries sent to close portals and kill monsters, and occasionally, retrieve stolen goods. While the closers collected the stolen property, the smugglers were imprisoned in a separate truck while their slaves huddled inside a huge tent. Keri and Chatterbox sat in the corner with the other prisoners.

The entrance flapped open as the biker entered. He tapped the bottom of his helmet as the electronic locks jingled and disengaged. When he removed the headgear, he revealed messy black hair that added to his rugged appeal. A man in his thirties with a long nose observed the mass of prisoners with small, grey sparkling eyes. His thin, dark-red lips stretched into a forced smile, highlighting his light goatee.

"Maxwell, leader of the Hairless Ape Guild, at your service," introduced the biker. "As you might've guessed, with our skills and abilities, we're closers—hired to retrieve stolen goods. We were also hired to find a boy named Charlie Chadstone. Does anybody here know who that is?"

The crowd turned to each of the boys who were with them; about ten boys total. They started asking them for their names.

At the back, Keri tapped the shoulder of the old lady she knew from the truck. "Grandma, what are they going to do with the boy?"

"Some rich family must've hired them to get their child back," whispered the granny. "Wish my son was rich too, instead of being a worthless drunk."

"The boy's parents are rich?"

She looked at her like it was the most obvious thing in the world. "Who else can hire closers?"

Keri thanked her with a half-smile and half-apologetic expression. She thought it'd be nice if Chatterbox was the Charlie they were looking for. If he was, she could've exchanged him for the bounty—or at least a ride home back to Zuobic. Then, she wouldn't have any problems. But who was Chatterbox, really?

After she had awoken, she found him clutching onto her. Her normal instinct when children approached her was to shoo them away. Contrary to popular belief, she didn't think they were cute or deserving of every adult's attention—especially with the crying and cutesy-looks. But with Chatterbox, she felt some sort of connection with him. Not just familiarity, but something extra. A psychic connection maybe? She could understand him without signing, like really having a conversation, even when nobody else seemed able to understand him. She assumed it was from a skill granted to her by the system. But something at the back of her mind told her that her guess was wrong. Moreover, she felt something odd coming from him. She didn't understand it, but she knew the condition: 'Protected from harm' emanated from the kid.

Keri shook the thoughts away. Too much thinking made her head hurt. Her sights then fell on the ruggedly handsome man in front of the crowd. She had to admit he was her type. His face reminded her of a certain knight, a king's guard, in *Love Me, Princess*—one of the capture targets. More and more, she felt like she was in a game herself with how the system rewarded her for simply meeting this person. That meant she could earn more coins by interacting with him, right? How though? *I'm overthinking this.* Shaking her head, her gut instincts told her she'd soon know. She focused on the best news: she earned coins. Though, there was something weird. If this man was #2, who was #1?

"There's no one here by that name," answered a woman who hugged her daughter and son.

Maxwell glanced at the boys again. "My bad, he's mute, so he probably wouldn't tell you his name—'cause he can't. Here is a photo if—"

"Here," screamed Keri, shooting her hand up.

His eyes scanned her. "I'm looking for a boy, not a girl, or what is clearly an older woman."

Keri stumbled to a stand, knocking a few people to the side. "Sorry. Uh yeah, not me...Charlie is here. But yes, I am a woman." He waved and pointed at Chatterbox.

Maxwell stared a few moments at her before waving her over.

Keri helped Chatterbox stand, leaning close to his ear. "Just pretend you're Charlie, you're the only mute guy here so they will never know," she whispered to him.

Chatterbox made a face, then sighed.

"What, you are Charlie?" she repeated what Chatterbox had told her. "I thought your name was Chatterbox?"

His head tilted.

"Nickname? What kind of nickname is longer than your real name? Whoever gave you that name is weird and has bad taste," she commented. "Anyway, this is perfect for me. Cause, you know, I'm like your guardian. Okay, pretend we're super close? Okay?"

He shrugged.

Her heart danced with excitement. It was great luck that the boy she rode with was the person they were looking for. She couldn't believe it. Score! "Come on, Chatterbox—err Charlie. Let's get back to your parents, with me, your *guardian*," she announced, with her hand wrapping around his shoulders.

When the two moved to the front, Maxwell wore his helmet again and began tapping the side of it as the linko jingled. "95% match," he said after the scan. "Thanks, miss..."

"Keri Bolo. You're welcome," she answered in an upbeat tone. *You can also pay me back with a kiss, but I would settle for grabbing your butt,* she thought as her vision slid down to his backside, which was hard and firm. Her hand slightly crept from her side.

Maxwell removed his mask again with a wary expression. "Is something wrong?" He eyed her hand.

"Nothing. We're just happy he can go back to his family now." She smiled, placing her arm around Chatterbox instead.

He made a perturbed face, then relaxed and faced the rest of the crowd. "The Apes will be leaving in an hour. You're all free to go, or do what you want to do," he announced to everyone.

"What about us?" shouted a middle-aged man.

"I don't care what you do," he said nonchalantly.

Yes, and leave us two together, thought Keri while licking her lips. *Can someone take Chatterbox away now?*

"You can't leave us here. We're in the middle of nowhere," reasoned the man. "We'll die out here."

The woman with children stood. "Please help us get back to our families."

Two more stood and pleaded. Then a few more shouted, asking to be helped. Soon enough, the tent was filled with screams for safety.

The grey tattoos of snakes on his neck came alive and spread up and covered the whole of Maxwell's face, painting it wholly black. His visage shifted closer to that of a reaper with his white teeth and glowing red eyes. A shadowy aura spread across the tent, causing the prisoners to shut their mouths and sit back down. Some, like the elderly and wounded, even fainted.

Keri wondered if the shadows were what was causing them to yield. If that was true, it wasn't affecting her. She didn't feel anything. Maybe it was the same as the bullets? Somehow, she couldn't be harmed. Was it something to do with her abilities? When she checked her status again, she assumed the odd *condition* was the reason she stood fine.

CANDIDATE STATUS:
Name: Keri Bolo| Profile: Maiden
Class: None | Coins: 150
Activated Fragments: Prima – F (innate)
Available Fragments Left: 2
Condition: Protected from harm*

The aura ceased as the tattoos over his face disappeared. "I was paid only to save this boy and get the goods back. If you want my help, pay up," declared Maxwell.

"But we don't have money," the man cried.

A spark gleaned from his now normal grey eyes. "Sign a contract with my guild then. In exchange for us protecting you back to the city, you'll work for us for a month for free."

"What? But that's—"

"That's extortion," shouted another man.

"Yes, it is," responded Maxwell. "So what?"

A few moments of silence hung in the air. "That's a lot of time," someone complained.

"And you're wasting mine right now. Don't like it? Don't care."

"I'll sign your contract." Grandma raised her hand.

Everyone stared at her.

The woman with children raised her hand as well. "We'll sign your contract. Please let the kids have easy jobs," she said in a defeated tone.

"There you go. Smart women." He waved at the entrance of the tent as two closers entered each with a glassy.

As the two women signed, the rest gave in. With no other course, each one signed the document electronically; DNA samples and photos were taken.

Maxwell then tapped Chatterbox on the shoulder. "Come on, your rich parents are waiting for you." He walked outside with the kid, guiding him from the back.

Keri followed a step behind. "Ah...question: Where are you taking us?"

He stopped and turned. "Us? I'm taking Charlie and those people to Zone Troef."

Her face froze. Did she hear right? This place was close to Zone Troef—that was one of the freezones. If what she knew from the internet was right, it meant she was literally kilometers away from Zuobic. How did she ever get this far back? Wait. What did he mean by *those people*?

"Can you say that again?" asked Keri.

"I was paid to take this boy home, that's it. You can go wherever."

She shook her head. "I don't understand. I showed you where Charlie was. I took care of him during our time together. I'm like his nanny."

"Please let her come," Chatterbox signed.

"Tell him," Keri urged the boy.

Maxwell had a placid expression. "I don't understand signing. If you want her to come, she'd better pay the cost. Your parents didn't cover a nanny."

Keri and Chatterbox exchanged glances. "He says let him talk to his parents over video, he'll convince them to pay."

"We're too far for network coverage. No calls here." Maxwell proceeded to the parked vehicles, dragging Chatterbox along by the arm.

Keri followed suit. "Doesn't your linko work here?"

"It's hooked up on our private network."

"Wait. I'm sure his parents will cover the cost. Just take me."

He opened the backseat of a jeep, carried Chatterbox and handed him to a fellow closer. "The transportation cost to Zone Troef is 2,000 credits plus meals. If you don't have the money, leave."

The cost was more than twice her monthly rent. It was a rip-off, but then again, she did have the money saved in her account. She was hoping to buy it with a new gaming console that attached to her linko. Being alive and safe was more important right now. "I'll pay. Do you take linko transfers? Or have a teller machine?" Her voice elevated a pitch higher.

Maxwell walked towards the driver side and got in. "No public network coverage." He shut the door on her.

"Please. I have the money. I promise." Keri banged on the window.

"Like I said, no money, no transpo." The engine started.

Keri noticed the rest of the freed people were being guided to the Ape's vehicles. She could steal one of the slaver's trucks that were being left. But the problem was she didn't know how to drive. And even if she did, she didn't know the way. Not to mention, she didn't have food to survive the travel. When Maxwell's jeep slowly backed up, she jumped over the hood of the vehicle and glued her face on the windshield.

Maxwell braked and shouted, "What are you doing?"

She gripped the wipers and the frame of the windshield tight. "Please, please, please, I'll do anything you want. Just take me with you, please." Her eyes reddened and snot leaked from her nostrils.

Maxwell stared from the window to the rearview mirror. At the back, with his fellow closer, Chatterbox had a pleading, sad face.

"Don't leave me here. Please. I'm too young and pretty to die," cried Keri. "I can't be monster food. Please."

He made a disgusted look, sighed, then opened the window. "I don't take late payments. Once we get to Troef, transfer me the money."

She sniffed away the tears and building snot. "Are you for real?"

"You have five seconds to get in. Five, four—"

"Wai-wait. Wait." She hopped off the hood and got into the passenger seat.

Chatterbox clapped in joy while the closer rolled his eyes.

"Thank you, thank you, thank you so much," cheered Keri. "You're so awesome, you're so great. You are the best."

"Fasten your seatbelt and hold out your arm." He took out a palm-sized device from his pockets.

"Do I get a reward?" she asked.

Maxwell slapped the device on her wrist. It quickly lit up, transformed into a bracelet and locked shut. "If you think about running when we get to the zone, I can find you anywhere."

Keri inspected the accessory, blinking with a faint red light. "Isn't it too early to be giving me gifts? I mean I just met you. But I'm not against a pretty piece of bling like this," she mumbled.

"It's a tracker," the closer at the back stated.

"If you try to pick it open, it explodes. If you run more than five kilometers away from me, it explodes. If you piss me off, it explodes." Maxwell changed gears and sped off.

"Wait. What?" shouted Keri.

Target lover #2 has claimed ownership of the maiden temporarily. Earned 50 coins. Total 200.

CHAPTER 10

KERI, ZONE TROEF

The travel towards Zone Troef wasn't at all that different from the previous one Keri had been in. She would still blab and complain about the deserted environment, the lack of radio reception for entertainment and the quiet company. None of the people in the car liked to talk. The closer kept most to himself looking over at his glassy, Maxwell mostly drove the car and told Keri off for being too noisy, and Chatterbox, well, signed.

When they stopped to camp for sleep or a nature break or simply to switch drivers, Keri would run off to the other closers or the freed people in the truck to chat with. Some of them tolerated her for the first breaks, but afterwards everybody avoided her or outright told her not to bother them.

Riding at the back with Chatterbox, Keri stared out the window with her face planted on the glass. "What are closers? They're like hired mercenaries, right? Why are they the only who can close rifts?"

Maxwell grumbled while driving while the other guy snored in his sleep.

"Oh, come on," she pleaded. "It's a simple question."

He looked back at her in the rearview mirror. "The monsters coming from the rift..."

"Outlier #2. I know that," she finished.

"Closers possess items, weapons or artefacts from the world inside the rift. Without those, they can't enter. "

"Oh. Ok it's like their key card to a building or apartment," she asked, tilting her head.

"You can say that. Plus, there's an issue with compatibility. If you get an item like a sword, not everyone can use that sword. If someone compatible with it uses it, all good. If someone incompatible does, well, you end up being cursed or injured—or whatever bad thing you can think of."

So that's why they are rare, she thought. "So you use your key cards, or items, to get into the rift? Can monsters come out?"

Maxwell steadied the wheel with one hand and drank from a water bottle with the other. "When the rift appears, it's only a one-way portal. Takes a while to become two. When that happens, all living things from the other side try to come through."

"What happens when that happens?"

"It means the closers that went in are dead and this shit happens." He nudged outside the window.

From the desert, they entered an evacuated town with empty houses, blown-up shops, destroyed parks and cracked, empty roads.

Keri recalled the news online mentioning programs from Zuobic helping everyone in the freezones: assisting with monster combat, providing shelter and food for refugees and more. "It looks bad. But I'm sure everyone's okay, right? The federates are helping construct more places for people to stay at and be protected from—"

Maxwell laughed. "Now, I get it." He placed the water bottle back.

She felt a tad annoyed, though she did not know why. "Get what?"

"Why you act like the way you do. You're a federate," he said casually.

She beamed. "Yes, yes, yes. I've been trying to tell people, but everyone keeps thinking it's a joke. I mean, I don't look like a soldier. I'm sure all the outside people just see soldiers. But yeah, I'm super federate."

The closer at the passenger seat awoke and scoffed. "Outside people?"

Maxwell slightly shook his head. "Sure. If that is true, I shouldn't really be suspicious of you."

"Of course. I'll pay you. I'm not rich, but I do have some money."

He nodded in reply.

Keri wanted to ask another question, but strangely the mood turned sour. Was it something she'd said? Did she do anything wrong? She didn't understand. Her head leaned back as she made herself more comfortable against the upholstery of the door. With an intentional nudge, she opened the system. She had gained 50 coins from something Maxwell had done. Was it always going to be like that? To earn coins, she had to make her targets do something to her? Interact with them? If so, then it really wasn't far off from *Love Me, Princess'* own system. It was exactly the same.

Her stare glued on the window of the soul shop. The choices jumbled in her thoughts: body, soul or mind. In the game guides for *Love Me, Princess*, it was always body that got chosen first. It was to enhance the main character's features so that they could catch the target's attention and go on a date. But with a sly look over at Maxwell, she huffed. Sure, he was definitely one of her types, the bad boy leader type, but she wasn't feeling him at all. He was just an asshole. She didn't care what he thought of her. Throwing caution to the wind, she selected soul.

> Purchased Soul Growth. Total: 0 coins
> Congratulations! Soul Fragment has been upgraded!
> Soul Fragment > Prima - E.
> Description: The maiden is the muse of the world. She has an affinity with Silaw, his blessings and the outworld artefacts.

She snorted at the notifications. Not that she was expecting anything big. The first purchase of growths was always a dud, even in the games. The least she hoped for was that she understood what the descriptions were. *Guess I have to farm for more coins,* she thought to herself.

After they passed the dead town, it was back to the endless desert and black hills. The boring view made Keri tired, so she closed her eyes.

When she awoke, they had stopped at an area with barely passable tents made of used clothes, curtains, broken pipes, tarpaulins, and ageing wood. They lined the area among grass, bushes and trees. Men and women wearing mismatched and dirty clothing cooked lunch over rusty pots and pans. Children and their parents cleaned themselves by the river and defecated next to the trees. As for the elderly and the wounded, they stared out as if waiting for something. Some stole glances over the vehicles that had stopped where Keri and the rest of the closers were. Their stares had a mix of hunger, pain and desire mixed altogether. But none stood or acted on it.

"Tell the guard she's with me, guest of the guild, if he asks," said Maxwell to his subordinate at the passenger seat.

The Ape nodded and left the car.

Keri felt a pain in her heart, though she did not know why. She felt like she was missing something important. "Who—why are these people here?" she asked.

Maxwell parked the car and sat more comfortably in the driver's seat. "Never seen refugees before, Miss Federate?"

"I know what they are and have been through. Where are the soldiers? What are they doing here? What if the monsters eat the refugees?" Her volume increased in anger.

He clicked his tongue. "If it were me, I'd have them working in the guild. Useless for them to be here without doing anything. And what are you mad for? Not like I wanted them to be here."

Keri stopped fuming. She unclenched her balled-up fists and breathed deeply. Why did she say that? "I'm sorry I don't know where that came from. I was just curious, that's all. I guess, I feel sorry for them." Even as she said those words, the feeling felt alien to her. Like it was not her own, but someone else's.

He shrugged. "I think I'm getting used to your nonsense."

She wanted to tell him off, saying it was not nonsense. Her lips ached to speak of these lives that are being wasted, that needed to be protected. Where was all this coming from? "Why are they here?" she asked.

He pointed over at the tall cement and brick towers scattered near them and after each kilometer. It went around the area and all the way as far as the eyes could see. Atop of each, one could see the noses of heavy artillery and missile launchers. The sight reminded Keri of the security walls Zuobic had that kept the zones closed from the outside.

"Zone guards. They protect the area from monster attacks," explained Maxwell.

The Ape returned into the vehicle. "Everyone captured is registered. Half of them live in Zone Rumaf and Shoef. The rest live here in Troef. She's the only problem," he reported.

"How am I the problem?" asked Keri.

Maxwell drank another sip from his water bottle, ignoring her. "Did you give them her tracking code?" He released the brakes and sped forward, nearing the closest guard tower.

The Ape nodded. "She's tied to you in the system. You'll have to register her before we remove the tracker."

"For how long?"

"What does that mean?" asked Keri.

"Twenty-four hours from now," answered the closer, also ignoring Keri's protestations. "If she doesn't get registered, the guards arrest her."

"What's going to happen to me?" she cried out.

A refugee banged against the other side of the door where Keri was seated. He was a thin man with broken lips and teeth and scars on his face. "My sister is sick. Please, someone help. Please get her a doctor. I can cook, clean, work at the mines, please." His dirty hands pounded the window.

Before Keri could even react, two guards soldiered forward and grabbed the refugee and pulled him back.

"Please, you have to help me. My sister is going to die," he shouted.

The two guards knocked him out with the butt of their rifles and dragged him away.

Keri grabbed the driver's seat and shook it. "You have to help him."

Maxwell acknowledged the guards with a wave as he continued. "And do what? I'm not a doctor."

"Then get one." She raised her voice.

"Who's going to pay for it? You?" he asked in a firm voice.

"I..." Her readied counterarguments drowned out.

"Doctors cost about what? 100 credits? Then, depending on the treatment, that's like, another 1,000 credits maybe. Recovery, rehabilitation, extra meds, another 1,000 credits? So around 2,100. Can you pay for that?"

Her eyes searched for his in the rearview mirror, blazing with anger. But she had no words to say anything back.

"What if the patient is suffering from #31? Oh, forgot you're ignorant and stupid," iterated Maxwell casually. "Outlier #31: diseases and conditions brought about by monsters, source or whatever shitshow is happening in this world."

She kept her mouth closed.

"That means, you will have to pay a sorcerer to heal the patient. No way a regular doctor could drug you up to fight curses and hexes. That's what? 2,000 credits for a spell? And that's the cheap one, if it ain't that complicated."

"We only have ten people in the guild who are registered sorcerers," offered the Ape. "Only three know how to heal."

Maxwell smirked. "And we have supply issues. What are you going to do then, Miss Federate?"

Keri broke away her eye contact from the mirror and looked outside. "They need help," she said after a big breath.

He shook his head. "I don't care if you help them after you pay. But piece of advice, Miss Federate, I wouldn't be broadcasting about your Zuosh rights if I were you. Unless you want everyone knocking on your door asking for help, just like that ol' man."

The car stopped in the middle of an expansive, empty flat land. Before Keri could ask for anything, the earth rumbled, and the whole vehicle started to descend. The ground beneath them was an elevator pulling them into darkness. After a few minutes into the unknown, light peaked out and surrounded them.

An expansive canyon came to view. In between the valley, a large city lived and thrived. "How?" Keri breathed. How could a city live underground with sunlight shining right below them? The ground she had seen was missing.

"The earth above are holograms mixed with soil installed with opacity shifters," explained the closer. "Tricks monsters and people from snooping."

The canyon had houses and shops indented at its walls, with two level platforms serving as walkways and streets on both sides. Steel bridges connected the left from the right, acting as the roads where people strolled, biked and drove mini cars. Stout coiled wires extended out through the lengthy stretch of the landscape, with cable cars traversing back and forth, carrying cargo or people. Placed at significant points, near a bridge or a guard tower, mechanical cranes lifted the capsule vehicles and placed them on cables on the lower level's platform, or the other way around.

Maxwell casually waved a hand about, "Welcome to Zone Troef, Miss Federate."

Chapter 11

Keri, Hairless Apes Guild, Troef

Over the next hour, the guild mostly counted and registered the names of the rescued slaves. They set up meeting rooms with their loved ones in their guild building. Keri, on the other hand, had to make a withdrawal at the teller inside one of the offices with Maxwell hovering behind her. She was charged 3,000 credits, instead of 2,000 like the rest because Maxwell attributed the upcharge to the *VIP Treatment* when she rode in the car with the guild leader.

Maxwell wore his helmet and checked his account. "Thank you for doing business with us. Please think of the Hairless Ape Guild if you have problems again in the future," he said in a forced rehearsed tone.

"Now can you get this off?" Keri dangled the tracker on her wrist.

"You need to be registered first." He removed his helmet.

"And where do I do that?"

"Maybe we can help?" a melodious voice said behind them.

A slim silver-haired middle-aged woman clutched Chatterbox at her side. Her face had deep wrinkles on the sides of her otherwise bright eyes.

"Miss Chadstone, I suppose everything went well?" asked Maxwell.

"Yes. Thank you again, guild leader," Miss Chadstone said. "You don't know how much this means to us."

"Just doing my job. Please think of us again if you have any more problems in the future." He flashed a cordial smile.

Why is he being this nice to her when he is such an asshole to me? Is he into older ladies? thought Keri.

"Hi, I'm Vivian Chadstone. Charlie has told me so much about how you cared for him," she repeated. "He told me you were new here. Maybe we can show you around? As thanks for helping him."

She looked from Chatterbox to Vivian and smiled. "Yes, yes, yes."

***

Keri stepped out of the zone hall with Vivian and Chatterbox in tow. In her hand, she had an orange card, which had an ID photo of her, and a blue card which was her bank card. She scratched the hard plastic with her green painted nails. It was her first time having these cards and felt kind of weird carrying them around. Worried about losing them, they headed to the electronics shop and bought a linko for her.

Inside the shop, Keri fitted the new device on her ear. "This is so much better. I'm just not used to the cards." She held the device and tapped each one of the cards. One by one their details and numbers were encoded into the hardware.

The saleslady approached with a glassy. "That's 800 credits ma'am." She smiled.

Vivian touched her linko with her right hand and placed her left palm over the glassy before Keri could move. "I got it."

"I got money now, you don't have to."

"It's the least I can do to make your stay here better." She lifted her hand and left for the door.

Following his mother out, Chatterbox shrugged.

"Yes, I'm thankful. But there's a fine line between helping and abusing." Keri's face crumpled as she left the shop. Normally, she knew she would accept such easy money, so why was she so against it?

"What was that, Keri?" Vivian stopped and waited for her.

She shook her head. "Just chatting to Chatterbox."

Her face brightened. "Oh, you know sign language?"

Keri tilted her head. "Uh...no?"

Chatterbox made a plain face and nudged his head.

She turned to him. "What do you mean I have to explain? Explain what?"

He waved his hand.

"That you can't talk but we talk? What? You're making no sense."

Vivian had a frozen face as she placed a hand over her son's shoulder. "Honey, what's going on?"

Chatterbox expressed his thoughts with his hands.

"You're saying she understands you without having to sign?" she asked the words slowly. "Honey, that's impossible."

His shoulders rose and fell.

"So you were born mute, and you don't know where your real parents are. And Vivian and her wife found you wandering near a rift two years ago. You can't remember anything before that? It's sad, but at least now you have a family," interpreted Keri. "Why are you telling me this?

"See? She understands me," signed Chatterbox to his mother.

Vivian looked from her son to Keri with a blank face. Then after a few moments, worry lines creased on the sides of her eyes.

"Miss Chadstone?" asked Keri.

"Follow me. And no more talking about this here." She grabbed Chatterbox by the hand and strode ahead towards the nearest cable car.

Keri nodded and followed suit.

The party of three got into the cable car and rode above the valley of Zone Troef. Below them, they passed the grocery stores, shops for household items, electronics, apparel and other common items. As the bartering noise died down, they entered a quieter commercial area. All the buildings had at least ten floors that descended underground. Signs on each structure announced they were guild houses, auction houses, trade offices, rune artisans, mech warehouses, weapons dealers, sorcerer towers—all seemed to be of the high-end and outlier variety.

The cable car stopped at the platform next to a twelve-story building with a sign that said 'Amazing Discoveries' in bold gold letters. Upon entering, rows of shelves greeted them, storing an array of items from swords, shields, armor to archaic textbooks, robes and staves. Hats, masks, helmets and other headgear hung on the walls. They passed statues of armored guards from silver to black knights—all in different designs and sizes.

"What is this place? What are these things?" asked Keri.

"Outlier #7, outlier treasures. Items from inside the rift or from monsters," answered Vivian. "Or as I would call it, alien junk. Don't tell Riley I said that."

"Riley?"

"My wife. The owner of this lovely junkyard." She stretched her arms around the area.

People entering the premises either brought an item with a face full of hope or left dejected and gloomy. Others without any items came with purposeful walks, chatting with the salesladies for the new arrivals.

Keri stopped at the end of the hall with everyone and waited for the elevator. "What's happening with everyone? Some look like they're grieving. Others look like they won the lottery."

As the doors opened, Vivian entered first and held the door. "I guess it does seem like that, huh?"

She walked in after Chatterbox. "Like a lottery?"

She nodded. "Everyone's trying their luck on the items. Everyone wants to be a closer."

"Oh, so are they checking if they're compatible with any outliers?"

Vivian scanned her retina and palm on the controls and tapped B10. "You guessed it. The requirements for closers are only two things: Either you're a sorcerer or an item user. And we both know that very few exhibit the power to feel source. Now, everyone wants to try finding their luck being an item user."

Her thoughts fled to the death-dream she had, particularly the princely man, the sorcerer, Lake. "Are sorcerers really that rare? Can you be both?"

She shook her head. "It's as you said, a genetic lottery thing. Some are gifted with manipulating source. Others are able to use the outlier items. Most people can't do either. People see it as a ticket to riches. Because the demand for closers is so high. With the increasing number of rifts and monster invasions, I wouldn't be surprised if the demand skyrockets." Her tone had a stiffness to it.

Keri shifted her head to the left. "Is that how you see it?"

She smiled a joyless smile. "It's certainly better to have the power to defend yourself than to have none at all."

The bell chimed as the elevators opened. The tenth floor was not any different from the first except there were rooms at the back and the displays were fewer and scattered about.

"I'll check on Riley if her meeting is done. Are you okay to wait here?" asked Vivian.

"That's fine."

"Give me a second." She left with Chatterbox towards the back rooms.

Keri moved around the wide empty room full of alien junk. The silence was a bit deafening since she was the only person around. It made sense to her, since this place seemed to only be for the owner and important clients, but with everything lying about, it didn't seem to be a quality space.

Her hand tapped the glass displays as she checked for the gold necklaces, jewelry and other accessories. She gagged at the prices, which ranged from 100,000 credits to 500,000 or more. Deciding it was out of her reach, she walked over to a coat racket. But as she felt each soft and hard fabric, the tags screamed one million, two million, or five million—everything was in the millions. The tougher it was, the more it cost. She snatched her hand back. Why were they even more costly than jewelry? Her feet backed up reflexively as she stumbled onto a steel casket by the wall. A sign at the lid of the casket said: For disposing. Keri's eyes twinkled. She bent, opened the casket and saw a pile of overflowing rusted and antique items. It was the clearance pile. Jackpot.

She drummed her fingers on her chin as she observed each one. They all appeared old to her, and none met her taste. Then a spark at the bottom caught her attention. Immediately, her hand dove in and pulled out a wooden tiki. She slipped it over her head. The system chimed:

Curse: Doom detected on artefact.

Doom: Wearer of object will suffer chest pains and lung deterioration in the span of 1 week and will die until this curse is removed.

Activating Prima. Maiden is unaffected by curse.

Affinity with artefact is in effect. Maiden may now use Doom.

"Freaking shi—ow!" Keri shot up to a stand but bumped her head onto the chin of a man who was passing by behind her.

"Hey, what's the big de—are you okay?" Her face changed from bubbling anger to cooling steam after getting a good look at the man.

A muscled hunk stood tall in his 182 cm glory. His biceps and chest rippled underneath his white shirt as he rubbed his stubble. His strong jawline, lips and nose contrasted with his kind, big eyes. "Didn't see you there. My bad," he said.

Though her head still hurt, she smiled. "No worries. Doesn't hurt much."

"You sure?" A slight concern etched on his face.

"Mhmm."

Vivian appeared from the room at the back. "Keri," she called out.

Keri stood there smiling at him like a dumb dog.

The man whipped his head from her to the back, then back to her. "Are you Keri?" he asked.

She extended her hand. "Yes, and you are?"

He shook her hand. "I think she's calling you."

"Yes, call me anytime." Her smile reached to her ears as she continued to shake his hand.

His smile made her insides melt. "I meant the lady is calling you."

"Oh right. I have to...yeah." She pointed back with her free hand and made unnecessary gestures.

"I need my hand back." He nudged towards his hand that she kept shaking.

She snatched her hand back and strode off. "Right. Yes. Bye."

"It's Wayne, by the way," he called out.

She glanced back, smiled, and went along on her way.

Vivian waved from the door when she saw her. "There you are. Come on in. She's ready to see you. I'll get some drinks—I'll be right back." She squeezed her arm after passing her.

Various mannequins draped with colorful clothes from casual, formal and battle attires lined the left side of the room. Boxes and shelves stuffed with different sized books were crammed in the corner. On the right side, desks and tables took up most of the space placed with crystals, gems, office supplies, antique figurines and other junk grouped together. As Keri entered further, her nose wiggled, itching from the dust.

A sound came from a mannequin that stood at 200cm tall with a white witch's hat, a sparkling blue shawl and a voluminous dark cape. "Hi, I'm Riley. Thank you so much for saving my super cute, super loveable son. I can't even begin to thank you," it said.

Keri stared at the weird doll from head to toe, squinting at it. She thought it was some sort of sorcery. "No worries. You know, you look nothing like I imagined." She shook the hand of the mannequin.

"It's the stress. People keep asking for appraising this and that—it's so hard to keep up. Everyone wants to be a closer nowadays," it said in a mishmash of run-on words. "It's insane, let me tell you. Don't get me wrong, business is booming—but with the monsters and the new things, I can't keep up."

She tilted her head. "Appraising? I don't get it."

"I'm an appraiser—it's my ability—my power. When I touch outlier items, #7, treasures, whatever you want to call it, I know what it's used for," it replied. "Business was so dead before—deader than the undead. Nasty skelly monsters, don't get me started when there was a rift outbreak. That was a killer. Anyway, I didn't get a new client in months—then this happened and all of a sudden, I get people coming by from god-knows-where."

Keri felt a bit pressured talking to a doll. Who knew an inanimate object could blabber so much without even moving its mouth? "Then you're a sorcerer?"

"Nah, I'm a designer—well I used to be—I'm a #14, an ability user. Don't tell anyone that. We're supposed to be a rumor, not real. I pass myself off as an item user, #8, which I kinda am as well, I guess. But the items and abilities I can use are really poor for combat, I can't even save myself with them—or my own son.

That's why I hired closers. Got the money anyway, no use for it lying 'round. Closers are good for that. Money and helping," it digressed. "I heard you were a superhero too, tell me about how—"

Vivian entered the room with a tray of pots and cups. "Honey, she thinks you're the doll. Get out from under the skirt," she interjected.

The large skirt of the mannequin lifted up. A plus-sized woman with short hair crouching underneath the skirt revealed herself. She rose to her feet with a solid build and her head just over the mannequin's. "Sorry about that. I'm not usually that stiff. Haha, kidding. Oh, hi Keri. It's nice to finally see you. Come're." Riley reached out and crushed Keri in a tight embrace right on her big bosom.

So the mannequin wasn't real? She had been talking to an inanimate object all this time, thinking it was a person? *Not like it is farfetched, I mean, outliers,* she thought to herself and then said, "Nice to meet you."

Vivian cleared away some junk and placed the tray on the table. "Stop crushing her and have some coffee. What do you like, Keri? Coffee or tea?"

"You're a kidder. I like that." She let go and smacked her back.

For a woman who Keri guessed was in her forties, she smelled old like crochet, grease and grass, mixed together. "Coffee please, milk and sugar," coughed Keri, recovering from the hit.

Riley was about to sit down at the table, but instead, she went around the mannequins, lifting the skirts and robes of each one. "So you can talk to Charlie? Wait. Charlie, come here. Talk to Keri. We have to see her power. Where are you? There you are." She snatched Charlie hiding underneath a skirt and slung him over her shoulder.

"No fair. You didn't count," signed Charlie while giggling. "I wasn't ready."

"Let's play later. Talk to Keri," she urged. "Talk to her about something she doesn't know about."

"Can I talk to her about my secret?" he signed.

Riley looked to Vivian for help.

"I think it should be fine," responded Vivian. "It seems like the three of you are all in the same boat."

Charlie climbed down from Riley and tilted his head while staring at Keri.

"Your ability is to prevent you from being harmed?" repeated Keri. Thinking about it, the time the smugglers tried to shoot her, the bullets simply passed through her. So she was right about Charlie. The condition in her status was Chatterbox's doing.

> CANDIDATE STATUS:
> Name: Keri Bolo| Profile: Maiden | Coins: 100
> Activated Fragments: Prima – F (innate)
> Available Fragments Left: 2
> Condition: Protected from harm*

Vivian stirred a cup of coffee and handed it to her. "Guns, swords, curses and spells don't really work on him. It is one of the reasons why we believed he'd be okay when he disappeared."

Keri sipped the coffee, warming her insides. "This isn't the first time this has happened?"

She shook her head as her long hair shimmered from the fluorescent lights. "It used to be a floor away when we found him. But as time went, he'd disappear next door, the next street, then the next block. It hasn't happened for a while, then this—the furthest and longest time he has ever been missing. It was more than a month ago."

Charlie shrugged.

"What did he say?" asked Vivian.

"He says he's sorry he makes you worry," interpreted Keri. "He doesn't know how to stop it."

She moved closer to him and knelt. "This isn't your fault. We will find a way for you to control it, okay?" She kissed his forehead.

"By the way, what are we going to do 'bout your ex?" asked Riley.

She rubbed her forehead. "I forgot about that."

"Ex?" asked Keri.

"My ex-husband is from the army, and I asked for his help to find Charlie. In exchange, he can run some experiments on him," explained Vivian. "I know what you're thinking—it's nothing harmful. Only non-invasive tests, so that we can understand his powers a bit more."

"You already found him. What's the problem? Tell him you don't need his help anymore."

"If only that was the case. My ex has a propensity to obsess about outliers. And 14s are, as you know, rumored to be true, but no evidence has ever appeared to prove it. Except for this little kiddo, my wife, and now you, Keri. Once he finds out about you, he will not stop—even at the cost of relationships and trust."

Keri noticed a hint of regret and sadness in her tone. "Wait. Let me get this straight: Outlier #8s are people who can use items from other dimensions or closers, and #17s are sorcerers. And now, I'm an unproven outlier category which is #14? Does that mean I can go inside a rift?"

"Closers is a loose term, sometimes sorcerers can be closers too as long as they are hired by a guild or to do a job inside the rifts," answered Vivian. "And yes, you can go inside a rift. Riley and Charlie tried it once with the Apes. It was only a minute though, just to check. I'm not going to risk my family's life for longer than necessary."

"Fair warning: Don't let her ex know you're one of us. Cause he'd be really interested in what makes you tick." Riley moved next to Keri as big black spectacles materialized over her face. Her big eyes even looked larger than before.

Keri took a step back. "Uh, what are you doing?"

Vivian carried Charlie by her arms and placed him on a chair. "She's trying to use her abilities on you. Her powers work on people too, not just items. She can unveil if someone is a sorcerer or closer, or can be one." She gave her son a cup of tea with milk.

Riley placed the spectacles over her head. "Try this on." She crossed the room to one of the mannequins, grabbed the blue sparkling shawl and handed it to Keri.

It wasn't really to Keri's taste but she swathed it over her. And as she did, her whole presence glimmered. Her skin transformed into the surface of a disco ball, shining and shimmering. "What's going on? Why am I—"

She snatched the shawl from her and exchanged it for a golden scale. "Now, this."

"What am I supposed to do with—oh my god, what's wrong?" As Keri held the scale, the two women fell to their knees.

Vivian struggled to say each word as sweat slipped down her face. "Ugh, Riley. Not that one."

"Enough. Let go," barked Riley with some difficulty.

Keri quickly let go as the scale fell to the floor. "What's going on?"

Riley heaved and looked at Vivian exasperatedly. "She's like me and Charlie, but she has an affinity with everything."

"What does that mean?" asked Keri.

"Closers can technically use and hold any outlier items they want. But some items have features that work only for people who have an affinity with it. Like the scale or the shawl, some cannot activate them. Or some can only bring a part of their power, not full," explained Riley. "Charlie and I can use some to their fullest, and others just a tiny bit. But for you—"

"—I can use anything? Everything?" finished Keri, followed by a nod from Riley.

Vivian rubbed her temples. "You're going to need a sponsor or a guild—to become your cover at the very least. Have you been in contact with the Zuobic army recently?" she asked.

Riley was sitting on the floor with both of her hands on her face. "Has anyone seen you using your powers? Or using a 7?"

Nothing came to Keri except for the incident with the hot guy earlier. "There is this one thing..." She fished out the tiki she snatched earlier and told them about using Doom on Wayne. Her recollection touched on the details of the system—how she suddenly had it after a weird dream and things were happening to her—now she had this weird ability.

After Keri told her story, both were silent, but after a few tugs from Charlie, Riley snapped out of it. "You might be a new outlier. A variant of an ability user, maybe?"

"I'm more concerned about that dream you had," said Vivian. "Dying there and coming back to life here. Are you okay?"

Vivian's concerned face made Keri sincerely consider her question. "I-I don't know. I'm okay, I think. I mean, it was just a dream, right?"

She grabbed her hands. "In my experience, things like this are rarely what they seem, especially with outliers. But this might be something bigger, and a lot of people will do anything they can to find out what this is. And with the lengths they'll go to, hurting you is barely the minimum."

Keri gulped at the words. "It's just like a game. Like a video game." She forced a smile.

"I'm thankful that you told this to our family, and we're forever grateful to you for saving Charlie. But do not tell anyone else." Vivian's voice was laced with tension and danger.

"I agree," added Riley. "For the moment, I don't think you should use your powers in public—or at least not until you know more about it."

A knot started to form at the pit of her stomach. But before her thoughts could follow, Chatterbox caught her attention. "Charlie's asking if the tiki was a bad one? Something people shouldn't touch?" translated Keri.

Vivian narrowed her eyes. "The cursed artifacts. Riley, didn't you tell me you got rid of those already?" she yelled.

Riley smacked her head and spat, "Shit."

Mechanical Source Powered Suit

Mechanical Source Powered Suits were invented by a famous scientist in Thetyx even before the first rift was sighted. He created the first mech to defend against the threat of invasion from their neighboring country. During the war, they deployed the first functioning mech, **Grey Wall**, as a deterrent for more than one thousand tanks that threatened to invade their city. Before hundreds of missiles and explosives could fire, Grey Wall zoomed through their defensive lines and destroyed the tanks. It destroyed all of them, including a fleet of fighter jets.

It continued the fight towards the invading country. Due to its abject condition, it stopped at a city midway. The nuclear powered mech then exploded and left a crater, killing more than two million citizens and enemy combatants. The invasion stopped at that point, and the mech was deemed powerful but unstable in battle. It was never seen in public again until Dr. Christopher Cervantes unearthed its design.

—*MechBoy Magazine Issue #10 p. 24*

Chapter 12

Lake, Army Headquarters, Aberkyz

The days that followed his talk with Cervantes were uneventful for Lake. Since his incident, Lake was banned from taking exams or classes in sorcery until he'd fully recovered. It would also last until the instructors could figure out what to do with a failed sorcerer. To fill his time, he spent most of it doing side jobs in the hangar or doing research. Like everything in his life, if there was something stopping him from doing something, it only needed fixing.

He holed himself up in the library, reading records and backlog reports of known and unknown outlier artefacts found in rifts. Nothing came up that could help him cast spells safely. Although, he did find spells that were *safe,* so to speak. Enhancement spells were rune sorcery that brought about temporary boosts in power. An increase in strength, speed, reflexes, focus—any aspect that requires action could be boosted. It could be cast on living things and non-living objects. They helped in most situations, but were not really ideal. They took a lot of energy from sorcerers. One strength spell could feel like a ten-rune spell. Practically, it was better to cast a combat spell instead.

As he rested his head on a desk in the library, he stared at his violet system. He had also been looking for anything that could possibly give him some answers about it, and instead he found that the system highly resembled the game *Love Me, Princess*. It made him sad when he had tried to play the game; it reminded him of Jella. But also, oddly, he wasn't that crushed by it, since he also recalled that strange woman in his dream where this had all started. She was cool in some ways, and funny too. Was this system related to her somehow?

Though he found the game to be too cheesy for him, he had learned this system was the same as the one in *Love Me, Princess*. Meaning, if this was real, he could have superpowers like the main character did. *I'm going insane,* he thought and sighed.

An email jingled from his linko as the monocle covered his right eye.

It was Major Cervantes asking to see him after lunch. His insides churned as he sat up straight. Was this the judgment he had been waiting for? He wondered if they'd let him stay on as a base mechanic if he got dropped from the training program. Maybe he could be an assistant instructor?

After lunch, Lake headed to one of the army's training facilities, up to its control room where he had been asked to be. "Student Deskenn, here as requested." After a salute to the soldier guarding the door and a scan of his palms, he was allowed entry.

Inside, thick bulletproof glass windows covered the front. It had a large view of the training facility below, where most of the soldiers gathered. Next to the window were the computer panels and controls, manned by tech administrators. Behind them were rows of ascending seats for viewers which were mostly other officers of the army. At the far end of the seats, in the corner, Major Cervantes sat alone.

Lake made his way to his superior. "Sir, you wanted to see me?"

"Have a seat, Student Lake. Let's watch the drill." Cervantes tapped the seat next to him.

He stared at him, at the seat, then back at him. After sitting down, he kept his back straight and shoulders back. From the prompts that popped up on screen, the conversations about who was better and the squads that ran around in the facility, he surmised it was an exam. But to what end he did not know.

"Relax, Student Lake, we're only here to talk," ordered Cervantes.

He pressed himself against the backrest to try and calm his nerves. It only worked a bit. "Sir, are you going to kick me out?" he asked, getting it out of the way. He didn't like lingering on a subject too long or making small talk. It was the most important subject to him right now, so why not ask directly?

The major pursed his lips and stated, "You have nothing to offer the sorcerer's division at your state, nor do I see any future contribution you could impart to the research and development division with only your mechanical skills. Good as they are, there are more talented, regular people."

Further training with his condition could help or assist other students in developing could make him stay. "Sir, I can try to—"

"If you're thinking about working around your condition or being an instructor's assistant, I don't see that as an option for you," he said as if answering his thoughts. "Your combat and mech piloting skills aren't anything special either. We have a lot of cadets who could do better than you."

Was that it for him? Three years studying and slaving away as a student, repeating the same year over and over again, all down the drain just like that? What about all of the exams and physical conditioning he had to do before just to qualify for this program? Was it all meaningless? His mental state took him back to his old home with his father. He pictured himself working under him, with his heavy hand and incessant blabber about his incompetence. The thought made him sick at the pit of his stomach.

"I'm giving you an assignment. You'll be the sorcerer engineer for the upcoming inner zone investigative mission: Mission #314-A," Cervantes cut through his worsening mental state.

Was he hallucinating? Did he actually hear a mission being assigned to him? "Sir?" he croaked.

"You've been here, what, three years? You're more than qualified to be an engineer in the field."

Down in the training room, the soldiers worked together to lift barrels, climb walls and unlock puzzles. Perseverance, confidence, and focus showed in their faces as Lake tried to process what the major had said. In every squad that used mechs, the standard composition had at least one medic and engineer. Usually, sorcerers only ever filled the role of medics because of their obvious better talents than regular doctors and necessity in missions. The other roles were filled by regular soldiers.

Combat sorcerers usually filled up a spot when medics weren't available, which was what Lake was aiming for when he graduated the academy. Sorcerer engineers were not unheard of, but they were rare—to the point that people talked about the possibility but rarely required them. Their main job was not only providing tech support to the team but boosting mechs and enhancement spells. He was already about to propose he could be good for a role that used enhancement spells, so this worked out great. So why wasn't he jumping up and down for joy?

"Sir I...I don't understand. I might make things worse," he squeaked.

Cervantes produced a glassy and showed the video of him in a scuffle with a masked man in the convenience store, then disappearing and reappearing. "Would you like to explain something?" His left brow perked.

From holding his breath, to a sigh of relief and then holding it again, Lake was weary and tired. "Sir, I..." He gave in and told him what had happened in his dream. It wasn't as if he could lie his way through the smartest man in Zuobic. The only thing he kept to himself was the system. He barely escaped criticisms of his poor performance; any suspicion of his degrading mental health would only serve to block him even more.

The major was silent for a while; his attention was at the front. The scenario of the training facility was converted from an obstacle race to an ambush of goblins in a local zone. The soldiers were supposed to assist both the holographic army that fought the goblins and the civilians being evacuated. Tony was one of the people being tested. He flew to the thick of the battle while others helped the injured.

"Do you know what happens to the zone if we fail to protect it?" asked Cervantes.

Lake wondered why he was being asked such a basic thing, but he did not show any kind of face expressing it. "A black flag is raised on the area. It means we and any civilians are prohibited from entering it," he answered.

"Do you know why?" he asked.

"Because there is a high count of monsters. Taking it back would be overwhelming for the team and counterproductive," he answered readily from what he had been told. "The army should focus on the other zones to protect, rather than waste time on lost causes."

"If that was true, why don't we simply nuke a zone and kill all of them in one swoop."

"The army should focus on the living zones to protect. We cannot waste time on lost causes," he repeated from memory.

His face and eyes shifted as exhaustion and worry surfaced, but it was only for a second. "Student Lake, what I'm about to tell you is for your ears only."

Lake felt a chill around him as he noticed his superior cast Silent Space. An invisible barrier surrounded them that cut sound from travelling out and into the enclosed space.

"Rifts break after some time, if they're left untouched. When they do, the monsters inside come out on our side," continued Cervantes. "After leaving them for weeks, boss monsters, their pack leaders, come out of the rift."

"Yes sir," he confirmed, as this was basic knowledge.

"If they are not killed within a few months, the zone disappears."

His face crumpled. "I don't get it, sir."

"The buildings, plants, people, air, the very land itself, vanish from existence," Cervantes clarified. "This exam we are watching is taken from the incident from Zone Estrez a few years ago. We failed to take it back from the goblin king. A lot of soldiers died fighting that monster, but we only managed to save 20% of the zone's population. The rest was trapped inside when the whole zone disappeared."

"What...? How...?"

"Zone Estrez was in between zones Daz and Fritz. When it vanished from our world, the lands between Daz and Fritz connected," he explained. "It made it seem like Estrez was but a fantasy. Though we have pictures, records, people we know from there—that very place ceased to exist in our reality. We call it deleted space, outlier #25."

"Why are you telling me this, sir? I'm nobody," admitted Lake.

Cervantes met his gaze. "Indeed, you are. But you are one of the living survivors of a deleted space. And as one, something in you changed. The exploding spells. I believe that is worth following through. You are worth following through."

Uncertainty edged at his heart. His whole life, people had only praised him for his good looks—a pretty useless trait when your friends and family were dying. "It should've been you," or "can your dimples kill monsters," were the words his dad usually said when he'd had too much to drink. And now, he was actually good for something? No, laughable. Give the spot to actual soldiers, the real heroes of the day, not him. It was hard enough passing the academy. Any hope for talent and change was stupid and unrealistic.

Cervantes took a deep breath and explained, "Outlier #25 happened again after Esterz. It was in Kermoz, eight years ago."

Flashbacks of his past from eight years ago came flooding back. He was around 12 years old when his dad and mom took him and his younger brother to the amusement park. They had left the car and started to walk to the entrance with giddy steps. A rift suddenly tore through the sky and monsters descended. Nobody thought a rift would open in Kermoz because of its ward generator. That mindset caught everyone off guard as pitch-black-skinned humanoid monsters with four arms and glittering cosmic capes descended. With a wave of their hands, earth cracked underneath, fire rained from the skies and the air froze to sub-zero temperatures.

The Deskenns ran for the car. His dad was about to help his mom and his younger brother inside it when Lake tripped and cried out for help. This caught his dad's attention as he rounded back and helped him up. As they turned back, a fireball blasted down and incinerated the car. Lake froze from shock while his dad screamed. His mom and brother were burning into crisp embers inside the blazing vehicle. His dad tried to reach for the door handle, but the road beneath him shook and cracks snaked towards him. He quickly retreated back into an open space and started running away from the scene. With tears flooding his eyes, he braved the random attacks, collapsing structures and dying Zuosh. Young Lake cried for his mom, but his dad kept hushing him, telling him that it'd be all right.

"Student Lake?" repeated Cervantes for the second time.

Lake broke away from his thoughts. "Zone Kermoz, I used to live there with my family. After I got into the academy, I read the reports. The army didn't defeat the monsters, the svartal—the rest of it was redacted."

Cervantes observed him for a moment before he continued, "We only had half a day of inspection before the whole land and space of Zone Kermoz was deleted. The whole investigative team was taken too."

He recalled the day he was recovering at the hospital. He obsessed over the TV, looking for any news about his mom, hoping for anything. "I remember the president announcing a program to clean up Kermoz, but it was deemed uninhabitable after. So they've labelled it as a non-living zone."

"Truth is, it disappeared eight years ago," he clarified. "But now, its back."

His eyes widened.

"Outlier #24, recovered space. Zone Kermoz returned to this world around the time the incident at WalkBy happened. I had a team investigate the zone, but only a few returned. They were attacked by monsters, causing them to separate. The mission you will carry out with a squad is to look for any signs of the separated team and recover them if possible."

The kind look of his mom and his playful brother's grin flashed before him. "Sir, I can't. I'm glad for this opportunity, but I-I can't."

He placed a hand on his shoulder. "Before, we thought that the only people that could enter rifts were sorcerers and item users—that was it. Recently a rumor started about people possessing powers to manipulate source but not from objects or runes—the outlier #14 theory. You know what I believe?"

"Sir?" He looked up at Cervantes. Usually cold eyes stared back, but there was a hint of kindness to it.

"You are an outlier survivor. If anyone is to prove the rumors true, it'd be you. Prove to me that you are one of them, Student Lake."

Lake's gaze shifted to the floor. "What about Jella? She was there too. Can't she do this? She's an actual soldier, I'm barely a sorcerer. I'm nobody," he repeated.

"I have a different task for her. Forget about her. As you said, you two are over. Focus on you. Why do you want to be a soldier?" he asked in a softer tone.

"I don't want people to die." The voice of his pops yelling and crying for his mom and brother while chugging a bottle of vodka flashed in his mind.

Cervantes squeezed his shoulder. "Then isn't it about time you make a difference? Lake, I don't know if you have realized it yet, but these things to tend to happen around you. You are in the middle of unravelling the mystery of outliers. Don't you owe it to yourself, to the army, to your nation and to me, to prove your worth? That finally, you are able to accomplish your goal in life?"

He looked up to him. "Sir?" It was the first time anyone had said that to him.

"You are worthy," he said softly.

"I'm worthy," he repeated.

As Silent Space dissipated, the noise and excitement from the test returned.

"By the way, that woman you were with, the one with green hair. Did you see her again?" asked Cervantes. "Or anyone else in that store?"

Look shook his head. "No, sir. I still think—I'm hoping it was all a dream. But after talking to you, I'm not so sure anymore."

"I'm sure they will turn up. Nothing is for certain." He half-smiled.

"Yes sir." When he saw his superior's confident look, he felt like it was true. No, he wanted it to be true. He needed it to be real.

"If you run into any of them, be sure to let me know. I'd like to interview them. Learn about their experiences."

"Definitely, sir." He beamed with positivity.

"Thank you everyone for participating," announced an officer into the microphone. "Congratulations to the top performers: Tony Gallagher, Osher Grace and Nikki Valson. The rest of the results will be posted tomorrow."

CHAPTER 13

JELLA, HOSPITAL WING, ABERKYZ

As the hospital doors opened to the ground floor, staff and visitors filed out and headed to the exit. Wearing a scrub suit and a mask over her face, Jella mingled with the crowd. Her eyes darted to the soldiers standing guard. They were inspecting the ones coming in, not so much the ones going out. It gave her a bit of hope, but she still steeled herself. She kept her head forward. Her motions were purposeful but unhurried, matching everyone's tempo. Her heartbeat raced as she crossed the door frame with everyone else. After a few more paces, she exhaled.

The open space of the roads welcomed her. The light of the morning sun wrapped around her skin, invigorating her. She smelled the fresh air and celebrated the feeling of being outside. It was so much better than being locked up on her floor. Something about being caged and bound like that didn't sit right with her. She longed to be free. This feeling and the thoughts that came with it were all because of who she was. She had slowly been recalling things from her past, and she knew that she didn't belong here at all.

As she took a step forward, a familiar voice said, "You'll ruin your life if you go."

Jella glanced back. It was that bitch-doctor Maggie who kept on insisting they were friends. At first, she was nice, talking about their times together, their conversations, their traditions, but after a while, she started *suggesting* things to her:

"You should take less missions when you get back to your squad."

"I think it's great you're eating carbs to get your strength back. But you don't want to be fat. Have more salad."

"Maybe you should stop piloting and do an admin role. I've said it before, but the battlefield is not a place for ladies like us."

"Where'd you get beer? Stop drinking that. It'll ruin your figure, not to mention your skin."

And when she was watching a fashion show of men in swimwear on television, Maggie turned it off and said, "You shouldn't be watching that. Men who look like that are bad for you. Like your ex."

Her ex. That was a weird one since she and Dr. Badez had asked her to record a breakup video for a man she didn't even know. She was sick and tired of doing things for them—Dr. Badez and this doll-faced bitch. Jella had wanted so many times to push them out the window when they met. Now she cursed herself for not doing just that before she escaped. "I've wasted so much time in that place. Nothing is wrong with me. I am healthy," she declared.

Maggie sighed. "Like I said before, your condition is different. You are healthy, yes. Too healthy. Your cells regenerate at an alarming rate. This is not good for the body in the long run. You will exhaust yourself."

She looked directly at her eyes. "I don't care. My body. My decision. You don't get a say—however smart and educated you are. Fuck you." She went on her way.

"Jella, come back. Please, I don't want it to be like this," Maggie screamed.

She completely ignored her. From a walk to a jog, then a sprint, her legs pushed her further and further away. Her whole being wanted to be rid of this place, of this whole event. Sure, her mind might not know where to go or remember everything in her life, but that's what gave her clarity. She knew that place was hell. And she wouldn't be able to leave if she stayed. It had to be—

Something stung her in the back. Her hand tried to reach for it, but she felt herself lose control and motion as she fell on the pavement. She tried to push herself—get back up, flail, struggle, anything, but she was frozen still. Her left cheek was against the dirt.

Maggie stopped beside her as she had her hand on her linko. "Target is paralyzed. Please bring in a hover gurney to collect her."

"I'm sorry," she said, after giving her report.

New footsteps sided with Maggie as Dr. Badez came to view. "Don't apologize. This is what has to happen for the good of mankind. Are you prepared?"

Jella tried to glare at them, but all she managed was a defiant stare against a line of ants that walked next to her face. Like them, she was powerless against the heels of someone bigger and more powerful. But unlike her, they were at least free.

Chapter 14

Keri, Roads in Troef

On the open road, Riley was driving her minivan with her wife in the passenger seat. Her eyes kept looking over at the sides of the road, overtaking cars whenever she found an opening on the road. Chatterbox was seated in the backseat with Keri who had a perturbed look. Keri understood the urgency of getting the curse off of Wayne, but why did it seem like it was more than just that?

As the car stopped for the stoplight, Vivian reached out a hand to touch her wife. "I understand you are in a hurry. But you have to be careful when you're driving," she said.

Riley shook her head. "Doesn't matter. Charlie's here. Nothing bad is going to happen to us. Right, buddy?" She looked at Charlie in the rearview mirror.

"Leave it to me, Mom," signed Chatterbox.

The car moved ahead once traffic cleared just a second before the red lights turned green.

Vivian rolled her eyes. "That's right, use your kid to run red lights."

"Um, I know I've done something bad. I'm sorry," said Keri. "But doesn't Wayne have time?"

She turned to the back seat. "Situations involving cursed objects tend to escalate fast in my experience. And don't apologize, it isn't your fault. If only someone had done what I'd asked them to in the first place."

Riley beeped her horn. "All right, all right already. It's my fault. Charlie, can you help Keri figure out the extent of her powers. The cursed artifacts are in the bag behind you."

Keri gaped at the blue backpack sitting on the floor next to Chatterbox. "You brought it here?"

"Relax, Charlie's here. His powers can keep the curse from activating. You're free to experiment," she said. "Get out of the road, stupid grandma!"

Chatterbox opened the bag, took out a ring and offered it to Keri. Once her finger touched the ring, the system tintinnabulated.

Curse detected on object. Maiden can now control the curse.
Curse description: Touched entity will suffer from weakness and fatigue.
Length of time depends on the source applied by user.

Keri felt her fingers and palms. She sensed a cold aura enveloping her hands. It seemed to dissipate and exist at her command. "I think I can use the cursed items or something. Like, I'm not affected by it."

After making a sharp right and making everyone tussle to the left, Riley looked in the rearview mirror. "Buddy, is it safe for you to take it?" she asked.

Vivian reached out her arm to the back. "I'll do it to be safe. Charlie, protect Mommy please."

Chatterbox put his thumbs up.

Keri looked at the arm with flawless skin held out to her. "Vivian, I don't—"

"Do it," ordered Vivian. "Testing things out and trying stuff is this family's thing. We won't know how to solve it if we don't try."

After taking a deep breath, she closed her eyes and clasped her hands. After a while, when she felt nothing, she opened them.

Target is protected.
Curse did not take effect.

"What happened?" Riley slowed to a stop from the building traffic.

Vivian retrieved her hand and checked herself. "I'm—I think I'm fine."

"You think you can undo the curse on Wayne?" Her large eyes shot a fierce look in the mirror.

"I think so," answered Keri.

Charlie handed Keri a golden clock from the bag.

Keri grabbed the clock with both hands.

Curse: Bright Terrors detected on artefact.

Bright Terrors: User will see ghostly apparitions of the dead at night. Artefact is unfit to be used by Maiden. Please increase Prima fragment to use. Artefact will now be depowered. Curse is absorbed. Artefact is now a regular object. Earned 50 coins. Total 150.

"No way," Keri exhaled.

"Keri, what happened?" asked Vivian.

She turned to Charlie. "Give me another."

Charlie pouted from confusion but handed her another item; a long, used quill.

Curse: Creative Madness detected on artefact. Creative Madness: The user will have flashes of inspiration for any type of art. Though when and frequency cannot be controlled. User beware. Artefact is unfit to be used by Maiden. Please increase Prima fragment to use. Artefact will now be depowered. Curse is absorbed. Artefact is now a regular object. Earned 10 coins. Total: 160.

From finding lovers, to absorbing powerful curses—was that the ticket into getting more purchases from the system? But the way she earned the coins seemed varied. Not all curses produced the same number of coins. This felt like the same system in *Love Me, Princess*. Whenever she interacted with objects in-game, she'd use them to progress the story or receive some sort of compensation.

Riley pounded on the horn, stuck in a deadlock of cars. "Freaking traffic jam. We're literally a block away."

"I think there was an accident up ahead." Vivian opened her windows and peeked at the sides.

"How are you doing there, Keri?" Riley turned to look from the front.

Keri closed the notifications by mental command. "I think I'm growing stronger if I absorb the curses."

"Stronger how?"

"Not sure yet. I think I have to experiment with it a bit more."

Vivian switched her stiletto for flats. "We don't have time to wait. Keri, come with me. We're going to run. Honey, catch up to me when you can." She opened her door and got out.

"Uh ok." Keri undid her seatbelt and jumped out of the car.

"Keep your linko open," Riley shouted.

Vivian nodded and sprinted off. "Come on."

Following behind, Keri ran along the pavement in the dark of the night, illuminated by streetlamps hanging from the walls of the valley. Crowds of people, bikes parked by the side and peddlers howling took up much of the space in the walkways as she squeezed through gaps and took care not to bump into anyone. Shop signs illustrated by bright lights conveyed their products and services. From item outfitters to rune tattoo parlors, monster butchers and closer arenas—the establishments were wide and varied compared to what she was used to at the night walks in Zuobic. Back home, everything about the outliers was blocked off and isolated except for what was shown on media. Everyone focused on their work, events, shopping, games—their life. All the stuff about monsters and rifts were all true. But at the same time, it felt unreal since they, the common citizens, only saw them on TV.

Vivian grabbed Keri by the hand and pulled her into an alley lit by dim signs and hypnotic neon billboards. The stores were smaller and narrower in size than the ones at the main road. Men and women scattered around, wearing jackets, cloaks and other dark clothes and fabrics, glanced in their direction.

A man in a suit and slicked back hair approached them with a smile. "Hello ladies, is there anything I can help you with? Some helpers maybe?" He waved over at the closest shop that displayed humans bound and chained.

Keri squinted at a skinny man wearing only tattered shorts. She gasped at his pointed ears and golden crystalized eyes. "Is that an elf?" she asked.

"They look like that, don't they?" answered the man with a flash of his bright white teeth. "This one claims to be a member of royalty from a fallen country. He says he is a celestial—the interpreters said something of the sort. Would you like to take a look?"

Vivian stepped forward. "Thank you for the offer, but we're looking to head to Promentos. I'm sure you can guide us? In and out. No trouble?" She placed a hand on her right ear, where her linko was, and held out her left hand.

As the man shook her hand, his eyes widened.

"We're in a bit of a hurry," she said.

"For you, madame and your friend: Pleasurable, discreet and safe. Follow me." He strode off quickly.

The two women followed a step behind. "What is this place? What is that elf?" asked Keri.

Vivian pulled her closer, locking her arms around hers. "Welcome to the red-light district. Trust no one. If you need something here, better have lots of credits. Be up front. No lies, no bullshit—unless you can pull it off." She gave her a hard look.

"And that celestial-elf thing?" Keri gulped.

"Outlier #32, humanoids. People find them inside rifts," she responded in a hushed tone. "They're rare. They're being sold as slaves."

She remembered being stuck inside the truck and trafficked. "Do they sell people too?" Her voice broke.

"Don't worry. Cluster RSTU, where Troef belongs to, do not allow human slavery," she responded. "Monster slavery, however, is very much legal."

"They're not monsters," she said, rougher than she wanted to, though still at a lower volume. The same heated feeling from Maxwell's car earlier came rushing back.

Vivian ignored her slight outburst. "That's debatable."

They stopped over at a medium-sized building with a blue sign that flashed 'Promentos'. Two big and heavily armed men stood at the door with frozen faces.

"Ladies, here you are. I've already informed the establishment of your arrival. You can head on in and enjoy yourselves," said the man in a jovial attitude. "Do you need help with your selection?"

"No thanks. Please wait for us until we are done," replied Vivian.

"Very well, madame. Do call me if you need anything. You have my number." He bowed his head.

The heavy scent of alcohol and cigarettes, and flashing strobe lights arrested Keri's senses as she stepped inside. Loud thumping music and a mish-mash of howling, laughing and arguing invaded her ears as she tried to acclimate with the assaulting environment.

"Stay here. Don't drink. Don't talk to anyone. Don't do anything stupid," Vivian shouted. "I'll be right back." She disappeared into a sea of people in the darker room.

As Keri's vision got more used to the room, the more she understood where she was: a bar. But this type of bar was something she had only ever heard about, but never really been to.

A tall man with a chiseled jaw strutted up and down the platform, looking at everyone staring at him. He ran his hand over his white shirt, lifted it up to showcase his ripped six-pack and then smirked at the audience. Women and men screamed. His hips gyrated to the sound of the beat as he slowly took his shirt off. His pecs bounced as he paraded his sweaty body, dancing sensually. He dropped to the ground on all fours and thrust his hips on the floor like he was making love to it. More screams and whistles resounded.

Keri stood near a pillar, mouth open and glued onto the performance.

"Hi, is it your first time here?" a male baritone voice coquettishly whispered into her ear.

She jumped back and turned. "Who-who-hi. Hello." She stupidly grinned.

Another man, shorter than the one on stage, smiled at her. He flashed his perfect white teeth and boyish charm. "Hi, do you need someone to show you around?" He reached for her hand. But instead of shaking it, he caressed her palm softly with his fingertips.

The move sent ripples down Keri's spine. "I-I-I'm looking for someone," she blurted out, a bit incoherently.

Keeping his eye contact, he placed her hand over his rock-hard chest. "Are you looking for this? Or maybe..." He slowly moved it down to his abs, making his way lower.

Vivian appeared at the side and snatched back Keri's arm. "No. She's not looking for anything. Thank you. Bye." She dragged Keri away onto the back part of the dance floor, near the backstage.

They exited into a hall leading to many corridors, leading to many rooms. Separated by curtains instead of doors, a couple howled in delight as they fornicated in missionary style. In the next room, a woman screamed in ecstasy as a man and a woman went down on her. Then, in the room on the left, an old wrinkly, fat man penetrated a hot, muscular hunk.

Vivian found an elevator at the far side of the hall and entered with Keri. "You're drooling," Vivian said. She tapped the button to close the doors.

Keri reached for her face and wiped the drool off in panicked motions.

Vivian sent a curious stare. "Have you never seen men like that before? What do you do in Zuobic for fun?"

She shook her head. "I...play games a lot."

Vivian bobbed her head in understanding. "Which one do you like? The hunky guy on the dance floor? Or the younger lean one?"

Both. The hunky guy in the mornings. Lean guy at nights. For over a week, was what Keri thought. But instead, she said, "Excuse me?"

"I'd do the hunky guy if I was single."

Her forehead scrunched. "But don't you like girls?"

Vivian smirked. "I'm fluid or queer. Before I met Riley, I slept with boys, girls, old farts, trans."

"Doesn't that get confusing? Like who you get attracted to?"

"To me, no. I'm attracted to people who I'm attracted to. Simple," she explained. "But for others, it takes some time getting used to. Had some exes that can't really get over the fact that I sleep with women, and some exes who think sleeping with men was a phase."

Keri's head tilted slightly. "You're with Riley, so isn't it a phase?"

"I am loyal to my wife if that is the question. But it doesn't mean I don't appreciate men and their beauty."

She recalled those times when she appreciated beautiful women and kinda connected that with her lust for men. "I think I get it. Must be fun having a lot of options," she said.

Vivian snickered, then scowled. "It has a lot of good moments. The ugly thing about it is that people assume I'm a slut. I messed around as much as any average man my age before. God forbid, if a bi-guy sleeps around it's all right, and I get labelled as a whore."

She felt a whole can of worms was about to burst out, so she tried to get back onto the subject and asked, "Um, why is Wayne here?"

Vivian breathed deeply through her nostrils. "Wayne works here as an escort. Today is his last day. He starts work with Amazing Discoveries tomorrow."

Before Keri could ask for more details, the elevator opened to a long, wide and airy tunnel. Stepping out, it reminded her of passageways she used to take for the subway with the tall ceilings and tiled walls.

"Most of the establishments here in Troef have access to the underground railway systems. Good for travelling and escaping if trouble ever comes up above," explained Vivian as she strode at a fast pace. "Of course, the underground would not be complete without its shady deals."

The long, airy tunnel opened to a spacious cavern almost the size of an amphitheatre. People gathered around a large steel cage. Some sat and watched over the descending stands, while others observed from the boxes hanging above.

In a steel-caged dome, an imp and a beetle double its size battled. The imp tried to catch the beetle with its giant hands, but it kept buzzing away. At a set distance away, the beetle would vibrate its wings and send a concentrated sonar attack and disrupt the imp's senses. Quick to recover, the imp would roll away before the insect chomped on it with its mandibles.

After the third try, the beetle was finally able to hit its mark. Its serrated mouth dug deep into the bony shoulder of the imp. The beetle buzzed in joy. But the celebratory mood only lasted for a moment as the imp pushed its horns deep into the beetle's abdomen. The horned beast rummaged through the insides of the insect from the hole it made. Then, the imp reached for its wings and ripped them from its body.

As the butchering continued, the crowd in the stands roared. They cheered and jeered on which monster they wanted to win.

Vivian pointed at a box directly opposite them. "There he is."

Keri spotted Wayne watching the fight with a middle-aged woman. They talked a bit before retreating away from the windows and disappearing inside. "Who's that with him?"

"Probably a client. Come on."

"What about Riley and Chatter—Charlie."

"I already sent them a message. She's tracking my linko."

The two women waded through the crowd, who burned with excitement and fervor. When the imp finally killed the bug, the audience jumped for joy. One man pushed Keri forward accidentally. She landed on another man, who elbowed her upon contact. Then soon after, a domino effect started. People kept pushing or pulling her away when she touched them. She suffered from hair pulling, knuckles to the back and pushes to her boobs until she flung out of the mass and onto the floor.

"Why does this always happen to me?" Keri groaned.

Vivian helped her up. "Are you all right?"

"I think so. Where to?" She massaged the painful areas on her body.

"This way."

The two climbed up a staircase into a quieter hallway. They walked further until they stopped dead between four different doors each leading to different rooms.

"I'll check the left. You check the right." Vivian went for the closest door to her.

Keri did the same. After knocking on the door, she opened it and saw four men gathered around a table, playing cards. "Sorry, wrong room." She closed the door immediately and went for the next one.

As she grabbed the handle to open it, she heard the lock click. Another try confirmed it wouldn't open.

Vivian arrived behind her. "Did you see him?"

"Not in the first one. This one's locked," answered Keri.

Vivian took out some hairpins from her hair and started picking the lock. "Let me." After a couple of pokes and twisting, the lock opened.

"Where did you learn how to do that?"

She placed the pins back in her hair. "Try opening outlier treasure chests every Tuesday for a year. Makes doors kid's play." She grinned.

Keri then realized there must be some real treasure chests closers brought in to Amazing Discoveries like how it was on games. She wondered if she would ever see one.

Vivian twisted the door and opened it. "Let's go."

Chapter 15

Keri, Promentos, Troef

Inside the large private box, a mini buffet stood at the side, offering cakes, cookies and other sorts of confectioneries. Opposite was the bar, complete with rows of rum, vodka, tequila and other alcoholic drinks. A mini fountain oozed with red wine next to it. Yellow and ambient lighting illuminated the medium-sized and cozy room, creating dramatic shadows all around. Soft, sultry music sang through the speakers, creating a mellow romantic vibe for the three occupants of the room.

A middle-aged, obese half-naked woman stood to the right of a big leather couch. An unconscious Wayne lay on the couch butt-naked, bound by rope. His limbs and body were tied together tightly, letting his big chest and penis hang out. On the left was a rugged man wearing dark jeans and a white undershirt. He had a long scar running from the back of his left ear to his collarbone. His arms, tattooed with red-grey runes, secured the rope tightly.

At the frame of the door, Keri blabbed, "Kinky. I mean—oh my gosh. This is so inappropriate." She covered her eyes with her hands, but kept her fingers spread out so she could still see.

"You were bringing company?" asked the obese woman.

The man raised a brow. "I thought you ordered room service."

Underneath her dress, Vivian unholstered a pistol and pointed it at the man. "Let go of Wayne and step back," she yelled.

"Isn't this a bit much? They're just having a three-way," said Keri. "We can totally take Wayne after they're done."

Vivian kept her aim. "This is kidnapping. Wayne hates BDSM."

Keri's ears quirked up. "How'd you know that?"

"We slept together. It was a long time ago," she reasoned. "Riley doesn't know about it."

"Say what?"

Vivian fired her gun on the ceiling to stop the man from moving toward Wayne. "I said back off," she ordered.

The man grumbled. "Lady, mind your own business if you don't want to get hurt." He stepped forward, crunching his knuckles.

She pointed at the man and shot him in the leg. A hole burned through his jeans. The tattoos in his arms glowed once, then a pop sounded. The bullet that was lodged in his thigh spat out from the hole and fell on the floor. The wound closed and recovered as if it was never there to begin with.

"Are we in trouble?" asked Keri.

Vivian fired more shots. "Get Wayne. I'll take care of this." The bullets decorated the man's chest.

Keri ran off to where the unconscious Wayne was. She tripped on the couch in a hurry as her face landed on his dick. Her face immediately backed up. She had never seen one this big before—actually, she had never seen a real live one before. The closest thing to the real thing she witnessed was porn, and it was never a good measure for real life. Snapping away from her lewd thoughts, she reached in for the bindings and tried to untie them. Her nails cracked after failing to undo one. "They're too tight," she yelled out.

After running out of bullets, Vivian threw the gun at the man, which did no damage. "Get a knife or something." She yanked her cross necklace from her neck as it transformed into a long glittery silver-blue sword.

Her head flicked from the bar to the buffet, spotting a small cake knife. She hurried to the bar and grabbed the knife. When she returned to Wayne, someone yanked her hair from behind, pulling her back. She let go of the cake knife and grabbed her head. It was the obese woman, now fully clothed. After the big woman pulled Keri close to her, she pushed her at the wall. Keri's head hit the wall lamp, smashing it into pieces.

"Wayne's mine! Fat-weirdo," exclaimed the obese woman.

Her fingers felt the warm red liquid trickling down her temples. "You bitch." Keri lunged at her.

The two slammed against each other and fell to the floor. Keri grabbed the woman's wide forehead and pushed it down, knocking her head against the floorboards. The woman retaliated with a knee to the vagina and a punch to her boob. As Keri cried out from the pain, the woman rolled her down so she was on top. The woman gripped her by the neck and choked her.

Keri gagged and heaved as she tried to get the woman's hands off her. As her vision blurred, her hands crawled at the sides of the woman's head. Her thumbs found her assailant's eye sockets and dug deep into them. The woman cried out and pulled away from her grasp. Keri crawled backwards and stumbled on the knife on the floor. She grasped it in her hands and lunged with it again. But her opponent quickly snatched a bottle and swung it at her. As Keri grabbed the cake knife and swung it back, it collided with the woman's bottle. Glass and wine sprinkled on their faces.

The woman was the first to recover and tackled Keri to the ground again. She wrapped her stubby fingers around her neck and squeezed. Keri tried to eye her again, but she was smarter now, and moved her face to avoid her fingers from reaching her sockets. As Keri's vision blurred, she caught a sparkle on her finger. The ring Chatterbox gave her. That was right. She hadn't given it back.

Keri activated the ring as the familiar cold feeling enveloped her hands, which were grasping her oppressor's arm. In a matter of seconds, the woman let go and toppled over backward. She was on her elbows and knees, heaving. Sweat dripped down her face, but Keri didn't relent. Once she could breathe again, she put both her hands on the woman's face. She felt something from the space around enter her, it stirred within then spilled out of her fingertips. Was this source? She was manipulating source, right? The phenomenon was so amazing she forgot what she was doing to the woman until she croaked and fell on the floor: her eyes open, mouth not breathing and body still.

After staring for a while, the commotion behind her jolted Keri back into focus. She proceeded to help Wayne. Clutching the tiki around her neck, she tried to activate it. When nothing happened, she prayed and then cursed at it in her head. Either seemed to have worked as a few notifications popped into view. She zoomed on one window that had the Doom curse.

Across the room, Vivian thrust her sword multiple times. Each blow went through the tattooed man, but he healed. The man countered with a couple of swings with his fist, which were easily parried by her. Each time she swung her sword, he would defend and get closer to her. After a few more exchanges, her back was pressed flat against the wall. There was no more room left to run. The tattooed man smirked in triumph. He raised his arm and swung his fist. Before it connected to her face, Riley appeared next to the man with Chatterbox hanging on her neck. She swung a large hammer, smacking him into the buffet table.

"You okay?" asked Riley, holding the hammer with both hands.

Vivian nodded, catching her breath. "Check on Keri."

"She's fine," Chatterbox signed with one hand.

"Riley!" she screamed.

The tattooed man exploded with a purple aura that pushed Riley back. She and Chatterbox stumbled to the floor and hit the bar. The man rose from the broken pieces of plates and wasted food with glittering earrings and two lanterns floating beside him. The left glowed purple with a sad face, while the right glowed orange with a manic face.

Vivian rushed to her wife. "Are you okay?"

Riley pushed herself and her son with the hammer with Vivian's help. "Yeah, Charlie took care of the damage. Are you—I can't move my hands," she said in alarm.

"What do you—my feet won't move," Vivian exclaimed.

Black spectacles materialized over Riley's face as she observed the tattooed man. "His name is Qahoon. His body is tattooed with minor healing runes. Those earrings are rare 7s. Gives him something called Lantern Bombs. Orange one explodes and kills people while purple curses them with paralysis," she analyzed.

"Anything there about how to get us free?" asked Vivian.

"No. Charlie, can you do something?"

Charlie struggled to sign but didn't move an inch.

Qahoon reached for his orange lantern, threw it at them, and it exploded. The fire and impact burned half of the room, incinerating the couches, marble floors and bar. As black smoke receded and gave view to the wreckage, Wayne stood in the middle, naked with shimmering hands. A shield with the pattern of swirls glowed from his fists and protected the whole of his body.

"Wayne?" Vivian coughed from the smoke, though still unable to move. The rest of her family were safe behind the shield.

Qahoon raised a brow. Another orange lantern appeared beside him, and he immediately threw it. The lantern exploded, but like before, the damage was negated by the swirl-patterned shield. He grumbled. The purple lantern emitted a ghost-like image and floated towards Wayne.

Keri snuck up from behind Qahoon and placed both of her hands on his ears. The ring of weakness activated. *I hope this works,* she thought.

The light from Qahoon's earrings vanished as he crouched. Sweat crystalized on his face as his breathing grew labored. At the sight of him weakened, Keri jumped away and cheered.

Qahoon saw her and growled.

Something was wrong. *Why isn't he keeling over like the fat lady? Is it because he's a closer?* thought Keri. "Sorry," she pleaded.

Qahoon hit her and made her fly across the room. Her back slammed against the wall. As he pursued her, Wayne punched him in the lower back and swung an uppercut that pushed him aside. Vivian appeared right next to the enemy and delivered multiple thrusts. She decorated his body with innumerable open wounds. Qahoon tried to defend with his arms and regenerate, but the rate he was wounded was faster. After her assault, Riley stepped in and swung her hammer down. Lightning sparked as it touched the ground. She raised it again and bludgeoned the man over and over again, until he was flat as a pancake of flesh and bones.

Riley placed the heavy hammer down and heaved. "Everyone all right?" she asked.

Vivian manipulated her sword back into a necklace. "Keri, Charlie?" she asked.

"We're fine." Keri rose from the floor with Chatterbox's help.

"Does anyone know where my pants are?" asked Wayne.

Riley spotted half burnt trousers on the floor. "I think these are yours." She tossed them over to him.

"Thanks."

As everyone tried to catch a breath, unbeknownst to them, an orange lantern slowly rolled over the floor. It kept on rolling silently until it reached the window and started to glow. When Chatterbox noticed the light, he tried to get their attention, but the windows abruptly exploded.

Qahoon, in his half-vegetative-half-regenerating state, tossed himself over the opening and fell off the box. Everyone ran to the window as he freefell down to the arena platform and slid to the side by the cage walls. Another orange lantern came upon the cage walls and exploded as well, letting the monsters rampage loose.

"Shit." Riley slapped her head.

"I'm calling Hairless Ape," said Vivian. "We can't deal with this."

"What about her?" signed Chatterbox, pointing at the obese woman.

Wayne checked her pulse. "She's dead."

Outlier #23: **Discovered World – Bisenti**

The books retrieved from the first rift were not just about sorcery. A lot of them depicted history about civilizations in a world called Bisenti.

In the text, sorcerers were revered as scientists and doctors—only a few delved into combat. Though powerful, the culture skewed to researchers that tried to better life through magic. Therefore, a lot of their spells went hand in hand with contraptions and devices made for daily life in comparison to modern electronics and gadgets. But after the first cataclysm, which looking by definition of the text, was the first rift, their world changed.

Like ours, monsters from another dimension poured in and invaded. In response, the sorcerers changed themselves and their career pathways. Combat spells, weapons imbued with enchantments, artifacts that granted inhuman strength and abilities—the list went on and on. These were but a few of the things that the sorcerers invented to combat the aliens that invaded their home.

—Outlier Cultural Studies Vol 1. By Julia Osori, Otherworld Pioneer Researcher

Chapter 16

Keri, Amazing Discoveries, Troef

A fresh afternoon breeze rustled azalea bushes and jacaranda trees as purple petals fell over the gardens. At the center, inside the gazebo, Keri sipped tea in a free-flowing and sparkling beige dress. Today was a good day. She had practiced horseback riding and cavalry combat in the morning, had lunch, then bathed. Now, she was having her afternoon tea. Maybe she'd brush up on her studies later in the evening, but for now, someone else took her attention away.

The elven prince bowed at the footsteps. "My lady, may I join you?" he asked.

"Of course," said Keri effortlessly. Was this another one of her dreams? Had she been playing *Love Me, Princess* until morning again? So much so that it was invading her dreams? *Whatever, let's just play it out.*

As the elven prince sat opposite her and the already-prepared tea, his expression changed, serious and perplexed.

"Is the tea not to your liking?" asked Keri.

The prince looked back and forth, inspecting his surroundings. "Where is this? What is this room? What am I wearing?" He fussed over his fit trousers, dress shirt and black jacket with gold trimmings.

"Prince, is everything okay?" asked Keri.

He looked up at her. "Prince? Who are you talking to, lady?"

"Lady? You shall not address me so casually," guffawed Keri. "I am Princess Keri to you in personal affairs, and Your Highness in public."

His expression wore an odd look. "Okay, is this drink spiked? Are you drunk? And where am I? Is this Zuobic? Or am I inside a rift?"

She exhaled, annoyed. "Okay, this is supposed to be my dream. You're sup-posed to be the dreamy prince. Stop being weird. You're supposed to woo me, and I'll pretend I don't care, then drop my handkerchief and you pick it up. And I'll be like, 'oh, Prince, you are so handsome,' and you'll be like, 'not as beautiful as you, my lady.' Not this weird thing you're doing. What's wrong with you?"

"Nothing's wrong with me, lady," said the elven prince.

"Quit calling me lady, my name is Keri!"

"And I'm not a prince, my name is Lake," he countered. "I live in Aberkyz, I'm a sorcerer in the army—I was prepping for my mission. But definitely not royalty. I'm not even from the empire."

She gasped, then squinted. "Wait, Lake? Are you from my other dream?"

"What?"

She began to retell the story of her death-dream in WalkBy. Halfway through, Lake interrupted, "You're that woman who followed me? I thought you were dead. In my dreams, you died."

"I know, I totally felt like I died," Keri agreed. "Not the best feeling, taking your dying breath."

A morose expression covered Lake. "I'm sorry I couldn't save you. If I had been stronger or better, if I had paid more attention in training, maybe—this wouldn't—I would be—"

"Prince, I mean, Lake, don't blame yourself for my death, that was totally my fault. I didn't know what I was doing—honestly, I don't know what I'm even doing now," she admitted. "But thanks to that other dream, I think I have superpowers now."

"Superpowers?" His head cocked.

She shrugged and told him about her experiences after the death-dream. "Yeah, so it's all because of the system."

Lake was silent for a few moments, then got up, paced, then looked over at the gardens. Keri was going to ask what was wrong, but then he laughed. Not just a simple cackle, but a heart-filling, belly-aching laugh. He doubled over, leaning on the gazebo's frame. He laughed until tears formed in his eyes.

"Is, um, everything fine?" asked Keri, wondering if the tea was indeed spiked.

He waved a hand at her as he tried to catch his breath. "I'm sorry. It's just that I'm overjoyed right now. You have no idea how badly this was haunting me. I thought I was going insane. Turns out, I wasn't the only one who saw the computer logs—or system." He told her of his own experiences with the system.

Keri listened. She was about to interrupt at some parts, but seeing how relaxed he was, she stopped herself. Before, in her last dream, he was uptight and focused on some objective, but now, the way he regaled her with his own tales, it was nice and easy. This was nicer than the sim dreams she'd had before, and so much more vivid and real. She patiently waited for him to finish.

"Do you know why we have this system? Why us?" asked Lake, sitting back down.

Keri shook her head. "It's pretty random, right? I mean, I was just at that WalkBy 'cause I was hungry. It's a weird dream."

"It's not just a dream, I think. I think it's our souls somehow being transported," Lake guessed. "Like right now. Look at us, talking in a dream."

She looked around her—the white paint of the gazebo gleamed against the light as she heard and felt the breeze going through the purple trees and her. "This and before—they're not just dreams, are they?"

"They're more like virtual reality. Do you think there are more people like us? With the system?" He got up from his seat and paced the gazebo.

"You mean, the other customers?"

"Yes, it makes sense for them to have it. We all got transported, or our souls got kidnapped?"

"Mmmm, maybe our souls crossed into a different world?" Keri suggested. "But yeah, I've never met anyone besides you. Have you?"

"Not really. You're my first one too." Lake stopped at the end of the rails and proceeded to be in deep thought.

Keri sipped her tea as silence hung in the air. "So, um, how are you?"

"Hmm? Oh, I'm doing okay." He leaned on the rails of the gazebo.

"Any plans for tomorrow?" Half of her hoped they could meet in real life.

Lake stretched his neck from side to side. "Tomorrow is the new mission. I still don't know if I'm ready, actually. I'm scared this new system will blow up, literally. I don't want to mess things up like I usually do."

She walked over and placed a hand over his. In her head, it was the right move—the princess would always comfort the prince like this. "The future is tomorrow's worries. The past is the worry we now regret. Today is the gift we receive to make no regrets—a present only we can give ourselves," she said and smiled. It was the perfect scene.

Lake looked at her with wonder and amazement. And could it be? A slight blush in his face? *I got you now,* thought Keri. *Ha ha!* That was the same line the princess used in the game. She couldn't believe she'd said it and actually pulled it off in real life—well, it was a dream or semi-dream—whatever. *Dating games do work in real life and dreams.*

Keri was still reveling at her accomplishment when, without any warnings, Lake leaned down and kissed her. His lips were soft and smooth, sending weird yet gentle sensations in her face and then body. Her eyes widened as a jolt within her wanted to—

Her alarm rang.

Keri awoke with a shocked expression on her face.

The mixed scents of fabric softener, citrus and soap effused from the fluffy pillow and silk bed coverings as Keri laid on her side. Sunlight streaked from the windows of her room, illuminating the tidy study and plush beige couch across from her bed. The walls around her mimicked nature with photos of landscapes and wall art of trees and flowers. Besides the low hum of the air conditioner, it was quiet and comfortable. Everything was so real, comfortable and present that her thoughts kept fleeting back to her dream with one question: *Was it all real?*

There was a knock on the door and Riley entered with a tray filled with her breakfast: eggs, toast and sausages. "Heya Keri. How are you? Still feeling sick? Hope everything is okay. Didn't really like the décor much in this room. But Vivian said you'll like it. I prefer lions and animals and the wild than trees and flowers." Her boots thumped against the floorboards as she made her way to an overbed table at the side.

Keri sat up. "No. Everything is great. Why didn't the maid bring it up?"

She placed the food on the overbed table and rolled it next to the bed. "I was coming up to talk to you anyway, so figured I'd bring it. Saves time. Anyway, are you good to talk? Does it hurt anywhere else?"

She shook her head. "The doctor you sent has been a big help. He says there are no more issues, I just need to rest."

Riley exhaled. "That's good. Good. Uh, I guess it's on to the next one. You can come in now," she beckoned at the door.

The carved wooden door creaked open as an embarrassed Wayne entered wearing jeans and a tight white shirt. "Hey, Keri. You all right?" he asked.

Keri's cravings deviated from one sausage to the other. "Uh, I'm fine. Are you fine? You're really fine." Unconsciously, underneath the sheets, her fingertips slid between her legs.

He walked closer to the bed with his hands inside his pockets. "Look, I'm sorry for dragging you into all of this. I never wanted anyone to get hurt."

Her lips stretched to a big smile. "Oh no. Don't think like that. I'm glad to help. And it was my fault you were there in the first place. Without that curse, you'd have taken those guys out, no problem. With your big...arms and shoulders." She leered from his package up to his torso.

He scratched the side of his neck before pocketing his hand again. "To be honest, I'm not entirely sure. This whole ability thing is new to me, you know? Plus, they spiked my drink. But you, you're the one with the incredible power to cure curses, right?"

Her face reddened. "I don't know about cure, but I can stop it if I have the artefact."

His face beamed. "Really? Can you actually do that? I'm willing to pay. How much do you want?"

You can pay with your body, thought Keri for a second before she realized what he was offering. "Can't you just hire a healer?"

Wayne made a pained face. "I had a client who fell in love with me. At first, she showered me with gifts: cars, equipment, protection. I was okay with it, but then she became more demanding, wanting me to be with her all the time, to serve her constantly. It was suffocating. I told her I had a life and other clients, and that made her furious. She gave me an ultimatum: her and her money, or she'd walk away. I've always managed with what I had, so it was an easy choice for me. I left her."

"Um, I'm not a love counselor or anything," admitted Keri. "This is out of my area."

He made a wry smile. "If that was the only problem, I wouldn't have gone crazy seeking help from people. After days of not seeing her, she asked me to meet up for closure. I agreed, thinking it was fine. But when we met, she started crying and apologizing. Then she gave me a parting gift—a reminder of our time together."

Riley cleared her throat. "Wayne has suffered a curse from this gift for months now. It's a curse from this choker." She handed her a glass box. Sitting on a small pillow inside was a black necklace with a metal engraving at the front.

By mental command, Keri brought up the notifications she ignored earlier. Details about Doom and revoking the curse came up, then something about a curse called Unloved.

> Curse: Unloved detected from target lover.
>
> Description: The wearer of this artefact will be cursed. Each time a person says I love you to them in any language, the person forgets all memories of the user completely. If the wearer attempts to tell them of the keyword in any form of communication, the person informed will lose memories of them.

After understanding the notifications, Keri said, "So people forget you when they say—"

"Don't say it," Wayne warned. "You have no idea what those three words have done to my life."

Keri felt a bit uncomfortable as the atmosphere turned sour.

He covered his face, sniffed and then gritted his teeth. "Sorry, I'm a bit on edge. It was fine when my clients said it, you know, role-playing and all. They'd forget about me. I thought it was okay, no repeat services needed. But when my close friends and family started forgetting—we're very open with each other—they'd say things like, 'Love you, man. Love you, bro.' And with just two words of the same meaning, *poof.* 'Sorry, do I know you? Are we close?' People in my life treated me like a stranger, and I didn't even know why. I begged them to remember or to get to know me again, but they hired people to keep me away." He slammed his fist against the wall, then let out a breath.

Riley patted his back. "Vivian found him drunk in the streets, starting fights. She remembered him from when she first moved to Troef. She used to buy his services."

Keri's face warped in surprise.

"Yes, I know they've slept together before," answering her quizzical expression. "Wayne told me after I saw his curse and explained the details around it to him."

Deciding it was better for the couple to figure out, Keri stared at the choker inside the case. "Before I do this, there's something you should know. There are some artefacts that are too much for me to handle right now. And if this is one of them, it might turn into a regular accessory without the curse," she warned them.

"Does that remove the effects of the curse?" she asked.

"I'm not really sure. This is all new to me."

"It's all right. Give it a try," said Wayne, after clearing his throat and wiping tears from his eyes.

Riley turned to him. "Are you sure, love? You know you aren't less of a man if you're afraid."

He shrugged. "The damage is already done anyway. At the very least, I don't think that stupid choker will ruin other people's lives."

"All right. Let's try it," Keri said after a moment.

She held the choker out and immediately felt the source attack her, then cease within a matter of milliseconds. Like a glove, her thoughts fit into the choker's power and control. She acclimated to the sensations for some time. Then, she noticed it. A tendril of source firmly bounded Wayne and the choker together. She could sense source in the form of strings from Wayne, binding and cursing people he cared about. Her thumb rubbed against the leather of the choker as she ordered the curse to terminate. With one thought, the strings that connected the choker and Wayne vanished.

> You have stopped the curse that plagued Target lover #3's life.
> Earned 600 coins. Total 760.

"I think that's it," spoke Keri.

"What do you mean, 'that's it'?" asked Wayne. Worry etched in his rugged and handsome face.

"Um, it's gone."

"But I don't feel any different."

Goggles materialized over Riley's face. "Hmmm, I don't see it anymore. Do you feel any different when you first wore the thing?"

His brows engaged and his mouth pouted. "I don't think so."

"Maybe it is gone. Why don't you try reaching out to some friends or clients that were affected?"

He snapped his focus to her. "Why would I do that? What if they push me away like last time? What if they hire people to keep me away again? I don't want to be locked up again."

Riley sighed. "What if they already remember you this time? Sad to see them wander around and not know what truly happened."

He didn't reply.

"If they don't remember you, we'll think of something else," she said softly. "But right now, the best way to test this out is meeting those who don't remember you."

After two deep breaths, Wayne stood straight. "I'll come back and let you know. Thanks, Keri." He reached for the door and left.

"Will he be okay?" Keri asked after a few minutes.

"He's strong. He'll be fine," answered Riley. "More importantly, will you be fine, love?"

"Me? All I needed was rest. I'll be fine to do..." Her lips stopped at that point. What was she to do? Everything was happening so fast, she barely had time to think about anything.

"Before you go thinking about what to do next, you have to know something. You know those people we stopped? That bomber man?"

"What about him?"

"He's a slave trader. He's after Wayne because he thinks Wayne is a 14. Like you, Charlie and me," Riley said. "Since Wayne came back from Zuobic a few weeks ago, I'm unable to read some details about him through my ability. Usually, I can see everyone's wellbeing represented in numbers. Health, source capacity, strength, intelligence, things like that. But I can't see his, love. The same way yours and Charlie's are both hidden."

"What's wrong with that?"

Riley shrugged and sat on a seat nearby. "Nothing mostly. But that slave trader saw you using abilities. He felt you use your abilities. They have a keen sense on people that display any kind of powers. He'll investigate you, and it won't be long until he figures out something's amiss."

"Is he going after me next?"

"Possibly."

"So people will try to catch me for money?" She hated the idea of being sold as a slave before. She thought it was just bad luck, but now there was a legit, good reason to be sold again?

"We're special, love. Not the type you'll like," answered Riley. "Especially to scientists, politicians, officers—we're tools for their dreams and whims. The Empire and Federation would pay millions for us."

A lightbulb lit up in Keri's head. "I'm a Zuosh citizen. They can't do this to me. If I end up in a slave prison, my country will rescue me."

Riley sighed. "Then this gets more complicated."

"It's not complicated. I have rights."

Riley slowly explained the laws that govern 16s, sorcerers, and 8s, item users. At the time that a person discovered he or she was a 16 or 8, they must register with their nation. This was made mandatory to have them help save humankind. If they were a new type of outlier, which was related to having abilities but doesn't qualify as a sorcerer or an item user, they must do so immediately. Those laws were similar to every nation, including the freezones. In Zuobic, the laws were stricter. They had to join the military as soldiers. If they were a new outlier, they had to immediately submit themselves.

Keri imagined herself wearing those puffy vests and heavy trousers. "Does this mean I have to be a soldier if I go home?" she asked, to which Riley confirmed. "No. Not wearing those heavy baggy clothes. All that discipline and order—no, definitely not. I don't want to be a soldier. Wait. What about you? Did you register?"

"Technically, I'm registered as an 8, like Vivian and Wayne," said Riley. "The mayor of Cluster RSTU is a good friend. He knows what I am and helped me make this establishment. For keeping my secrets, his office and soldiers enjoy some of my items and services."

"Great. That solves it. Give me that damn form, I'm going to register as an 8."

Riley pushed herself up from the seat and moved to the over table. "Not so fast, love. You're a federate, the only way you can register here in Zone Troef, a freezone, is if someone sponsors you. And you, being a 14, an ability user, is a big risk for any organization—that's what Vivian keeps reminding me over and over again. If someone finds out they're keeping a 14, zones, nations and armies will come after you." She helped herself with Keri's coffee.

"Can't Amazing Discoveries sponsor me too?"

Riley made a downcast face. "Sorry, love. I would if I could. We're full of me, Charlie and Wayne. Any more, and I don't think the mayor would like it. I've already maxed out my favors with him."

"Is there another way? I don't want to be a soldier back home."

"Well, you can register as a freeperson. You can use a different name and identity. But we only need to find a suitable organization to do that for you. I think I can ask Vivian to look into it. But you're going to have to train your abilities. I imagine if you want a decent organization to keep your identity, you have to let them know how you'll help them benefit.

"Think about it and let me know what you want to do. You can chat to Viv as well. Have to get back to work now, love. Get some rest."

Objectives:

1. Investigate Squad A's cause of disappearance in Kermoz Zone.

2. Recover collected data from engineer

3. Rescue separated members of Squad A.

Squad B Leader:
Captain Falon Rochel

Squad B Members:
Osher Grace - First Officer, Scout
Tony Gallagher - Second Officer, Mech Pilot
Nikki Valson - Mech Pilot
Maggie Alkido - Sorcerer (Medic)
Lake Deskenn - Sorcerer (Engineer)
...

#314-A
MISSION BRIEF

—*excerpt from mission dossier*

Chapter 17

Lake, Kermoz

Three vehicles travelled on a road filled with cracks and debris, heading towards Zone Kermoz. Two carrier transports zigzagged slowly on the road, hauling two mechs with a third livable caravan trailing behind, which had all the members of the active squad.

Falon rode in the passenger seat discussing details about the mission with the driver. Wearing the standard skin suit with a vest and cargo pants over it, she had red fiery hair that was tied in a ponytail.

Seated right behind the driver, Lake sat alone. He noted the single purple spade patch sewn on Falon's shoulders. It was her rank, signifying her captain status. She was a true and experienced soldier—his Squad Leader. They'd had a good exchange of words earlier. Basically, her expectation of him was to maintain the mechs, weapons, communications and recordings—a true support for the team. For the fighting and healing, she was heavily relying on the mechs and the other sorcerers with them.

With her shining black hair, Maggie sat at Lake's opposite side, looking out at the window. When he had been in the hospital, she came in, asked him questions and examined him, then left. No hellos nor acknowledgments. Today was no different. Not like he wanted things to change. To Lake, Maggie was part of the past that he was trying to get over quickly. Jella had made her statement clear, and now he had to live with it. It was not like he could beg her back. She was right. They weren't a good match.

Speaking of matches, the dream about Keri, the soul virtual reality, the level of detail she recounted about her experiences were far too real and tangible for his subconscious to ever make up. A quick social security check netted him results of a few Keris in the public database. But after searching for photos, he found a Keri Bolo: orphan, worked at Padala Services and was missing. It was her—he had no doubt about it. Her stories mentioned being accidentally transported to the freezones—was that why she was still recorded as missing? He made a mental note to try to find her after this mission was over.

His train of thought halted as Falon climbed out of the passenger seat and moved over to the back, where all the passengers were. "Okay Squad B, we're getting close to the site. I'll repeat the plan." She held onto a railing next to the door and punched buttons on a control panel next to it. A holographic map of Zone Kermoz materialized from the ceiling. She continued:

"Our team starts at the central station, then the tunnels and search underground. We have no radio support once we go underground except for linkos connected on our intranet. I trust you've at least memorized the general area of Kermoz. We have a total of eleven people, including two mechs and two sorcerers. If we encounter monsters, don't hesitate to escape if your gear can't kill them. Leave it to the mechs or the sorcerers."

"Any questions?"

Some of the squads shook their heads while others said no.

Falon turned off the holographic map. "Check your equipment again. I don't want you dying because of carelessness. Stupidest way to go out. ETA ten minutes." She headed back to the passenger seat next to the driver as she answered a call from her linko.

As everyone checked their gear again, Tony moved and sat behind Lake. "How did you do it?" he asked.

"Do what?" asked Lake.

A glint sparked in his eye. "Did you bribe someone to get this mission? Figured you'd grease some wheels. See if they saw your sparkling engineering skills you'd get to stay in the army or something?"

Lake felt tired of Tony's antagonizing behavior. For someone so good at being a soldier, he had a shitty personality. "I'll get out of your way, and you do whatever, okay?" he tried to diffuse the conversation.

"I'm surprised Major Cervantes didn't write you off from the squad list. You really got a good hold on Captain Falon," he whispered. "Do you have some deals with her? You tappin' that on the side? Everybody loves a pretty face huh?"

Osher, who had long-tied silver hair, stared at them with his grey eyes from the back seats. He was polishing his already shining rifle. "Tony, stop bothering our engineer. I'm sure he has the skills to prove his worth," he said aloud.

"Just catching up. We're from the same year in the training program," replied Tony, with his eyes glued onto Lake. "Ain't that right?"

He looked at him squarely as his jaw tensed.

Their linkos chimed. "We're arriving. Prepare yourselves," Falon announced.

He snickered. "Guess we're almost there." He moved back to his seat and waited.

The odd conversation halted as everyone ambled to their seats and strapped their seatbelts. Lake exhaled the breath he had been holding. *Someday Tony was going to get what he deserved,* he thought to himself. As he let go of the frustration, a new feeling braced him. Just as anxiety gnawed on him from entering Kermoz, the system alerted him:

> Contested Area Entered. Candidate Confirmation Started. Area Coordinate: Outworld Kz-S01A.
> Declaration of Owner: Defender. Confirmation Completed.
> Visitor: Hero Candidate. Declaration of Visitor: Invader.
> Alert: Please acquire Outworld Kz-S01A.

Lake read the intrusive message from the system a couple of times. But none of what it said made sense. Feeling confused by the system prompt and the situation earlier, he turned it off and focused on reviewing his support runes.

Darkness mostly loomed over the subterranean station, with only half-working vending machines and flickering fluorescent lights installed on the cracked walls giving any light. Squad B made do with the flashlights configured into their guns or helmets to light the way. The stuffy air and fusty trash triggered involuntary coughs and sneezing from a few of them.

At the front of the formation, the two mechs, the Red Giant and Silver Fox investigated the broken carriages. With a height of ten meters each, they were easily comparable to four-story buildings, but with the spacious tunnels they reached about a third of the vertical clearance. Most of the other soldiers shuffled behind them and searched where the two mechs were too big for.

Lake was a bit slower than the rest because of the heavy and large backpack he wore containing most of his equipment. He crossed over a turnstile and closed in on where most of the soldiers were.

Maggie blocked his path. "I don't care how you got here. This is my ticket to get the Major's attention for top secret projects. I suggest you twiddle with your screwdrivers or twirl your wrenches, whatever you need to do. I want a proper sorcerer-engineer. Don't mess this up for me." She turned and left.

It should've been you, boy. Your younger brother was smarter than you, were the words that echoed in Lake's head. It was one of his father's many nuggets of wisdom growing up.

Lake noticed the ranks of everyone in the squad. Their patches were all green, sergeant-level. The only blue ones were the younger ones. But all of them had three spades already. One more and they would rank up, leaving the private category. He had no star at all—what was he even doing here? Maggie was right. He'd only be in people's way. His hands gripped his backpack as he moved a step back.

His back bumped against Falon after a few more steps. "Sorry, Squad Leader, I didn't see you there."

"You okay? You look like you've seen a ghost. Are there ghosts here? That means we have to use magic. Bullets don't really work on them." Her face changed from concern to steely.

He shook his head. "Uh, no. No ghost. Just nervous."

She patted his shoulder. "That's all right. First missions are always tough, but this is just recovery. I'm sure not many monsters are going to be here. Come on, scout saw something." She pushed him forward.

With his supervisor at his tail, Lake yielded and marched ahead.

"Sorcerer Lake, I read about your file," she said. "About your family. Are you sure you're okay to be here?"

He looked down on the ground as he walked. "That was eight years ago, Squad Leader. I've made my peace with it," he said in a soft voice.

She nodded. "If you say so."

Further into the tunnel, mangled human legs were stuck between tracks covered in grey goo. The cloth on one leg had a patchwork of Zuobic's national flag—a cog, fist and anemone interwoven in an arabesque design. The team huddled over the remains.

Falon headed closer to inspect with Lake. "What do we have?" she asked.

Piloting the Red Giant, Tony was analyzing a sample of the goo. "Scan shows ten monsters that excrete the same substance according to our database. Only two of which live underground. It is either a shadow drake or ghost spiders."

"Eww, spiders. I hate spiders," said one of the soldiers. "Wish it was drakes."

"Yeah, drakes are better," said another soldier. "Put cumin or curry on them, and they'd dissolve like gravy. Easy kill."

"There are no nests nearby outside the walls," stated Maggie. "Did the outposts get breached?"

"Maybe a rift opened up underground?" suggested Tony.

"Doesn't the ward generator take care of that?" responded another.

Lake noticed Osher and Falon exchange hard stares. It would seem like not everyone was informed that Zone Kermoz had returned from another dimension. There was a separate brief that he received for this mission, which was labelled top secret. It was the initial aerial scans and findings Squad A did before they went missing. All seemed normal above ground, but there were seismic activities underground. Hence, Squad A headed below.

"Too early to tell," responded Falon, quieting everyone's conjectures. "But it's good to know we're dealing with level-0 monsters."

Monsters and beasts were categorized by intelligence level. Common monsters, those that had the basic instinct to kill and feed, were rated as level-0. Leaders and bosses from these beasts ranked at level-1, and the ones that exhibited intelligence on par with humans rated as level-2.

"Squad Leader, better get over here," reported Osher through the linko.

Veering from the train tracks, the goo trailed to a large hole in the wall where Osher knelt silently.

With the team behind her, Falon crouched next to the hole. "What's in there?" she asked.

The sniper wore black goggles that scanned through walls and hard surfaces. "Cavern up ahead. About five to eight passages that lead deep underground," said Osher.

"Enemies?" asked Falon.

"I can't see any from here. I have to be closer."

"Mechs?" she asked aloud.

"Nothing on vibrations or source frequencies," answered Nikki, who piloted the Silver Fox.

Falon crossed her arms. "Let's go deeper then. Engineer, start the cubex for recording. Squad, prepare for attacks."

"Yes, Squad Leader," everyone answered.

Carefully, the squad entered the hole in their formation: the Red Giant and Silver Fox in the front followed by the scout and the rest of the team. The cubex was a small black cube the size of Lake's palms. He hung it around his neck as it activated and recorded his surroundings. Following everyone, his thoughts drifted to the next task he should do. As they entered the large cavern, he rested at a corner near another passage. He put his bag down and started going through his supplies and equipment. He wanted to be as ready as possible.

"Do not move, engineer," shouted Falon.

"Ma'am?" he asked.

From her back, a mechanical baton transformed into a bow. Tattoos of red runes slithered from underneath the sleeves of her skinsuit up to her fingertips. She caressed the arc of the bow and drew a red arrow. The arrow zoomed and struck a shadow above Lake. A wail sounded as a knee-tall white spider with multiple blue eyes revealed itself, pinned on the wall.

"Ghost Spider," exclaimed one soldier.

"Squad, we are under attack. Enemies are level-0 monsters. I repeat, under attack. Prepare for battle," yelled Falon in a confident tone. "Red Giant, scan the area."

"Ten lifeforms within a 500-hundred-meter radius—no, twelve. All coming from the passages up ahead. All level-0," Tony reported from his readings on screen.

"Scout, hang back and snipe the closest ones," she ordered. "Use the mechs to block the passages. The rest kill anything that gets into our formation and figure out how to plug the holes."

Osher found a secure location in the corner while guarded by one soldier. He switched the settings of his goggles and aimed in the dark with his large rifle. "I'm in position, re-focusing senses...target found," he announced.

"Fire at will."

Deep inside a passage, a black hole materialized above the ceiling. Next to it, a translucent and monstrous form hung upside down. A bullet passed through the hole and hit the monstrous form as a ghost spider revealed itself and fell. The monster bled from a gunshot wound between its many eyes and twitched as it died.

Lake gazed at the rifle Osher used with amazement. It was a rune weapon type of gun. Rune weapons were the creations of Major Cervantes using monster cores to create a specific spell when a weapon is used. In Osher's rifle, Shadow Through was being cast whenever he pulled the trigger. Shadow Through was a spell that opened a hole between two places where the caster could see. The first place was at the nozzle of the gun, and the second was where the sniper wanted it to be. In this case, through the many walls his goggles could pierce and see through, he shot his rifle right at the heads of the monsters.

"First target dead," Osher reported. "Locking on second target."

"Keep going," ordered Falon. "Sorcerers, we need to see the enemy now."

Maggie cast Revealing Ring. Light circles expanded throughout the left side of the cavern in beats of two. As it hit the shadowed recesses, droves of spiders unveiled themselves.

Lake threw liquid grenades at unilluminated areas from his pack. The explosion sprayed glow paint everywhere and marked the invisible spiders which were immediately gunned down by his team. He then charged at a passage, absorbing mana at the same time. When he was ready to summon sorcery, he blanked.

He was about to cast a spell but quickly recalled he wasn't supposed to—not unless it was an emergency. As an engineer-sorcerer, his job was to support everyone else and not to attack, especially with his condition. Each combat spell could wind up killing him instead. His head blanked. What was he supposed to do? He grunted and decided to throw a couple of low-strength grenades instead. Rocks and dirt quickly filled the passage and blocked the entry after a small but loud explosion.

Maggie rushed to his side. "Stop that. Ghost spiders have poor eyesight but have highly sensitive hearing. That explosion might attract the whole nest."

His eyes widened. He knew what the characteristics of ghost spiders were, though he didn't really think about it at that moment. "I didn't mean to." His tone was laced with guilt.

She stepped forward and cast a 3-rune spell aiming at the passage. Stalagmites erupted from the ground and jammed into the ceiling, covering the hole. "Do you think you can do that without losing control and hurting yourself?"

Before he could answer, Tony reported from his scans, "Stop the explosions. A lot more are coming."

Maggie glared at the engineer.

Lake made a pained face. He just wanted to be useful. "Sorry. I—"

"I don't care," she interrupted. "Do it right or get out of the way."

More ghost spiders popped from the holes and assaulted the mechs and members of which were the closest ones to the passages. Tony responded by activating a sonar call only monsters could hear. The nearby spiders detoured from the soldiers, blasting them with bullets and attacked him instead. He hacked with his big red sword, but the number of spiders overwhelmed him, crawling over his back and torso. They tore through Red Giant's armor with multiple slashes from their piercing legs and deadly mandibles.

"Need some support over here," exclaimed Tony. "Red can't take this much damage."

"Engineer, defense enhancement on Red Giant." Falon shot one arrow that pierced and killed three spiders in a row.

Lake gathered source in his palms with complete ease. A bit of confidence flourished in him since enhancement spells were technically harmless. If he overloaded the spell, he would not blow up but would be more enhanced. He wrote two runes that glowed green and clapped his hands. Once he released the spell, he aimed for the mech. A fresh green breeze enveloped Red Giant.

Tony's eyes widened after checking the status of his mech on screen. "Speed buff? I need defense, damn it."

"No, I cast Troll—" He stopped his words midway. The last rune he wrote was of the third rune for the Earth Spikes spell, not Troll Skin. He mixed up the two spells.

"Forget it." With additional speed, the Red Giant moved like a speedy ninja, completely defying its heavy build. It dodged the attacks of the spiders with grace and sliced through their bodies with its giant sword with swiftness and ease. Though the monsters were many, with increased movement, the mech decreased their numbers in no time.

As the onslaught died down, the squad had some time to breathe. The scattered members moved back closer to formation as the others covered them.

Falon released another arrow on a crawling half-dead spider and ended it. "Scout, are we seeing the end of it?" she asked through linko.

"Negative, Squad Leader," reported Osher. "It's only the initial wave. More are coming."

"I need those holes blocked."

Four spiders appeared from one hole. Large steel blades slid from Silver Fox's arms as it met the monsters head on. As it tangled up with two, Maggie froze the third with a spell while the others gunned down the others dead.

"We'll keep them busy, Sorcerer Maggie," said Nikki. "Please take care of the holes."

Maggie nodded as she hurried to a hole and cast Earth Spikes.

Five more sprouted from another side. Lake had an idea and threw an oil grenade at them. The ends of the grenade spun in both directions as it spurted oil in a straight line. When a stray bullet hit it, flames flowered from the oil and created a wall. It slowed them even further while burning them to death.

Even though the squad's firepower was formidable, the spiders kept coming. As the corpses piled on the ground, the living ones pushed further. At every second that passed, the party was slowly being driven back.

Falon drew one big, overcharged arrow and released it. It passed by a line of three spiders and punctured a big hole in all of them. "Mech, report." She drew another arrow and did the same thing, this time, killing four.

Red Giant picked off a spider on its back and cut it in half. "There seems to be an increase of nine to ten spiders every minute, no signs of stopping," stated Tony.

Falon's face darkened. "Anyone have a large area of effect damage that does not explode? Or damage the walls?"

Everybody mulled over their own arsenal as they fought. Lake thought of one he could try, but he hesitated to bring it up. He could not afford to mess up and be the cause of the mission's downfall.

Maggie had finished plugging in another hole. "Frozen Wave. Freezes everything for 50 meters in diameter," she volunteered.

"How long is your cast time?" asked Falon.

"Two minutes."

"Make it one."

"Yes, ma'am."

She knocked out three more arrows and killed seven more spiders. "Everyone, have a timer for one minute. All of you, protect Maggie. Before ten seconds are done, run back near the exit. Engineer, block them. Scout, find a safe spot already and give us cover from there."

Osher stopped sniping and found a spot at the back. Meanwhile, blue colored source twinkled beside Maggie. As runes formed, arrows and bullets decimated the spiders that dared to approach her. Already at the back, Lake created more fire walls from oil grenades, preventing a direct path.

At the remaining open passage, the spiders poured out incessantly. When they closed the distance to their female prey, their march slowed. Icy frost manifested on their hairy legs.

Maggie, glowing blue with runes, breathed out.

Six floating runes vanished. A blue-silver mist crawled outwards and froze every spider, rock and dirt it came in contact with. Alerted by the danger, the other monsters ran back to the passage. But the cold air swept with purpose, slowing everything down. It reached the fastest amongst them and encased them in a blanket of icy death. Like the heaviest of winter days had arrived, the whole cavern was covered with frost.

Maggie fell to her knees, heaving and sweating.

"No signs of incoming spiders," Tony read his scanners.

Looking through his goggles, Osher announced, "The spiders furthest away are running from the hole. They don't seem to like the cold."

Lake came to Maggie's side. "Are you okay?"

Sweat dripped down her face. Her hands shook, and her skin paled.

He assumed she was suffering from hypoetheria—a condition where sorcerers experience the symptoms Maggie was showing. It occurred when they use too much source, more than their body could handle. "You have to rest. Recommendation says three hours at least," he said in a lowered voice.

Maggie stared daggers at him. "Do you not think I know that?" she hissed.

"Are we going back, Squad Leader?" asked Tony through linko.

"There seems to be a big nest down there," said Falon. "I'll only proceed if everyone is well enough to."

"Red Giant is fine. We're ready to go, Captain." Tony spoke for himself and his two buddies.

"No problems here," said Osher.

The others voiced their confirmation, since they only suffered minor to no injuries and could still carry on.

"Sorcerers?"

Lake and Maggie exchanged weird looks.

Maggie forced a smile. "We are able, Squad Leader."

He frowned at her.

"Good. Looks like we're continuing," declared Falon.

Chapter 18

Lake, Underground Train Station, Kermoz

As the squad headed deeper below, Lake had one eye on Maggie who was clearly slower than before and had another on his system. Due to the intensity of the battle earlier, he had not had the chance to look over the multiple notices his system had sent. Apparently, he had earned a lot of coins from killing the ghost spiders. Though not all of the monsters vanquished counted as his kill, every time he helped kill one, he earned rewards. Even the ones Red Giant killed counted, due to the effect of his buff.

CANDIDATE STATUS:
Name: Lake Deskenn | Profile: Hero | Coins: 410
Activated Fragments: Storehouse – F , Hero's Retreat – F (innate),
Available Fragments Left: 1

He'd had a hunch before that monsters were the key to him gaining coins, and it seemed to be true. By thought, he perused the many fragments and items he could buy. Though the mission so far was a mess, he felt curious about purchasing one. He didn't know what it could bring to his life, but it would definitely be amazing. After all, Cervantes did mention that he was at the center of all of this. Maybe the system had some truth to it? Not just a linko mind hack.

The squad stopped at another tunnel that seemed to open wider as they got deeper. Osher broke away from the formation and crouched at the opening. With his shoulders leaning against the wall to his left, he used his goggles and scanned ahead, relaying what he saw:

A wider cavern existed twice as big as where they were. Multiple skinnier spiders tended to hundreds of eggs. A few cracked and tiny hairless spiders broke free, squealing. The adult spiders fed them drops of blood from chopped human remains.

In a corner, people hung inside cocoons made of spider silk. Judging by the heat they gave off, they were still alive. The spiders offered human parts from the cocoons to a ghost spider, ten times larger than the rest. The large spider, of which seemed like the queen, as batches of eggs ejected from its rear.

"A big giant spider mama, huh?" asked Tony. "Means a rift opened here."

"The queen looks new," said Nikki.

"What do you mean?"

"Spider-Queens get fatter as they mature. This one looks to be like a bigger version of the small ones—still slender and all. It means it hasn't been long since it became queen."

"This place has been untouched for years, the report said. Maybe it died?"

"Could be. From what though?"

"Can you confirm if they are Squad A, the investigation team?" asked Falon.

"Their clothes match the standard uniform," answered Osher.

Falon moved closer to the scout. "How many are left alive?"

Osher opened his mouth, then closed it back again. "They are—what the..."

"Scout?"

"Definitely alive," he said with sweat running down his forehead. "The ones breathing don't have arms and legs."

"Anyone know how long ghost spider prisoners last for?"

"Two to three weeks give or take," answered Nikki.

Tony searched and read from the database. "She's right. Adults last for three weeks—children, teens and elderly, around three days at most. The webs produce anesthetic effects. The longer it is applied, the stronger it is."

"That explains why they haven't gone into shock or death with no limbs," breathed out Maggie.

"Despicable bastards," cursed Tony.

"What do we do now?" Nikki asked.

"The right thing to do is to save them," suggested Lake.

"Sure. Maybe if someone follows their orders," Tony said in a condescending tone. "Maybe we'll stand a chance against a whole colony."

Lake clenched his jaw. "That was an honest mistake. I will try better."

Tony shook his head and turned away.

Falon stared ahead and thought out loud, "A whole nest of level-0 monsters and one level-1. Odds are against us. We're pulling out," she announced.

Lake opened his mouth for a moment to protest. But realizing he was out of place, being the lowest rank with the least amount of experience, he kept his down and started to prepare like the rest.

"Wait," Osher interrupted.

The squad stopped midway and focused on him.

Osher continued watching through his goggles. "There's a...rift? Something's coming out."

"Is it another mama spider?" asked one soldier.

"Nah, it's probably a different monster," countered Tony.

From a crouching position, Osher staggered back and fell on his butt. "It saw me. It saw me," he exclaimed.

"Bro, what's wrong?" said Tony from his linko.

Osher scratched his neck as he struggled to breathe. He pulled his goggles off. His eyes reddened and veins protruded from his temples. He choked and heaved, then passed out.

Falon rushed to him. "Squad B, stay in formation. Medic," she ordered.

Maggie sided next to the scout and began inspecting him.

As the two women huddled over the scout, Lake's heart threatened to burst from his chest. His breathing increased as his hands started shivering. What was this? He knew he was not anywhere near his source conversion limit, so he should not be experiencing hypoetheria. But what was happening to him? Then, as the feelings intensified, he understood what it was. Fear. "We have to leave." His lips trembled.

"Can't you see someone's injured?" said a soldier.

"Medic, what's wrong with him?" asked Falon. "Administer healing, now."

Maggie tried a healing rune, but it fizzled out before it completed itself. She then produced a bandage from her pack and wrapped it around the scout's head instead.

"That is not what I asked for, medic," barked Falon.

"Squad Leader, we have to leave, now," demanded Lake.

"Stand down, engineer. The wounded comes first."

Around him, he felt a violent source leak from the entrance ahead. Like it was a soft start to a horrible and dreadful song. It crept up as the moment passed. The hairs at the back of his neck stood. His breathing slowed and then stopped. The song's beat dropped. "Too late. It's here," he exhaled.

On their left, a shadow skittered forward. Slender human hands felt the air as a hooded woman crossed through. Her black skimpy outfit accentuated the paleness of her skin and her white hair. She pulled down her hood and revealed eight red eyes on her face. Each eyeball zeroed in on one soldier, flaring with alertness.

Falon released arrows without warning. It hit the ceiling, burying the entity under rubble and dirt. "Retreat now," the squad leader commanded.

For a very brief moment, they stood in shock. But the next, they realized the order had been given, their bodies moved like it had rehearsed a thousand times. Silver Fox led the way with most of the members in the middle. Carrying the scout, Red Giant brought up the rear with Falon following close behind.

Falon let another volley fly after as she retreated. "Keep going." Every attack caved the underground passages further.

Squad B reached the first cavern where they had fought the horde of spiders. Most breathed hard, but otherwise fine, except for Maggie who crouched to the ground and whose sallow complexion made her look like she had jaundice. But however worse she was, it could not compare to Osher whose eyes were bleeding the whole time. The bandage was so soaked that the red had fully replaced the white.

Falon emerged from the tunnel. "Engineer, bomb the tunnel," she shouted.

Lake rolled multiple remote-controlled bombs into the tunnel. After distancing himself, he detonated them. Dry earth and hard rocks covered the pathway with a boom.

"Everyone well?" she asked.

Red Giant placed the scout on the ground gently. "First officer needs help," he said in a slightly panicked tone.

Nikki observed their medic. "I don't think Sorcerer Maggie is well," she said.

Maggie struggled to stand upright. "I'm fine."

Falon's face hardened. "Engineer, heal the scout."

"Squad Leader, I am fine," she repeated. "I can do my job."

"Ma'am, I'm not familiar with healing spells," Lake admitted.

"Don't let the Starless Sorcerer heal the patient. I'm the medic. It is my job. He doesn't even know anything about healing." She gesticulated her arms.

"A medic who cannot heal is useless," stated Falon. "Teach the engineer a healing spell."

"Squad Leader, with all due respect, I won't let someone who blows himself up heal the First Officer," stated Tony with conviction.

"What does that mean?" asked a soldier.

He hastily retold the story of Lake blowing up the training center with his own spell.

Criticizing eyes filled with doubt and uncertainty befell Lake. The slightly biased opinions of his squad seemed to change to unreadable and confused expressions.

"Maybe it isn't a good idea after all," said a female soldier. "Maybe he can wait until we get out of here?"

"We can radio in for help outside," suggested another soldier.

Falon looked past nothing and breathed deeply. "Teach the engineer, Sorcerer Maggie," she ordered.

"But, Squad Leader," pleaded Maggie and the others.

"Are you refusing direct orders from your superior?" barked Falon.

"No, Squad Leader."

Maggie waved Lake to come with a downcast face. "Do you know Mending Touch?" she asked.

Lake knelt beside her. "No."

"The first rune is like the forward direction rune but inverted. The second is an unequal sign with a slash instead of a straight line," she instructed. "You want to gather source at the tip of your index finger, not your palms."

As he raised his right hand to start, the foreboding feeling seized his body again. His heart thumped loudly against his chest and the hair on his back stood. He wrote the two runes with desperate strokes. Then, repeated them again.

"That's not Mending Touch," complained Maggie, looking at the runes he produced.

Revealing Ring was a 2-rune spell. He intentionally ignored Maggie's complaints and strengthened and expanded the spell, casting it twice. Pulsing light illuminated around them and reached for the walls. When it hit the furthest soldier from them, the woman with eight red eyes revealed herself behind him.

Maggie gasped.

"Get away," screamed Lake.

As the soldier turned around, six large spider legs emerged from the woman's back. The hairy legs punctured him from head to toe in consecutive strikes. It bore holes in the man like a knife to a fruit with red juice leaking out. The monster then lifted the corpse and tossed it aside.

"You asshole," screamed Tony.

Red Giant brandished its sword and met the Spider-Woman head on. With sweeping strikes and stabs, it took advantage of its size to intimidate and overwhelm the enemy. The Spider-Woman defended with only four hairy legs while standing in place. After a few exchanges, the half-human arachnid grunted. She used a fifth leg and struck the mech on its left leg. Then, all of the spider legs struck the Red Giant's lower limbs, each drilling a hole through it and holding the giant in place.

Falon removed her vest and skin suit, exposing her back muscles and a red tattoo of wings and runes through her sports bra. "Eject and retreat, Squad B," she ordered.

Smoke escaped from the cockpit as the latches opened. Tony's seat ejected from the mech and catapulted back. The multiple red eyes of the Spider-Woman focused on the fleeing chair. It started unhooking itself from the Red Giant. The monster disappeared in a flash and reappeared above the flying chair. It caught the chair with its legs and brought it down to the ground.

Next to the entrance, Silver Fox collected Osher and Maggie with both hands and retreated with the other members following behind.

The tattoo on Falon's back came alive. Red wings made of aura sprouted from her shoulder blades and fluttered on both sides. Extending her bow again, she plucked a feather from her wings, placed it on the string and pulled it back. The feather transformed into a scarlet broad arrow. "Let him go," she called out.

The monster tilted its head to the side. With a scoff, it hurled Tony right back to the remains of the Red Giant. It strode to her new prey just as Falon let the arrow sing. Mid-flight, it transformed into a bird made of fire and engulfed the enemy.

Instead of escaping, Lake leaped towards the Red Giant and found a bleeding and half-awake Tony. He pulled out a knife and began cutting the straps of the seat around him.

"Starless Sorcerer, pull back," coughed Tony. "Help Osher."

Once the pilot was free, Lake carried him over the shoulder. "I'm helping you first," he said.

Up ahead, Falon pulled out another arrow and continued her attack. "What are you still doing here, engineer? Go," howled Falon through her linko.

From the wreckage, he gazed over to a battle that seemed to be one-sided. He wondered if Falon was indeed winning. But looking at it closely, the Spider-Woman only stood there taking the blow, not doing anything.

"It's fireproof," murmured Tony. "The impact is keeping it from attacking."

Lake gulped. Out of all the people in their squad, Falon was the strongest attacker they had. With her bow, that he believed to be a rune weapon and her rune tattoos, she could easily destroy mechs and tanks with her fire power. But that wasn't working at all. This monster was impervious to fire. What should they—he was reminded of Maggie's Frozen Wave that drove away the spiders.

"Ice. We have to fight it with ice," said Lake aloud.

"Do you know a spell?" asked Tony.

He gave a once-over at the wreckage of Red Giant, inspecting the destroyed legs, but otherwise functioning torso. "No. I can't cast one. But I..." He moved next to the mech, laid the pilot down and typed on the control panels.

The internal specifications and status of the mech appeared on the screen. Red marks flashed on its lower limbs, yellow on the torso and green on the head and chest.

Lake made a fist-pump. "It still works." He popped the lid of the main engine, located below the seat and started fidgeting with Red Giant's internal mechanism.

"What the fu—are you—" Tony coughed up blood.

"Every mech has a cooling system. It just so happens that I've installed the newest version to Red Giant. Best one ever—it can last for months, even years, operating without adding coolants," he explained. "If I can somehow reconfigure the monster core and power the cooling system instead of the main engine and overload the system, then maybe—"

"—you'll have an ice bomb," finished Tony.

From his pack, he dug out an electronic pen that could solder and cut metal at the same time. "Yes. Maybe." He took a moment to take in what was he doing before diving back in again.

As fire birds collided with the monster continuously, sweat poured from Falon—on her back and on her face. Her breathing was labored, and the speed at which she loaded her bow with her burning abilities slowed. The red aura behind her that fluttered as if they were real wings diminished in size and intensity.

After one arrow, she, for the nth time, reached behind her aura of wings and plucked a strand and placed it on her bow. As her arm stretched back to pull, she involuntarily let go. The arrow vanished as she bent and heaved. Big, deep breaths came slowly in and out of her. Her head bobbed a couple of times before she stood straight again. She then repeated the attacking motion. But just as she lay hold of her aura, the blaze evaporated. She fell to her knee and puked water and saliva.

"Squad Leader," voiced Tony from his linko.

"Please hold tight," radioed Lake in alarm. "I'm almost there."

The Spider-Woman appeared behind Falon, tilting its head. As she raised her head to look at the shadow towering over her, a spider leg struck her from behind and punctured through her core. It slid up and down as blood flowed from the wound and onto the ground.

"Live," Falon mouthed to Lake.

Squad B's leader, with the last of her strength, climbed closer to her killer and embraced it. She locked her fingers together and bound the monster close. The red wings blazed again from behind her. Instead of extending out, they wrapped Falon and the Spider-Woman. As it cocooned them both, the aura transformed into fire—from a simple spark to a raging inferno. A pillar of flame stood in the darkness of the cave, scintillating in beauty and destruction.

From the wreckage, Tony gasped at the display of fireworks. "Captain Falon..." he murmured.

Lake continued with his reconfiguration. "Squad Leader." As he focused on the screen, on his periphery, he saw his leader dying.

The fire glowed bigger and brighter for a few more minutes, covering the ceiling and the space around it. Then, it receded and wilted. From a full tower of flame, it dwindled to a stick by the second, and finished to embers on an ashen corpse of a previous living soldier. Next to the dead was the living—an unharmed monster with the appearance of a pale-skin woman with eight red eyes and six legs from its back. The Spider-Woman flicked its spidery leg that was stuck into the dead as Falon disintegrated into smoke and cinder.

Tony cursed under his breath. "How long 'til you get this rolling?" He pushed himself to stand, groaning and wincing.

Lake finished cutting some boards and adding new lines. He proceeded to connecting the wires on the cooling system. "Five minutes? Wait—Where are you going?"

Tony spat blood. "Buying the stupid Starless Sorcerer time." Lightning crackled around his boots as blue rune tattoos swam over his feet, moving in and out of his footwear. From his right leg, he unholstered a baton that mechanically transformed into a spear. His stance shifted to a semi-crouch with one leg forward, weight on his back leg, spear on both hands and pointing forward at his enemy.

The Spider-Woman's many eyes focused on Tony as she tilted her head.

In a flash, Tony vanished from where he stood with traces of electricity crackling over pebbles. The next moment, he appeared behind the monster and swung his spear. The blade almost hit the monster's pale skin, but its hairy spider legs blocked it. Just as the other spider legs moved to strike, Tony disappeared in a flash again. Hitting, dodging, and hitting again—that was the tactic the soldier used. From all directions, he tried to get in solid swings but quickly escaped after. Though his agility was beyond superhuman, no strike ever landed.

The Spider-Woman grunted. When Tony appeared behind her yet again, this time, it was she who vanished and surprised the soldier from behind. Spidery legs struck both his feet, drilling holes in his ankle. When it let go, he fell on the ground face first with a thud.

Blood pooled around Tony's lower body. "Damn, bitch." Once the Spider-Woman towered behind him, he gripped his spear tightly, turned and stabbed it forward.

The Spider-Woman parried the spear away with its arachnid leg as it hurled away and struck a wall. It grabbed the soldier with its human arms and stared at him with its many red eyes.

Veins bulged around Tony's temples as his eyes reddened. "Aaaaaahhhh," he screamed and cried blood.

On the Red Giant, the configuration was set and a timer for the bomb's detonation appeared. Lake wasted no time after his setup. He cast the runes for Earth Spikes and targeted the Spider-Woman. After the runes twinkled to life, he clapped them into his hands and slammed them onto the ground. Something stirred within him, the same unbridled feeling over source when he had cast fireball in the training room.

Instead of stalagmites sprouting from below, the Spider-Woman's feet changed to stone. The condition crept slowly up to its knees and then onto its hips. It let go of the soldier and stared at the sorcerer with all of its eyes glowing a brilliant red. An invisible wave of source shot from its eyes and onto his own.

Hero is affected by curse. Due to unstable source conditions, curse does not take effect.

Its face expressed a slight surprise at its curse not working. As the petrification reached its hands, it said, "@~!34^$@."

> The soul of a hero is a candidate. Congratulations for unlocking Soul Fragment: Otherworldly Languages – N/A.
> Description: Candidates comprehend otherworld languages.

"I made a mistake. This world has its candidates awakened," the Spider-Woman said before its whole body was turned into stone.

Seeing the statue of the monstrosity, Lake made a stupid grin. After hearing Tony groan, he snapped back into reality and stumbled forward to where his colleague was. He pulled Tony's arm and slung it over his shoulders again and dragged him up and away.

"Is it dead?" asked Tony, his bleeding eyes closed.

Sensing the tremor from the beat of his heart and the violent energy coursing in his immediate environment, he doubted it was. As he neared the exit of the cave, he heard the crumbling of stone behind him. He looked back.

The Spider-Woman broke away from its petrifaction. It glared at the sorcerer with blood lust. With robotic steps, it pursued them as its legs slowly recovered. Just as it passed the wreckage, Red Giant exploded in ice. Freezing temperatures and frost covered the immediate vicinity of the explosion, blanketing it in glacial beauty. Once again, the monster was turned into a statue—this time not of stone, but ice.

"Now, it's over," Lake exhaled.

Tony mumbled fast asleep.

As the engineer stepped forward, a laser beam shot through his shoulder, creating a clean, sizzling hole. He fell on his knees and released Tony, catching a glimpse behind him.

Though the Spider-Woman was frozen, its eyes floundered erratically on its face. One of its eyes lost its red glimmer and seemed to have died. Another eye sat still glowing brighter than the others.

The hairs on Lake's skin stood. "It's firing another shot." He tried to get up, but his wound, the load of his bag and Tony, all weighed him down.

A laser beam fired and carved a clean hole from the back of his left shin.

He howled in pain.

Two red eyes died. Six writhing ones remained. A third flared red hot.

Lake struggled to rise on his feet, suppressing all the pain that screamed within him. Panic urged him to let go of Tony. He needed to survive. But a part of him held on. He wanted to save a life. No, he *needed* to save at least one. It was not going to happen again. He was not going to let someone else die. "Please, just this once," he pleaded to no one, maybe to himself—maybe to anyone that could hear.

> Emergency Alert! Hero's Retreat activated. Finding escape route. Escape route found.
>
> Due to rank, fragment cannot initiate freely. Finding alternatives to initiation.
>
> 410 coins available.
>
> Would you like to use all coins and initiate?

Without even thinking about it, Lake screamed, "Yes."

> Initiating...

Rows of runes surrounded Lake and Tony. It went around them, creating a cylinder full of markings. The writings glowed in pink as an arcane formation materialized beneath and above them. The letters revolved slow at first, then fast. It spun quick enough to be barely readable as a bright light exploded from each text, blinding the entire area. When it receded, another laser shot forward, but the two had already vanished from the depths of Zone Kermoz.

Love Me, Princess!

Orphaned and waiting tables at a pub, follow a young maiden as her world is turned upside down when the royal family whisks her into the palace and brings her news that changes her life forever. She is the long-lost princess of the Sword Empire.

Multiple date scenes with different choices and outcomes.
Three love targets for the princess to pursue with separate endings.
Two additional targets from DLC.
Customizable main character through items, fashion and skills.
Variety of mini games available: puzzles, tower defense, card games and more.
Gallery collection for all scenes, uncensored.

WARNING: for adults only +18

Join the princess as she learns noble etiquette, faces intrigue and politics, and most of all, searches for her one true love.

Platforms: linko-gamelink, Glassy-Play

—*Love Me Princess, Game Back Cover*

Chapter 19

Keri, 8F Infirmary, Amazing Discoveries

Spending most of her mornings playing in her room, Keri realized more and more that the soul system operated like the RPGs she played, taking shape as the *Love Me, Princess* system. Her interactions with Maxwell and Wayne reinforced that idea. If she really wanted more coins, she'd have to pursue the men around her fervently.

The game's interface was open while the soul system floated next to it—two screens juxtaposed. Her eyes bored on the coins and the three options:

Soul Growth - 500 coins

Body Growth - 300 coins

Mind Growth - 300 coins

Like *Love Me, Princess*, it seemed the cost for growth increased per purchase. This appeared a bit random in the game, but mostly the ones that get purchased a lot usually doubled its cost, forcing players to not over-invest in one upgrade. After checking her coins, she selected Body.

Congratulations! You have purchased Body Growth.

Total coins 460.

Your reflexes and agility will increase after your body undergoes changes within a day.

"Fudge brownies," she cursed.

Her expectations leaned towards getting beauty improvements: big boobs, glowing skin or a heart-shaped face—something like that. She wasn't sure reflexes and agility would get her in bed with any of her target lovers, but maybe it was one of their kinks? She could only hope. In any case, with the threat of slavers, monsters and being experimented on, this kinda worked? At least she wouldn't get stomped by stampedes if she was agile enough.

An audio message arrived on her linko. When she touched her earlobe, the message from Vivian played; "Come have lunch at the kitchen in the residence."

Keri made her way into the kitchen while playing around with the system some more. She discovered the help menu. It told her a lot about how the system functioned, which she knew quite well already from her gaming experience. She went through her system shop as she operated the elevator. All of the fragments she had available previously were greyed out. The only ones left for her to choose were: Increase Mind, Increase Body and Increase Soul. She rolled her eyes over the screen. First, fragments that acted like skills and now options to increase her stats? This was becoming more and more like a game. She would've been ecstatic at how her life was changing if it weren't for the fact that she had been kidnapped—and she may be kidnapped again, or even experimented on.

Making her way to the kitchen, she grumbled at her options on the screen. After getting stomped by people, being thrown against a wall and being dragged everywhere, she was sick of it. Her finger selected the Increase Body. If ever the slavers or army were going to hunt her down, she was not going to go along with it willingly. She was running—hopefully this option would give her the means to do so.

Vivian was standing in the kitchen halfway through opening the fridge. "Is something the matter?" she asked. "You look like someone dropped a bomb on you."

Keri half-smiled. "Oh, no. Just figuring out my abilities. I'm still kinda confused."

Vivian took a cake from the fridge and placed it on the bench. "About that, I think we should talk. Let's have cake." She took out plates and utensils.

"That sounds serious. Am I in trouble?" She sat on the stool.

Vivian sliced a cake and served it. "Of course not. I'm simply worried about everything. I know we agreed to keep it all a secret and private, but frankly, after the incident with Wayne, your secrets will come out sooner or later."

"What do you mean?"

"When I first met Wayne, he was normal. But after coming back from Zuobic, you know, to try and find a cure for his Unloved curse, he changed. He was stronger and almost superhuman. And that incident at the arena, I've never seen someone exhibit that much power without the help of an item."

Did Wayne have a system too? Does Vivian know about it? Questions juggled around Keri's mind as she continued to devour her cake. "You think I'll be powerful like that?"

She served herself a slice and sat on the opposite stool. "Not sure what to think. Riley's appraisal is limited on you and Wayne. She says the info is incomplete. It's like...Charlie all over again. I was thinking it might be the system you're seeing, but Charlie doesn't have that."

"What's his story?" Bits of icing and bread appeared stuck on her teeth.

"You already know we found him two years ago—"

"Near a rift," she interjected. "I'm guessing his parents were killed by monsters as well?" In the news she watched back in Zuobic, there were always clips about children being orphaned due to monsters killing people.

Vivian played around with her food for a minute before eating a slice. "That's half of it. Truthfully, closers found him inside the rift."

"You mean, he was kidnapped and brought in?"

"He was from inside the rift. He is an outlier. But we aren't sure if he's a 14 or maybe a 32." Slight unnoticeable worry lines creased at the ends of her eyes.

Keri gaped then realized there was food on her mouth, so she continued chewing and gulped. "Is he one of those elf-people?"

She shrugged. "We don't know. Riley and I happened to be on the site where a rift was closing. The guild had already defeated the boss monster, and we were both collecting the items from inside and back out. That's when we saw him. A lost little boy." She stared out blankly at space.

She continued to eat her cake while the news sunk in her mind.

"He looked at us and pointed at Riley's sausage roll. She was eating while working. Riley liked her snacks and she wouldn't part with them that easily. But she did that day," continued Vivian. "He was so hungry that he ate it all in seconds. Then asked for another. Of course, Riley had another one. So she gave them until she ran out. Riley picked him up and told him we'll take him to the department that handles orphans. But on the way there, in our car, we were passing through city ruins and an old building collapsed and fell on us."

Keri nodded and continued eating the cake, engrossed in the story.

"I thought we were going to be crushed to death or buried underneath, but that didn't happen. For some odd reason, we were next to the rubble, safe and sound inside our car, and Charlie was glowing. He protected us. Then it hit me. I said to Riley, 'We have to protect this child just like he protected us.' So we decided to adopt him instead of letting him go. Whatever he was, 32, 14 or some other outlier, we didn't care. He's our boy, and we're a family.

"I don't know why we did the collection that time at the rift. We usually just get people to do it for us, but that day, we decided to do it ourselves. It was the best decision that we've ever made.

"I'm sorry, Keri for unloading on you. I am sure you have enough on your plate to be thinking about, besides listening to a mother's woes."

Keri shook her head. "Oh, this is great. I mean, not you almost getting killed by a building, but talking to you is. It's nice talking to someone like this. I didn't really have anyone back home I could talk to."

She took another bite. "No friends? Or family?"

Keri shook her head. "I can't remember my family much; all I know is that they died from a rift when I was young—one of those orphans. I got by with social welfare and government programs. Uh, I do have people I talk to at the warehouse, but they're not really friends. Maybe my addiction to games is why I don't have any."

"Charlie is attached to you. Besides the way you communicate, I feel like there's more. If you want to, you can stay here with us. If you don't have anyone to go back to." She reached out and clasped her hand across the table.

Something stirred in her chest. "What about rent, food or bills?" She was warming up to the idea of staying here permanently. Something in her pushed her to find out what this system truly was. In order for her to do that, she had to explore her abilities. Where else would she be free from the threat of experimentations and slavers other than the freezones?

Vivian returned to her cake. "You can work as a closer, you know. All the 7s—the weapons, the artefacts, the monster remains—all of them fetch a very high price. If you become one, money won't be a problem," she urged.

"What about the slavers and scientists?"

"If you become a closer, you will have to register with a guild. A guild gives you cover when you use your abilities. People will simply think you're a sorcerer or you possess an abundance of items."

"That will shoo them away, right? I won't have to worry about them?" Uncertainty coated her words.

"I believe so, more so if it's a powerful guild."

Keri finished the remainder of the slice. She hated fighting, not because she was afraid—well yes, it was because she was afraid. She admitted she was definitely afraid of dying. But won't her new abilities give her some sort of protection? Especially if she got more coins. Being a closer did mean she could get her hands in more outlier items. And if she did fight, won't she just stand in the back and help people if they've been cursed?

"I think this should help you decide." From her pocket, she placed a gold necklace with a tiny sword for a pendant.

"Does this turn to a big sword too?" asked Keri. "I don't know how to use one."

"It's called a Trainee Sword. Whoever can use it will slowly learn swordsmanship. You'll be a master in no time."

"Are you sure? This sounds like a really good 7," she said with a tight grip on the necklace, hoping she wouldn't ask for it back.

Vivian waved a hand. "It is absolutely fine. Besides, this is a loan. Once you're done, give it back and you can use a real sword next time."

As Keri wore the necklace around her neck, a sensation enveloped her—as if her palms touched the handles of a lever. At one command, she knew she could summon the blade on her neck into a full-sized sword of any kind. This definitely was handy in a fight if she was suddenly pit in the front. "If I become a closer, and I can't register with Amazing Discoveries, who do I go with?" she asked.

A glint sparked in Vivian's eye. "I take it that's a yes?"

"Uh, it's not a no?"

"I can work with that."

Chapter 20

Keri, Hairless Ape Guild House

Keri waited behind the sliding doors leading into the training room of the Hairless Ape Guild. Vivian had asked her to stay outside while she had a conversation with its leader. She snorted at the thought of working under Maxwell in his guild. His incorrigible attitude made her skin crawl.

"You can come in now," Vivian messaged in her linko.

As the sliding doors opened, a vast open room with nothing but space greeted her. Right at the corner near the entrance, there was a break area where multiple seats and benches were laid out. A number of people, mostly men, sat and talked at the benches—all sweaty and in their training clothes. Her eyes darted over to two men she recognized from her rescue. Both of them had their tops off as they headed to the drink station. One drank from a water dispenser while the other pulled a bottle filled with a yellow liquid in it from the fridge. As their lips touched their drinks, liquid spilled carelessly down their chins, to their hard chests, and trickled down their ripped abs, ending on their skintight training suit trousers—almost wetting the area near their bulges. She bit her lip.

"You want to join us?" a baritone voice sounded behind her.

Keri turned and salivated some more. Wearing only black tights, Maxwell patted himself dry with a towel. He started around his neck, sliding to his square ripped chest, passing over his pink nipples, down to his navel and around his six-pack abs, and then right up again. On second thought, Keri might not actually find it bad to be under him.

Maxwell's eyes swiveled from head to toe. "No," he said firmly.

The trance she was experiencing from the hot and sweaty men around her broke. Keri resented herself for even considering doing anything with this jerk.

Vivian stood next to the guild leader with crossed arms. "What do you mean, no? She has potential. She can use any item she wants," she argued.

"Does she have rune tattoos?" asked Maxwell.

"What are rune tattoos?" inserted Keri.

Grey tattoos on his neck came alive and swam all over his face. "These are rune tattoos." A slight pressure dominated the space around him for a second before it disappeared as the runes retreated to normal aesthetics.

She gulped at the momentary displeasure.

"It gives closers more skills for combat. Sorcerer runes and symbols are tattooed into your skin, then they inject a serum made from monster cores and other ingredients into your blood. All of these things have to be very, very compatible to you," explained Vivian. "It is a highly dangerous procedure. It mostly works for 8s and 17s. But for the others, there is a very high risk. I don't recommend it."

"Please no needles or surgeries or anything like that," squeaked Keri.

"You want a pussy like her to join us?" asked Maxwell.

"Not getting the procedure is not cowardice," countered Vivian. "And I don't appreciate that word being used in front of me."

"She can't fight. She doesn't have experience in the outside world, let alone monsters. She is a liability," he asserted. "Look at her. She's not even pretty to look at."

"We want you, Miss Vivian," hollered a member from the bench.

A few agreed with howls and cheers.

Keri was reminded of why she didn't have friends. She always wound up being friendly with the prettiest people. And when people saw them together, insufferable remarks came. It was nicer in games; at least in there, the target lovers noticed only her—wanted only her.

"I've given her the Trainee Sword. She can fight," said Vivian, ignoring the cheers.

Maxwell crossed his arms and then snapped his finger. The floor beside him opened as a rack filled with weapons elevated. He grabbed a katana and held it up. "Let's see what you've got."

Keri's brows scrunched. "You want me to fight you?"

"Go ahead, Keri. Use the sword," urged Vivian. "You can do it."

"See? Pussy," said Maxwell. "I don't need women in their thirties acting like spoiled kids in my guild. Especially ones who can't decide on a hair color."

She stared daggers at Maxwell, grabbing onto the necklace. *I don't care if I trip or hurt myself. You will get it,* she thought. The tiny pendant-sword transformed into a jian with a green hilt.

> Trainee Sword unlocks Swordsmanship – F soul chip.
> Description: Trains the user to properly handle and master a sword over time. Fragment has congruence with Body.
> Would you like to combine chip with fragment?

Her thoughts on vengeance halted as she scanned the system's notice. Though she did not comprehend what congruence meant, she agreed. It sounded powerful to her.

> Please wait while fragments are updated.

As she read the notice, a shadow loomed in front of her. By instinct, she hoisted her armed hand up. The jian blocked the attack from Maxwell, but the jolt caused Keri to stumble a few steps back—almost falling down.

Maxwell clicked his tongue. "I wasn't even trying." Holding the katana with both hands, he attacked again.

His swings were simple downwards and diagonal strokes. To the trained, his movements were obvious and could easily be blocked. But for Keri, each blow caused a numbing impact. Her arms jiggled as she held the sword with both hands. Every advance he made caused her to retreat a good distance away. He swung his sword again. It met the other blade as it slid down at the start of the jian's hilt. The katana swirled and pried the blade off, completely disarming the owner. Keri, in a panic, tried to retrieve her sword from the floor. But the tip of the katana arrived next to her face. She traced the blade back to its owner with a cloudy expression.

Maxwell turned to Vivian and asked, "This is a fight?"

Before Vivian could speak, Keri replied, "Let's do it again. I wasn't ready."

He retracted his blade. "Is this your best defense when monsters attack you? 'Hold on, I'm not ready'?"

"She said give her another chance," shouted Vivian from the break area.

Keri checked the new notice and smirked when she recovered her sword.

> Update complete. New Fragment Swordswoman Body available.
> CANDIDATE STATUS:
> Name: Keri Bolo| Profile: Maiden | Coins: 460
> Activated Fragments: Prima – F (innate), Swordswoman Body – E
> Available Fragments Left: 1

Maxwell kept his focus on Vivian. "This is a waste of—"

In a swift and calm movement, Keri dashed to her opponent and swung her sword from below with one hand. Maxwell blocked the attack on his leg by reflex. Before he could recover, she pulled herself back and delivered another attack by twisting her body in the opposite direction. The attack was blocked again. But Keri did not stop, initiating another three-sixty-degree movement in the same direction, pushing the opponent back. When it was blocked, yet again, she stabbed her sword forward, flung it three times across and finished with a swing from below. She quickly jumped back.

There was a collective gasp from the guild members. Some pointed while others clapped and cheered.

"Was that a fluke?" a member asked.

The last attack grazed Maxwell slightly as blood trickled from his arm. A slight quiver from his runes on his neck healed his wounds. "Let's have some fun then." With both of his hands on his katana, he advanced and attacked.

Like before, Maxwell's attacks were big and wide, but fast and more aggressive. But unlike earlier, Keri didn't block with difficulty. She evaded when it was a good distance away from her or parried when it was too close. When Maxwell got really close, Keri gripped his arm with her free hand and pulled him forward. She then twisted her body around and kicked his back.

He staggered forwards for a few beats before he regained his balance. "That was okay. Girly strike, but okay." He smiled and growled at the same time.

Just as Maxwell swung his sword, Keri met him head-on and flicked her wrist, twisting the jian in multiple circular spins. It slashed at his arms, spraying blood on the floor. She then stabbed his gut and pulled the blade back, causing him to kneel. Quick and agile, she stepped on his knee, shoulder, then stomped on his head and jumped over him. When she landed, she kicked him from behind.

Maxwell tumbled to the floor with dots of blood staining all over. As he got up, the black runes on his neck flooded his face, completely enveloping his skin, from head to foot. Steam escaped from his mouth and flared nostrils. A heavy pressure weighed on the immediate surroundings.

One of the members at the bench, who had large eyes and with black circles around it, rose from his seat. Keri remembered him from the car ride. "Boss, you're overdoing it!" he yelled.

All of a sudden, the air lightened again. The runes receded. Maxwell inhaled deeply. "All right. You can fight."

"She's in," cheered Vivian.

"She can register with us, but she's on the reserves list," he clarified. "We have too many members in offensive."

Breathing hard, Keri returned next to Vivian. "What does that mean?" she asked.

"They need support members more," she explained. "If you were a sorcerer or healer, you'd be in the active roster."

"Forget about being in the roster, I'd beg you to help us every time," stated Maxwell.

Vivian hugged Keri. "Don't mind him. It doesn't matter. You're in."

Maxwell returned his katana to the rack. "Deeg, register her. Keep a lid on her abilities as well," he ordered.

The man with black circles around his huge eyes answered, "Yes, Boss."

Target lover #2 has increased his respect towards you. 100 coins earned. Total 560

"Oh," chirped Keri.

Inside one of the guild offices, Deeg sat at the head of the desk, facing Vivian and Keri. Both of them read the copies of Keri's closer registration contract and guild membership. As one of the major guilds in freezones, Hairless Ape had the right to sponsor 8s and 17s. Vivian and Deeg discussed the contracts further, changing the terms and upping the benefits for Keri, including a higher pay that was triple what she'd earned working in Zuobic with the potential to grow even more. Though her future income made her happy, Keri's eyes glazed at the legal terms the two uttered, wishing she could watch a movie or play a game instead. "My name is Mary Bolo?" she asked, reading her false identity.

"On paper, yes," confirmed Vivian. "She's a missing person in Zuobic, right about your age. She matched your name and physical characteristics. Her immediate family and relatives are all dead—no one's going to come looking for you."

"But the same last name? Isn't that going to get me in trouble?"

She disagreed with a wave of her finger. "Bolo is one of the most used last names in Zuobic. You'll be fine."

"You realize we are doing you a favor, right? Being an outlier 14 is not something to take lightly," stated Deeg.

Keri nodded. "I do. So why are you taking the risk? I mean, I'm grateful, yeah, but why?"

"My boss thinks you're some kinda investment. Plus, he hates Zuobic, the army to be more specific. So anything to cockblock them, he'll happily do."

"Uh, thank you?" she replied.

Deeg took a long look at her and Vivian before sighing. He then gathered the papers and handed a copy to Keri and sent a digital copy to her linko. "That makes it official. Welcome to the Hairless Ape Guild." They shook hands.

Chapter 21

Lake, Grocery, Quisix

In an abandoned, warehouse-sized grocery store, Lake waded through the aisles with his backpack open. Though dust and webs covered the shelves, he wasn't picky on what he took. Canned and boxed food that were a little out of date fell into his pack, as well as gauzes, antiseptics and sanitizers.

It had been four days since he had been transported into Zone Quisix. Zoning areas were established a hundred years ago, around the time the first rift happened as part of an effort to remap areas that humans still occupied. First letters stood as the nomenclature for the actual city or place, while the last ones indicated the nation it belonged to. Therefore, Z was for Zuobic Federation, H for Halton Empire, and F for the free ones—the independent capitals.

X or Xcilan, however, was a small country that had long disappeared. Its last area, Zone Quisix was overrun by monsters breaking from rifts right around the time he started in the academy—at least that was what the public believed. But according to top secret files, which Lake had access to recently, Zone Quisix fit the outlier #25 category, deleted space.

As Lake moved to the next aisle where water bottles were, he reviewed the last notifications from his system:

> You have arrived in Outworld Qx-S04D, Contested Area.
> Candidate Confirmation Started. Area Coordinate: Outworld Qx-S04D.
> Declaration of Owner: Defender. Confirmation Completed.
> Visitor: Hero Candidate. Declaration of Visitor: Invader.
> Alert: Please acquire Outworld Qx-S04D.

Judging from the similar text he got from entering Zone Kermoz, this area was ruled by a level-2 monster similar to the Spider-Woman. Going further, he thought the only way he might be able to get out of this place was to 'acquire' the area. And to do that, he gathered, it looked like he had to defeat the boss monster. How was he gonna do that? He barely survived fighting the overpowered arachnid.

He bagged bottles of water. "Out of the pan and into the fire," he said to no one in particular.

Once done, he activated his S-glove. From scrap parts from unused devices, Lake modified a training glove and added a computer that went up to his elbow. A screen placed on that part of the arm displayed a map of the area with two indicators: one was where the glove was and two was where his hideout was located.

Just as he was about to leave, a tingle shot up his spine. He immediately ducked down. Ever since fighting with the Spider-Woman, his senses had sharpened. He was aware of the monsters around him. The stronger they were, the more pressure he felt. From the shelves, he peeked through the juice bottles.

A bipedal lizard with the height of an average man wearing leather and steel armor around its shoulders and legs stood near the entrance. Its shield and spear glinted as it held them both in its upper limbs. Taking a step forward, its tongue flicked out, sensing the air around it. As it did, it crept closer and closer to the liquid aisle.

Though Lake had not moved an inch, he panicked on the inside. These types of lizards tasted the air to feel out their prey. However quiet or motionless he steeled himself to be, his scent was going to get him caught. Sweat dripped down the back of his head as the lizard's movements stopped right before the aisle. It licked its lips a couple of times before turning around the corner.

Without hesitating, Lake grabbed the ankle of the lizardman and activated his S-glove. The lizard shook as bolts of electricity coursed its scaly blue-green body from the sorcerer gear. When he let go, the monster fell back, and he immediately ran to the door. Just as his hands touched the handle, he froze. Two more lizardmen paced the abandoned streets. He ducked down when one turned his way. On his hands and knees, he crawled to the back part of the store in a hurry. Once he was out of view from the windows, he stormed to the back door to the employee area. With one step toward the exit, the first lizard lunged onto his path and swiped its spear down at him. Lake quickly rolled aside and evaded the attack but suffered a slight cut to his leg.

As he rose from the floor, he took out three small grenades from his cargo pocket and threw it on the salivating lizard. Upon contact, a tiny boom exploded and grey goo wrapped around the monster, impeding its movement with a slimy and poisonous liquid. The lizard tried to bite and claw the engineer, but the goo held strong and slowly dissolved its scales.

The small explosion had alerted the two lizards from outside, and they jostled into the grocery. Their slit-like eyes focused on the back of the store, right at Lake's head. They hissed upon seeing their comrade struggling, then charged at him.

Hearing his heart pound, Lake breathed deeply and murmured to himself, "I got this. I got this." Green runes sparked to life at his fingertips. When three formed in a row, they fizzed into fading glitters. "I don't got this," he said and looked up.

Barely a couple of meters were left before they reached him. Lake stumbled into the employee area with his back, shutting the door behind. His fingers reflexively locked the door as he spotted a dining table to his right. Just as he placed the table to block the door, the lizard bodies slammed against it on impact. Seeing through a circular glass peephole atop the door, Lake saw the lizards change from using their fists to their weapons. A spear went right through the wooden door. A second jammed in. Then a third, followed by another, and another. Pretty soon the door would crumble into splinters.

Once again, source floated around the engineer. Three runes shined in a row of green light before disappearing in a clap. As he brought the energy down to the ground, spikes pushed up and broke the tiled floor and the door into pieces. It stabbed holes into the bodies of the lizards, skewering them in place. Though unable to go further, the two snapped their jaws and slashed their spears, hungry for revenge and blood. Lake gulped at the large teeth and claws that would have been his end had he not cast in time.

Feeling relief wash over him, he hurried to the back exit of the store, passing through the lockers and the cargo bay. Out in the alley, he crouched over a large trash bin and took a breath, reorienting himself with his map and where he needed to go next. The display led him onto a back street and onto the main road. After checking left and right, his face froze. Both ways had lizardmen patrolling. He checked his pockets—all he had left were large, loud explosives. If he were to use them, he'd give away where he was.

"Think, think," he whispered to himself. There has to be a spell that could take these guys out. If he was Maggie, he'd use Frozen Wave, but the complexity of that spell was too much for him. And even if he could pull it off, he risked freezing himself as well. If he was Major Cervantes, he'd blast the area with a rain of fire. But he was him. He was the Starless Sorcerer—no, he was Lake. Just Lake now—not a student nor a soldier, not since his absence and failed mission. He was a good—no, he was a great engineer, and a barely passable sorcerer. What would someone like him do to get out of this place? Wait. He didn't have to fight all the monsters. He just had to safely leave.

Source roused around him, glinting and waving in a soft cyan glow. He wrote three runes in the air. When he finished, he gathered them in his palms gently and blew into it. From where he knelt, mist condensed and expanded around him.

The spell, Mist Clouds, blanketed the back alley first and shaded the grocer next, then the nearby shops and then the roads. The sorcery spread, covering everything up to the third floor of the shops, blinding the view of the lizards that roamed around. They hissed at the creeping fog. Some tried to forge ahead, but their sights and the smells through their tongues were dark, icy and cold. After a while, they stopped, observing the expanding mist. It went on and on until it covered more than a kilometer in every direction.

Satisfied by his cover, Lake took out a pair of red goggles from his pocket and put them on. Thermal view was activated. Ahead, he could see the heat signatures of all living organisms. With careful and quick movements, he traversed the rundown town away from the monsters and back to his hiding place.

Less than an hour later, he arrived at an abandoned mech shop at the border of the town. It was a big warehouse that could house six mechs, but only three currently sat in the bays. When he first got there, he thought he could use the mechs to fight off the monsters, but all of them only functioned at about 50% of their capacity. Either there was an internal circuitry issue, or the parts were destroyed or missing.

Lake went directly to the back of the shop where the kitchen and living quarters were. He unloaded his salvaged goods into the pantry, then opened a canned of soup and placed it in a bowl. Taking packs of first aid kits, the bowl and a water bottle, he headed into one of the offices.

In a shirt and shorts, Tony sat on the couch, waiting. Bandages wrapped around both his legs and eyes, covering his wounds. At the sound of footsteps coming in, he asked, "Thought you were coming back later?"

Lake placed all the stuff he carried onto the coffee table. "Ran into some lizards. Had to leave." He sat next to him and reached for the bandages on Tony's head.

He flicked his hands off his face. "You should've let them eat you." When Lake didn't answer, he added, "Leave me alone."

"I'm not going to leave you," he replied for the nth time. The past few days had seen Tony barking to be left alone. And through Lake's own stubbornness, he kept saying no.

Tony pointed to his legs and eyes. "There's no point for me, can't you see? I'm already dead," he yelled.

He tried to reach for them again, but he stopped. There was no use if he was in this mood again. "I'll come back later." He rose to his feet and headed to the door.

"Leave me alone." He patted around him for anything he could grab to hold onto. His hands found the bowl of food and threw it. The bowl smashed into the wall as beans scattered on the aging paint and wooden floors.

Closing the door behind him, Lake heard shouts and other stuff being flung across the room. His hands tightened into fists. With just a thought, his system appeared before him, rolling back to the day he was sent to Zone Quisix.

> You have saved a living soul.
>
> 100 coins earned. Total 100.

"No. You have to live," Lake whispered.

Closing the system, he headed for the kitchen and fixed his own meal. After, he made his way into the other office to a similar couch. While eating cereal mixed with powdered milk and water, he stripped naked. Cuts and bruises on his body gleamed red against the fluorescent lights. He jumped into the bathroom next door and showered. As water washed off the dirt and blood, he constantly drew runes for healing—the same ones Maggie had taught him. The constant stream of water from the shower coincided with the steady flow of healing energy from his own sorcery.

Lake had learned that it took him significantly longer to experience hypoetheria, unlike others back at the academy. On average, adept sorcerers could cast up to twenty basic spells before they tired out and needed rest. But to Lake, his twenty was around fifty or so. He attributed it to his fragment: Storehouse. Though it was useful, he was ashamed he lacked the potential to maximize it. He thought if Maggie or Cervantes had the ability, they'd surely save a lot of people. After turning off the shower, he dried himself with a towel. Exhaustion weighed on him with each step as he retired to his room.

From under the coffee table, he pulled out an old notebook. He had written down a list of necessities and crossed out the supplies he had gotten. While continuing to eat his cereal, he penned a new list of weapons and other things he'd need to survive. Once he filled a page, his eyelids fluttered closed.

Chapter 22

Lake, Living Area, Warehouse, Quisix

Noel Deskenn sat on the couch with a glass filled with whiskey from a half-empty bottle. He snorted and cackled at the jokes playing on the glass screen before him. The comedian discussed the implications of picking up a girl at a bar—how to spot the mentally unstable ones to easily get them to bed. As the critique of desperate, lonely women in bars played on screen, the doorbell rang and he heard a thud. Noel grimaced at the disturbance to his precious entertainment. He was about to call for Lake to answer the door when the show on the screen cut into a commercial. A slew of curses later, he opened the front door. A meter-tall and wide box laid atop the welcome mat. With a perturbed look, he dragged and kicked the box inside his house. Slashes and cuts mangled the box from a knife he had procured from the kitchen. After tearing it apart, his hands pulled out a new and packaged uniform from the army. His face bubbled red.

"Lake, get out of here, you son of a bitch!" shouted Noel. "You useless piece of crap."

Dripping wet, Lake emerged from his room with a towel wrapped around his waist. "What is it?" he asked, leaning against his own room's door.

Noel crossed the room, threw the uniform at his face and forced him against the door. "What the fuck is this? Are ya a soldier now, huh? Ya think you're some bigshot now, huh?" His saliva spewed everywhere as he pressed harder on his chest.

He twisted the knob to his door and immediately stepped back as his dad fell on all fours. "I applied to the academy and got in." He quickly dressed into a pair of jeans and a white shirt.

Sweat trailed over his red face. "Fucking dumb kid, ya did that on purpose. Help me up." He moved to a sitting position.

Lake ignored his father and went to the closet. He rolled out a filled suitcase and an empty duffel bag, then started filling it with his uniform, tools and some nanochips he had been working on.

The excessive drinking on the couch had deteriorated Noel's health. He was heaving and panting as he tried to pull himself up. "You have no right to enlist in the army. I am still your father. You need my consent."

"Today's my eighteenth birthday," he replied. "I don't need you or your drunk consent."

Noel grabbed mech figurines from his desk and threw them at his son. "Leave then. Fucking ingrate. Ya think I need you? You're nothing but a useless kid. Ya hear me?"

After packing some of the toys he liked, Lake moved to the living room. "The army wants me. They passed me." He transferred all of the things inside the box into his bag.

"Ya think they want ya just coz they passed you? They don't know ya like I do," he shouted from the bedroom. "Once they find out you're a useless, snotty, stupid kid, they'll throw ya out."

Ignoring his dad, he rolled his suitcase from his bedroom to the living room.

Noel followed him out and yelled, "Six months. Six months and ya'll be crawling back into this house begging me to take ya back."

He then grabbed his duffel bag and opened the door.

His voice lowered in a deep, wrathful tone. "People will die because of ya. Just like your mom and brother."

Lake's jaw tensed as his hands tightened around his bags. His heart pounded and his vision darkened. He turned about with raging red eyes. All too suddenly, he lost all thoughts and his body moved on its own. His feet crossed the distance between him and his father. The bags fell on the floor with a thud. A motion carried his whole left limb and fist into his dad's face. A cracking click sounded as knuckles wrecked the nose and teeth. The force sent him toppling back, knocking him out cold and lying on the floor. Lake breathed heavily. A stain of blood glistened on his fist.

His second hand was about to move for a second hit, but a familiar voice spoke at the door, "That was intense."

The sound pulled his senses back to the present. He turned and saw Keri in a green shirt and cap. "What are you—why—Padala Delivery Services?" he read the printed logo on her uniform.

She looked from his dad to him. "I delivered the package. I work for a courier company—I mean, I used to. Not now. But I was also in the back office, never on site. I think this is a dream. Again. But not. Can we call it a pseudo-dream?"

He shook his head. "It's a memory. My eighteenth birthday, the day I left my dad's place."

"Wow. This was your birthday?"

Lake breathed deeply, trying to calm his rage. "I left home, boarded the train and asked if I could stay at the academy early. They kind of allowed me to, but I had to help in the kitchens and clean for food and spare cash."

A few moments passed where Lake just stared at his father and Keri waited at him. After a few head scratches, fiddling with her uniform and stretching, she finally asked, "Do you want to celebrate?"

Again, his senses returned. "What?"

"Your birthday. Do you want to celebrate your birthday?" asked Keri.

"Now?" His brows creased.

She nodded. "Yeah, why not? We're in a pseudo-dream, right?" She grabbed his hand and pulled him out the door. The moment they crossed, they exited to the outside, in the middle of an amusement park. Carousels, bumper cars, roller coasters and other rides entertained a mass of people, children and adults alike. Joy and anticipation filled their faces. Their laughter and chatter plus the park's music produced a festive atmosphere.

"The Kermoz Rainbow Amusement Park? This is your idea for my eighteenth?" asked Lake. "I haven't been here since I was twelve."

The dreary start to Lake's day turned into a night full of lights and excitement. He almost couldn't react from amazement, but he just could not understand what was happening. He tried to put logic into it, but when Keri's arm roped around his and she forced him to try the roller coaster, it was out the door.

The sensations of the roller coaster were real. Not real like real life, but real enough that he understood it. But it was also kinda like a dream, intangible and always moving—truly like virtual reality. That's as far as he got into analyzing the situation. Because for the rest of the time, he bumped cars with Keri, impressed her with his throwing skills and won her a big monkey. They ate ice cream while on the carousel—he insisted that the best flavor for ice cream had always been vanilla because of its versatility and that he disliked rabbits. Lake viewed them as useless animals who were only there as a food resource and to procreate. That's why he got the stuffed monkey instead of the rabbit.

"Thanks for this, Keri," said Lake as they both sat on a bench, sharing chips.

She shrugged. "It was too sad. Birthdays are supposed to be fun."

There was a quiet moment that came between them. His past feelings and the kiss they shared appeared in his mind. Like before, he acted on it. No use thinking about it too much. It was a pseudo-dream, after all. His lips pressed against hers, and again he felt his insides rouse with delight. As he pulled back, a commotion caught his attention.

The people around them stopped. Worried and blank looks plastered their faces while some pointed to the sky. He focused above as well, seeing a rift tore through space. Humanoid monsters with black forms and dazzling capes descended.

"No," Lake exhaled.

Keri's puckered face finally rested as she swiveled and looked at what everyone was chattering about. "What is up—" Her eyes widened. Then she reached for her head and screamed.

***

Lake jolted awake with sweat soaking through his singlet.

Tony leaned by the door. "Is something happening? You were shouting," he said.

He evened his breathing. "Nightmare... Did I wake you? Was I loud? Did monsters hear me?" Each question rose in pitch.

With his hand by the wall, he walked closer to him. "Chill, Starless. If monsters heard you, we'd be fighting them now."

Lake sat up on the bed. "Had a dream about my dad, and... Anyway, it isn't a good one."

"Is he dead?"

He shook his head.

"Are you gesturing something?" He stopped halfway and raised his brow.

"Uh—sorry—I didn't—"

"I'm gonna be blind my whole life, might as well get used to it," cut Tony. "What about your pops? Drug addict, alcoholic, rapist, slaver, dead?"

"What makes you think it's any of those?"

He shrugged. "Isn't it always like that?" He finally reached a seat and sat.

Lake leaned back and sighed. "Alive. Alcoholic. Abusive. Gambler. He'd hit me when he was not in a good mood—which was almost all of the time. But he was never home a lot, so it's fine. You can say I grew up alone and was a part-time punching bag." He chuckled without the humor on his face.

"Tough. Mom wasn't around? She left your asshole dad?"

"Dead. She died with my little bro from a monster attack in Kermoz," he admitted with a grim expression. "My dad gambled the money we got from my mom's insurance and subsidy from outlier deaths in the family."

Tony's ears perked at the sound of Kermoz. "Is that why you joined the army? To escape your dickhead pops?"

"Part of it. The rest was me hoping I can prevent people from going through the same thing. Funny right? In my head, if I got in, I'd learn to be strong, and when I was strong, I'd get to save people—a lot of them," he answered. "But look at me now: failed mission, defeated team, dead leader, stuck in another dimension, with a lot of lizards, and no escape."

"At least you're not blind and limping," he added.

The misery Lake felt stopped for a second as pity emerged for both him and his teammate. "How about you? What's your deal?" he asked.

"Pops was always away on missions, so he was never around. Cause of that, my slutty mother left him for her boss," he said casually. "When I reached eighteen, my dad fell into a coma after an accident and died—at least that's what the army told us."

Lake frowned at that statement. "Is that not true?"

"Maybe, maybe not. All I know is that my dad wasn't in a coma," replied Tony. "I saw him a couple of times in the hospital, and he was fine. He was taking some new type of drug the military gave him. Said it'd make him stronger. But weeks later, he died."

He felt sympathy for him. "You think the army did something to him? That doesn't sound right."

He grumbled. "Doesn't matter what I think—I got into the army, so I can find out the truth of it. But now...I don't know." He rose to his feet and started his way to the door again.

Lake rose from the couch. "Here, let me help—"

"Piss off, Starless," he interrupted. "I can do this myself."

He sat back down. "Uh, okay."

After a bit of stumbling and tapping on the walls, Tony reached the door. "Thanks," he said in a barely audible whisper and left the room.

Lake noticed some of the first aid kits were missing and then smiled.

> Monster slain x 3. Earned 50 x 3 coins.
> Total 250.

Lake's face crumpled. A notice about slain monsters? And there were coins too? After thinking about it, a light bulb sparked in his head. The lizardmen he had trapped earlier were probably dead by now. Maybe they hadn't escaped and died from blood loss? So aside from saving people, coins could be earned by monster-killing.

Excited, he then opened the system shop at a thought. Most of the items and fragments were greyed out, except for a few ones at the cost of 200 coins.

> Soul Growth - 200 coins
> Body Growth - 200 coins
> Mind Growth - 200 coins

At pure instinct, his finger reached out for the Mind. Maybe the condition in his brain would somehow magically be cured by this unknown system?

> Congratulations! You have purchased Mind Growth. Total coins 50. Due to user's affinity and use of source, new fragment received! Mind's Eye
>
> - F.
>
> Description: More than feeling, source is revealed through sight.

After reviewing the notification, he assumed the change in fragment must have had something to do with the tingling sensation whenever he was close to monsters. He then tried Mind's Eye. Light specks appeared before him. They were soft and almost unnoticeable. After blinking a few times, they disappeared. When he focused again, they were there, twinkling or still, almost like dust he noticed when the morning sunlight hit the window. From the corner of the room to the ceilings and floors, the motes of light were everywhere. He rose and tried to touch them, but they passed through his hand, unaffected, unlike water or air, as if they were holograms.

With his Mind's Eye open, he called for source in his grasp, like he would when casting a spell. The specks of light congregated together in quick motion, creating wavelengths of light swirling around him. The manifestation of sorcery in his hands, in which people could normally see, was colored green. While the source dancing around the green, which was only visible to him, was white. When his fingers started drawing runes on air, the white light changed its movements, from a delicate flow to a raging, erratic noise. A smile crept on his face as he saw the intensity of the strobe lights. He wondered what it would look like if he cast a spell.

He left the room and made his way into the center of the warehouse, where it was most spacious. When he stopped, ready to cast his spell, he noticed a faint aura coming from one of the mechs. It was surrounding it, almost enveloped by it. He walked closer to it, then noticed the mech beside was emitting light much like his sorcery. Neither was green nor white, but bluish in color, much like the ocean.

Lake climbed the mech to where the main engine was. A dwindling monster core sat at the center of the main engine, hooked up to multiple wires—it was the source of the mech's power. Upon closer inspection, he believed the used core could barely power up the software of the mech, much less run the whole body since it had been used too much. Normally, engineers would discard these types of used cores. But after touching it, he noticed threads of light dancing around it. It was similar to the wavelengths he saw when he cast a spell.

By instinct, he touched a few of the threads, braided them together, and attached them to the wire. The moment the source touched it, the mech's system came alive. Then, after braiding another, and hooking it up as well, the function of the body parts was restored. He could now operate the mech—at least the bits that were still operational.

"No way," gasped Lake.

It blew his mind that this small, dying core could power up the whole mech. How was that even possible? The moment he asked that question, for some reason, he knew how. The source within the core was enough. Knowing that made him feel odd.

Proceeding with his experiment, he touched the other strands of the core. His fingers braided a bunch, then weaved in the braids. His thoughts flew around the spell Lightning Flash, which was a basic lightning spell that he had failed to produce over his time in the academy. Minutes flew by as he created a woven fabric of source. He attempted to connect it to the mech, but for some reason, he knew that was wrong. Instead, he attached it to his S-Glove.

Electricity crackled around his glove and then exploded. Smoke and fire followed. As he had done dozens of times in his life, he quickly put out the flames with an extinguisher nearby and checked himself for injuries. But after all that, a stupid grin split his ashen-covered face.

Though the spell exploded, he had finally managed a way to create rune weapons. He marvelled at his research and looked at the other mechs who glowed faintly with different colored lights. The possibilities of what he could do raced through his head. Maybe he had a chance to get out of this prison world after all.

Chapter 23

Jella, Lab Room, Aberkyz

Cold. It was freezing inside the tank where she floated. Her naked entirety fully sensed the mix of chemicals she was immersed in. Her breathing mask kept her from drowning or gagging. Not that she could, even if she wanted to. She had no control over her motor systems. Arms, shoulders, legs—nothing. She willed her toes and fingers to move, but none stirred. She tried this exercise when she had the strength and the will to, which seemed to be a few hours every day. After some time, she surrendered and commanded the only part of herself that she could. Her paintbrush stroke eyes fluttered open halfway.

Maggie stared at her in her white robe. She had her arms crossed with a sullen look in her eye. "I know this looks like I'm tossing aside our friendship, but you should have said yes and stayed. If you'd just let us do the tests, none of this would've happened. It could've been like the old times; you and me, together."

It was fortunate Jella had no recollection of those times. If she did, her need to end this bitch would probably lessen.

She sighed. "What am I saying? Ever since that stupid Lake came into our lives, it's been, *Lake needs help with his homework. Poor Lake is being picked on. Lake has no family.* It's honestly hard to compete. I'm sure if you've seen him watching that video of yours, you'd remember everything again."

Bubbles escaped from her mouth device.

The volume of Maggie's voice increased. "Has that pretty face blinded you that much? You could've soared higher in the ranks without that fool. Major Cervantes could've given you better missions. Given you several rune items. Or is it the dick? Was it that big? For someone so accomplished and so beautiful, you could've had anyone. But you chose the Starless Sorcerer?"

Jella's eyes fluttered open and close a few times.

"You're right. He's good with machines. I admit, he helped me out, and the squad. Fine. But stealing you from me and ruining our friendship—I won't forgive him for that." Her tone was icy.

She closed her eyes every so often to rest. Keeping them open taxed her.

"Don't look at me like that," said Maggie with spite. "It was your choice—choosing a stupid man over me. I've done so much for you, Jella. The least you could've done was honor that. But what can I expect from someone spoiled like you? You've never been good at relationships. If only you listened. Stupid, stupid Jella. You deserve this."

The water in the tanks was still except for the air that came through from the pipes into her nose and bubbles escaping from the sides of her face.

"You'll rot here. And I won't stop Dr. Badez or anyone in the research team from doing what they want to you. I'll even help because you deserve it."

Speaking of the devil, the door to the lab opened and Dr. Badez entered in a white lab coat over a grey skirt and blue blouse. Without her usual surgery cap and mask, her short locks dangled free. "How is she?" she asked.

Maggie glanced backwards to acknowledge her presence and returned to her screen. "Her cellular regeneration rate falls in between highs and lows with a median of seven hours," she reported.

She walked right next to the tank. "Good. If I increase the samples we're harvesting from her, about two or three more times, will you have complaints?"

She shook her head. "This is for the people Zuobic and the soldiers. I won't stand in the way."

Badez looked at her in surprise. "I see. I wasn't expecting that from you. I know you are headstrong, but she is your close friend, isn't she? Some might say best friend?"

"If her memories were intact, she'd want this. She's always had a hero complex." Her lips parted to a smile.

Badez nodded. "I'm not going to lie. That does make me feel a bit better about all of this."

"You're doing the right thing, doctor. I support you. Jella supports you." She beamed.

Jella observed her body, seeing her chest, stomach, shoulders and feet. Patches of removed skin, cut muscles and missing toes looked back at her. Blood was coagulating on her wounds at a visible rate. It was as if an unknown force was healing her.

"Doctor, any progress with the project?" asked Maggie.

Badez rubbed the glass. "The prototype of the drug is being developed as we speak. And a new line of defense is also being created. All because of her."

If ever I do get out of here, I will rip both of your heads from your necks and feed them to monsters, thought Jella.

Maggie smiled. "I'm glad."

"Yes, the two projects are going well," agreed Badez.

"May I ask about Jella's family? What do I say if they ask questions? I know its officially reported that she's on a mission, then on leave and another mission again."

Badez crossed her arms and tapped her elbows. "Though her family is rich and powerful, if we tell them she went missing inside a rift, they will most likely not pursue it further. I'll work out the details with the Major later. If they ask you, defer them to me."

Fucking bitches. Let me out! Jella screamed in her mind.

"Yes doctor," answered Maggie.

"How are you doing lately?" Badez asked in a warm tone.

She shook her head. "I'm fine, doctor. A bit shaken up by the mission. But I'm glad that my team survived and is recovering. I just wish the others had made it out alive too." Her voice cracked as if threatening to cry.

When did you grow a conscience?

Badez reached out and squeezed her shoulders. "I can certainly understand that. Take as much time as you need."

She wiped her watery eyes away. "Thanks, doctor. But I like being here. Helping."

Let's swap places then. You stay here, and I'll run off.

Dr. Badez smiled. "That's good. We need more doctors like you. Especially since we've received a report that the missing ability user has been found."

Maggie's eyes widened. "Do you mean the people from WalkBy?"

She brought out photos of the people that were involved in the incident. "Yes. A slaver has reported a person that exhibits talents much like an ability user would, like Jella. The Major is reaching out to his contacts to secure both of them as we speak," she explained.

"Why don't we get them ourselves? We have cadets better than those lowlifes."

Pot calling the kettle black.

"I'm inclined to agree. But it's all politics," Badez replied with a shrug. "We can't have the Zuobic army turning up at a freezone's doorstep without just cause."

And keeping me like a fish is just? Dumb bitch.

Maggie pointed at the photo of the lady with colored hair. "This ugly, weird looking one, she's federate. That's more than valid for us to get them ourselves."

"Yes, but we risk exposing their identities," said Badez. "Last thing we need is someone finding out their abilities, or worse, knowledge we are yet to uncover."

She sighed. "We wait then?"

"We wait."

Let me out!

CHAPTER 24

LAKE, MECH BAYS, WAREHOUSE, QUISIX

Filthy with grease and dirt, Lake soldered a microchip into a circular plate equipment on a workbench. He was building a battery source from the stocks and leftover mechs in the shop. Across him, at the next desk, he had Tony's spear laid out in separated parts. He had disassembled it to try and copy and improve on the design. Like Osher's rifle, it was a rune weapon. The rifle had the spell of Shadow Through, which enabled the gunner to shoot through very small holes that connected two different spaces, cutting the distance and time it travels. The spell in the spear wasn't as sophisticated as Shadow Through. Still, it gave the blade a distinct sharpness that was able to fillet monsters that regular swords could not.

He placed his tools down and took off the face protector. "Here comes the hard part." He popped an almost depleted monster core into the socket of a circular steel plate-like shield.

He squinted and stretched his glove-protected fingers. Immediately, threads of lights came into view surrounding the core, moving like seaweeds underneath the ocean. For the shield, he chose the spell Light Dome. The specks of light floating around him, the source, swarmed and changed into a blanket of waves that entered his body. His fingers proceeded to write the runes for the spell. When the four runes were complete, he placed the spell in one hand. Instead of releasing it, he plucked the threads from the core and tied it into the spell. After threading the core into the spell, he carefully released the energy, expecting the core to absorb it. Instead, the spell imploded and the core's threads retracted.

Lake groaned from frustration. Threading the core into the spell was a failure. He had previously tried rune writing into the core itself and using the tendrils to form runes—which were all failures as well. He thought maybe it was the way he had designed the batteries. Maybe it wasn't at a quality where the core could absorb the runes and function at a hundred percent. So he had made designs that were significantly better than the others. The latest one on the plate was, at least what he believed, his best version yet. But nothing worked like he wanted. After rising from his seat, he kicked a pile of broken parts.

Tony ambled over with an umbrella as a walking stick. "Bad time?"

Lake took off his gloves and threw them on the ground. "I'm having issues getting this damn thing to work. Did I wake you?" He heaved calming breaths.

He shrugged. "Does it matter? When I sleep, I see darkness. When I wake up, still nothing."

"Sorry, I didn't mean to—"

"Cut the crap, Starless. I'm blind. Not a basket case," he interrupted. "What's bugging you?"

He ran his hand over his hair. "I'm trying to make a rune weapon. Not working out great."

Tony moved to the bench and touched the plate and a pair of boots. "You do know the army's R&D teams make one weapon. Not a just a single person. At least five people made my weapon, not including the source—is this my spear?" His hands moved to the half of the handle of his spear.

His back leaned against the remains of a mech. "I was using it as a reference. I'll put it back together when I'm done."

"Tch," he sounded. "It's fine. Not like I'm using it anytime soon. So what's got your panties in a twist?"

"I don't wear panties," growled Lake.

"Then stop acting like a pussy and spit it out."

"The core's programming is not taking the runes I've set it into. At first, I thought maybe the capacitor isn't large enough or the transformer can't handle the source," he explained. "But after the upgrades, I don't think that is the issue."

Tony found a seat. "Can you turn the 'not nerd' filter on, please?"

"Oh, you mean the dumb dictionary?"

He smirked. "That's funny."

"Basically, it's a rune issue. I know there is no problem with the device, it's the rune itself," Lake stated. "I don't know how I can put the spell into the weapon."

Tony started to unzip his trousers.

Lake's forehead creased. "What are you doing? I'm not into men, you know. Gay people are nice. Some have hit on me in the past, even wanted to pay me, but I never said yes. Even if I was, not the best time for sex."

Tony removed his trousers completely, followed by his socks, leaving his underwear on. "Relax, you're not actually my type either. I go for emotionally stable and talented people. I'm here to inspire you, not sleep with you." Starting from his thighs down to his feet, runic tattoos glinted in blue ink, except for parts that were covered with bandages.

Lake knelt down next to Tony's legs and observed them. "May I?" His hand hovered.

"No homo, bro," he joked.

Lake rubbed his fingers across the leg. "It's amazing. Runes that sorcerers never use, they broke it down into fine details. Like this one, it's the movement and speed and characteristics of electricity, it's a whole four rows, but when we write, it's only one character. No one casts spells like this. It's so detailed."

"It's also a bitch putting on," he shared. "I had to take a drug that lets my body get used to the ink and source. That drug was no joke. I was coughing, sneezing, headaches, vomiting. When they finally tattooed me, I broke into hives and a fever. And that's only for one row. I was in bed for two months."

He pulled out his cubex from his pocket and started taking photos. "I don't understand. You're a good mech pilot. Why do you need to be tattooed? Only closers need to do that. Did you want to be part of the closer divisions? Unless you're an 8—an item user. But with a rune weapon, I'm guessing not," he conjectured.

Tony was quiet for a minute, letting the engineer examine his leg. "You know I was looking for any lead to my dad. I got this idea that maybe I could get some intel in R&D if I signed up for a tattoo."

He transferred the photos into a glassy standing on the workbench. "Did you find out anything?" He zoomed into the photos and started analyzing them.

"Nah, it was a stupid thing to do," he said in a somber tone.

An idea popped into Lake's head. Instead of casting a spell and hooking the threads into it, maybe he should make a medium to attach the spell much like that of tattoos and then hook the threads. "I think I'm going about this the wrong way," he murmured.

Tony put on his socks and trousers. "What's this all for, anyway? You gonna raid a communication tower or something? Call for rescue?"

His brainstorming halted. "About that, we're not actually in the lawless lands." He had lied about their whereabouts so that his teammate would not have another thing to worry about.

"What are you not telling me?" Tony's voice deepened.

"Remember I told you that a rift opened up suddenly at our feet?"

"Yeah. We were transported into Zone Quisix. What about it?"

Lake shared the details of deleted and recovered spaces, outlier #24 and #25. Then explained the mysteries surrounding Zone Kermoz and now Quisix.

His voice rose higher. "There's no way out of here..."

"Sorry, I—"

"I said quit being a pussy and apologizing," Tony cut in. "These pieces of junk, what are all these for then?"

"There's a lot of lizardmen who patrol around," he answered. "I can't defend myself against them."

He laughed hard, but joy was not present. "We're fucked, aren't we? We're stuck inside a rift with nobody else and no contact with the outside world. I'm blind, limping, useless. And you're shit at fighting. This is shit." He rose to his feet and made his way back to his room, tapping the umbrella from left to right.

Lake thought about telling him about his system, or at least the notice of taking over the dimension. Maybe that would at least give him some hope. "Tony, I'm trying to—"

"Man, don't. Just don't." He closed the door behind him.

As he heard things flying around inside the office, Lake went to the bathroom and splashed water on his face. While he looked at his drooping face from exhaustion and lack of sleep, he thought about what he could do to solve his rune dilemma. He guessed maybe a circular or spherical cover around the core etched with runes could produce the results he wanted. If he wanted Light Dome to be the spell, then the runes couldn't be simple like he'd cast them. After drying himself with a towel, he gathered source and walked back to the work bench. He wrote a part of the detailed version of the spell on air. Eight runes shimmered before him, which only meant that source should be converted to light. For some reason, these eight symbols before him were easier to maintain rather than the simple ones. Was it maybe because it carried less source to write and less commands for it to do anything?

> Congratulations! Due to life experiences the fragment Storehouse has evolved to Source Blessed – E.
> Description: An intimate understanding of source. Your existence will adapt and change to handle extreme source exposures.

Surprised by the sudden notification, the spell burst into a bright light for a few seconds before disappearing completely. He scratched his head and slightly blamed himself for losing his concentration. At least it didn't go haywire.

> Congratulations, you have achieved all requirements for growth. Your soul is undergoing a qualitative change.

After a few moments, the system jingled:

> Your soul has grown. It now understands the concepts of source and the various materials it resides in. An additional fragment is available. Please further your achievements to ascend to a higher plain of existence.
> CANDIDATE STATUS:
> Name: Lake Deskenn | Profile: Hero | Coins: 50
> Activated Fragments: Source Blessed – D, Hero's Retreat – F (innate), Mind's Eye – F
> Available Fragments Left: 2

"Qualitative change? What does that mean?" he found himself asking.

> True definition consists of 500,000 words. Would you like to read?

"What? Isn't there a short description?"

> Searching for semantics suited for candidate. Abridged version found. Qualitative change is the milestone the soul reaches for growth and development in order to reach its full potential as a candidate to lead the new world.

"Wait. Why is the system answering my questions now?" He thought about all those times he asked it all sorts of questions and it never really answered anything. He believed that it was a one-way mechanism, sort of a display monitor of what was happening, not a two-way communication device.

> As the soul grows stronger, it is able to handle information beyond human understanding. Lesser beings are not able to handle life-altering data.

"Nice to know even the system thinks I'm a lesser being," he digressed. "What is a candidate?"

> Candidate Description: A being born from the old world, unique from the rest of the race, able to grow to its full potential to lead its followers to the new world.

"What is the new world?"

> The new world results from the transformation an old world undergoes. These entail a change in environment and the genetics of living beings, such as the highly dense presence of source, introduction of new species, new elements, etc. These changes open the old world to vulnerabilities that lead to invasions from other worlds depleted of their own source, natural resources, the worldless and more.

He deduced that somehow being a candidate had something to do with rifts in their own world. Somehow the rifts were a sign of change, and candidates were supposed to lead them to change? What? "As a candidate, what's my mission? What do I have to do?"

> To lead your followers to the new world.

"Followers? Am I a pop star now? What's a follower?"

> People who have selected to follow a candidate.

"That doesn't make sense," he said and tried other ways to ask his questions. But the replies of the system gave vague, incomplete details. He then asked it to expand on the answers.

> Soul is at its limit. Please grow soul potential by increasing fragments and life experiences to unlock more information. The stronger the soul is, the more life-altering information it can handle.

He cursed at the automated response. For a second, he thought he was onto something. But it turned back into a pumpkin before he had discovered anything substantial. At least now he had an inkling of what to do. It meant he needed to kill more monsters to grow stronger.

By mental command, he opened the shop. The three growth upgrades were still there, now a bit more costly, as well as the gems he usually ignored. Concluding his coins fell short for any kind of purchase, he shut the shop down. All this system business was for next time; first he had a job to finish.

Back at the tattoo photos again, he started drawing on a design for a rune case where the core would sit. He started editing the runes on the photo. For some odd reason, he knew there were better runes that could draw on more power and were more efficient to use. He backed up and looked at his work. A grin cracked on his face. Though he had not produced any actual working prototypes, he knew for once, he was on the right track. He had hope.

Chapter 25

Keri, Travelling in J-Law

In the passenger seat, Keri checked herself in the mirror inside the sun visor. The person staring back at her was still her but different. She had lost a bit of fat, and her aura had a slight edge to it. The Swordswoman Body had been taking effect these past few days. Today, it seemed like it was at its peak. She was not only stronger, but lighter. Her sword movements were faster and more fluid. The downside was that her body was developing muscles that made her look manly. She didn't know how to feel about that. But at least she didn't need her cat glasses anymore. When she woke today, her eyes were clear. She could see properly without them on.

Wayne, who was driving the car, entered an abandoned town in the middle of the desert. "Those runs you've been doing every day seem to be working."

Keri half-smiled. She'd started running not to lose weight, but because she could. Back then, running made her knees and soles ache because of her imbalance and weight issues. A sprint around the block would kill her. Not to mention, she hated how her tummy bounced up and down. It didn't look or feel good. But now, she was agile and athletic. It felt like she could climb flat walls and leap from building to building—not that she had tried. But she sort of wished she could. Will the system grant her powers like that?

"You didn't have to drive me all the way to my first assignment, you know. I'm okay getting a ride with the rest of the guild," stated Keri.

He smiled. "Being your guide to your first closing is the least I can do. After pulling me out of that curse, I don't mind serving you forever."

After Wayne had returned to Amazing Discoveries, he confirmed the curse had been lifted. The keywords no longer stripped his loved ones of their memories of him. Moreover, the forgotten memories had returned to them, making it seem like they had never experienced it at all. It left Wayne to fill in the gaps of what had transpired before.

Keri bit her lip. "What kind of services do you provide?" Though her thoughts turned dirty, she didn't outright ask for anything like that.

Wayne thought for a bit before saying, "My first thoughts were going down on you, 69 or missionary—whatever you're into." Keri was about to scream *yes*, but he continued on, "But on second thought, I think this deserves more than sex, you know. Like something special. I don't mind taking you around so you can get used to freezones like this. Or I can be your closing partner. I used to do closing admin and logistics part time, so I know a thing or two."

She regretted the moment passing without her saying what she really wanted. "Sure," she said unenthusiastically.

"Riley asked me to inspect some of the artefacts. If I participated, I'd get to choose items firsthand, and not just rely on what the guild gives us. It saves Discoveries some dough. And it kinda works out." He parked the car inside a parking building.

She looked out the window. Besides their car and a few vans and trucks from the guild members, it was basically just them. "Where are we?" Further out, the few shops and houses were dilapidated and abandoned.

"This is Zone Bref. It's been deserted for years now. Rift is that thing over there." Wayne pointed directly ahead.

At the outskirts of the small town, near the welcome sign was a tall portal that glowed green. Crackles of source surrounded it as the main body shimmered brightly.

"The one in the news was orange. Why is this one green?" she asked.

Wayne turned off the ignition and leaned on the wheel. "That's a torn rift. Monsters get out into our side when its orange and yellow. Blue, green and the others, they're still inside."

"Ah, yeah, I saw other colors as well. Violet and indigo mean they're new ones, right?"

"Mhmmm. And easier to close, with less enemies inside."

"What about the red ones?"

His face turned to stone. "Means the boss is coming out and there's no way to close it anymore."

"Oh." She wondered about the refugees on the outskirts of Zone Troef. Was a red rift the cause of their grief?

Wayne got out of the car and unloaded their bags from the boot. "Come on." He handed a backpack to Keri as they moved closer to the site.

Besides the looming green danger, a hundred members of Hairless Ape were busy running around the rift, preparing for the closing. A big part of their numbers belonged to non-combat participants. They provided support and other necessary help before and after the combat teams entered the rifts. Administrators coordinated with the different teams on when to enter the rift, according to the strategy given by the closing leader.

Rifts allowed entry to only qualified closers, which were basically sorcerers, item users—and unbeknownst to the public, ability users. Any civilian who touched them would feel a wall instead of a way through. Each rift had a limit on the total number of people and the ratio of 17s, 14s and 8s that could enter. There was no hard-fast rule of how many or what type of closer could enter, only that the closer it got to turning red, the more people it accepted.

Keri walked up to a woman administrator who was looking through her glassy while talking to her linko. "Hi, I'm Keri and this is Wayne, from Amazing Discoveries. Where should we—"

She held her hand up and continued talking on the line. After a long minute, she placed her attention on them. "You're in the reserve team, Team J. All of you are there." She pointed to a van with a sprinkle of her fingers.

"Thanks." Keri walked away with uncertainty.

She smiled mockingly. "You're welcome."

"What's her deal?" she grumbled as she made her way to the van.

"We're the reserve team. The last team to enter," answered Wayne. "They need to put the powerful teams first in case the rift caps the number. We only get to enter if one team doesn't show up or had an issue with their members."

Keri sent glares at the administrator when she wasn't looking at them. "When does that ever happen?"

"Almost never?"

She pulled and adjusted her pants and the skin suit she wore underneath her green vest. "We still get paid, right?" she asked.

"Of course, we're here," he replied. "You look really uncomfortable."

She scratched her neck. "The damn skin suits. It's like I'm back in ballet or something."

When they reached the van, Wayne unloaded his bags at the back. "When did you take ballet?" he asked.

A princess should always be graceful. No matter the place or time, learn to act with grace and posture, her mother's voice echoed in her head. It was a fading memory that she could not pinpoint the time or place it had happened. She barely even remembered her mom's face.

"I'm not really sure I did," replied Keri.

Wayne shrugged, opening one of the bags. "These things aren't really my thing too. That's why I leave it until the last minute to wear them." He changed his white shirt into a sleek body suit made for defense, then added a vest and an outlier chest plate. The way his muscles rippled with every motion highlighting his pecs and abs sent involuntary currents down Keri's lady parts.

She bit her lip. She imagined how it would feel to lick his body.

"Nice view huh?" asked a chirpy voice behind her in a whisper.

"Definitely," she half-moaned.

"You like 'em big huh?" the voice replied.

"Mhmm—what—who?" She turned around and saw a lanky, tall guy about her age with a big grin.

He reached out and shook her hands. "Hi, I'm Ivo Vork. Team J's leader, also known as the bench warmers. Because, y'know, we warm up the bench cause we're here all day. I kid. I kid. You must be the new ones," he said animatedly.

"Keri," she croaked in reply.

Ivo grinned and whispered, "Don't worry, I won't tell a peep to anyone. I wish you two the best. Hee hee."

She blushed.

After dressing up, Wayne walked over and shook his hand. "Wayne Gorsbi. We're from Amazing Discoveries, it's our first time closing. Hope to be of assistance."

"Oh, so you're new too. It's raining new men and women," he responded. "If you're excited to go in, not gonna lie, we might stay here forever. You look like you're itching for a challenge, with your *biiiig* muscles."

He scratched his head. "Nah, we can hang back. We're not the only new ones?"

"Definitely not. Most of our old reserves got promoted to other teams and they're in other rifts right now. Except lil' old me. Huhu. I kid. I kid. I love being in the reserves. Makes my wife happy knowing I'm always safe, and useless." He pretended to cry, then grinned.

"I'm sure that's not true," said Wayne.

"You're a nice man. And big too. Oops, I've got a call from the admins. You two should meet the team. They're all new too. I'll be with you in a jiffy." As his linko lit up, he excused himself and started talking.

The two looked expectantly at their new team. But as they approached the members, they avoided their gaze and sauntered off.

"They don't look welcoming," said Wayne.

Keri stepped closer to a big woman with big red curls wearing a cloak, half hiding her face. "Hi, I'm Keri. I'm new here. What's your name?" she asked.

"I'm Queen. Sorry I'm really shy. Bye." Queen covered her face fully with her cloak and left.

Wayne sided with her. "She's kinda odd."

"I think I've seen her before," she said.

"I don't think I know her," said Wayne. "Anyway, got everything you need?"

She thought about the items the Chadstones had given her for protection: Trainee Sword necklace and Weakness Ring. Both of which were already worn by her. Additionally, she had been given two more items: a small flute pipe and an old large brown wall clock. The pipe could call for winds, of which she wasn't sure what for—Riley joked it'd be more than a fart. While the second one was a wall clock, to which it could somehow help with the wounded. But Riley warned about its overuse, so she had to use it sparingly.

"I think so," answered Keri.

Ivo got off his linko and called everyone's attention. "Hey Team J, I've got good news. We're going inside the rift. Isn't that swell?"

Keri raised her hand. "I thought you said we never enter?"

"Well, there's a first time for everything," he replied. "One of the teams is running late and some of them can't be reached. Don't know why, but as they say, the show must go on."

"That doesn't sound good," said Wayne.

Ivo stomped his foot. "Aw, don't be a party pooper. This is our chance to do something good. To save our friends and families from monsters. Let's go."

Wayne and Keri exchanged worried glances as they all hopped inside the van. They sat close to the front, with Ivo in the passenger seat next to the driver.

Past the rift, a haunting view of a mountainous region of ash, black soil and dark rocks welcomed them. At the tallest mountains, numerous towers of steel stood and almost pierced the clouds as they coaxed lightning from the storm clouds that brewed overhead. Thunder and intermittent rain filled the atmosphere with danger and uncertainty. As the vehicle moved away from the rift, its color transformed from a luminescent green to ash grey, indicating that it had reached the cap of people and had temporarily closed. For it to open again, the lord of the rift, which was the boss monster, had to be killed.

> Candidate Confirmation Started. Area Coordinate: Outworld A1-D01S.
> Declaration of Owner: Defender. Confirmation Completed.
> Area transformed into Contested Area. Visitor: Maiden Candidate. Declaration of Visitor: Invader.
> Alert: Please acquire Outworld Qx-S04D, A1-D01S, A2-D02S.

Keri frowned at the notices on her system. What did the coordinates mean? And how did she acquire them?

At the front of the van, Ivo tapped on the settings of the radio as he had his other hand on his linko. "Good day, this is Ivo from Team J, substituting for Team F. Does anyone copy?" he said.

From the speakers, Deeg spoke, "Deeg, from Team B. Ivo, why are you here? Where's Team F?"

Ivo relayed the circumstances surrounding Team F.

"Not good. We have most of our healers in Team F," said Deeg. "Did you at least bring medical supplies?"

"Yes sir-ee, we brought 'em all and some food just in case," replied Ivo.

"Good. I'm sending you the coordinates to Team A. Please assist them."

"You got it. Heading there right away."

The van headed to the given coordinates through the heavy weather. The closer they got to their destination, the heavier the rain poured and the darker the surroundings got. They had to turn on their rooftop, fog and auxiliary lights.

Inside, Keri poked Wayne who sat beside her. "Are healers that important?" she asked in a low volume.

He sighed. "You know they are. Healers are more important than doctors because they can heal people faster, and cure poisons and curses. Like you, you're important. I'm sure that's why you got into Hairless Ape."

She slapped his arm. "You're just saying that 'cause you're trying to be nice."

He frowned. "Not really. Healers are the real support of closers. Without them, they won't last in battles that take days. And I don't need to be nice to tell you that you're important. You are." He looked straight into her eyes.

She turned away and blushed. "Okay. Thanks." She took out a glassy and pretended to fiddle with it, but in reality, she opened her system.

CANDIDATE STATUS:
Name: Keri Bolo| Profile: Maiden | Coins: 460
Activated Fragments: Prima – E (innate), Swordswoman Body – E,
Available Fragments Left: 1

She checked her status and noticed the line for condition had disappeared. Since she was far away from Chatterbox, his protection didn't cover her. She hadn't seen the kid for a while. He didn't even say goodbye this morning. She wondered if he was upset about something. After making a mental note to talk to him when she got back, she opened the system shop.

Again, the area and gems sparked her interest and confusion. She'd look at the help screen later to understand how this worked. For now, her sights dangled over growth upgrades. She didn't know what could help in this situation. But since it looked like any would make some sort of difference, she decided to choose the mind this time around—not really caring that their costs spiked from the last purchase.

> Congratulations! You have purchased Mind Growth. Total Coins: 60.
> A qualitative change is happening with your mind and how you interact
> with source. Process is on-going.
> Awaiting external stimuli and data in order to proceed.

"I wish this came with a manual," she breathed out.

"Me too," answered Wayne.

The two locked eyes for a moment.

"I was looking at a new bag that has so many colour options in it," she lied with a big grin.

Wayne scratched his head. "I was checking good gear for myself. Armor and stuff."

They both spoke at the same time, stopped and returned to what they were doing in a more secretive manner.

After feeling a bit weirded out, she read the notifications on her system again. If it had been like the Swordswoman Body, would she have to wait until she used another item? Would the new upgrade fuse itself with the item? If so, why didn't it fuse with the Weakening Ring? She grunted in annoyance. Figuring all these things out was what she didn't like about *Love Me, Princess'* system. She was content to just play the game and leave all character customization and upgrades to chance. That was fine and dandy if this was the game, but this was her life. The only thing she could think of to beat the randomness was doing a shit-ton of upgrades. But to do that, she needed to be rich. Her 60 system coins mocked her poverty.

She leaned her head on the headrest. Was absorbing accursed artefacts and doing favors for her targeted lovers the only way for her to get coins? She glanced at the man beside her, and she noticed the big bulge in his pants. Her thoughts wound back to her first time meeting him. How it was so huge. If she gave him a blowjob, would she earn coins? That was a favor, wasn't it? She massaged her jaw, thinking she might not be able to take it all in. It was not as if she had practiced these kinds of things. Maybe a handy would work? Then what about Maxwell? Was his dick big as well? With the way his personality is, being so money-grubbing and a jerk, she felt like he was overcompensating for something. So maybe a small dick?

A large, monstrous cry broke her internal penis monologue.

The ruins of a castle came into view as a dark-blue dragon-like entity wrapped itself around it. Thunder and lightning illuminated its menacing size as it rested on the castle like a throne. It howled atop and sprayed breaths of ice on its enemies. One of its wings was cut and could not fly anymore. Five guild members, including Maxwell, brandished their swords and spears to damage the large monster bit by bit. While avoiding its tails and claws, they slashed and struck at it. They persisted with small but fast attacks until the beast's strength waned. The wyvern persisted with an ice breath that was neither fast nor far enough to catch its assailants.

"They look like they're handlin' it," said Wayne.

"Yes sir-ee, that's our guild leader right there," chimed Ivo. "We should be ready just in case they need backup."

The van was parked a distance away from the battlefield. The reserves hopped off and kept a close watch on the fight.

Still on the castle, the wyvern cried out in rage. Hales of ice, the size of a car, poured over. Team A, full of vigor, moved at their top speeds. Some blocked or split it with their blades, while some jumped or hopped away. But the continuous rain of ice, its speed and gigantic size, had left them little to no room to maneuver. One got hit at the back; two had frozen limbs, and one was blasted away by the impact. Maxwell managed to land on the wyvern's head and pierced his sword onto its skull. Blood spurted from the wound. A grey aura blazed around him as he put more pressure on his sword and drove it deeper into the cranium. The wyvern cried in death, defeated.

Bloody and dirty, Maxwell pulled his blade back out with a heave. He curled his fist and raised it to the air. His teammates cheered in victory.

Ivo clapped and screamed for joy. "All right, reserves, time to do our job. Let's get Team A to the van and help treat their wounds." From his pockets, he produced a small lamp, the size of a keychain, and summoned a magic flying carpet into existence. He hopped on and began moving the injured on it.

Completely opposite to the reserve leader's enthusiasm, the members moved at a glacial pace, making their way to the members of Team A carrying bags of medicine, medical equipment and using their own 7s as well. One could call fireflies to light up the rainy night with a whistle. Another J-member served water for everyone to drink from a canteen that never emptied. And another had a backpack vacuum cleaner that vacuumed the important remains of the wyvern to be taken back outside for monster butchers.

Wayne walked towards the castle as he shined a flashlight above the wyvern. "He's gonna fall." He immediately dashed ahead.

"What? What's happening?" Ivo's voice trembled as he gnashed his teeth.

Maxwell's eyes fluttered back as he let go of his sword and teetered at the edge of the wyvern's head. Some reserves close to him started running towards him as well. Team A tried to help, but their injuries hampered their approach.

The guild leader closed his eyes and completely lost consciousness. He tumbled down the wyvern's head then shoulder and rolled to its back. His vest ripped against its many scales and snagged against its thorny tail. He dangled unconscious almost fifty meters high.

"Damn it," cursed Wayne. Sweat dripped on his face as he raced against time.

With his weight, Maxwell's vest completely ripped apart as he slipped off the monster and tumbled next to the castle. His arms and legs smacked and chafed against the walls as new and older wounds opened wider. The sleeping Maxwell kept falling with an angelic face and not a care in the world.

"Somebody, do something," Ivo screamed. The weight carried by his magic carpet prevented him from flying faster.

A soft green light glimmered close to where the van was. Accompanying a musical sound, a green cloud coalesced around Maxwell. His high-speed death-plummet slowed to a graceful floating descent. The cloud carried him close to the van, right into Keri's embrace, like two lovers reuniting again.

The members all stopped and gaped at the startling event.

Maxwell roused from his sleep. "Huh—where—what?" His face was dangerously next to hers.

In some odd way, the moment felt different to Keri. It reminded her of the ones she had seen in movies where the two leads met, where everything else didn't matter, and they finally kissed. The flute pipe stopped glimmering as it left her lips. Her eyes closed and her mouth puckered.

He looked around at their situation and frowned. "Keri, let go." He struggled from her embrace while she held on tighter. He flailed his hands and pushed her face away until both lost their balance and fell to the ground.

The rest of the members rushed up to help them.

Ivo knelt beside him in a rush. "Guild Leader, are you hurt anywhere? Hey, I need a stretcher and a scanner," he shouted.

Maxwell waved them away. "I'm fine, just tired." With a member's help, he rose to his feet and made his way onto the van.

Ivo was right next to him yelling for the other reserves to help the guild leader. "Show's over. Reserve Team, let's help Team A recover. Those who aren't medically trained, please collect the core and other useful parts of the monster," he announced.

Wayne helped Keri to a stand. "What was that?" he asked.

Keri dusted herself off. "Riley's flute-thing. I think it can control the wind?" As she headed back with everyone, she felt faint and lost her balance.

He quickly put his arms around her and steadied her. "You okay?"

"Just need to rest."

"Okay. Let me help you." Without warning, Wayne bent down and hoisted her in a princess-carry.

She wanted to protest out of embarrassment, then realized it was rare for her to get such treatment. Maybe she'd let it slide this time. Instead, she asked, "I'm heavy. You sure you want to do this?"

"Not heavy at all." He adjusted her to have a better balance of her weight that made her closer to him.

The warmth of his body and the hardness of his biceps and chest sent alarming sensations throughout her own. She turned her blushing face away. Was she going to misinterpret this gesture as well? She silently reprimanded herself for almost kissing Maxwell. *I couldn't help myself. Who knew he looked so cute when he wasn't bitching about everything?* she reasoned.

"You should try taking it easier with your abilities," said Wayne. "You're probably suffering from hypoetheria."

"Hypo—what? Is that the one they put in soap," she joked, knowing full well hypoetheria was a condition people suffered from the overuse of source and abilities. She considered it to be the loss of MP (magic points), like in games.

"It's not funny when you're in a bad situation and you can't use your powers." Keri reviewed the latest notices from the system.

> Stimuli and data have been recorded. Waiting for more input.
> Congratulations! Target lover #2 learned to appreciate you for saving his life.
> 200 coins earned. Total 270.
> Congratulations! Target lover #3 earned your respect. 100 coins earned.
> Total 370.

Seems like there were other ways she could interact with her target lovers, just like in the game. A blowjob may not necessarily be needed, but she kept it at the back of her mind. After all, any advancement or interaction could convince a target lover to get closer if the specific action was what their heart desired. Getting closer to them meant earning more system coins.

Chapter 26

Lake, Streets in Quisix

An area in Quisix, once famous for its many tall artistic buildings, dancing night lights and musical theatre, now housed a variety of lizardmen in its destroyed and crumbling buildings. The green-colored monsters, the melee warriors, carried shields, swords and spears, while they patrolled and guarded the entrance. Each patrol had at least one of the blue ones—archers who carried large steel and wooden bows and crossbows.

Weaving through the alleys, Lake ran at full speed. Five green lizardmen chased after him while blue ones raced in from another street. The green ones quickly stopped, aimed and fired. At the onslaught of arrows, Lake activated the plate equipment he had been working on, he named L-Shield. On his right arm, the lights and mechanism of the shield activated and made a whirring noise. As the arrows reached him from above, a dome made of light encompassed his whole being and barred the assault of projectiles. Still on the move, he dashed forward, then rounded a corner.

Lizardmen followed suit; their group growing in number. As the distance between them threatened to narrow, Lake released pebble-sized grenades. The feet of the ones in front exploded, rendering them immobile. Others that followed tripped over them while the rest leapt over.

Glancing back, he diverted more strength in his legs and squeezed his core, trying to push himself further. His heart pounded and his lungs heaved. Signs of his dwindling endurance and strength started showing. He took a left, then a right, before stopping at a closed lot surrounded by tall buildings on all sides.

He looked around. They were in front of him, filling the sides and finally behind him—there was no way out; Lake was surrounded. The lizardmen caught up with him, even the ones that had tripped earlier. They had their blades at the ready, hissing. At the sight of their cornered prey, their slit eyes widened, their shoulders hunched and legs half-squatted—they were ready to kill him. One screeched in what looked to be exhilaration, then leapt at him, but was met with a lightning bolt that blasted it away.

Lake discharged a lightning spell he had installed in his S-Glove. His new fragments led him to place more spells in his equipment without the need to cast it himself. Now, he only had to push the buttons for them to execute.

The other monsters grew hesitant as they zeroed in on Lake's crackling hand. They squawked at each other as if arguing about who would attack first. But their chatter ended as the ground tremored. A giant, bulky green lizard, two stories tall, stomped and made itself known. The others fell aside and created an aisle to let it through.

"Didn't see that one coming," Lake murmured to himself.

As if responding to him, the giant roared in rage, pointing at Lake. It then approached him in big steps, with the other lizardmen trailing behind it. Lake discharged another bolt. It zoomed in and hit the huge monster with a bang. As the flash waned, the giant came off unscathed, with only a black mark and scuff on its belly. It howled a deafening, irritated cry. In response, the other lizardmen behind did the same, bellowing a chorus of hair-standing wails. Waving their arms, the earth shook as the horde charged at him at full speed.

Though their movement was fast, the seconds felt like hours for Lake while sweat beaded on his face. He waited, unmoving and unflinching. His peripheral vision darted over to a white line near the start of the empty lot. The ground shook harder and the lizardmen's sounds grew louder as they neared him. Once the giant faced him, it struck down with its oversized hands on him. At the same time, the last of the lizardmen crossed the white line.

"Game over," he said.

His boots lit up. The wind spell installed on his new boots activated as he high-jumped into the air. Passing the height of six stories, he landed right on the rooftop of the back building, away from danger. The lizardmen stared at him dumbly, mouths gaping open in confusion. He then pulled his left sleeve back, revealing the panel of his S-glove. A red dot pulsed at the glass panel. With a wide grin, he tapped on it.

Down below, four cylindrical steel devices attached to corner posts glowed. It released lines of light that connected with each other. Once they created a rectangular perimeter, a strong downward force manifested within. A weighted force worth ten tones pushed down on all matter inside the rectangle. Rubble broke into small rocks, cars smashed into pieces and bins squished like tin cans. For the lizardmen, they fell to the ground face first as their hands and legs broke. Though most were unharmed, all of them were pressed down unable to move. Even the giant was rendered helpless, with its fat pressing against the hard cement.

Lake steadied his pounding heart with deep breaths. With a calmer feeling, he unholstered his pack and opened it. He tossed a large grenade below that exploded upon impact. Then after, another rolled in, adding to the fire and the sounds. For good measure, he even added some cooking oil to the mix. He kept filling the lot with grenades as the cries of the lizardmen echoed around, reached a height, then died down.

As the fire blazed on, Lake crouched at the ledge, watching them burn. He was satisfied that he had caught them, but he doubted his current skills right now could take on the boss of the area. Maybe with the growth from the system, he wondered if he might be getting closer and closer.

> Monster slain. Earned 50. Monster slain. Earned 50.
> Monster slain. Earned 50. Monster slain. Earned 50...

The buzzing continued on for quite a while as the monsters all died. When it stopped, the fire had been reduced to mere embers flickering around the lot, leaving a scene full of charred remains, ash and soot.

Lake jumped back down using his boots. Unstrapping a knife from his straps, he bent and stabbed the closest lizard. Most steel blades would only take after multiple tries, but this one had a sharpness spell installed in it, so it only took one try for Lake to sink it deep into the monster's scaly skin.

He made a circular incision in the chest and chucked out the flesh and bones. Once it was open, he picked out a red rock off the cadaver—the monster core. Though it appeared more like a quartz crystal or tektite, to Lake's Mind Eye, it glowed a strong brilliance as source concentrated in it. He tossed it into his backpack and started on the next.

When Lake harvested the last of the cores, a foreboding feeling slid down the back of his neck. Quickly, he high-jumped back to the building and crouched as four green lizardmen came rushing in. They stopped after seeing the remains of their brethren—their tongues slithering with spite. Behind them, a tall red-scaled lizardman strode in the middle wearing burgundy robes. Much of its head was covered by its hood. Its eyes were wrapped in a red blindfold with intricate patterns. Most of its face was covered except for its long snout, showing its mouth full of sharp teeth.

Lake recorded the scene with a cubex. The small cube sat lightly in his palms, taking everything in.

The red lizard revealed a golden wand from underneath its robes. With a few archaic whispers from its mouth, the wand glowed as a soft white light exploded out. Before it reached the building, Lake had a sudden impulse to write a rune he only knew meant 'pass-over'. It was those trivial runes that were never really used in battles, but were translated for the sake of it. As the light reached the rooftop, it split apart around Lake's surroundings and skipped over him. It was as if there was an invisible wall that blocked the light.

Below, the red lizard stashed its wand away, seemingly finding nothing. It flitted its tongue in and out of its mouth before relaying its orders to its brethren. The greens collected the blades that had not been burnt. Once they were done, they left the lot and made their way to one of the biggest roads in the city.

Lake jumped from the current rooftop to the next and kept a watchful eye over the group. He was a good enough distance away that they would not notice him trailing behind. Whenever they stopped at a corner or street and inspected their surroundings, he'd crouch and hide under the ledges. They never left his sight as he moved overhead. This made him realize that he needed some type of tracker or vision equipment—a task for when he got back.

When the number of lizardmen patrols increased, Lake stayed a further distance away. The group he was following ended their patrol at the arts district. Theatres, museums and art shops lined the street. Over at the end, the biggest and most popular movie theatre stood with a tall triangular roof and rainbow-colored glass walls. Holographic posters and banners plastered the establishment of the last film it hosted: *Xia Meron*—a biopic of the early life of Zuobic's female president.

As the large double doors opened, two red-robed lizards strode out and greeted the group he had been following. They talked for a moment before the first red lizardman went into the theatre and a new one replaced it to start the patrol again.

Above an apartment building, Lake was leaning at the ledge with his peripheral vision on the theatre. He accessed the panel of his S-glove and pinned the location of the theatre. He also noted the other buildings surrounding it. After taking notes, he slipped away from the scene. He promised himself he'd go back there to investigate further. Using his S-boots, he jumped away and made his way back to the mech shop.

The sun was setting by the time he arrived back at his makeshift home. After disarming the alarms he had installed, he entered and put them back up again. He made his way to his work bench and placed a backpack full of cores on the desk.

Tony sat at the dining table, eating from a cereal box without the milk. "Took you long enough this time," he said out loud.

Lake made his way into the kitchen, bringing another pack. "You're eating now." He unloaded the food supplies from it.

"Did you know that a linko has a function that identifies products off shelves? It reads the name, price, nutritional value and where closest to buy it from? Just have to carry the camera around." He played with a cubex in his hands.

He stocked the shelves with more cans and boxes. "It gets data online. I'm surprised the servers here still work. Probably a child server or cached system."

"You seem to forget I'm not a dumbass nerd like you," replied Tony. "What happened to you out there? You were out later than usual."

He grabbed a can opener and fixed himself a can of beans mixed with lunch meat. "I think I might know where the boss is." He relayed how he followed the red lizardman on patrol.

After finishing a box of cereal, Tony opened a bag of chips. "What does that do? This isn't a rift world. We are not going back to ours if you kill the boss."

Lake chewed on his food and let it go down before he said, "No. But this place goes back to us."

He stopped munching. "What—that's not—What?"

"Tony, if I kill the boss, this place, this whole area comes back to our world. That means we don't have to be stuck here." His voice was slow and steady.

Tony put the bag of chips down. "How do you know this? Are you messing with me? Do I look like I wanna be messed with right now? Did I put on a shirt that says stupid? Huh?"

His jaw tensed. "I was going to say trust me, but I don't think you'll believe—"

Tony slammed his fist on the table. "Damn if I do. You don't make sense, Starless."

Lake breathed deeply in and out. He licked his lips and opened his mouth to say his truth, but instead he agreed, "It really won't make sense, but I honestly think it's crazy—"

"Out with it," he cut off. "I decide what I want to believe."

His fidgeting fingers stopped as he stared at him for a moment.

Tony relaxed his shoulders. "I already think you're a weirdo with issues. Anything else you say about you, all the more that I think you're just crazy." His face cracked with a smile.

He calmed his nerves and anxiety. "I'm bad at explaining, so I'm telling you what happened..." He started his dream, then the accident at the training room and everything else involving the system since.

After the story, he drank a glass of water.

"You're not going to say anything?" probed Lake. "Don't you think it's insane?"

"I...expected something more." He crunched loudly on the chips.

"What?"

Tony waved his hand across. "Man, look around you. We are stuck in a dimension ripped from our world. We fight monsters from another world. You have magic—kind of. I can run super fast. A video game in your head isn't as crazy as it sounds."

Looking at Tony's perspective, Lake thought he was right. "Am I an outlier?" he asked.

Tony shrugged. "What did Major Cervantes say?"

"I only told him I had that dream. And things have been different. He doesn't know about the system." Lake resumed eating his meal.

His brow rose. "He didn't ask you about it? Like details? And he just let you go? Did he install a tracker on you?"

"What are you saying? Why would he do that?"

Tony threw the empty bag of chips aside. "It might be on your linko."

"What are you trying to say?"

"If you value your life, you'll do your best to shut up about the video game in your head," he said in a deeper tone. "Unless you want to be the army's next lab rat."

"The army isn't like that. They take care of their own." Lake felt heat rising from his body.

"I have a tattoo on my legs that put me in bed for weeks. How do you think they got through this level of tech without breaking a few eggs?"

Lies. In his mind, these were all fiction. "You're wrong. The army's—no, Major Cervantes wouldn't do that. I know he is a difficult person, but he believes in people. He trusts his soldiers. He's the best scientist to ever live in Zuobic—no, the world."

"Is that what he said to you? He said he believed in you? That you are the key? You are worthy? Which one was it? It changes over time." Tony's questions flooded him with no room to speak.

Lake was tongue-tied.

"I overheard him telling the same thing to my dad before he died in the hospital," he spoke in a somber tone. "It's the speech he tells you when he wants your life."

The reasons he thought of in his head to prove him wrong all paled in comparison to his colleague's own.

"Don't talk to him about this video game thing in your head. The last thing you want is to be a research subject for the nation's advancement bullshit." He rose from his seat and fumbled his way back into his room.

Lake was left alone with doubts and uncertainties. He convinced himself that all the talk was Tony's way of coping with what had happened to his father. As he moved to the workbench, he decided to focus on what he could do—getting out of this place. He opened the system again.

CANDIDATE STATUS:

> Name: Lake Deskenn | Profile: Hero | Coins: 1050
> Activated Fragments: Source Blessed – D, Hero's Retreat – F (innate),
> Mind's Eye – F
> Available Fragments Left: 2

After checking his coins, he went to the system's store. The three upgrades stared at him again:

> Soul Growth - 850 coins
> Body Growth - 850 coins
> Mind Growth - 1000 coins

He was blown away by how these upgrade prices kept jumping up. Did that correlate somewhat with the growth and changes he experienced? At first look, it seemed like a scam. But then again, to somehow change himself to something better to help himself and people—giving himself that chance—wasn't that the real scam? A scam he could definitely benefit from, despite the rising costs.

As a cheapskate most of his life, who opted for free meals in the cafeteria and denied Jella's help with anything money related, he leaned on the Soul and Body as potential next purchases. When he had asked the system for more details about each, it responded:

> Possible results for Soul Growth: Increases the candidate's soul; unlocks abilities that manifest the soul or evolves fragments of the soul type. Also increases fragment capacity of the soul.
> Possible results for Body Growth: Grows the candidate's physical functions; unlocks abilities that manifest the use and extension of the body or evolves fragments of the soul type. Increased constitution against hypoetheria.

He read over the descriptions for the 850 upgrades. The randomness of what he was going to buy made him apprehensive to actually select anything. It wasn't like shopping for outfits or food—this was about surviving here in a deleted space. He needed something that worked in his favor.

After a few sighs, he settled for Soul. He had no fragments that related to Body anyway, so there was no chance for an evolution to happen. He figured Soul had more to offer for him.

Congratulations, you have purchased Soul Growth for 850 coins. Total coins 200. Due to likeness with current fragment Source Blessed, Source Blessed shall ascend to Soul Weaving – B.

Soul Weaving - B. Description: The whole being is closer to understanding the mysteries of the source. He is able to manipulate its very fabric, producing varied effects between objects and other souls.

CANDIDATE STATUS:

Name: Lake Deskenn | Profile: Hero | Coins: 200

Activated Fragments: Soul Weaving – B, Hero's Retreat – F (innate), Mind's Eye – F

Available Fragments Left: 2

After reading the notices, he assumed nothing had changed. He felt as he did before. Grabbing one of the cores he had extracted from the lizardmen, he used his Mind's Eye. As before, he could see tendrils around it. His hand moved by instinct as he tugged the strings. From the new core, he attached a blue-colored braid to his L-Shield and a red one directly at the back of his neck. After doing so, a realization hit him. He had just touched his soul.

With a slight mental command, the L-Shield roared to life as a dome of light surrounded him, protecting him from attacks from all directions. His face widened again with a stupid grin. At another request through the soul connection, the dome expanded in size. It increased as much as ten times its size, almost reaching the ends of the walls and ceilings. A slight glimmer caught his attention as the core he had been using dimmed and seemed to grow smaller. He ceased his experiment as the light dome faded.

He closed the shop, satisfied by his new fragment. Ideas raced again in his head for what he could do this time, but then they all stopped. What Tony said was bugging him. He unhooked his linko from his ear and disassembled it. After a minute, a tiny chip that was unnecessary for the communication device to function sat before him on the table. The function of the excess part was to send data of its geographical location without any control hooked onto his linko. The tiny tracker inanimately mocked him for his stupidity.

"No. This doesn't mean anything. He was only looking after me. He doesn't want anything happening to me," he mouthed to no one in particular.

Though he believed his words to be somewhat true, he took the chip and smashed it into pieces. He rested his head in his hands, filled with thoughts of self-doubt and uncertainty.

Chapter 27

Keri, Outworld Ai-Dois

The day-long journey towards the canyon was not without its dangers. Tribes of lizardmen occasionally ambushed the two teams. Always at the front, Team A received the brunt of the attacks while riding their dirt bikes. With their blades, they skillfully dispatched any attacking monsters and left them for dead. Then, Team J would stop at each cleared battle and harvest useful organs from the lizardmen, including their precious cores.

During that time, Keri would help with harvesting—she had learned to butcher monsters from Ivo. At first, the blood and guts nearly made her vomit, but after a few tries, she found it tolerable. She guessed what she was doing was better than being on the frontlines and in danger. Her first priority was her own safety, but that also meant she was losing her chances of earning points. She didn't know if she'd step up or continue on the sides.

Maxwell walked towards Keri. "Keri, do you have a minute?" He was wiping his sword clean from the blood and guts of a lizardman.

Keri was lugging a bag full of leather armor and shin guards. "Yeah, just getting these things back. What's up?" She continued towards the truck.

"About the other time, I'd like to reward you with what you did at the wyvern battle." He paused at certain moments, looking as if he was unsure of what he was saying.

"For catching you so you wouldn't fall to your death?" she said while grunting at the heftiness of the bag.

Maxwell clicked his tongue. "Can we not say it like that?"

"Why not? You fell. I caught you. What's wrong about that?"

He forced a smile. "Nothing. Clearly nothing. Anyway, what would you like as a reward?"

"Reward? I don't know. I wasn't thinking of one," replied Keri. "You fell, so I caught you."

His pulled-up smile twitched. "Got it. If you think of anything, let me know." He left with stiff shoulders and a rigid walk.

"What's his problem?" she breathed out, annoyed.

The teams camped for the night to rest with watchers taking turns throughout the night. Soon as morning came, they packed their bags and headed out again before finally arriving at their destination.

The storm had cleared and left a blanket of gloomy clouds by the time they reached the canyon where the dimension's overlord lived. A clear, shallow river cut through the middle of it. On its left, three of the wyvern statues stood with their claws out, holding bowls, expecting the offerings needed to summon its lord. On the right, two other large statues waited.

The guild leader had instructed the teams to collect the cores and place them on the statues. The intelligence mentioned that by doing this, the boss would show up and defeating it would close the rift.

Max radioed new directives as the other teams arrived as well. Team A to E would be battling the boss; Team J would stand back and observe. Team J parked near the river, far enough from the fight but close enough to lend a helping hand. As the teams spread into the pre-planned positions, silence covered the canyon.

"They've placed the cores," Ivo announces over the speakers.

For a couple of minutes, nothing happened. Then, a shriek sounded from above. A large dragon with five heads descended from the storm clouds. Its size was more than ten times bigger than the wyverns. The heads all faced the statues and blasted it with their breath. Each head exhaled an elemental breath: fire, lightning, ice, wind and poison.

The teams all took cover under their shields, behind the statues and the Water Barriers their few sorcerers created. The breath extended for a minute before it cleared. Once it did, they charged ahead.

The front-liners, who used blades split themselves, taking on a head each while the ranged fighters barraged the body of the beast with exploding and penetrative bullets and arrows of magic. Behind a statue, three sorcerers gathered in a circle and composed a spell together. On another statue, two more supported their team with spells for protection and cover.

The Hairless Apes were like huge sea waves. Their attacks splashed against the dragon from all sides and hit it hard. When the heads retaliated, they retreated with haste. They put constant pressure on the beast, piling wounds and cuts on top of each other. The guild leader brandished his gigantic sword with two hands and slashed down at the fire-breathing head. Then, Maxwell stabbed the poison head with his sword with the same killing technique he had done earlier.

The other heads cried out in pain, grief and rage. Runes appeared and swiveled in midair. They were aligned in patterns of diamonds, squares and circles and rotated. The guild's scanners warned that a dangerous level of attack was coming from the heads.

"How long?" asked Maxwell in his linko.

One of the two sorcerers who supported the guild studied the thirty runes dancing around the three other sorcerers casting. "It's ready," he reported.

"Do it now."

Stepping into the circle, he cast another string of runes around the circle they had created. Once all glowed together and the spell was ready, they concentrated into one ball, shot above and vanished. Then, with a spark, a web of light sprouted out and covered the whole wyvern. It wrapped the wyvern from head to toe. As the web restricted the creature's limbs and wings, it landed on the ground. The three heads ceased their breath attacks, but even after that, the spell the wyvern started continued.

Blue beams rained down and the patterns disappeared. The melee members of the guild managed to block and evade the initial downpour, but the ones that followed and kept coming proved to be more and more difficult by the second. Meanwhile, the sorcerers were blasted and hit multiple times. Having just released a spell, they had been the most vulnerable. The ranged fighters ran for cover before the attack. But they still received small wounds and cuts.

As the rain of banishing beams continued, Team J maneuvered their truck, dodging the lights and burning rubber. Once they arrived at the nearest injured fighters, the door opened and Wayne, Keri and the rest of the members came out. They hauled them back to the trucks with medical equipment. Inside, a few sorcerers and doctors started attending to them.

At the behest of a doctor, Keri patched up the members with gauze wrappings, antiseptics and painkillers inside the truck. The first few cases she got were mild and were easy to help—a few open wounds and bruises. But as the fighting continued, the ones she received bled all over the truck. Still, she persisted and did as the doctor instructed. As she pressed on the open wound of a team member, the earth shook.

"What's that?" Keri blurted.

"I need a medic on the battlefield," Deeg broadcast through the linko.

The doctor with Keri reached for her linko and said, "Can you guys get that? My hands are full."

After a few minutes, Deeg announced again, "We need a medic, now."

The doctor tried her linko again but could not reach the other support staff. "Patch him up like before. I'll be right back."

Keri stared at the moaning patient, whose guts peeped at the side of his torso. "But he's dying," she protested.

"Do what you can." She grabbed her backpack and fled the truck.

Keri stared at the burn marks and open wounds. "Do what I can?" She had zero medical knowledge apart from what she had learned, what could she do? By practice, she repeated the steps to patch the wound. But no matter how much roll she placed around the wound, the blood kept gushing out and the guts peeked out of the hole.

"Shit," she cursed.

She continued wrapping the wound to no success. The organs and blood kept coming out. After another wrestle with a pack of gauze and towels, she finally stopped the bleeding. But after a few beats, the patient's skin grew pale by the second as the statistics screen bleeped in a louder alarm.

"Shit, shit, shit." She looked around her, hoping for help. Everyone dealt with their own dying patients.

Keri reached for her linko. But the second the linko was connected, the sound of the wyvern's howl reverberated across the link and another quake shook the entire area. Her right ear deafened for a moment as the truck rumbled. After the sonic boom, another alarm from a display screen screamed. A patient next to her was dying; their heartbeat was fading.

"No—no, no, no—please don't do this to me." She reached her hands instinctively to the other patient. But as soon as she did, the blood from the previous one started gushing out again.

Soon as her hands returned to the wounded, a third alarm sounded. "No, not you too, miss. Please, don't die yet." She wanted to try for the linko again, but as her hand moved away from the wound, the blood soaked through again.

Then, a fourth alarm sounded. A patient was seizing.

Her head spun from one dying member to another, trying to find out why they were dying while keeping the wound of a patient from bleeding further, also figuring out how to leave one patient and attend to the other and trying to reach for her linko all at the same time.

"Wait!"

A clock made of light appeared above her and the patients in midair. The second hand was moving by the second until it froze, and the screaming of the alarm and seizing of the patient stopped.

Her face crumpled. For some odd reason, she knew it was okay to let go. And as she did, the wound did not bleed out. Time for the patients had stopped. She knew they were safe for now, but for how long? Her knees unexpectedly gave out as she held onto the wall for support. Sweat trickled down her face and the pace of her breathing increased. She felt it. Source entered and escaped her body continuously as the clock above her existed and stilled.

She was about to reach for her linko yet again, but the doors to the truck opened. Wayne appeared at the entrance.

"Wayne, get help. I can't hold out for long," she requested.

Wayne didn't reply. Instead, he stepped inside the truck and immediately fell to the floor. Keri rushed to his side. Upon closer inspection, she had only noticed now the cuts and bruises on him. She gasped. A large sizzling wound burned his back.

In a panic, she quickly extended her powers over him and stopped his wounds from getting worse.

Queen entered the truck. "I wouldn't worry much about him. He'll pull through," she said in a deep, almost male voice.

Keri looked up with knitted brows. "What are you—"

She took off her hood and the wig she had been wearing. A man with a scar at the back of his left ear and red-grey tattoos on his arms revealed himself. "Hey, remember me?" asked Qahoon.

It all came back to Keri. He was the man who was chasing after Wayne. "Hello, I need help. There's an intruder here." She reached for her linko.

An amused look displayed over Qahoon. "Shout all you want, missy. It's not gonna work. This jams all other signals but mine." He produced a small phone-like device from his pocket.

If she could not reach people for help, what could she do? Could she fight him head on? But what if he tried to kill Wayne and the other patients? "I don't understand. You wanted Wayne, why are you trying to kill him?" she asked.

He further entered the vehicle. "He actually killed some of my guys, you know, the rest of Team J. We were just trying to subdue him. He'll be fine. He's a tough cookie. Not sure about you."

She realized that the rest of the people in her team were probably slavers as well. "What are you planning to do?" She kept Wayne close to her.

Qahoon smiled, showing off his golden incisor tooth. "When you sealed the curse on my lantern, I thought that was an odd item you might have. Better steal it from you and kill you. Then, I see you moving fast and slowing down the guild leader, I'm like, damn, this bitch might be an ability user, just like big boy over here. And lookie you now, pretty impressive." He looked at the clocks with great interest.

"Screw you," she hissed.

"You know how much one of you cost in the Federation or the Empire? I'm going to live a long, good life."

"You won't have a chance," she said with conviction. "Once Maxwell kills the boss, he's coming after you."

He removed the cloak and the fake boobs he had been wearing, revealing a singlet and jeans underneath. "I admit the guild leader is a tough guy, but with all of his medics gone, not sure they'd survive that fight."

Keri was conscious of her Training Sword dangling on her neck, ready to use it whenever. "You killed them? If they die, how are you going to leave?" she asked.

He produced a palm-sized duck figurine from his pockets. "This is a Mandarin Duck; it comes in two. If you put source into it, all things around it, in a meter, will magically teleport to the other one. Pretty cool huh? Freaking rare too. After last time, I planned my getaway." He walked closer to her until they were next to each other.

"So you have it all figured out?" she growled.

"You betcha. Now, we should go."

Once he reached his hand out to her, Keri transformed her necklace into a short sword and slashed across, creating a shallow cut on her opponent's arm. "Don't you dare." She placed Wayne behind her with the rest of the patients.

He licked the blood slipping down his arm. "I like a girl with spice, you know that. It isn't really bad if she's got some meat in her." He winked.

She charged forward with another slash and succeeded in pushing him back a few steps. "I said get...back," she huffed, feeling her strength drain away.

Qahoon raised a brow. "What's the matter? You're new to this huh? Don't know how to conserve your strength?" His left earring gleamed as an orange lantern floated next to him.

"What are you doing? Put that away." She threatened him with her sword.

"Do you know that I can control the explosion of the lantern? Could be big. Could be small. Do you think this truck can handle a big one?"

"You won't do that," stated Keri. "You'll get hit by the explosion too."

He giggled. "Didn't I tell you? All explosions and curses these babies put out don't affect me at all. It's why they call me the Zombie Bomber. Get it? I do a suicide bomb, but I don't die."

This wasn't right. This was not how it was supposed to go. With the dwindling power she had left, she gathered her energy and steeled herself. But as she set her mind to it, her control faded.

The clock in the air started to move. The second hand started moving again as her body grew cold. No, this was not it. She had more fight in her. Deep inside her, she reached for more energy. The second hand stopped for a few moments then moved again in a slower pace. Each second in the clock was equal to half of a second.

"My clients don't really like damaged goods, so I've got some healers who can patch you up if you get injured," offered Qahoon. "Just a small warning: they can't put back fingers or legs. You know how it is. What will it be?"

She wanted to speak, to call out for help, but her mouth would not move. All her strength was diverted into keeping the clock from moving and maintaining her attacking stance. Not a muscle in her moved. As her breath grew shallow, memories of the dying moments she had experienced at her death-dream flooded back. Would she wind up dead here as well? No, she didn't want that. But she felt helpless and stuck. She didn't know what to do. Why did she always end up in situations like this?

"You look like you're about to faint. Are you scared?" asked Qahoon curiously. "Oh right. You're still trying to save them."

Her body collapsed onto the floor as she went on all fours. The sword clanged with a loud sound. Keri breathed in deep and hard. Though her body gave in, the clock stood still. Her vision blurred.

He grinned. "Looks like you're almost out of time. Tell you what, I think I'll bomb this place up. Just so you don't wake up in the middle of transport and try to escape."

Keri's situation felt like a bad ending in her sim-games. She didn't get her kiss, she had not stolen any of the men's hearts, and most of all, she and the leads were dying. No, just no. This was not her time. Damn it. If she was going to die, a villainess should be the one killing her for the attention of the prince. Not some low life slaver. This was not how the story should go.

"Boom," the bomber whispered softly.

The light from the orange lantern brightened from a soft glow and increased into a blinding light. It surrounded the whole vehicle and exploded. The whole truck blazed into fire, smoke and debris.

A notification chimed.

Chapter 28

Keri, Canyon, Outworld Ai-Dois

As smoke and debris clouded the air, Keri lay on the ground, battered and dirty but otherwise fine. More than fine, she believed. She was great. Her strength slowly returned to her in pulses as she felt a different kind of power course through her. She pushed herself off the ground, taking note of how she moved. She was, in all meanings of the word, healthy. Before she prodded more on her own condition, the state of the wounded and Wayne interrupted her thoughts. Her head twisted around, but the thick smoke and embers blocked her sight. As panic rose in her, it was easily quelled. The power she felt seemed to extend around her. Somehow, she knew they were fine. Feelings were unreliable for her; she needed to know, to see if what her gut was telling her was true.

She reached for a hand around her and felt Wayne's big biceps quickly. Was he alive? If he was, was he okay? Was he going to pull through? Keri felt him with her hands, trying to find his chest. In another time and situation, this would have sent her to the sky, but now she only tried to feel his heartbeat, to know if he was safe. When she could not, she placed her head down and tried to hear it. Thump. Thump. Thump. A smile crossed her face. He was alive.

As the smoke cleared bit by bit, revealing wreckage and embers, she gasped. A circle filled with weird symbols and a huge clock brightened the ground where the people lay. Small golden sparks floated around the guild members and Wayne. At the center of it all was Keri, whose source fed the glowing marks as it ticked each second. Next to her, a notification on the screen was waiting to be read:

Flute of the Breeze has been consumed. Life O' Clock has been consumed.

Essences of artefacts are being remodeled to Maiden's needs. Please standb y...

Congratulations! A new fragment is born. Time Trade – C. Description: (1) Vary a matter's perception and experience against real time. (2) Trade time between matters. (3) Misuse can cause negative effects on a candidate. It is recommended to increase Mind and Soul Growth to avoid these.

"What does this all mean?" she whispered to herself.

As the circle of light dwindled, it left her and the others healthy and sound. Other than dirt, their bodies had been healed of the wounds and cuts like they'd never been harmed in the first place.

A few meters from her, Qahoon rose from the rubble and dusted the dirt off of him. "The explosion doesn't work on me, but it still blows me off. I hate doing this. Whoever made this thing, should've made it—you're fine?" He gave her a perturbed look.

Keri immediately grabbed her Trainee Sword. But there was nothing to grasp around her neck. Her eyes darted around and discovered the sword lying a meter from her. She jumped for it. As her hand wrapped at the hilt of the sword, a boot stomped on her fingers. She cried out from the pain and let go.

Qahoon grabbed her by the hair and pulled her head off the ground. "Stupid bitch. How'd you do that?" he asked.

Her eyes burned with anger. "Eat shit." She balled her free hand and punched his balls.

He immediately let go and cried out, "Damn bitch."

Keri staggered forward to where the sword was. She picked it up from the floor and turned to attack. But as she swung her blade, the orange lantern appeared on her and exploded. She was knocked back.

As Qahoon approached Keri, he picked up her sword on the ground. "I'm sure someone will still buy you even without your hands." He swung the sword down on her.

Before the blade connected, an arm wrapped in blue fire blocked its contact, and another flaming palm struck him on the chest and sent him flying away. "Get your hands off her," said Wayne.

Pain throbbing in her back, Keri looked up at her savior. "You're okay," she said.

He picked up the Trainee Sword and returned it to her. "Thanks to you."

"I didn't do—"

He placed a hand on her face. "It was you, I felt it. I know it. Ever since I became a 14, I can sense source. Can't you?" His big kind eyes bore onto her.

Oh my gosh. Is this my romantic scene moment? This is it, isn't it? He's gonna kiss me, she screamed in her head, imagining an orchestra playing music for the special kiss. "I do. I feel it."

"Your source has always been different from others. You've always been special, Keri. From the first time I saw you." Wayne inched his head closer to her face.

Keri puckered her mouth and gradually closed her eyes. Under her eyelids, she sensed something brightening. *Was the sun coming up? Is this that scene in the movies? Wherein the lead male and female kiss? The clouds part and the sun shines on the land?* But what was that heat? It felt more like her body temperature was rising and something was burning? Was she on fire? She shot her eyes open.

A ball of fire the size of a house lit the murky skies before them, and it grew bigger by the second. In the middle, the orange lantern burned the brightest.

Keri raised her hands up as a clock traced itself with light before the ball of fire. "Look out," she yelled.

Wayne turned around. "What?"

The growth of the ball of fire stopped as the roaring fires around it slowed in motion. The rate of time surrounding it was reduced to tenths of a second.

"Why'd it stop?" Qahoon fed it more of his source but its growth was stunted.

Keri felt her insides being torn apart as source flooded into her and converted it into the energy that sustained the frozen time. The rate of consumption sucked more out of her than the previous ones. "This is harder than healing people. Help," she said with gritted teeth.

In a heartbeat, Wayne's feet were enveloped in blue fire as he leaped into the sky and dove down behind Qahoon. The tremor caused the slaver to fall on his knee.

Using that moment, Wayne slammed his palm on his enemy's back, creating a deep burn mark between his shoulder blades. Air escaped the slaver's lungs as he fainted to the ground. The large blast stopped and the orange lantern vanished.

Keri exhaled with exhaustion as she rested her back on the debris more comfortably. "Is he dead?" she huffed.

He lifted the slaver's head with both hands from the ground and twisted it. "Now he is." Then he let go.

"Why'd you—he wasn't moving—maybe prison." She covered her mouth, unable to comprehend what had happened. Guilt blossomed in her heart. She had a hand in this man's death. No, but it was Wayne who did it. She had nothing to do with—but she wanted it to happen. A part of her desired it so.

Wayne was right next to her. "This is life here. Kill or be killed. We don't have walls and fancy tech that protect us like in Zuobic."

"Couldn't you at least take him to—"

"He's a slaver. If I didn't kill him and he's tossed into jail, he'll be hunting us again for the money and revenge."

Keri's mind raced of all the consequences and things she had done. "But what if someone finds out? I don't want to go to prison. I—"

He embraced her. "Shhh... This is a different dimension. Once it closes, it's gone forever."

Was this reality now for her? All the power and the system—they were all fun and exciting. Defeating monsters thrilled her. The thought of growing was just like a game. But now, she was killing people? And she'd almost died?

From the rubble, movement stirred. Wayne approached it with caution, but after checking on it, he quickly cleared the debris. Ivo rose from the wreckage. He was dirty and coughing, but otherwise healthy and full of energy.

"Where is Queen? I must report her," exclaimed Ivo. "She has violated closer laws and tried to kill me. This is unheard of. Truly."

"He won't be coming after you for a while." Wayne motioned to Qahoon's dead body.

"He?" His gentle face wrinkled.

"Her real name is Qahoon. He was a slaver out to get me and Keri." He moved over to another area as he spotted and helped another member getting up.

"A slaver? That is appalling." Ivo assisted him.

"Thanks to Keri, we're fine." He moved to the next closer that roused.

Ivo smashed his fist into his palm. "Right. Keri. I remember Queen saying something about kidnapping and selling her before he plunged a knife in my gut. Wait, how did Keri help us?"

His intense expression softened. "She can heal."

"Really? I thought it was only sword stuff and curse nullification? You can heal too?"

"I guess so," said Keri.

Ivo rushed and knelt before her. "I am truly thankful you saved little old useless me. Thank you for not letting my wife become a widow."

Keri's building guilt crumbled at the voice of Ivo's appreciation. "I...only did what I could."

The recovered and waking closers listened in and started asking questions about what had happened. Wayne was quick to tell them the gist of what they'd missed.

Ivo grabbed both of Keri's hands and shook his head. "You helped us all. We wouldn't be here without you."

"Thank you, Keri, for saving us," said a sorcerer.

Guilt and appreciation tore her apart. It was something she didn't understand how to deal with. She had to get away from this place. These people, with all their smiling faces, this positivity was not something she could bear. She did something wrong, but she was being thanked?

"AAGGGOOOWWW!!"

Like an answer to her heart, the dragon howled as the battle raged on. Quickly, everyone rushed towards the sounds of blades clashing and explosions.

Chapter 29

Maxwell, Outworld Ai-Dois

Previously, the dark-blue dragon had large wings and five heads that breathed different elements. Now, it had only one head and no wings, crying out as it battled a spearman and Maxwell. Electricity spouted from its body as bolts shot off in various directions. The two closers leaped back, dodging the electrifying rain.

While executing swift movements, Maxwell accessed his linko. "Report," he ordered through a broadcast channel.

Hidden behind a boulder, Deeg fired off cannons with another member. "There's only two of us left. The rest are incapacitated. The others are missing, including the medics," he said.

He parried a few bolts away with his katana enveloped in a grey aura. His other sword was stuck at one of the heads. "And Team J?" he asked.

"I can't reach Ivo nor the people from Amazing Discoveries," he answered. "Looks like a jammer has been placed. It seems like one of the new reserves might've been the cause of it."

Maxwell took cover behind the remnants of a truck. "What are our options?"

"I'm out of shells," intruded the bomber next to Deeg.

"The only thing to do now is to gather the trucks together and make them explode," suggested Deeg. "But I don't know if we have enough explosives for that."

"I brought extra ones in the truck. They should be good for that," shared the bomber.

"Would that be enough to kill it?" asked Maxwell.

Deeg watched clips of the recording he had made earlier from his cubex. "Should be enough if it makes a sizable impact."

"But what about our members?" asked the spearman in the guild channel. "They'll be caught in the explosion if we do that. We have to rescue them first."

"We don't have time for that," Deeg argued. "The trucks are too far from us. Getting all of it together and rescuing people—can you stall the dragon until then?"

The spearman was quiet for a moment, but he continued, "There has to be a way. We can't let our comrades die here. Guild Leader, please."

Maxwell closed his eyes. Was there no other option? Was sacrificing his members, the very people who he treated as family more than his own worth it? His hands turned into fists.

"Ah, it stopped its lightning attack and it's coming for us," shouted the bomber. "What do we do? What do we do?"

"Guild Leader," screamed both the spearman and Deeg.

Maxwell released a heavy air. If he could at least save three people against the whole many, maybe that was the answer? Still, at this rate, he was no better than that man. He swore to himself he'd be better than him. "Deeg, take the truck and—"

An explosion hit the head of the dragon before it had a chance to reach the bomber.

"What was that?" asked Deeg.

Ivo, Wayne and a sorcerer were flying around the dragon on a magic carpet. "Guild Leader, we're back. Sorry we're late," reported Ivo through his linko.

Shaking away the damage, the dragon howled in anger. Electricity started sparking in its mouth, ready to shoot. Wayne stepped off from the magic carpet, wrapped in blue fire, and plummeted down. His feet stomped onto the dragon's head and closed it shut, making the beast gulp its attack.

Wayne tumbled off from the head and onto the ground. He readied his fighting stance with burning fists.

From afar, a group of people gathered together next to their fellow members. The ranged attackers bundled together with the bomber and Deeg, continuing the onslaught from a distance. Two joined Wayne in close combat and kept the dragon at bay while the rest assisted the wounded and unconscious and started bringing them next to a working vehicle.

"Where—what happened to you? To all of you," Maxwell blurted.

"The new members of Team J were all slavers, Guild Leader. They were after our new recruits," reported Ivo. "Sorry, I was supposed to know my team the best. I let you down."

Maxwell stared up at the magic carpet with a blank look and then hardened. "No, it's my fault for approving their memberships in the first place. You've done nothing wrong."

"No, Guild Leader, its mine," intervened Deeg. "I reviewed their applications."

He shook his head. "This isn't the time to take the blame. How did you recover? Are the slavers dead?"

"Oh, about that, it's all thanks to the miss over there." He waved to a muscly and chubby woman who arrived next to all the wounded members in the van.

A woman with green-pink hair stood at the center of all the injured and unconscious with ragged clothes, a dirty face and crooked glasses.

A frown emerged from Maxwell. "Keri? What are you—"

A gentle aura radiated from her as a luminescent flowery pattern blossomed beneath her. It stretched to 20 meters in length and width as symbols traced themselves inside. Above her head, a clock made of light appeared as its hands moved in an anti-clockwise direction. The speed was slow to start but kept picking up pace. As time reversed, the wounds on everyone around her started to disappear. The dirt that covered them also vanished together with the rips and tears on their clothes and armor. Slowly, they roused from their sleep.

"What is...I feel...I feel so good," one gasped as she checked her condition.

"This—I feel alive. This is great." A man leapt up to stand and flexed his arms.

More and more, as everyone woke up, they were startled by their great recovery. Strength, endurance and vitality returned to them like they had woken up from a good night's sleep and had not battled recently.

"This is crazy," chimed Deeg, who was showered with a trickle of the power from where he stood.

Surprise and shock painted everyone's faces. Some jumped up and down while others tapped and rubbed on various places where their injuries had been. The more they tested their renewed, healthy bodies, the more flabbergasted their expressions became.

Any closer who had closed a rift and battled monsters, acted like injuries were just a common cold that happened occasionally. To treat it, they sought meds, doctors and sorcerer-healers for help. Whatever the case, rest always came with the treatment plan. No shortcuts and no exceptions. The body needed time to recuperate, to regain its lost energy and to recover from trauma. But now, as they cracked their bones, stretched their muscles and shuffled their limbs, they discovered a panacea to all their sufferings and pains, now and in the future. No other explanation could be made, other than magic.

"What do we do now, Guild Leader?" asked a recovered member.

Maxwell grinned. "Hairless Ape, bring down the dragon," he broadcast with a strong, drumming voice.

Everyone cheered in agreement. Strength and vigor radiated from each individual. The sounds caught the dragon's attention as it charged in a different direction. But this time, more than just the three people, including Wayne intercepted, together the guild met it head-on. Their skills and expertise shone through the battle as energy blades, swift shadows and flashes happened all at a rapid pace. The multi-headed dragon was defeated through blood, glory and power.

Chapter 30

Lake, Warehouse, Quisix

Wearing goggles, Lake was welding a back piece of tech to a used mech that was attached to a hangar bay. From the head to the torso, it was a 10-year-old model that had scratches and rust on it. Amongst all the junked mechs in the warehouse, this one had the least problems. Its current limbs were all sourced from five other mechs, each dating back further than ten years.

Tony walked closer to him, using a retractable stick the engineer had crafted for him. "What are you doing?" he asked.

"Building you a mech," said Lake as sparks flew from the welding torch he held.

He snickered. "Funny. Is it another trap? Or a drone?"

He turned off the torch and raised his goggles to his forehead. "What's so funny about that?"

Tony frowned. "Are you really building me a mech?"

He climbed off the back and stepped onto the levelled platform of the hangar. "Yeah. I'm building you a mech." He climbed down the ladder onto the ground.

"How the hell am I supposed to pilot a mech? I'm blind," he howled. "Before you even start with the accessibility plugins for linkos with audio bull crap—we both know that isn't the best way to handle weapons and grenades. It can't keep up with auto-targeting—what if I use my agility boost? What then? Should I wait for my linko to describe the walls that I'm running into? Or should I wait until it identifies the type of monster that is going to eat me?"

Lake raised up his hands in surrender. "What's with you? Did I eat your lunch or something? Are we running out of food?"

He clicked his tongue. "Nah, it's just...I've been at it with this stupid blindness for days. I've been going through all the accessibility devices that could help me fight, but there's nothing really out there." His shoulders sagged.

He tapped his shoulder and guided him up the ladder. "Come on," he said.

"Where are you taking me?"

"You'll know soon enough. Trust me."

Tony snarled but continued up the ladder and hopped into the cockpit with Lake's help. "This feels familiar. Am I in Red Giant's cockpit?" he asked.

He stood next to the seat as he fitted the pilot with gloves, boots and a helmet connected to the mech. "Sort of. Found an older model of Red Giant. Fixed it up with parts I scavenged here and there. The mainframe and software is still very much like your old one, so there shouldn't be many issues adjusting to it."

"Adjusting to it? I'm blind, in case you—"

Lake knocked the crown of his head "Quiet." He summoned his Mind's Eye. The threads snaking from the core installed in the mech revealed themselves in the gloves, boots and helmet. They wrapped intricately within the equipment and around the wires.

"Do that again and I'll—" He closed his mouth shut and stared into nothingness.

He assumed that Tony was feeling the same sensations he had when his soul strings were being tugged. If he were to explain it, it was like someone was looking deep down inside of him. Everything was laid bare. When he did it to himself, Lake felt like he understood himself more because he could actually reach towards his own true self—the core of his humanity. For Tony, he wondered how it was for him—to be bare in front of someone—mind, body and spirit.

Lake reached out to the glowing aura surrounding Tony and plucked a soul string from his arms. He connected it onto the glove strings. He wounded them together like a neon rope, tensile and beautiful. Afterwards, he went to the boots and did it again, weaving, turning and stretching. Dots of perspiration showed on his face and his armpits. Despite knowing what to do and being confident in the procedure, his heart pounded. After all, there was no telling if this would work on Tony—or that nothing of consequence would arise.

Hours had flown by when he had finished. Lake straightened his posture then leaned to the wall of the cockpit. "It's done. How are you?" he exhaled.

From a blank face, shock surfaced on Tony. "What the hell was that all—"

The mech shuffled on the hangar, rocking the inside of the cockpit.

Lake placed his hands over Tony's shoulders. "Stop. You're moving the mech."

Tony sat still. "What are you even—I don't understand—what did you do?" The volume of his voice increased and decreased from shock and confusion.

"I connected your soul to the mech. Everything you do; reflects back at the mech."

"What does that even mean?" As Tony shifted to his right where he could hear Lake's voice, Red Giant cranked to the right as well. A look of anxiety came over him. He turned to his left. Red Giant followed suit. As he lifted his right arm, the cockpit creaked with the mech's motions.

"Do you get it now? How do you feel?" Worry etched on his face.

"Everything I do, the mech copies it?"

Lake nodded. "Yes."

The Red Giant curled its right arm and tested its fingers. "I can't move my left side," he said.

"Oh. I haven't connected your left side yet. I thought it'd be best if we tested your right first."

Tony elbowed his squad mate with his left arm and struck his gut. "You could've told me all of that before you did anything."

He clutched his stomach. "Ow. I'll ask next time. Was too excited."

He played around with the arm some more and raised the right leg. "How did you come up with this? Is this because of the video game in your head?"

Lake shrugged. "It's one of the skills it gives you—or in this case, fragments. It lets me see into people's souls, I guess."

"It sounds creepy, but I like it." A delighted energy surrounded him like a kid playing with a new toy. But after a few minutes, his shoulders sagged and he stopped moving.

"What's wrong? Don't you like it? It's the response time, isn't it? I was thinking of putting electro-motors to compensate for it since the hydraulics are too slow. It'd be nice if there was an actual mech shop here. Everything here is so outdated."

"That's—that's not it," Tony murmured.

"Maybe if I practice weaving a bit more, I can increase the muscle to thought ratio," rambled Lake. "But I don't know if you can take the long practice though. You might get tired or lose focus. And if I practice on myself, I feel like I'm not getting the most out of the experience learning—"

"That's not it," he snapped. "Do I have to spell it out to your nerdy-ass brain? I can't see, Lake. How can I pilot this mech if I can't see where I'm going, what I'm shooting? I can't see."

Lake squeezed himself next to the cushioned seat and reached for the control panel. "Oh yea, forgot about that." He fiddled around with the system for a bit as more lights around the cockpit brightened.

He tried to shove Lake away from him, but the space in the cockpit was tight. "Hey, that hurts. Get off me." The mech rocked in the hangar in response to his struggles to make room.

He pushed himself to the back again. "One last thing." He flicked a switch on the helmet.

The main screen of the cockpit blinked to life. Various colors showing status screens of different parts of the mech flourished as well as a square map of its immediate environment.

"There we go," said Lake. "What do you think?"

Silence covered the atmosphere. For a while, Lake wondered if it was actually working. He did all the testing and calibration. What Tony should be experiencing was the visual output of the mech inside his head. What people envision when they close their eyes and dream—that's how he could best explain it. There was no data coming from the eyes itself. Everything was directly fed to his optic nerve from the head apparatus he had invented and weaved into Tony's soul. He was confident for a while. But then minutes flew by and Tony was still quiet. His heart raised. Was it really not working? As he was about to speak, a tear tracked over Tony's eye.

Lake gulped. "Does it hurt? Does your head hurt somewhere? Is the intensity too much? Or is it too unclear? Can you make things out? I saw it in my head—it was fine—do you feel like throwing up? Or—"

Tony cleared his throat. "This place is really wrecked, huh?"

"What?"

He sniffled back some tears. "Thought it just stinks, but I had better places to live in when my brother and I were movin' round."

Lake crouched next to his left. "So you can see?"

"I can feel your face hovering over me," he commented. "But yeah, I can see what the mech sees."

From his S-Glove, he took out a wire and connected it to the control panel of the mech. He started jabbing buttons on it as more windows flashed on the screen. "Good. Now I can get a baseline from your experience and adjust accordingly." A list of things to do and how to do them populated his head as he busied himself with the mech.

Tony wiped away the tears that wet the helmet. "I know you didn't like what I said about Major Cervantes. Didn't mean to do that."

He stopped typing midway. "You were right. He has a tracker on me. It's the same one used for prisoners and monsters. It's probably one of the highest-grade ones."

"You good?"

"I...don't know. I want to know why." Lake continued where he left off.

Tony cleared his throat and smashed his fist into his hand. "All right. Tell me how I can pilot this thing."

"Pilot it? I was only helping you to see and move."

He smirked. "Really? I'm a soldier, Lake. I was born for fighting. If we're going to leave here, as you said, we have to defeat the boss of this rift. Teach me. I don't care how long it takes or how hard it is. We're gonna leave this place."

A bit of hope sparked in his heart. For the longest time, he was here, the plight they were in was gnawing inside of him. All he could do was build and try, but now it strangely felt like the chance they had was more of a guarantee rather than something that may or may not be. "Did you just say my name?" he asked.

"Did you miss your nickname? Don't worry, you'll always be the Starless Sorcerer to me."

Congratulations! You have saved a precious friend from self-harm.
200 coins earned. Total Coins: 300

He was taken aback by the sudden notice. It seemed like saving people's lives was indeed a hero's job. The number of coins from slaying monsters proved that. But what was more, Tony was thinking of committing suicide? And he stopped because of him? He let that thought sit with him for a while as he returned to his work with a smile on his face.

CHAPTER 31

KERI, NEAR THE RIFT, OUTWORLD AI-DOIS

"Shit. I killed someone," said Keri, resting and waiting at the passenger seat on one of the team vans. Technically, it was really Wayne who did. So she shouldn't feel guilty, but why did she?

"Is this going to be my life now?" she asked herself.

The blood, the violence, the killing—she was slowly getting used to it. And dare she even say it out loud, it felt good. It felt good to have power—to fight back. Most of all, nothing felt better than being needed and wanted. The way everyone looked at her when she saved them, it was a tingly sensation. Not like the sensation she got in her lady parts when being touched by Wayne, but more like a soft warm caress in her chest. Was this what the system wanted for her? To be someone who helps people?

She glanced at the side mirror. Wayne was selecting the important parts of the dragon's carcass to bring back to Amazing Discoveries. Her lips perked up. Maybe it was all on in her head, but they were about to kiss earlier, right? It wasn't a dream, not like her dreams with the sorcerer?

Her mind still couldn't make sense of those dreams. She felt like a different person in those dreams. At the same time, the conversations, the laughter, the experience—it wasn't some simple nightly illusion. It was fantastic. But at the end of the day, they were all in her head—just a very realistic fantasy.

Wayne's figure reflected in the mirror as his arms flexed when they lifted the monster parts. The juicy man stopped her dilemma. This was real. She realized something then and there:

"Oh my god, what will he do if I ask him out? Wait. I'm the woman, shouldn't he ask me out? Who cares? If Wayne asks me out, I'm definitely saying yes. Wayne is strong, brave—and those chest and arms." She closed her eyes and imagined Wayne flinging her against the wall, grabbing her by the neck and sucking on her mouth. *Break me, daddy.* Her tongue darted in and out.

The door to the passenger seat opened. "What are you doing?" Maxwell stared at her with knitted brows.

She coughed and adjusted her mouth and jaw in an awkward manner. "M-m-mouth exercises. I grit my teeth when I'm stressed. Helps with the pain in my jaw. When can we go?" She smiled brightly, hoping to divert the topic.

His face held questions, but instead he responded with, "We're excavating the core now. Once that happens the exit rift will open nearby. Then we can leave."

"So, the rift only opens when you get the core out? Not when the boss monster dies?"

He scratched his neck. "It's a trigger thing. Scientists believe that the rift wants us to harvest the core. They say it's what's keeping this whole dimension together. If we get the core, it disintegrates."

Keri nodded her head. She waited for him to say more, but there was only an awkward silence that hung in the air. "Is there something else you need?"

Maxwell took a slight step back. "Right, uh, about earlier, what you did..." He avoided her gaze.

"What about it?"

"I'll make sure to investigate the slavers. You're in my guild now, so I've gotta make sure you're protected. Perks of being an Ape," he rambled. "Just have to snuff out anyone else that may know."

"Okay. Thanks," said Keri. "Is there more?"

He cleared his throat. "And, uh, tengs," he murmured.

"What? Sorry, I didn't hear you."

"Tengyu," Maxwell whispered under his breath.

"Can you repeat that again? I didn't get that."

He growled. "My men are very grateful for what you did back there. You might think that this is your fault, but guys like that are everywhere. They won't hesitate to make a quick buck on you."

Keri's heart warmed. "I appreciate you saying that."

He nodded, turned and left.

Congratulations! Target lover #2 appreciates you for saving his comrades.

600 coins earned. Total 910.

The driver's door opened as Wayne hopped in. "Was that Maxwell?" he asked.

Keri shut the passenger door. "Yes, he was just thanking me, I think."

As she turned to look at him, his face was right next to her. He kissed her. Shock seized Keri as her eyes enlarged. But every moment that passed, she found herself savoring the sensation. She let herself get carried away and let her eyes drop. Moisture and warmth rubbed against each other as the sounds of lip-locking and the heat of Wayne's body threw Keri into a current of heated emotions. His mouth parted slightly as his tongue slithered into hers for a beat. It was as if it was checking its surroundings, testing if it was allowed entry. She responded by biting his tongue with her lips. He kissed her strongly again as a reaction, then parted from her slowly, leaving her mouth glistening. Keri still had her eyes closed and mouth moving as if the kiss was still happening.

"I've been wanting to do that for a long time now," exhaled Wayne.

"Hmm...what? Why are we stopping?" Keri pulled him in for a swift peck.

He broke free from her after planting a third one. "Wait. I wanted to say, I know I'm not the best guy for you. I'm an escort and I know that has a lot of bad rep—"

She lunged in again and slobbered all over his mouth, moving to the cheek and ears.

"I want to tell you that—wait—wait." Breathing hard, Wayne pushed her off of him.

Keri pouted. "Is there something wrong? I'm not getting the wrong signal, am I? Didn't you want this? Is it me? Do I have bad breath?"

He shook his head and tried to catch his breath. "No, you're good. Really good."

She brightened. "Really?"

He nodded.

"What's wrong then?"

Wayne reached a hand to her face. "I really like you. I really, *really* do."

A dumb smile crept over her face. "You like me," she snickered, then snorted.

He smiled back just as silly. "I do." He kissed her again, putting more passion in his lips.

Congratulations! You have captured Target Lover #3's heart. 1000 coins earned. Total 1910.

Please continue to deepen your relationship with #3 and the other targets to earn more coins.

Keri glanced at the notification. She frowned while her tongue was still in his mouth. What did the last lines mean? Did she have to date all of them at once? Was there an end-goal to this? Like boyfriends? Or Marriage? Was her life really becoming a sim-dating game? Not that she was complaining.

Wayne broke the kiss and looked over to his right.

Area Coordinate: Outworld A1-D01S cleared. Candidate Participants: Maiden and Slayer.

Earned 1000 coins each. Total 2910.

Outworld A1-D01S has become ownerless. Rights to tunnel dimension Outworld A1-D01S will now be transferred to victorious candidates.

Would you like to claim for ownership or waive your rights? Yes | No

Time Remaining to choose: 4:58s

"Slayer?" Keri questioned.

"Maiden?" asked Wayne at the same time.

The two locked eyes and frowned. After a few beats, Keri gasped while Wayne's brows perked.

"Are you the Maiden?" asked Wayne first.

"Slayer?"

"How did you—Where did you—Did you always have the logs?"

Keri adjusted her glasses on her face that was ruined from the kiss. "Logs? You mean the system? I don't know. Less than two months? You?"

"About the same time. Is that where you got your powers?"

"No-yes," she said quickly. "Wait. Is that fire thing your fragment?"

Wayne's face lit up. "Yeah, Flame fist. Does it look like a martial arts master? I've wanted to be all kung-fuy and beat down monsters since I was a kid, y'know?"

"You look like a badass—fiery and everything."

He scratched his head and reddened. "Thanks. The clock thing is helpful too. Saved everyone."

She blushed. "Thanks. It's Pace of Time."

> Time Remaining to choose: 1:08s

"Do you know what this rights thing is for?" asked Keri.

He shook his head. "Barely have any idea what I'm doing with these logs—system thing. I'm just happy it makes me strong, y'know?"

"Should we just accept it?"

He nodded.

> Slayer Accepted. Maiden Accepted. Slot Choices shall commence.

A three-by-three slot machine appeared in their vision and started rolling. Each cell in the machine was named either Slayer or Maiden. The speed of revolutions of each slot increased by the second. The first slot stopped at Slayer, and then the second, Maiden. After a breath, the last slot eased at Slayer.

> The result is 2-1, in favor of the Slayer. Slayer acquires rights for Outworld A1-D01S.

"Do I own this place now?" asked Wayne.

"That's what it says," replied Keri. "What do you do with it? Is it like real estate? Are you going to live here?"

He scratched his head. "I...don't know about that. Never actually owned a house before. Grandpa and I kept moving from place to place, y'know?"

The door opened as Ivo popped in. "Scoot over. We're gonna take our much-deserved leave now." He positioned himself in the driver's seat.

Wayne and Keri squeezed together. Their shoulders locking together felt uncomfortable, so they adjusted themselves and found that having his arms around hers was the best position they could make.

"You two okay over there? Can't decide if you guys look like sardines in a can or new lovers," stated Ivo. "Anyway, I promise it will be a short ride. We only need to cross the rift."

The two blushed at each other and looked away.

"Did you collect the core?" asked Wayne.

Ivo started the engine. "Sure did. It's at the back as well as the other stinking parts of the dragon."

Keri noticed a rift that materialized ahead. "Did the exit pop up after we got the boss' core?" she asked.

"Sure did. 'Nother hard day's work done." He sped off.

The trucks and other vehicles of the guild exited through the rift, crossing from multiple directions. The portal likened to a pillar of light, two-story in height. It was a pillar that split space and functioned as a doorway wherein all sides could be exited or entered. These were the common rifts; the ones with black holes did exist but rarely appeared.

Return rifts were always white in color, a sign it was leading back home. But as Keri's truck, the last of the guild's vehicles, was inches to the exit, the rift pulsed and brightened.

Area core found. Candidate presence found. Rift redirection initiated to next area.

Please proceed with caution.

"Stop the truck!" Keri yelled.

Ivo heard Keri and whipped back at her, but his feet continued to step on the accelerator, causing the vehicle to exit the rift. Once the truck was halfway in, the white glow of the rift changed to red.

Chapter 32

Lake, Furniture Storage, Quisix

At a large, abandoned furniture storehouse, Lake was screwing a valve into the sprinkler system in the maintenance room. It connected to several drums twice his height and build. They contained bicarbonate powder, rice flour, vinegar and cumin. One look at the recipe and some would think he was creating some kind of sauce or dough, but that was far from the truth. According to Zuobic research, the combination of these ingredients was a deadly poison to most reptilian lifeforms in the rift.

For the first days he planned with Tony, both of them discussed the many explosives and weapons they could use. But Zone Quisix was a city of culture, so the stock of those things was limited. But during his supply runs, Tony had asked for curry since it was one of his favorite foods to eat back home. That was when it hit him. Lake had read somewhere in passing that cumin was a deadly substance against reptilian monsters. After checking the localized internet, which was still functioning, there were recipes for poison specific to lizardmen, drakes, kappas and a few other draconic species.

After fixing the mech, the two soldiers came up with a plan using the poison, hence the drums. The mech was handy to have around for carrying most of it. But they had to be careful since the lizardmen patrolled the roads occasionally.

"How are we doing?" Tony buzzed in through the linko.

"Done screwing them in," replied Lake. "Now I have to test them."

Inside his reassembled mech, he rested atop a tall apartment building next door. "That has to wait. Something's happening at the theatre," he replied.

"What?" He placed a wrench down and stood.

"The lizards are fighting."

Grabbing his backpack, he hurried out of the maintenance room and out of the storage house into the side streets. After a few blocks, his boots activated, and he high-jumped onto a small building's rooftop. He leapt through a couple of roofs before ending up at the apartment where Tony waited.

The new mech, aptly named Red Giant 2.0, pointed to the open road in front of the theatre. "See, there."

Lake pushed his goggles from his head down. The zoom and heat features activated. Missiles fired and explosions waved through the city streets as lizards fought against humans. "Are those closers? How did they get here?"

"Saw a bright light next to the opera house a few minutes ago. Must be a rift," answered Tony. "We going through with the plan?"

"You think they'll help?"

"They don't look like they will last."

Lake pushed his goggles up his head again. "Do we help or not?"

"This is your plan. I'm following your lead," he responded. "You're the Squad Leader, for now."

Lake's plan was to get the lizards to notice him by creating a big explosion. That way most of them would run after him. But now, it seemed getting their attention would be hard. But in hindsight, leaving them and waiting for the enemy numbers to decrease was not such a bad idea. 'That's wrong' Lake thought to himself. These abilities were given to him for a reason. It was telling him to go grow and save people. Becoming the hero that he wanted to be—he was not going to go against that.

"I'll stay here and cover you while you help them and draw the enemies in," suggested Tony. "You know well enough that this guy isn't the best for running tactics."

"Wait. How'd you know I'm going to help them?"

"You get quiet when you want to do something stupid."

Lake's face crumpled. "Not sure if that's a compliment."

"They're probably capable—you know we don't have to help them."

"I'm not doing this as a soldier. I'm doing this for me."

Another loud explosion sounded as debris flew up the sky and whooshed into different directions.

Lake switched his backpack of tools to the weapons lying next to Tony. He armed himself with his shield and explosives. "I'll be right back." Bright green lights sparked on his boots as he leaped onto the buildings heading over the theatre. As he landed in an apartment building, he spotted a masked man battling lizards.

The masked man cut a lizard's forearms with a katana. He then slashed the chest—blood spurted out and it fell dead. A second one attacked from behind as he blocked with his blade. After he dealt with one after the other, another entered into the fray. He was dealing with a growing horde by the minute.

Lake leaped from the roof and activated his S-Glove. A chain of lightning struck one lizard and rebounded to three others. Some of the reptiles next to them got shocked as well. With a clear path to escape, the masked man took it and ran to where the hero had landed.

"Are you okay?" asked Lake.

"Let's talk after we deal with this." Tony's stance readied with his blade as the rest of the monsters surrounded them.

He wrote two runes in the air in practiced movements as it glowed blue. When the lizardmen seethed in anger and rushed them with their swords drawn, Lake clapped his hands. A wave of water appeared and pushed the enemies back. Electricity then sparked from his glove as he touched the surface of the water trail. All of the enemies were shocked to death.

The masked man quickly ended them with a swift puncture to the heart. "Nice job. The name's Maxwell." He flicked the blood off his blade and then sheathed it.

> You have saved a living soul and slain monsters.
> Earned 500 coins. Total coins 800.

He dug through the dead bodies for their cores with a specialized dagger he crafted. "Lake."

"Rune weapons, huh? You don't get a lot of those in the freezones. You a Zuosh soldier? You look like a soldier." Maxwell removed his mask, eyeing his equipment.

He harvested cores from corpse after corpse. "Academy student. Got stuck here through a 5 in the middle of a mission. 'Bout you?"

"Rift within a rift, same damn thing. What are the odds? My team just killed a dimension boss, exited the rift and here we are—give me a sec." He listened in on a linko call. After a beat, he put his helmet back on and ran off to an alleyway.

With his abrupt exit, Lake curiously followed after. They reached the ruined plaza, away from the theatre. In between the spacious and modern architecture and colorful streets, there was a battlefield. Green lizards crossed blades with closers as blue ones found their targets amongst the people from high ground. Seeking cover inside shops and vehicles, sorcerers manipulated the elements to block arrows and heal the wounded while sharpshooters culled the beasts from the apartment windows.

From the alley they had emerged from, lizardmen charged in on the two of them. Maxwell was quick to put himself in the middle and deal with them. He slashed one monster after another, advancing forward, grey aura sizzling around him. Behind him, Lake fried two archers that aimed at them with an arc of lightning. The two men then marched ahead with fast slices and electrifying bolts, hacking down lizards as they moved.

Lake then felt an imbalance of source in the direction of the theatre. The air felt like it was growing heftier. "I'll be right back," he said. With a nod from Maxwell, Lake leapt over to a high building and landed on a roof until the sight beyond was clear from the fray. Between a large gap in the wall of the theatre, which he assumed was the result of a large explosion, a sparkle of red and purple light coalesced. He put on his goggles and zoomed in further. At the stage of the theatre, three red lizardmen wrote runes in their hands. When one was complete, it settled on a glowing magic circle on the floor. After a few more runes converged on it, a lizardman materialized into reality and joined the fight. "Shit," he cursed. The monsters were summoning more warriors.

Tony radioed in, "Hey, what's happening out there?" After being updated, he added, "What's the plan? Can you get inside and stop them?"

"I can get in from above. It's after that, I'm..." Using his Mind Eye, he saw source concentrating in the magic circle from all around in various colors. Then, there was an addition of a thick red string coming from the red mages.

"Why'd you stop?"

"They're summoning something big," Lake reported. "I can see them using their own life source."

"Why'd they change tactics?"

He looked below the streets. The number of lizardmen had significantly dwindled. "The closers are winning. I think they're veterans."

"They sound all right. Told you they could handle it."

"They look tired. The closing previously must've drained them out. I gotta stop the mages."

Using the roofs, Lake made his way to the building behind the theatre. He landed on the alley at the back with a slight stomp, noting in his head that the boots were a little noisy—he'd have to fix it for next time. After a quick search, he found the back entrance of the theatre and tried the handle. It clicked at his touch and squeaked when he opened it. Careful, slow and alert—his body moved to those words, a mantra he picked up from training. Inside, he sought immediate cover behind a moveable platform. His eyes adjusted to the dark background lit only by the lights from the stage. Sounds of incomprehensible whispers and inhuman chatter droned on and on. He moved closer, wading through the mess of black crates piled after the other, tiptoeing over cables and poles, and ducking from the occasional contraptions and props left hanging. He let out the huge breath he'd been holding when he touched the hems of the stage curtains.

One, two, three mages, he counted in his mind. The same number he'd seen from afar. A quick scan with his goggles revealed no other heat signatures other than the three he was targeting. Circles over circles, archaic symbols and unfamiliar runes shimmered on the ground and floated in the air. To his naked eyes, it was beyond his schooling. Maybe Major Cervantes could decipher this, or Dr. Badez. To him, it was more than he knew. But what of his Mind's Eye?

Strings of light streaked from everywhere and poured into the circle. Like before, a red highlight cut through the others and flowed from the red lizards themselves. Lake gulped. A deep abyss opened within the circle with three eyes staring out. It caught a glimpse of him staring back and snarled. He stopped using his Mind Eye as the pounding in his chest increased. He felt like he was being eaten alive.

One mage broke away from the sonorous chanting as the two continued. It spotted him and slithered forth. Before it could do anything, Lake shot a lightning bolt at it. The mage caught it with a glowing spell in its hand and crushed it. He stared in shock but dove away as the lizard shot a ball of fire in his direction. After rolling on the ground, he threw a canister at its direction. The same thing happened. But as the monster's clawed hand crushed the metal can, olive green smoke poured out. The scales of the lizard melted at a rapid pace as it howled in agony. It blubbered a wind spell to remove the rest of the smoke, but was cut short when Lake blasted it with another bolt of lightning. The mage continued to melt and gasp, turning into a puddle of goo in a matter of seconds.

Just as he rose from the floor, a second lizard pulled away from the ritual and cast a barrier over its remaining comrade. It then glared at Lake and conjured icicles above him. Lake activated his L-Shield. A plate of light blocked the continuous deadly rain. From hails, to icicles, to boulders, different forms of ice assailed him from all sides. He moved the shield from left to right to front and so on, but the impact pushed him from all directions and the splatter of ice cut through his battle suit—which was already fairly damaged to begin with.

As it continued, his injuries increased, and the L-Shield's dome flickered. The S-Glove's panel indicated that the battery was running out—it was time to change the core. His fingers doodled runes in the air, readying a counter-spell, anything to break the assault. But as he scribbled the last rune, the L-Shield gave out, letting the brunt of the ice attack through. Boulders and rocks rained on him in full force. He was pushed to the ground as his injuries grew.

With ice lowering his mobility, he found he could only move his hands, which fumbled in his pockets. The air grew colder as another spell started, and this time, it was a bigger and larger icicle. His heart beat faster as he dug deeper, finally touching an explosive; but his frostbitten hands prevented him from clutching it. "AAAAGGGHH," he cried with gritted teeth when he forcibly held the grenade. He clicked on the trigger and pulled it out. It rolled slowly and noisily in the mage's direction.

The grenade exploded away from the lizard, but the impact disturbed the casting as the icicle launched at the barrier instead. The barrier wavered for a moment, but the lizard outside reinforced the spell and strengthened the barrier.

It seethed in anger at his attempt. After a short chant, source converged in its hand, readying another ice spell but quickly fizzled out. It tried again, but it died down even faster.

"Out of juice, huh?" mocked Lake with shivering lips.

The lizard approached him with careful steps, sniggering. From its robes, it produced a dagger. As it raised the blade high above its head, a sword punctured right through the mage's chest. It tried to look behind, but a knife punctured it from the back of his neck that went through its mouth. Once the sword retracted, the lizard fell onto the floor dead.

Maxwell was behind, flicking the blood from his blades. "You okay?" He helped him up.

"We have to kill the third one," Lake said, leaning on the closer for support.

The third mage continued to recite incantations until its eyes and mouth sparked with a bright light and gave out. The lizard fell on the floor dead, leaving behind the circle of magic coalescing by itself.

"That was easy," said Maxwell.

"It's here," warned Lake.

The magic circle opened a black abyss as a clawed leg surged through and stomped the floor followed by another. Then a crocodile head popped through with three eyes, where the third one was situated on a fin sticking up on the middle of its head. The head cocked in their direction and roared. Its behemoth body wriggled out of the small hole with difficulty, trying to free itself.

"That bastard's huge," said Maxwell. "Almost like a dragon."

"How are we going to stop it?" asked Lake.

"Not here." Maxwell moved him away from the impending doom.

Lake wanted to go back and kill the beast. It was his fault for not stopping the mages in time—he had to fix it—but he let himself be assisted by Maxwell. Outside, the road was filled with bodies of dead monsters. Some closers were stabbing the dying lizards while the others marched towards the theatre.

"Get back," Maxwell yelled. "Apes, Boss formation—tank type!"

Deeg ran up to him. "Who's tanking?"

He motioned for him to take Lake from him. "I am. He needs first aid."

After slinging Lake's arms on him, he said in a low tone, "Leader, you are not in a position to tank. Our shields are on the truck with Ivo, and your greatsword is damaged."

"Did you find them?"

He shook his head. "No answer in linko. We'll have to search around."

"Do that after we kill this thing."

"Leader, you don't look good. Leave it to the others." Concern was written in Deeg's eyes.

Maxwell glanced over at the other blade-wielding closers. He raised a brow. "Deeg, I look better than them."

"I've got a shield you can use," volunteered Lake. "I only need to replace the—"

The whole front of the theatre collapsed as the crocodile crashed onto it with its hulking slimy and scaly green body. After shaking the debris from its head, its three eyes focused on the small prey in front of it. It roared and the sound carried out to the whole plaza, shaking some of the dirt, glass and ground. It made Lake's knees give out; thankfully he leaned on Deeg. But catching a glance at him, he looked close to running. Instead, he made his way to cover with the rest of the closers who seemed to be sorcerers and snipers. They were not in good shape either. They were battered, bruised and exhausted, like they had been in a fight before this and they had gambled their lives on it and had no more chips left to play.

He spotted Maxwell, who stood alone in the middle of the street. From observing him earlier, he thought of him as an expert fighter—the best he had seen yet. Even the veterans from Zuobic he knew could not compare to Maxwell's battle instinct and reflexes. And yet his composure seemed to waver as he gripped his blade. A katana that looked ready to retire with how chipped and dull it looked. Hope was hard to find.

The crocodile stared at Maxwell, licking its long, slender blue tongue. Its head tilted, seemingly amazed at and eager for its prey. Then, it swiped its front leg forward. Maxwell dodged the attack and tried to counter but another attack from the beast's tail swiped him away. His back slammed against a car. As the beast approached, he got up slowly while coughing up blood. He assumed his stance again, ready for another beating.

Lake wanted to help, but what could he do? He could barely move his body let alone cast runes. *There has to be a way to kill that—poison—if I can get the drums to it maybe we can kill it*, he thought. Just as he reached for his linko, it buzzed by itself.

"Am I too late for the party?" radioed Tony.

The sound came first—a high-powered engine accelerating at top speeds. The smell of burning rubber followed it. In a flash, the mech flew through everyone's vision, cutting through the road and slamming against the giant crocodile. Red Giant's armed arm stabbed the body of the beast with a retractable blade and clung onto it. In its other hand it was carrying a drum, which it then tossed into the monster's wide roaring mouth. When it snapped shut, the cumin solution burst out, spilling everywhere. The head, the body, the limbs—all of it started to melt at a visible rate.

"What's that?"

"It smells like...curry?"

"It's cumin poison," Lake answered the questions of the closers. "Lizard monsters are deathly vulnerable to it, like a poison."

The Red Giant stabbed its now free hand on the melting gut. "See ya later, ugly." The cockpit opened with the sliding of the mech's back. The pilot chair turned around and tilted on an angle. As the motors revved to fire the chair, it suddenly stopped.

"What's happening?" asked Lake in the linko.

From the distance, Tony struggled on his seat. "I'm stuck. Damn button isn't working."

The melting crocodile bashed the mech in a flurry. It crushed the arms and body and brought it down to the ground. The fangs snapped at the head, wiggled it and tore it from the body. The action caused the pilot seat to unbuckle and rip apart. Tony fell down the ground and rolled over. As the crocodile spewed the inedible metal aside, it spotted the human crawling away. It reached for him. But instead of grabbing it, it settled for a swipe from its claws as Maxwell intercepted and attacked the beast. He executed more swings to block the lizard further. The crocodile simply slapped him away unbothered by the cuts before continuing.

A barrage of spells, missiles and bullets attacked the beast from all sides. The closers had launched their attacks and slowed the opponent. Maxwell rose from the rubble and engaged the crocodile again, executing powerful yet clunky swings from behind. After a few more minutes of non-stop attacks, the giant monster howled its last breath and fell down with a thump on the ground. Covered with wounds, it continued to melt until half of its body was turned to slime and smoke sizzled from it, smelling like lead and methane.

Lake limped-rushed to where Tony was. After a few falls and tumbles, Deeg caught him and helped him over. Tony was looking up, breathing slowly, lying in a pool of his own blood.

"Did we get it?" Tony smiled with his bloodied face.

Lake tried casting a spell. He managed a single rune for first aid—something he had been studying in his free time. The spell lit up for a moment and graced the soldier with specks of light. The cuts and bruises on his body grew smaller, only by a few inches—not enough to save him.

"We need a medic here," shouted Deeg.

"Why are you looking at me like that?" asked Tony.

"You can see?" Lake gasped.

He smirked. "Kidding. You weren't answering. Had to get your attention. Guess I'm not going to last, huh?"

"You're going to be fine. We're going to go back." He tried casting again, but the effects were similar.

"Sure. That sounds nice. Listen, can you do me a solid?" Tony stretched out a hand.

Lake clasped it from air. He urged himself to talk to him, not to give up. But he felt him slipping away. Something about the source around him, dwindled.

"Can you check on what happened to Osher and the rest of the squad?" he asked. "I hope they got away. So, my sacrifice wasn't really wasted, y'know?"

Tears fell from the side of his face. "Sure," he sniffed. He knew what was happening. Not just by looking at him, but feeling the source around him. It was waning.

"Thanks, Starless. And, stay away from Cervantes, okay? He's a crazy mo-fo."

Lake continued to cast the spell. There was no way he was going to let his teammate go. He was a hero? He was supposed to save people. Not let them die. On his tenth try, his condition activated and released an overpowered heal. Soft light wrapped around the soldier. The injuries closed at a visible rate.

"That feels warm…You're not bad, Starless." Tony closed his eyes.

"Tony? Are-are you okay?" Lake stuttered. A spark of hope lit in his heart. Maybe he had done? He was okay?

Deeg felt the pulse on Tony's neck. His face darkened. The medic rushed over to their side battered and bruised. She quickly checked all of his vitals using devices and a quick mobile scan. After doing all of that in less than a minute, the medic's shoulders sagged. "Time of death: 23:43-DD08," she announced.

The worry lines on Lake's face flattened. His eyes lost their intensity, replaced by a hollow look. "What did you say?" he spoke calm and deep. As the medic turned her head away, Lake tried to yank her, but Deeg grabbed him by the arm, pulling him back.

"Did you hear her? She's crazy. She doesn't know what she's doing. Obviously, she's new," Lake babbled to Deeg who only nodded, and uttered words he did not comprehend. Was the medic incompetent? Did she hurt her brain in the fight? His heart resented her words.

"Take it back. Do you hear me? I said, take it back," he yelled at her a few times. He saved Tony, didn't he? He cast heal. He felt the power overwhelm him like it did when he first cast Fireball. Why didn't it work? Tears blurred his vision. A hollow pit slowly opened deep within his heart. He pushed the odd sensation away, grasping on the fiery and chaotic emotion that came along with it. "Fucking, look at me you fake. You take that back," each word thundered, deep and guttural.

Deeg motioned her to leave, and so she did. He and other closers held Lake back who struggled to reach her. He pushed hard, not a concentrated push, more of a wild and instinctive action; but the combined efforts of the men overpowered him.

Lake's vision narrowed as his attention was all on her. The liar. The fake. The incompetent pretender. "Come back here," he yelled. Tears wet his entire face. "I'm not done with you—you noob. He is not dead. Tony is not—" A huge wave of exhaustion and stress overwhelmed his body and mind causing him to collapse in the closer's arms. He passed out.

Chapter 33

Lake, Hotel Room, Quisix

Lake woke up in an unfamiliar bed. White beddings, beige walls and pastel interior pieces surrounded him. He assumed he was in a hotel in Zone Quisix as the window's view was of the art plaza and the banners of Xia Meron's biopic. But he didn't know how he'd gotten there.

Maxwell was sitting at a desk table next to him. His right hand pressed on his ear as his left tousled at a glass tablet. Lake thought of asking where he was, but then everything that had happened came back to him—from the setup of the trap, the closers and Tony. "Where's Tony?" he first said in a croaky voice.

"There's some canned soup over there and water," responded Maxwell. "You should get your strength back up."

He ignored the meal on the bedside table and repeated, "Where's Tony?" This time there was more urgency in the tone.

Maxwell placed the tablet down and eyed the grieving man. "My team has put his body in a bag and placed it inside our transport. We'll deliver him wherever you need him to go to. Back to Zuobic, if we have to."

Lake tried to get up but instantly regretted it, so he just leaned back on the headboard. "I have to see him."

"It helps no one if you pass out again—even the dead."

He grumbled on the bed, feeling helpless and useless.

"Why don't you tell me how you got here?"

"How does that help me?"

"It doesn't, but maybe, if we compare notes about how we got here, we can figure out how to leave," Maxwell said. "You do want to get back home and return your friend to his family, don't you?"

Lake gave in. There was no point in keeping information to himself—not with what had happened. He told Maxwell about the fight against the Spider-Woman, then told him about the lizardmen patrols. He mentioned that he had a theory that if they managed to defeat the caretakers of the dimension—the red mages—they'd be able to leave.

"They're dead now. Guess you were wrong," said Maxwell.

At the side of his vision was a blinking square bell icon. When he willed the system, it opened to multiple notifications. Most of them listed his win against the lizardmen and saving closers, which earned him coins that totaled to 3220. But what got his interest was:

> You have defeated the red mages of Qx-S04D. You have earned 2x Elixirs of Health.
>
> Description: 1 dose will restore a person's health, stamina and mental strength to optimum levels and cures all ailments and curses immediately. Has no effect on the dead.

Lake summoned one small glass flask in his hand—about 100ml of red viscous liquid. Tears stung the sides of his eyes. This thing could have been Tony's lifesaver. If he had only looked at his system early, maybe... He raised the item up and was about to throw it when Maxwell grabbed his wrist and stopped him.

"What are you—what is that?" asked Maxwell.

"Leave me alone." He tried to pull his arm back, but he was very weak and only managed to slap Maxwell.

Maxwell successfully pried the bottle away from him. "I have only seen two of these in my life—one at an auction and another back home. This is really rare. How'd you get this? Why didn't you use it earlier on your friend?" He put the item up against the light, inspecting the fine craftsmanship on the glass. As the sun hit the red liquid, purple specks glowed inside—a sign of its authenticity.

"I didn't know I had it," he murmured.

"You're pretty daft not to know you had something like this. Did you hit your head?"

Lake thought of an excuse to tell the man. But after a moment, he sighed. He was done keeping it a secret—he didn't really care for it if people started knowing about it. "...and that's how I have it," he said after divulging the existence of the system in his head.

He looked from the flask in his hand to Lake on the bed. "I see..."

"Think I'm crazy?"

"Far from it. I'm jealous."

"Jealous?"

"Yeah. The world is shit right now, people are dying, and you have this power. Do you know how many people out there wish they got something to defend themselves with?"

"I don't have anything to show for it," reasoned Lake. "Half baked-mechs, toys that barely work, and sorcery that fucks up. What power do you think I have?"

Grey tattoos surfaced over Maxwell's face. "And what about us? The ones who tried the surgery just so we could have this. Then there's the people who didn't even live through it—good people who only wanted to survive—to live with their families." Hurt laced each of his words.

"Should I be happy then? That I got my friend killed?" Lake's voice got louder and shakier. "And I can't even save him despite this stupid thing in my head? These powers I should be so proud of?"

"You have the actual chance to save people," Maxwell said. "Maybe not Tony, but you saved us. I don't know where that game thing came from. But man, it says you're a hero. To me and my team, we wouldn't be here without you."

Lake's ears reddened a bit. "I don't get you. Are you mad? Or are you complimenting me?"

He shook his head, paced for a bit and then sat on the bed. "I-I honestly don't know. This is too much for me but you have a real chance here. Not to disregard your friend's sacrifice, but people die all the time, regardless of whether you have your powers or not. I'm mad because if I was in your position, I'd be doing more...instead of this."

A moment of silence came between the two. Neither spoke nor thought of anything.

Maxwell sighed. "I should leave. Get your rest. I'll have people patrol the area—might be another red mage out there we missed."

"Wait." Lake read the last notification he had.

> Zone Qx-S04D is owner-free. As the candidate who defeated the defender and owner of Qx-S04D, you are free to take possession. Would you like to acquire the area? Yes | No

He answered yes in his head.

> Zone Quisix is originally from Silaw (Hero's world). It will now revert back to its original state under the protection of Hero.
> A default protection barrier is installed in your area for 730 hours. Please purchase special items in the store to continue protection.

A big article popped up at the side. He scanned through it and understood that the protection given to his area prevents rifts and unaffiliated entities from entering his domain. The only ones allowed were his followers or the undecided. When he asked what that meant, the system replied:

> Affiliation refers to entities (followers) who have sworn their allegiance to a candidate.
> Please increase your fragments and authority to unlock further description.

"So does your system say anything else about how to get out of here?" asked Maxwell.

After reading it further, Lake's brows perked up. "We're home," he said.

"What?"

"It's hard to explain, but since the bosses are dead, I basically own the place."

Maxwell messed up his already messy hair even more. "The surprises just never stop." He sighed.

"If you go out at the end of the zone, there's like a wall preventing you from going further."

"Tell me about it. I got there, and it felt like we're birds in an invisible cage."

"Yes, but now it goes on and on, back to Zuobic, or the freezones. Me taking over, puts us back into our dimension."

"If that's real, that's good news. I'll get my people to check it out." He reached for his linko and gave orders to patrol the outskirts of the zone again.

Lake continued to read more of the article as his mood darkened.

"My boys are on it. We'll hear something in a while," reported Maxwell, getting off the linko. "What's that look for?"

"You know when there's good news—"

"What's the bad news?" finished Maxwell.

"No invaders, monsters or people are allowed in Zone Quisix, except for me and people who are neutral."

"I don't know what neutral means, but that doesn't sound bad."

Lake sighed. "The only exception is the previous owner. He has the privilege to take it back within 24 hours," he summarized from a long description from the system.

Maxwell crossed his arms. "Didn't you kill them? The magical lizards?"

"They're, I guess, sub-bosses. The real one is in another dimension still."

"If we kill the big daddy, then we're all safe," he said nonchalantly. "How do we get there?"

"I can open a rift into that dimension. As long as I am the owner of this area—it's connected somehow—you're coming with me?"

"I have another team that's missing. We've been tracking them for three days. No signs. Best guess, they're probably in there," he explained. "Besides, I'm kinda curious about what this system thing is for."

Lake's experience with the Spider-Woman resurfaced in his mind. He had this feeling that they would face something similar. "I've been asleep for three—no—I'm not going there and having someone die on me again. You're not coming with me. This boss is beyond anything you've faced before."

Maxwell chortled. "What are you, my babysitter? I've been doing this a lot longer than you. Thanks for the concern, but you can keep it. Besides, you look like you're the one who needs babysitting." He tossed the elixir back to him. "Drink this. We'll leave in 12 hours," he said.

"We can't go in there, guns blazing. Don't you have a plan?"

"You got 12 hours for that too."

CHAPTER 34

KERI, OUTWORLD A2-DO2S

The air was musty and humid, suggesting rain would soon come. Though clouds clustered above the skies, none looked ready to pour as specks of sunlight cast through. It pierced some shadows in the vast pathways, but then was impeded by dark trees and its circling branches and crumbling towers with its stone arches. Their height stretched far above the hundreds in meters. Down below, nothing was even. Rocks gathered to make hills, and in between, roots the size of trains waved up and down. The occasional pond or stream flowed through, then the upheaving started again.

Though the atmosphere oozed with fear of the unknown and suggested the utmost care—those were far from Keri's mind. In her head, everything was...peachy.

As she followed Wayne's lead, her focus was glued to his shirtless back that she likened to a well-oiled machine as he moved. The muscles stretching back and forth—something about that was tantalizing. *This hot beefcake is into me? I'm not that gorg, am I? Or is it my personality?* Her focus returned to the sculptured movements of Wayne's back as it tensed and he glanced her way.

"Here, grab this," she heard him say.

"Don't mind if I do," she purred and reached for his back.

He handed her a long, sturdy branch. The fantasy in her head broke apart. "What?" she croaked.

"To help you with hiking," explained Wayne. "The hills aren't really helping with this humidity."

She couldn't remember what the conversation was about but figured she just said yes to it. "Thank you," she replied without thinking.

As she leaned on the branch to walk, she slipped forward. Wayne caught her in an embrace. Keri was made very aware of him, his body heat, his sweat and the hardness of his muscles. It took all her self-control not to melt into a puddle.

"Careful," he said as his face was next to hers.

"Mhmmm…"

"You have really nice eyes."

Keri glanced away for a second and then returned the stare. "You have a very nice back."

He smiled as his face moved closer to hers. She closed her eyes and puckered her lips. *Woooh round 2! Yeah! Come to me, baby.* The moment his lips touched hers, Keri opened her mouth and darted her tongue in his mouth, slobbering all over his face.

Ivo yelled into their linko, "Hey guys, I'm back." He was flying in their direction on his magic carpet. Keri tore away from Wayne as he gasped for air. "Sorry to break the hot steamy make-out session, but I brought guests to watch—or not."

A dozen green lizardmen trailed behind him with blades drawn as they traversed the uneven land with agile leaps and runs.

"What—what happened?" Keri asked.

"I-I-don't know," screamed Ivo. "I was just looking around and they suddenly came at me. Maybe I flew above their home?"

Wayne stepped forward. "Ivo, get Keri out of here."

"What about you?" asked Keri.

"I'll deal with them."

"I can help too. I got time magic and a sword—like a maho shoujo." She summoned her Trainee Sword and posed with her free hand in the air as she imagined she was in a poster in one of her games.

Ivo floated above them. "Ah—what now?"

"You know, magic girl. Except I don't have a staff. They always had staves in the games and anime. Is there a staff I can buy?"

As the lizardmen neared, Wayne ordered, "Ivo, now."

Keri swung around her sword. "But I got magic and powers too. I can help."

Wayne glanced at her and smiled. "No need for you to dirty your hands, babe. I got this." His pecs bounced.

Ivo reached out a hand. "Oh, he definitely got this. Come on, love."

As she settled on the ascending carpet, Keri felt slightly uncomfortable. But that melted away as Ivo patted her, telling her not to worry. The lizardmen leaped at Wayne, the only person still on the ground. Blue fire blazed over his hands.

Wayne launched a lizard into the air with an uppercut. He followed up with two punches for the next monster. Jabs, crosses and uppercuts flew from left to right with licks of fire catching on the monster's scales and armor. Some suffered from one-hit-knockouts, while the others that rose for more died on a second punch—with a flaming crater singed deep within their torso.

The blue lizardmen appeared from a distance, seething over their fallen brethren. They nocked their arrows and fired. With burning hands, Wayne swirled them around and created a mark in the air that shielded him from air attacks. He then followed it up with a fiery stomp and knocked the archers away. Then a flurry of kicks stopped the stragglers from getting away and ended the surviving ones.

The magic carpet flew back over to Wayne as Keri quickly hopped off and ran to him. "Are you o—kay?" She stopped midway to get a good look at his body glistening from blood, guts and sweat. Though he smelled like burnt meat and charcoal, she wanted to take him away and eat him.

"Did you see that? I was like pow and boom. It was awesome. I was awesome." He flexed his arms.

She felt his body heat rising and covering him as she neared him. "You looked so cool killing all the bad guys. Like a hero in the movies."

"I'm the Slayer," he corrected with pride. "It's all because of you."

"I didn't do anything," she said, but thought, *You didn't let me do anything.*

"You're my girl. You gave me strength."

Then the slight tantrum in her head washed away when he dropped that line. His words gelded her into submission. "Not just your girl; I'm your Maiden," she found herself saying out loud instead of just thinking about it.

He smiled, moved a little closer and then the two collided again. Their tongues and mouth dipped into each other's and sucked as the world around them faded into nonexistence. She hopped onto him as he caught her by the waist and they continued exploring with their hands and mouths. After a few minutes of heavy panting and rising libidos, Keri heard a buzz behind her. She ignored it a few times, but it kept hounding her until she realized it wasn't coming into her ear; it was in her mind.

"Do you hear that?" Keri parted her head from him but still clung to his arms.

"Took you long enough. You two are really getting hot and heavy," said Ivo. "It was awkward for me, but I know what it's like for new couples—the honeymoon stage. My wife and I used to get it on like..." He continued to reminisce as the other two paid attention to something different.

Wayne frowned. "I did. It's like not in your ear, but in your ear, you know?"

Keri removed herself from her *boyfriend*—she giggled at the thought. Forcing herself to focus, she felt a strange pull to her right. "It's over there." She pointed.

"Let's go." He strode over in that direction.

Ivo abruptly stopped his monologue once he saw them move and followed quickly from above. "Hey, wait up. Where are we going?"

"I don't know," replied Keri, but she still went.

The journey to wherever it was they were going was long. After a few kilometers, Keri would ride with Ivo on the carpet to rest. But after a few minutes, they had to go back to walking since Ivo's capacity to use source was limited. He informed them that the heavier the load and the longer the flight, the more the artefact took a toll on him. Since he had not had a complete rest, jumping from one dimension to the other, he was at his limit.

Between walking and flying, the party also had to deal with occasional ambushes from lizardmen. Sometimes arrows would rain down at them from above or sneak attacks would come from under roots or behind rock formations. But in every situation, Wayne would intervene with his fiery fists or his yin-yang shield. The first few times felt chivalrous and exciting for Keri when she got saved, like it was in the game, like she was a real princess. But after a while, it got boring. Here she was with all these time powers and a super sword—and yet she was just decoration? Did princesses lead such a boring life like this? Putting that aside, the coins! Since Wayne was killing all the monsters, like a slayer would, there wasn't anything left for her.

It feels like a bus without the rewards, she thought. 'Bus' was a game slang for players who get levelled by high-ranking players without doing anything.

Ivo was rummaging through his backpack while the two of them rode the carpet. "You falling asleep inside a rift? You'll get nightmares if you sleep here—and wrinkles! I kid. Hee hee," he said.

She turned to him with a half-asleep face. "Just tired," *and bored,* she added in thought. "Hey, does your wife ask you not to do some things?"

He pulled out some chips and fruits and started munching. "I tried helping around the house once, when I was on break, didn't end well. She said I was bad at doing all of them, so I stopped doing. Why'd you ask?"

She thought about explaining her predicament but decided against it quickly. "Nothing. Can I have some?"

"Sure."

Their journey ended when there were no tree growths to be seen; instead, a spacious clearing greeted them at the size of twice a football field. The large roots had all gone, but the ground still proved uneven with all the rocks. A tall structure stood in the center for all to see. As their feet carried them closer, the features became prominent. It was a humungous crystal the size of ten-story buildings. A purple light glowed at the center, and at every blink, a hum sounded.

Ivo drifted closer and closer at the crystal. "What do you think that is?"

"I don't know. It kind of looks like an overgrown monster core?" Keri ran her hands on it, feeling both coarse and smooth.

> You have reached the center of Outworld A2-D02S. The lord of the realm
> will be notified.

"Get away from there," shouted Wayne from the ground.

"What?" asked Ivo.

Keri re-read the notification, grabbed his arm and squeezed. "Let's go," she pleaded. Ivo nodded and they drifted back closer to the ground. Soon as he was able, Wayne hopped on to the carpet and all of them sailed the air away from the large crystal. When they neared where they had come from, another alert chimed in.

> Dragon-Knight S21 receives notification. Crossing initiated.
> Time until full cross: 24:59. Please prepare.

The two candidates read their respective screens and then exchanged worried looks.

"What's going on? You both look like you've seen ghosts. Are we fighting banshees or poltergeists? The undead?" asked Ivo. "Just let me know, so I can psych myself up."

"Stop here," ordered Wayne. Once the carpet stopped, he got off. "I want you two to fly away from here as far as you can."

"What? Why?"

Keri hopped off as well. "He wants to fight the boss monster by himself. I'm not leaving you behind."

"How'd you guys know that?" Ivo looked from her to him.

"We have about twenty minutes until it gets here," Wayne read from the notification. "This is not like the other lizards; this is the boss. It's like what the Hairless Ape faced. It might be even bigger and stronger."

"Exactly. How are you going to take something that big on by yourself?" Keri argued.

"No. This is no place for girls." His voice grew bigger and louder.

Keri's face burned. She had enough of being sidelined for the past half a day. Her title was Maiden, and the system gave her superpowers. It was unfair to sit around and do nothing. She wanted to swing her sword around and use magic. Sure, she wasn't the best fighter around—and she'd probably run for the hills when it got too difficult. But no one else was here to help them. She might as well try and get herself out of this mess—and damn the world if she was going to let her coins get passed up again. "I am..." She stopped when a dazzle of light caught her eye.

"What about you?" asked Wayne.

Ivo pointed behind him. When they all looked, a violet rift tore through the space behind them and two people crossed through. Both of them were familiar to Keri; both of them, handsome. One exuded leadership, strength and experience; the other displayed youthful energy and an air of inquisitiveness—both had sex-appeal that would make any woman wet with delight. But one particular man needed no introductions, for she loved and dated this man in her waking moments and in her dreams.

"Hello," said the elven prince.

> Target love #1 rediscovered.
> 100 coins earned. Total: 3010

Chapter 35
Lake, Center, A2-D02S

The notification flashed on Lake's vision, but he was too distracted by the woman in front of him. It was her. Her appearance looked to be slightly different from his dreams, but there was no denying it. Should he reach out and ask? Just to be sure. But he felt so sure already. But what if it isn't her? *I could be wrong,* he thought while Maxwell caught up with the situation.

"We've got around seventeen minutes until it gets here," announced the big buff guy.

"How'd you know this Dragon-Knight is the boss? And that it's coming here?" asked Maxwell.

"We...just do," answered the woman, briefly meeting the others' eyes before focusing on him again.

Lake quickly glanced at his notification. She and this big guy were candidates just like him. "You're her. The girl in my dreams. Keri, right? I was going to try and find you, back in Zuobic, but stuff happened." He started approaching her.

She moved closer to him as well. "You were? Sorry, I'm staying in Zone Troef now, so you won't find anyone there. Also, it's a pseudo-dream."

"Right. Pseudo dream." He brightened at the word.

"How'd your mission go?"

He nodded in glee. "I screwed up and now I'm stuck here. Told you I was going to mess it up." As she stared at her, he finally noticed the change in her body from the last time he saw her. *She must've had a tough time surviving,* he thought.

"But you're still alive, right? That's saying something."

"You're alive too," he agreed. "How's the gaming going? Still like being a princess?"

"If I'm stuck at the castle, not doing anything, not so much. I think I might want to be the hero this time."

His brow raised. "You want to save the princess? I thought you want to be the princess?"

"Can't the princess be the hero too?"

"She sure can." Unaware of his own movements, he was now right next to Keri.

She recalled the throwing games they played in the amusement park, in the pseudo-dream, and said, "You're really awesome with throwing. Why didn't you become a baseball player? You could've been a star."

He chuckled. "I used to play back in high school. Never really thought of pro. Besides, haven't you heard? I'm the Starless Sorcerer. So I probably won't be a star."

"Stars are overrated anyway." Her eyes sparked.

"We can play some time."

"Baseball? I'm not good at catching things. But I'm good at running. Does that count?" Her gaze gave him the feeling of wonder and calmness.

"Oh, it definitely counts," he replied with another smile.

The big buff man forced himself in between the two, grabbed Lake's hand and shook it vigorously. "I'm Wayne. Keri's boyfriend," he announced.

"Boyfriend?" asked Lake with a surprised look.

"Boyfriend?" asked Maxwell at the same time. "When did that happen?"

All eyes fell on Keri. "Uh yeah, I guess, I mean, we were—are together. Just now," she answered with a hint of uncertainty and embarrassment.

Lake kept shaking the big man's hand, wondering how Keri could fall for this oversized buffoon? He certainly was packed and probably spectacular and dependable in a fight. But there was nothing princely about him, the way that Keri would probably like. *Why am I thinking like this?* he thought to himself.

Aaah, my hand, he pulled his hand back from the crushing pain. *What is his problem?*

"How much time do we have before it gets all kung fu fighting again?" asked Ivo aloud. "And where are the others?"

"Ten minutes," updated Keri with a flustered expression.

Maxwell quickly shared his story. "I left them all in our dimension. Better me than the rest of us if we do get stuck," he finished with.

Ivo gasped. "Why did you leave everyone behind? We're the bench warmer team. We can't possibly defeat the boss by ourselves."

"Don't worry your ass, Lake's got a plan."

"Yes sir." He stood at attention.

Behind Lake was a hover-cart with drums of cumin-water that followed him around. He grabbed a backpack from the cart and pulled out water guns, explaining what the concoction was and how it affects lizard-type monsters. "We need a way to deliver the poison. I brought water guns but that isn't enough to make an impact," he added.

Ivo raised his hand with enthusiasm. "I, leader of Team J, will carry out that task. I will fly around with the drums and pour it over the boss."

Lake looked to Maxwell for guidance, to which he nodded. "Now, we need to pin it down somehow," he said.

"You think this thing will work on the boss?" asked Wayne with obvious disbelief.

"It should if it's a lizard type," said Lake. "I also added some ingredients that would hurt naga, drakes and other reptiles—it should work. The army has proven this works."

"This is a boss in a rift out to kill us. It's not coming for curry like in a restaurant. It wants human meat. Besides, no one here trusts your army."

Maxwell walked between the two. "I've seen it in action, Wayne, there's no need to worry. Even if it doesn't, we have a plan B." He gestured for the second hover-cart following them filled with explosives.

Wayne looked from Maxwell to Lake. "I say we pound it. None of this meal-crap." He cracked his knuckles for emphasis. He eyed him contemptuously, as if to say his plan was useless and pathetic.

Keri cleared her throat, cutting the tension. "I'm volunteering to hold the boss down," she announced.

Lake smiled and was about to answer yes, but Wayne grabbed her shoulder and declared, "No. You're going to be hiding behind the trees. Let the men handle this."

She shook her head. "I can do this. I've done it before. Might not be easy, but who else is going to do it? You three are like DPS—I'm sure you can tank, but I can cc."

"What are you talking about?" asked Wayne.

Lake connected the dots with the lingo of his classmates who played games. "She meant we're too focused on attacking and she has the ability to hold the boss. If she can, that's great, I'm sure she'll be careful," he explained.

Wayne glanced at him and scoffed. "I've got this. She's not going near that boss. She's staying far-far away."

"I'm a candidate too," pleaded Keri. "This is—"

"Medics at the back, not at the front," Wayne interjected. "Wait for us to be done."

Lake placed a hand on his arm. "Big Guy, let her speak. She's as much responsible for this fight as the rest of us."

He brushed the hand off him. "Big Guy? Who do you think you are?" he growled.

Maxwell let out a sliver of his grey aura, cutting through the building tension. "Stop bickering, kids. We've got a real big problem."

Everyone looked ahead as the large crystal at the center of the clearing began shining. "Two minutes to zero," announced Keri.

Ivo floated next to the barrels and started placing them onto his magic carpet. Lake caught sight and quickly helped out. "How much can you carry?" asked the hero.

"About three, I think. I'll have to go back for the rest of it," answered Ivo.

"Ivo, ride out to the crystal now. Lake, escort him," ordered Maxwell. "Keri, you hold the boss, but stand as far away from it as you can."

Wayne huffed, "Maxwell, she's not going to fight—"

He held out a hand in Wayne's face. "Last I checked I'm still the leader of this mission. If you're worried about her, guard her. I'll dance with the boss."

Chapter 36

Keri, Center, A2-D02S

The minutes turned to seconds as Ivo arrived atop the crystal. Not long behind him was Lake, leaping his way closer. As the crystal increased its brightness another level, Keri and Wayne stopped a kilometer away from it while the guild leader was still trying to get closer. A tall man with clawed reptilian feet, hands and black bat wings spawned in dazzling green armor. Its face was perfectly human and beautiful, save for the four horns sprouting from its head, its slithering forked tongue and lizard eyes that observed its new environment.

Dragon-Knight has fully crossed. Please defeat the boss of this dimension.

Cold sweat dripped at Keri's back. Her brain ceased to have any other senses than her trembling. She resisted the urge to run. Wayne stood right in front of her with the same uneasy expression. But when he glanced briefly at her, it hardened. He readied his fists. She looked at the others and saw the same firm expressions; even Ivo seemed determined. She couldn't falter now—she had to do this.

"Keri," said Maxwell over the linko.

The source around her instantly poured in her entirety. When she raised her arms, Keri let it rip. A magic circle that resembled a clock illuminated the ground where the Dragon-Knight was. As the enemy flapped its wings and gained a distance from the ground, it froze in its ascent like a video played in slow motion.

"Ivo," the guild leader commanded.

Hovering right over the head of the Dragon-Knight, Ivo poured the poison-filled drum. As soon as the brown-yellow liquid touched the horns, it melted visibly. It opened the scales of its neck and made gaps in its armor, the hands, the wings, the legs—its whole body sizzled as the cumin water spilled over the humanoid. It roared a monstrous howl, sending shivers down everyone's spines, but no matter how their hearts pounded, they continued their plan.

After finishing one drum, Ivo poured out another. But with every second that passed, the struggles of the enemy intensified and Keri's arms grew wearier as the source she absorbed increased. A tinge of a headache crept up the base of her head—she had been converting source far too fast for what her body could handle. The strength of the monster was too great to be bound. "I can't hold it much longer," she said into the linko.

Wayne quickly turned to her. His face was a mix of worry and anger. "Stop it, Keri. I'll take care of him," he urged.

"Stick to the plan," radioed Maxwell. "It's working."

"She just said she can't hold out. Are you deaf?"

"Come on, Keri. Keep it steady. You can do it."

Keri focused on Maxwell, who was close to the boss. Though she could not see his face, she knew he was looking at her. Somehow, she found her strength and poured more energy into it. She tasted blood.

"Your nose—you're bleeding—stop it," shouted Wayne. "She's hurt. Let her stop."

"I'll help." Runes of light twinkled around Lake as his fingers danced in the air. He then threw light on the ground; it snaked towards the humanoid. In a flash, stalagmites rose from the ground and trapped the boss within a circular cage made of earth.

Keri felt her struggles ease for a bit. "That was new," she said.

"I didn't think it'd work, but I get lucky sometimes," answered Lake.

The luck lasted only for a breath when Keri felt the atmosphere boil and steam. Javelins made of green and black crystalline material manifested around the Dragon-Knight. As it roared, the crystals shot out in all directions. One headed straight for her.

Wayne intercepted the attack with his blue-flamed fist, shattering it into pieces. "Enough, Keri. Get back." More javelins soared in their direction as he tried his best to knock them all away, but bits and pieces cut him.

Maxwell parried the attacks with precision and strength as the brunt of the attack came at him. Ivo had to stop pouring poison and drove the carpet out of harm's way. Lose shards cut the hems and poked holes at the edge. Then he lost control and crashed on the ground. Lake tried to run and help him, but he was stuck defending from the onslaught of crystals.

Keri briefly glanced at the others and carried on. "I can do this," she said.

"I said get back." Wayne fought more of the javelins away.

"I can—"

"You don't know how to do this," he screamed at her with wide, intense eyes.

Keri closed her mouth but met his gaze. Anger bubbled up inside her.

"It's launching another attack," warned Maxwell.

As the rain of crystals lessened, the Dragon-Knight opened its mouth wide. Rays of green and dark light gathered before it and consolidated into a mass of energy. It grew bigger in size and deeper in color as the seconds fleeted. Keri tore herself from Wayne's obstinance as she gawked at the enlarging mass.

Maxwell changed tactics from doing simple parries to attacking. He hacked away at its limbs, wings and torso, covering every inch of its body with wounds, never stopping. As he kept on, the mass stopped growing, so he continued even more vigorously than before.

Lake was leaping from the distance, getting closer to the Dragon-Knight. "Get out of the way." He threw his backpack at the boss. Once Maxwell backed off, he unleashed a lightning bolt and hit his bag.

Time seemed to slow as the bolt collided with the bag and set off an explosion. The moment the blast touched the Knight's skin, it pushed itself to release the massive ball of light. The ball floated down and simply vanished, like a blob shifting into a dot. For a few breaths, nothing happened. No sounds, no disturbances, no explosions—save for Lake's backpack. It made her think that maybe the worst had passed and they had succeeded.

Then suddenly, a white, blinding light replaced everything—no, erased everything. Like a large bomb, it took up everything in sight, swallowing all of the clearing and beyond. The last thing Keri saw was Wayne pushing her down on the ground and activating his yin-yang shield to protect them.

She heard a sound too. But it was too loud for her ears to discern or describe. From her normal hearing, she only heard ringing. She felt the heat as well. It was the kind of heat like when a hand hovered over a stove, then touched the fire, then pressed the whole palm on the burner. And just when they pulled out, a force slammed their head onto the burning grate.

The whole clearing, starting from the broken crystal, to the surrounding trees and bushes, was destroyed. Smoke, dirt and debris scattered around everywhere as the attack shaved the hills and ranges into a flat landscape.

When the air cleared, everyone was spread out on the newly culled land—some were beneath rubble, and some were exposed to the sun. A bit further off from the middle of the impact, where the black-green blast first touched the ground, Keri lay in the dirt with notifications sparkling over her vision.

Congratulations! You have defeated the Dragon-Knight. You have increased available fragments to +1.

You have earned 2000 coins. Total coins: 5910. You have earned the item: Soulsword.

Rights to tunnel dimension Outworld A2-D02S will now be transferred to participants.

Would you like to vie for ownership or waive your rights? Vie | Waive

You have chosen to stake your claim. If any other candidate vies for ownership, a lottery roll will commence.

Time left for other participants to claim: 4:59s

Keri tried to get up, but a stinging pain from her neck to the whole of her spine kept her from moving. Instead, her vision wandered, seeing Wayne an arm's length away from her buried in dirt. Half of his shoulder was blown away and his whole right arm and left hand were missing. She searched for the others, spotting their sorry states. All of them were injured, ragged flesh, broken bones, missing limbs, and unconscious.

By instinct, she reached for her power and activated it—a piercing pain cut across her head. Unable to cradle the pain, she only stopped and panted. Blood dripped from her nostrils. Seeing none of her friends were moving, she tried again and again, until it felt like her head would split open. "Aaaagggghhhh," she wailed as clocks made of light floated above herself and everyone. A faint aura permeated over everyone's skin as source manifested in drops. The tiny globs would vanish and reappear as their bodies incrementally repaired itself with every pass the clock hands did in a counter-clockwise direction.

As she pushed herself further, blood dripped from her nose. Her vision blurred and her breaths shortened. The floating clocks vanished into inexistence and left the bodies whole and out of critical condition, but miles left until full recovery.

Congratulations! Time Trade has upgraded to Rank B. Area of effect and strength has increased; source required to use has decreased.

Description: (1) Increase or decrease a matter's perception and experience against real time. (2) Trade time between matters. (3) Reverse the adverse effects on a matter. (4) Misuse can cause negative effects on the candidate.

Please increase Mind Function to avoid effects.

Congratulations! You are officially the owner of dimension A2 with tunnel D02S.

Once you claim ownership of areas within your home world, Silaw, your territories will merge.

A portal will now open to your home world.

Your mind has reached its limits in source conversion. Your senses will shut down temporarily to recover. You will be unconscious until your mind and body recover.

Please do not attempt to use fragments or any abilities relating to source during this time.

As her vision surrendered to darkness, the last thing she heard was Wayne stirring and then calling her name, before she surrendered to sleep.

CHAPTER 37

LAKE, APARTMENT, UNTEF

Lake paced the living room inside the apartment he was staying in at Zone Untef. It had been four days since he had returned from dimension A2, or D-A2 for short, the lizardmen dimension. The last moments he remembered from his time there were the big explosion from the Dragon-Knight. Next thing he knew, he was awake with a healthy body but a completely torn up outfit. The boss was vanquished and the rift back to their home world lay before them, shining white. Keri had been the only casualty, unmoving and barely breathing. Before he could even come close to her, Wayne scooped her into a princess-carry.

"This is all your fault," the big man barked. "Stay away from Keri, if you know what's good for you."

Those words made him freeze. Was it his fault again, that someone had died? Had he not tried his best to save everyone? Was it wrong to push Keri to feel strong and fight back the way he wanted to feel about himself?

Lake followed the two lovers out of the rift and came out on the other side. Groups of closers assisted them immediately. He felt distant from her, and he didn't know how to bridge that gap. Maxwell came to his side and said, "Keri is in good hands. Come with me. There are some things we need to discuss."

After that, Lake settled in this apartment the guild had offered him. He rested on his bed, munching on fries and fried chicken. His freedom was revoked until Maxwell sorted out his presence in the freezones. This meant there was no town exploration, shopping or talking to free people. For all the things he needed—food, clothes, spare parts, etc.—Ivo delivered them on his spare time. Lake imagined having a strange federate who was both a 14 (ability user) and 17 (sorcerer), who had come from a 25 (deleted space) was no easy discussion with the authorities. He more or less understood why he was being kept indoors.

His waking hours had mostly been spent exploring the system's coin shop. A lot of it was about increasing his abilities if he had the coins to spare. Now his interests fell to the items he had previously ignored:

> Area Claim Crystal. Description: Binds a whole unclaimed area or 1 grid or 20 sqm, including space above and below to a candidate. Cost: 500 coins.

This appeared to be a red gem with gold floating rings around it.

> Area Shielding Crystal. Description: Protects a whole claimed area or 1 grid or 20 sqm, including space above and below for candidate. 730 hours per consumption. Can be used multiple times to increase duration for 1 area. Cost: 1000 coins.

Similarly, this was a gem, but blue with silver rings.

He had used one Claim Crystal on their travel to Zone Troef with the Apes. He had claimed the freezone Pugof, which was inhabited by a few small communities that were inside caves and beneath the ground. There wasn't much as far as military or economic resources, but the population still counted in the hundred-thousands.

Further into his experiments, he found that Quisix and Pugof were connected by space and his will. Without actually experiencing it, he knew for a fact that there were certain places in Pugof that would lead to Quisix and he could move those doorways around. By mental command, he could open rifts within his territory leading to several areas. The only caveat was that he had to be in his area to do that. He could not open a rift in a space he did not own. The link he had with A2, the Dragon-Knight's dimension, was also severed once he returned to his home dimension—the system mentioned that there was a candidate who owned it already, Keri.

For a split second, he thought about Keri again, like he had for the past few days. He kept inquiring about her, but Ivo mentioned that he had no word either, since she was being taken care of by their partner company, Amazing Discoveries in Zone Troef. As much as he wanted to see her, he could not. He had to be patient and keep to what he was doing.

A red gem with golden rings materialized in his grasp before quickly disappearing.

> You have consumed Area Claim Crystal. Current Area: Zone Untef has been claimed by Hero.
>
> Areas Claimed: Quisix, Pugof, Untef

A knock on the door sounded as it opened and Maxwell walked in wearing jeans and a black leather jacket. "Bored yet?" he asked, entering the place.

"Was thinking of breaking the door and flying out," said Lake.

"I'm sure you could. Appreciate you staying put. Let's chat." He placed a six-pack on the coffee table and some grilled meat and seafood on skewers.

Lake sat on the couch. "Did you feel something here by any chance? Like a source or something?" he asked.

His expression hardened. "Is there a rift coming?"

He waved his arms. "Nothing like that. Just something, anything weird?"

Maxwell crossed his arms and scratched his chin. "Other than me having a beer with a soldier, nothing else odd. Why?"

He assumed claiming an area went unnoticed by anyone who didn't have access to the system. "Never mind. You don't like the army?"

"Not when they're exercising their rights to close rifts out of their territory, steal 7s from hardworking closers—and the occasional pillage a village so our team doesn't go hungry. Not that I'm a philanthropist, believe me, but there has to be some human line somewhere."

Lake shook his head. "Reports don't say anything like that. If they did, that's grounds for suspension."

He relaxed on the couch opposite the hero. "The little people don't make it into your fancy reports."

"But that's—"

"—wrong?" finished Maxwell. "That's not the half of it. Stick around, and you'll get to know more about your precious army. Anyway, I didn't come here to rant about the bastards. I come bearing good news."

He pulled himself away from the growing interest he had in Zuobic's odd behavior. "What news?"

"I got the mayor to clear you for a month's stay with us without having to notify Zuobic. Got you a new identity as well." He opened a can of beer and handed it to him.

"Why?"

He opened and sipped his own beer. "Technically, the mayor of Cluster RSTU knows you as a researcher in outlier technology, who is selling your services to Hairless Ape for a month. RSTU stands for the zones Rumaf, Shoef, Troef and Untef."

"I guess it's easier to pass me off as a worker than a 14—hell will break loose if they found out I'm a 17. No contracts, questions or tests."

"And easier to get rid of you if Zuobic ever finds out."

"You'll put all the blame on me," he guessed. "Act like it's all my fault."

Maxwell clicked his tongue. "Exactly. If we hide you, we've got to be able to get rid of you easily. Keep our hands clean. You know how it goes. You owe me 500k credits, by the way."

Lake snorted and spilled his beer. "For what? This place isn't worth 500k. And I am a trainee."

"*Was* a trainee. Now you're unemployed, a refugee and in hiding," he corrected. "The money is for all the bribes I had to give to keep your stay here quiet and smooth. Haven't even added my fixer fee for arranging everything. That's another 100k."

Zuobic gave importance to missing federates. Rewards were given for any information relating to them and even more so for their whereabouts. A sorcerer and academic graduate were on the higher list of priorities. Like Keri, a lot of people would pay good money for the return of someone like him. "I'm guessing I don't have to sign a contract if I'm a researcher. If I can't kill monsters or close rifts, how am I supposed to pay you back?" he asked.

Maxwell produced a glassy from his jacket and laid it on a table. "Your project."

Lake went through the images and files. "These are low-tier weapons and mechs. What do I do with these? They're outdated—the worst to combat outliers."

"These are what my guild uses."

"Uh, on second thought, they look okay. Passable," he chirped.

He waved a hand. "They're shit, you're right. That's why I want an upgrade. I want all of them to be rune weapons. Make them the best to combat outliers."

"Uh, I don't have the materials nor the blueprints for all of these. Zuobic has complete control over them. Even if I have them memorized or something, I can't break the law. They'll imprison me for stealing intellectual property rights, and hunt you down for carrying the same tech."

"I'm not asking you to use their tech. I'm asking you to make new ones."

"New ones?"

Maxwell sipped his drink before he stood and went over to the open closet where the L-Shield and S-Boots were kept. "Searched for these things—and they haven't come up anywhere. The Empire, Federation, freezones—no one has these weapons. So the reasonable conclusion is you made them."

"You want these? But these are prototypes I made on the fly. They haven't been through stress tests, ballistics, accessibility, or more tests that I probably don't know of. Are you sure?" Lake's brows bridged together.

He returned to the couch and rested his legs on the side of the coffee table. "I don't make business deals I'm not confident in. I'll take care of all the materials, and I'll pay you market price for each device you create. I'm inclined to leave you with the creator rights, but since you're in hiding, I'd like them too—or at least the manufacturing and distribution rights. Up to you to decide."

"How much would they cost?"

"Market price for your shield, 50-60k credits. Boots around 30-40k as unique items. Price goes down if they are made public."

Lake gulped even more beer. This was an unprecedented offer. He had never thought the things he created were of any use to other people than himself. He always thought there were other outlier items and rune weapons that surpassed his in terms of use, design, power—everything. Was all of it worth this much? Was he worth that much?

"Out of curiosity, why don't you want to go back home?" asked Maxwell.

Tony's warnings about Cervantes' human experimentation chimed in his mind. "I'm not sure if there's something there for me anymore. I never quite felt like I belonged."

Maxwell nodded. "I see. Anyway, I also got the mayor of RSTU to extend your stay indefinitely if you'd fix and upgrade their ward generators. You'll be paid for all your services on a weekly salary on top of food and lodging. Of course, we'll take care of the rent for the facility and equipment you'll need."

"Did you leave that for last to put pressure on me?"

He smirked. "Pressure is offering you a team of your own to do all those tests that you mentioned and assist you with whatever you need, courtesy of the Hairless Apes."

He gaped. "What?"

"Fifty people all under you. Serving your nerdy desires to their fullest."

"How'd you manage to get a lot of people like that?"

"We've got a lot of resources here. How'd you think we built this Cluster? And, once they found out they're building new tech, rune weapons—a lot of people wanted to help. Good people," emphasized Maxwell. "Hell, if you wanted, there's a bunch of them who'd join you. I was just afraid you couldn't handle them."

Lake would be lying to himself if he denied having any interest in it. He had access to a facility, a fifty-man team and more! Why was he hesitating? He was scared of the army and all of its rules—no, he was scared of Cervantes. But after his experiments in the lizardmen dimension, it felt like he was on the cusp of something extraordinary—something beyond him. "You've got a deal." He held out his hand.

He shook hands with him. "A deal is made. I'll have Ivo draft a contract. By the way, about your friend, results should come in any day now," his tone turned from jubilant to careful.

Tony's body was currently in the mortuary on a freezer undergoing the autopsy for his death. Lake had been having nightmares ever since his death. He had been distracting himself with the system and the internet for quite a while now just to put it out of his mind, but it had not been easy.

Lake nodded but then asked, "Is Keri doing okay?"

Maxwell sighed. "She hasn't woken up yet, but the doctors say she's stable with no physical problems."

"I see."

There was a moment of silence before Maxwell popped another can of beer. "She's Keri, she'll bounce back from this in the most weird and annoying way possible." He handed him a can and a skewer.

Lake smirked and helped himself to the drinks and food. "You're right."

Chapter 38

Keri, Kermoz Youth Center (Eight years ago)

A twenty-two-year-young Keri tucked a seven-year-young Chatterbox in a bed at the Kermoz Youth Centre, an orphanage. He had been crying the whole day, and it was only now that he had stopped. She patted his head, left his room and went down the stairs. Two children were busy playing games in the living room as she passed them on the way towards the kitchen. Her feet stopped at the door frame. "Hey Fynn, is dinner ready?" she asked a tall, lanky older man with an oval-shaped face who was behind the counter.

Fynn was the owner and manager of the orphanage, and Keri was working here part-time as a course requirement for her Community Welfare Degree. "Almost there. How is he?" He poured chopped carrots into a pot of broth and continued cutting veggies.

Keri's parents brought Chatterbox in this morning from inside a rift. Both were soldiers and worked in the social welfare division of the military. They were in charge of missing people and civilians who were affected by outliers. "He finally calmed down enough to sleep. Tomorrow, hopefully, he can say what happened to him. Maybe we'll find out he's just like us. Not a 32," she whispered the last statement.

"You know the chances of that are slim. Especially since Portia brought him here. But I don't care if he is. He looks like he's a good kid, and if he needs a home to say in, he is welcome here," declared Fynn. "Get them ready."

She nodded then moved to the living room, watching the kids play on floating screens. One had big black eyes and blue scales on his skin, while the other had small horns poking out of her hair. By military decree, her parents would usually send these beings from the rift into the R&D division to be tested until their bodies gave up or were preserved for who knows how long. But when they encountered children like these, they brought them here instead.

Her gaze softened as she said to them, "Hey, you two, enough playing. Go wash up, dinner's almost ready."

"Yes, Keri," the two happily obeyed, leaving the consoles and other devices in a mess.

As she was about to clear them up, the front door opened and a plump woman in a red army uniform with long wavy brown hair entered. It was her mom, Portia. "Keri, come on. Let's eat. Your dad's at the hardware store. He'll be a bit late." She carried shopping bags and walked straight into the kitchen.

Keri shook her head. She was always very strict and directly to the point—no hellos from her. "Coming, Mom. What's this?" She entered the room as a glossy paper bag waited for her where she always sat.

Fynn glanced over at it. "Is that what I think it is?" he asked.

Portia rolled her eyes. "Oh hush, Fynn."

Keri's heart skipped a beat as she opened the bag. "Is it...it is—*Love Me, Princess!* Oh my gosh. How'd you get this?" she squealed.

"I'm awesome," she stated. "And the fact that a colleague from marketing knows the developers of the game. She owed me."

She hugged her tight. "Thank you, Mom. I can't wait to play this."

"How a child's game can make you happy, I have no idea." Fynn set the food on the table

"It's not a child's game. It's for adults only. It has very mature themes," Keri said defensively. "Plus, this is game-of-the-year edition. Five never before played DLCs are included—plus two new romance targets have been added—all of them are gorgeous men."

"You mean, it's like porn? But a game, so game porn."

Her face cringed at the words. "Eww. Stop saying porn. Not the same. This is very adult and mature oriented. Ugly Blaire has rated this as the best relationship guide for maturing young adult women." She brought over silverware and plates.

"Why would you trust someone named Ugly Blaire?"

Portia took out big plates of pork and rice. "It's a lifestyle company on the internet. Get with the times, Fynn."

"Mmhmm," sounded Fynn. "Keep spoiling her, and she'll never find a boyfriend."

The door opened and a medium-built man with big ears entered. "Hi, love. What are we talking about?" He kissed Portia and opened a can of beer from the fridge.

"Xander, are you fine not having grandchildren?" asked Fynn.

"What is this about?" Xander whispered to Portia.

Portia gestured to him that it was nothing and that he should start eating. "She's young, let her do what she wants. She'll have time for real romance later. And besides, I saw the previews, it has interesting lessons about relationships."

"Porn giving relationship advice, what has the world come to?" gasped Fynn. "At least tell me there's a hottie in your school?"

"I don't think they're very interested in me. They like big boobs and slim waists. Not this." Keri gestured an arm over herself.

Fynn served the vegetable stew he'd made. "Oh, come on, don't put yourself down like that."

Portia started with the pork. "That's fine, honey. Let the boys play for now. Once they get serious and get their hearts broken, you'll have a line of men running after you."

"Is that what happened to you?" Fynn asked Xander which was confirmed with a nod while he chewed.

"I'm fine with my sim-men," said Keri. "Besides, I have my degree to finish. Then I'll get into Zuobic's Social Welfare Services."

"Sim-men?" Fynn chuckled. "You know what that sounds like?"

Portia slapped his arm.

"Aww."

Her father looked at her with a glint in his eye. "Are you sure you don't want to work in the army? Good pay," Xander urged.

"No to fighting," insisted Keri.

The two kids entered the dining room, walking straight to where the food was.

"Hey, greet our guests first before you eat," Fynn told them off.

The two were forced to wave to them before eating.

"You don't have to be on the frontlines," said Portia, resuming the conversation. "Your dad and I are perfectly fine doing paperwork at the office. Right, honey?"

He moaned a confirmation with a full mouth of food.

Keri grabbed a plate of her own. "They're still gonna have to train and do physical stuff, I don't wanna do that."

A bright flash illuminated through the windows from outside and then receded. Everyone peered through the windows. Above a broadcast tower, which was a few blocks away from their home, a rift manifested in the skies, covering almost half of Zone Kermoz. Humanoid monsters in capes, who had multiple arms and legs descended onto the streets. Their sudden entrance and bright capes caused a few cars to swerve and crash into poles, buildings and each other. Some passersby took photos and recorded it on their cubex, while the few stationed military police readied their guns and called for help.

Portia had her hand on her linko. "I need an extraction team at my location. Yes, lock onto my signal." She went to the front door and locked it shut.

Keri opened the window and poked her head out. "Dad, are those rift monsters?"

Xander had been checking his gun when Keri called for her. After holstering his weapon, he crossed the kitchen and pulled her back by her blouse. "It's dangerous outside. Get the children together and stay in a room until we get you." As he closed the window, a bright red wisp slammed into him. He fell to the timber floor with a thud.

She raced to her dad's side. "Dad!"

Lying flat on the floor, his eyes propped open as red mist enveloped his skin. "This body should do for now." He investigated his arms and legs, coming into a seated position.

Her face crumpled. "Are you okay?"

Portia entered the kitchen. Her head snapped from Keri, who was kneeling on the floor, to her husband, who rose to his feet. "Love, what happened?"

"Yes, I am very well." He drew his pistol, pointed at his wife's chest and fired. Once she was down on the ground, he shot two more. A bullet punctured her shoulder and her head.

Keri screamed as she ran to Portia, "Mom!"

"You look like you're a potential candidate," said Xander, pointing the gun at her.

"Mom, wake up. Come on. Mom." She shook her, hoping she'd open her eyes and tell her everything would be all right—her dad was just a playing joke.

Fynn stepped in front of Keri and cast Dome of Light, enveloping them in a spherical shield against the bullets. "You do not belong in this world. How could you have breached the outworlds?" he asked.

Xander shrugged, his eyes glowing an unnatural red. "Don't stall for time. I see your master's vessels are right here." He pointed a gun at the children at the corner. One of them was glowing gold.

"No!"

Two bullets shot right through the boy's head and chest. Some of the blood from the boy sprayed Keri's face. Keri focused on the body. Any thoughts in her head stopped dead, just like the child she had loved and cared for lay still.

The golden mist surrounding the boy vanished completely, then circled around the little girl. Gold specks dotted her skin.

Xander smirked. "Sorry, no second passes." Before he could shoot the girl, Fynn released the shield and cast a fireball at him.

Xander's right hand glowed and projected a red force that ate away at the fireball and swooped over at the little girl, devouring her whole. The red force left her dried, aged and dead in half a second. "Non-vessels don't really last, do they?" His whole left arm was desiccated and lifeless. The gun he held dropped to the ground. It was rusted and chipped, like centuries had come and gone.

Runes flared to life around Fynn, swirling and bright. When they came together, violet lightning crackled toward the enemy. Xander glanced at the man before disappearing, electricity hitting nothing but the wall. Xander reappeared behind him and grabbed his neck as a red mist devoured him until he was a corpse. He let go of the orphanage owner and familiar, another dead on the floor.

Xander grumbled as he inspected both his arms hanging lifelessly, inoperable. "Now what do I do about you in this state? It'd be easy if you weren't marked by your Will, like everyone here. I'm surprised this weak man was unmarked." He walked towards Keri.

Keri remained staring out, unresponsive, next to her mom. Tears streamed down her bloodied face as she hiccoughed.

Xander kicked her as her face rested on the ground. The sight of the lifeless and aged girl and Fynn stirred something inside of her. The boy and Portia's bodies knocked on the walls of her shocked state. Wails, sirens and gunfire from outside slowly brought her back. The scenes of alien monsters pouring from the sky, ravaging the people and her family in chaos lined up inside her head, like a movie being edited. She viewed each one of them closely, comprehending each one as much as she could. When finally, it made sense to her. Finally, the film was no longer cut, strewn, or paused. Finally, she had a full view of the picture playing out right in front of her—the horror movie which was her life.

"Goodbye, candidate," said Xander.

She screamed.

He stepped on her back; the red mist was quickly ravaging her. But before it could eat her vitality whole, just before half of her body was sucked dry, a golden force pushed Xander and tossed him against the wall.

Chatterbox stood at the kitchen entrance wearing his blue airplane pajamas. With a determined face a child of his age could never have, he growled while hugging a penguin stuffed toy. "You are not welcome here," he said.

Xander smirked. "Guess you had another vessel stashed. My bad. I'll come for your candidates next time."

"You have broken the laws of the universe. Leave at once."

He cackled. "I didn't break anything. Your people opened the door. I was only stepping—"

Chatterbox's eyes crystalized and glowed gold. Specks of yellow light surrounded Xander and flashed. His body disintegrated to dust, leaving a red mist which the yellow mist caged in the middle and brought over into the penguin stuffed toy.

Fear, confusion, then worry washed over Keri's face as she stared at him in her half-vegetative state. "Chatterbox?" she spoke softly.

He turned to her with a vertical wrinkle between his brows. "I am not Charlie. I am not the Chatterbox you named. I am Silaw, the Will of this World. Do not try to force yourself to do anything. Your body and soul have been damaged greatly. I can only mend your body in my current state. It will take decades for you to fully heal—or you can heal it yourself once you form your fragments. But with your soul damaged, it will be difficult."

All the words he said seemed like the same babble a child would say, but deep inside she knew this was not the real Chatterbox.

His sights focused outside the window. "Come. There are other matters we must take care of." He touched her as both of them disappeared from sight.

CHAPTER 39

KERI, KERMOZ (PRESENT)

Keri opened her eyes, taking in the soft light from the lamp next to her. The plain white ceilings, the large window displaying the rising sun and the many devices and screens hanging on the wall were all familiar to her—she was in one of the many rooms for recovering employees in Amazing Discoveries. Rooms like these were common for establishments who dealt with rifts. They'd rather have the facilities on their grounds than to go to a hospital, hiring medical staff as needed.

The dream she just had; it was a memory of her past.

Keri Richforth was her true name. Bolo was the last name the children got when they arrived at the orphanage. The name was from *Love Me, Princess'* main character, Princess Bolo. She'd picked it out after Fynn had asked her what a good temporary last name would be for the kids. Fynn registered a fake *Mary Bolo* as his sister, and the orphans were her children. Also, the children got temporary names from her until they selected one of their own. Chatterbox was the name she gave to Charlie at that time, hoping he'd talk more.

When the army found the scene of her past, she remembered telling them her name was Bolo. They assumed she was a relative of Fynn's wife. Was it months, or years she was in a recovery institution? The doctors recommended her to start working somewhere, slowly rebuild her life and socialize back into society. That was when she found herself in Padala Services and playing games the rest of her life.

Was that it? *I think I've forgotten something. Something important.*

Her mouth craved the sour and salty taste of the pork and rice Fynn had always made. Phantoms of the children's warmth and lightness haunted her empty embrace. Echoes of her name uttered by her mom and dad trembled in her heart, wishing she could hear them one more time. Tears ran over her face. She grabbed her head. There was more she could not recall. More of her life was hidden from her. *What's wrong with me?*

From the shadowed corner, Charlie emerged. "Like I've said before, your soul is damaged and it is still recovering," he said.

This young boy who had not aged in eight years was the same orphan from before. "Chatterbox? You're talking with your mouth—not inside my head. No, you're not him. You're Silaw," she corrected herself after the soft golden glow within his irises looked back at her, wise beyond his years.

He nodded. "Part of your memories were damaged when your soul was absorbed by the Will. Hypoetheria triggered the damaged memories to resurface. It is not a complete recovery. Give it time."

She recalled the red wisp that entered her dad in her dream. Was that another Will of another world? The same entity as Silaw? It destroyed his family and her. Why does she know all these terms? "Why? Why did it want to kill us?" she asked with a hoarse voice.

"You are the first candidate of this world, the Prima, the Maiden. You are the maid that helps all of the other candidates in my absence. The Will was incomplete when it crossed over—a small fraction of its true essence. At that state, it could not harm me, so it went after you, my vessels and my familiar, Fynn."

A surge of information poured in her head. She knew more details about the Wills of the World, the souls, candidates and the system—which used to be called a guide in other worlds. She remembered in other worlds it appeared as pets or guardians. And somehow in this world it appeared like a video game? "The Will of the World—that's the story Fynn made up. For the kids? He had me memorize it to tell everyone. Is that real?" Her voice strained.

"Did you give me this system? Why'd you pick me to be this maiden?" continued Keri. "I never asked for this. My parents died because of this. Because of you!"

"Your soul needs rest and recovery. Converting source at your limit caused your soul to shake," explained Charlie/Silaw. "You tapped into the recovering part of your soul."

She remembered the fight with the Dragon-Knight. That was when she had pushed herself to her limit, and because of that, her suppressed memories returned?

"My family died from the rift because someone opened the tunnel directly through our world without the outworlds. We were not protected," vocalized Keri, concluding the scene of her past. "I know this because those are the rules Fynn told me about. So, all along, he knew and he was preparing me for this."

"Your memories are and will be confusing," repeated Silaw. "They will all sort themselves when your soul has completely healed. Give it time."

"Why can't you just tell me? You're standing here right now. My memories don't make sense."

"I've already helped lift the veil as much as I can without hurting you or this body," answered Silaw. "This child is nearing his limit. The seal is causing me—us to wither."

Keri understood parts of what he said and at the same time was confused about all of it. "I don't understand. Tell it to me straight. Stop being all mysterious and weird."

"This is my limit. Earn more coins and shape your fragments further—build your authority. Then, when the time is right, I'll see you again."

"What are you—I get what to do—I think, but it's not the same."

"Be strong." Silaw closed his eyes.

The door opened and Vivian entered. "Charlie-baby, what are you doing here? I told you Keri is asleep. She won't have time to...play. You're—you're awake." She looked from her son to the patient awake in the bed.

Keri forced her focus from the boy to the woman. "I'm awake."

"You're awake." She crossed the room and hugged her.

Surprised, Keri hugged her back. "I'm awake," she said again.

Vivian pulled herself back. She wiped away tears forming in her eyes. "I'm sorry. I'm usually calmer—together. But it's all—you're awake."

Her face crumpled. "I am awake. Is waking up really such a good thing?"

She reached for her linko. "Honey, get in here. She's awake."

"You're awake. We can start playing again," Chatterbox signed.

Vivian patted Charlie. "No baby, she needs time to rest and recover. Her muscles are probably sore and weak."

"What are you..." Keri tried to get up to show her she was fine, but her legs gave out. Her whole body felt unsteady and weak.

"Careful. Did you go deaf too?" Vivian helped her back to bed.

"No, I heard you—I just—"

The door slammed open as Riley, wearing dirty overalls, gasped. "I can't believe it. She's awake." She lunged forward and gave her a big hug.

Riley hugged her tightly. "Too tight," said Keri, tapping on her to stop.

Vivian pulled her wife back. "Honey, do you want to risk her sleeping again? She might go for a whole year."

She made a cheesy face. "Sorry, got too excited. One month is enough for us."

"A month?" yelled Keri. "I slept for a whole month?"

"It's actually thirty-five days and seven hours. We thought you were never going to wake up. But the doctor said you were completely healthy physically, so must be something to do with source conversion or something," Riley guessed. "Maybe it was like a really, really bad case of hypoetheria."

The new information regarding the outliers crept into her mind. Surrounded by people close to her who had helped her, she thought they deserved to know—especially about Silaw. "There's something, I—"

"Did you know you were a big pooper even when you only have liquid stuff entering you?" Riley interjected. "Boy, did your poo stink."

Chatterbox gave a disgusted look.

Vivian elbowed her. "Honey, not the best morning conversation. Keri has just gotten out of coma. Go ahead, Keri. What did you want to say?"

Their eyes focused on her, making her heart thump. She thought about what would happen if they knew who their son really was. Would they be sad? Angered? At her? Or Charlie? "The things is... I...I was wondering where Wayne was," she asked, thinking maybe next time she'd bring it up, but definitely not today.

"Oh, he's on a mission," answered Vivian. "Glad he's away. He'll definitely run back all the way here once he finds out you're awake."

Keri made a confused face.

"He was watching you like a hawk, saying weird cutesy stuff like: 'Baby, come back to me. You belong with me.' It was for days and days—and then finally Riley convinced him it wasn't good for him to stay here."

"I got him off his butt and demanded he get to work," explained Riley. "He was stinking so bad even the rats were fleeing from him. He was so downcast and irritating—it was a nightmare having him. It was like a ghost hanging out by your bedside—scary, but stinky."

She turned to her. "Speaking of which, are you going to tell him?"

She shook her head. "And risk him running back here when he just left yesterday? No, thank you."

"You're probably right," she sighed. "Keri, dear, we'll wait for him to come back. Please try not to contact him. It's been very hard for him being stuck here waiting for you. It's nice for him to get some fresh air."

"Okay," replied Keri.

"In the meantime, are you hungry? How about some waffles?"

Chapter 40

Keri, Outskirts of Troef

A dance song played in Keri's linko as she jogged above the valley of Zone Troef. The beat started with riffs from electric guitars while the wind embraced her glistened face. When her legs gained speed, the song entered its refrain. By the time the drums kicked in with the chorus, she was sprinting down the rough road, traversing around the rocks and debris on the flatland. She was doing forty km/h as she felt the runner's high. But she knew she could do more and be more. After waving to the security up on the guard tower she passed, she broke into a run, hitting forty-five km/h. Then her senses all attuned to her breathing, to her muscles, and to her technique. Her mind tapped into the source around her and converted it into her own power. The scale of the time stream split into fractions against her own time. Each kilometer she crossed that would've normally taken her a minute to achieve, was done in half the time. Then it decreased to a quarter of that. Dissatisfied, she kept cutting her time over and over. In no time at all, she approached the next guard tower and eased her momentum.

As she stopped and caught her breath, Vivian exited the tower, bidding good-bye to the guards who were on duty. She casually touched their arms and laughed coquettishly. "I have to run now. You know, busy, busy." She winked at them and left the guards starstruck with a full bag in both of her hands.

"Those scones were delicious, Viv. Wouldn't mind some more tomorrow," said one of the guards.

"I'll swing by. Have a good day, boys." She strutted over to her car.

In the mornings, Keri would run from Amazing Discoveries to the top of the valley to train her abilities. Once she was done, she'd meet up with Vivian, who was doing her rounds over at the towers, trading. The guards would always battle stray monsters that got close to the living areas. That meant they had an overflow of monster parts and items. She'd hand some of the items that Riley appraised that could be useful to them in exchange for unappraised 7s or beast remains to be used for crafting. Discoveries would either resell them or make them into something sellable.

Keri opened the passenger door. "I don't get how you can make them like that. Look at them—they're like puppies, eating right out of your hands."

"Boys are easy. Either they want food, drink, money or booty. If you can give them any one of those, you'll have their attention." She slammed the trunk close after placing her bags in.

"If it's so easy, why can't I get a simple kiss?"

"Your problem is that you're waiting for him to make a move, and you're half expecting he'll get your cues."

Whenever Keri and Wayne were together, she'd often hint to him that she wanted to have sex, like the options *Love Me, Princess* gave her when she was faced with the target men in a sexual scenario:

1. Drop a handkerchief.
2. Reveal the hems of your dress.
3. Fix your hair and makeup.

She tried all the options above. The first one, she actually tried dropping a tea towel, because she didn't have a handkerchief, to which Wayne casually picked it up without saying anything. The next day, she tried again after buying a handkerchief, but like before, he just picked up. He even added a warning that she should be aware of her own stuff because she kept dropping them.

The second option, she went a whole week wearing an ankle-length dress. Every time they would walk outside together, she would lift her dress and reveal her knees. At the end of the week, Wayne bought her two short skirts. Keri asked the reason and he told her, 'You look like you were hot in those dresses you wear, so I bought you two cool ones.'

For the third option, despite having her hair dyed all the time, Keri was not used to putting on makeup. One night, she'd brush her hair and put on makeup she'd bought at a cosmetic shop down the market. As both of them were about to go to bed, Wayne questioned her face; he wondered why she needed makeup at this time of the night. She simply said she was trying it on—to see how it looked on her. To which he responded, 'For Halloween?'

Vivian snickered in the car as Keri told the story. "Do you maybe have a picture of yourself when you did that?" she inquired.

Keri strapped on the seatbelt around her. "Why?"

"You know, for Halloween? To drive the bad spirits away?" Vivian laughed.

"Not funny, Viv. I really tried to look pretty."

"I'm sorry. I didn't mean to offend," she giggled. "Maybe don't do makeup for now."

"You're not helping."

She sighed as the car hopped on to a mechanical ramp and descended. "Look, Wayne's used to women telling him what they want. His clients are all vocal about what they want since women don't have to pretend around him. He's paid to do exactly as instructed."

"So you're saying I should pay him?"

"I mean, you should just tell him directly."

"Just tell him? *Wayne, I want to have sex*," she stated like it was the most normal thing in the world. "Will that work?"

"Have you tried it before?"

"No, but—"

"Stop with the buts and try it. If it doesn't work, worry about it next time," interjected Vivian. "How's the training?"

"Thirty kilometers under thirty minutes." Keri looked out the window when the car emerged from the ramp mechanism. The cranes plucked the cars from ramps and placed them on the bridge roads all while maneuvering away from cables cars zooming across the sky. Free people moved about in shops and cables busy with their daily life. Meanwhile, the platforms near the gates above were crowded with refugees pleading to enter the living areas. When she first got here, she felt saddened by all of it. But now she understood, the freezones, despite its thriving people, were short on resources. They barely held it together except for the guilds who were defending the transport of goods and keeping security together for farmers. Meanwhile, her home country, Zuobic, was at peace with all of the technology they'd developed keeping them safe. Would it kill them to share a ward generator, she thought as the RSTU cluster was still experiencing some rift incidents at the edge of their borders from the news she got.

"That's past human limits. You're definitely a 14," said Vivian. "I don't think we should spar any longer. With your speed, you should be practicing against other closers or monsters."

She thought the same. In the afternoons, she spent her time in the free clinics to help out with the wounded and cursed to improve her source-control. On her free days, she sparred with Vivian to train her body. "You know I can't do that," she said.

"Wayne is obstinate like that. Spectacular in bed, but too stubborn in everything else."

"Is that why you two didn't work out?"

"He was a rebound—the first man after my ex-husband. Eight years ago, I ended my long-term relationship and moved here. I met Wayne, found him easy and refreshing—he was sort of my palette cleanser."

Keri turned to her with a somber expression. "Riley knows about your ex but not Wayne?"

She nodded. "My ex was such a big part of my life, it's hard to keep that covered. But for Wayne, I don't really count him as one of my exes—more like a real good friend. Someone who taught me self-respect and to find my voice again—someone who taught me how to open my heart again to others."

"I can't believe you thought like that. You're gorgeous, you're nice, you're cool."

Vivian patted her lap. "Thanks, Keri. I appreciate you saying that."

"Hey Vivian..." The truth regarding Charlie settled at the tip of Keri's tongue.

"Give me a moment." She eased the car until they parked on the side street next to Amazing Discoveries. "Yes?" she asked with a kind expression, waiting patiently for her.

"About Charlie..." Her voice lingered while she thought, *There's an entity living inside him named Silaw who is the personification of the Will of the World, our world called Silaw—both are named the same. He's also kind of a brother to me cause my family found him the same way you did. You're also right. He's an outlier, #32, humanoids from rifts, also a vessel. I'm not super sure, but I think 32s are good vessels.*

"Yeah, it's been hard," Vivian continued the conversation.

"Hard? Has he been disappearing again?"

She nodded. "Not that long, a couple of hours within the day. But when he comes back, he sleeps for hours. I honestly don't know what's going on," her voice croaked.

Her thoughts fled to Silaw, urging her to be stronger and find him. Did that mean she should find him when he disappears?

"I'm sorry, what was it you wanted to talk about?"

Keri aborted all plans to tell Vivian about Charlie and instead asked, "About Lake, how is he?"

"Like I said before, he is working for the Apes. Though I haven't seen him since I haven't visited them in a while," she said. "I'm not so sure you should be seeing him."

"Why?"

"Not my place to tell you what to do, you're a grown woman, after all. But soldiers—Zuobic ones especially, aren't really the best partners. They're too caught up with saving the world." A lonesome expression surfaced on her face.

"But there's nothing going on between him and me," Keri explained. "We're just friends, I think. I hope he considers me as a friend."

"I know. But the way he looked at you—asking about you—especially when you were in a coma, that man wants you. Definitely more than friends."

She blushed. "I really just want to thank him for his help."

She shrugged. "Okay, whatever you say. I have a meeting with the Apes at the end of the week. Do you want me to ask about him?"

"Yes please." She hopped off the car and waved goodbye as she drove off. Passing through the back entrance, she made her way into the elevator all the way down to the basement floor of the residences. She exited the elevator and went to the apartment granted to Wayne as part of his work benefits. She had been living there after she was released from the infirmary floor.

After scanning her fingerprints, the door slid open. She noticed Wayne's boots and bag on the floor. "You're home. They said you'd be home tomorrow." She entered and made her way to the fridge for a glass of cold juice.

"Mission finished fast." Wayne left the toilet and started unpacking his bag.

Keri rested on the couch in the living room. "You, Ivo and only two other closers, escorting a caravan group of fifty people from two super far clusters, was fast? What about the monsters? Were there any?"

"Two dozen ogres and two building-sized ones."

"Did everyone die? Did you escape?"

After taking his shirt off, he grabbed all of his dirty clothes and went to the laundry room. "I killed them all."

"What? How'd you kill giant monsters?" exclaimed Keri.

Wayne returned butt-naked with his big dong hanging magnificently. "Watch this."

"I'm watching." Her eyes glued onto his penis.

A ghostly knight in shining silver-blue armor enveloped in blue flames materialized behind him. "This is my spirit knight. I call him Azure. He's my new fragment." The knight summoned a large mace and a shield and assumed a battle stance as Wayne's pecs bounced. "I look jacked, right?" Veins popped all over his arms when he flexed them.

"Mhhhm..." She wiped the drool off at the side of her mouth.

He relaxed his muscles as the knight vanished. "After I killed the two, and the system thing showed, I claimed the area. It said G-law is under my control, or something like that. Anyway, did you want to grab lunch somewhere? I could eat a horse." He headed to the bathroom.

He is naked in the shower—what do I do again? Right, be direct. Say what you want, she thought. "I-I want to...have sex," she whispered.

"How about the café next to the red bridge? You like that, don't you?" shouted Wayne as he turned the shower on.

Is he ignoring me? No, he didn't hear it. Louder. "I wanna have sex," she repeated in her normal speaking voice.

"What was that?" yelled Wayne over the running hot water.

"I want sex," she shouted at the highest pitch she could.

Suddenly the shower turned off, then a moment of silence ensued. Wayne popped his head out the bathroom door. "Did I hear that right? You, you want to have sex?" he asked with a serious face. Water dripped from his hair and face.

Now that he was staring at her, she turned beet red. She couldn't bring herself to say it again, so she nodded instead. The next moment, Wayne was already in front of the couch with his dong rising to a salute, making Keri blush. "I don't know...how to..." Her sentence was cut short as Wayne intruded with his mouth and tongue.

After a few motions of lip-locking, he came up for air. "Are you sure you're okay? You're not sick or going to pass out?" he asked.

"I'm fine." She gulped as he felt the heat of his face and body over her.

They continued to kiss. Keri went along with it. She didn't know how much time had passed, but her body went to a whole new temperature level as she became wet from arousal. He explored her with licks and kisses as he removed her clothing piece by piece, with each touch making her shiver from ecstasy. The moment his head arrived at her groin, she pushed him away.

"What?" he asked.

"I-I'm sweaty down there. I just ran." She couldn't look him in the eye.

He smirked.

"What?"

"You're cute."

"What? Heyyy—ahh!"

He scooped her up in one swing and entered the shower. After gently placing her in the tub, he turned the nozzle and let the hot water stream in. He rinsed both of them off for a good while, then stopped. His hands dabbed itself on soap then caressed her vagina. He smoothly pushed his index finger in and out of her vagina, then added another finger, then a third. All the while, Keri was panting heavily with her arms slamming against the wall. "Awo awo awo," she barked. Wayne made a weird expression but kept going. After four fingers were sliding in and out easily, she cried out, "Aaawwwooooooo!" She leaned on his chest.

"Did you...?" whispered Wayne.

"I-I think so," she replied.

He smirked. "Get ready for the next round." His dong pressed against her.

Her tits perked up. "I'm ready," she panted. *This is it, yeaahhh,* she screamed in her head.

After a few rounds, Keri exited the bathroom with a robe over her— clean, refreshed and exhausted. She collapsed over the bed with a silly smile on her face. "That was—oh my—I want more—but I'm so tired. Wow," she said to herself.

> Congratulations! You made sweet love with Target Lover #3 for the first time. 2000 coins earned. Total 7910.
> Please continue to deepen your relationship with 3 and the other targets to earn more coins.
> Congratulations! You have made love for the first time. 2500 coins earned. Total 9410.

Her eyes widened at the notifications and once again she was reminded of Silaw's advice—the reason she was training herself.

Wayne came out of the shower with a towel over his waist. "How are you?" he asked.

"It was...wow."

He got into a fresh pair of jeans. "Glad you liked it. We should grab lunch and maybe come back for a second round, what do you think?"

"Yes, definitely," agreed Keri, rising from the bed. "I could definitely eat pancakes or bacon or waffles and cake maybe."

"Got my pay from the last mission. I'll buy you anything you want."

"Uh, about that, I was thinking...I'm ready to go back to work," she voiced with enthusiasm. "Maybe the Apes have a new rift they want to close, I think I could really help this time. Every morning I'm—"

"Is Maxwell asking you to come back? I thought we agreed I'll cover for you while you're recovering. I can do both my job for Amazing and yours for the guild." He cut in as he wore a tight blue shirt.

"Uh no, he hasn't asked. It's just that I've been running a lot and training with Vivian daily. She said I'm ready to face monsters and—"

"You don't have to," he cut in again.

"I want to."

He shrugged. "I earn enough for the both of us—more than enough. I have a car we can both use. We've got a good place. Is there anything you want to buy? Is it expensive? Another car? New clothes? Shoes?"

Keri frowned. Wasn't she explaining herself properly? "I don't need to buy anything—maybe a new game or a new battle suit—something not so tight. But that's not what I really mean. I want to close rifts—defeat monsters. I'm a candidate just like you."

He crossed his arms. "Aren't you happy doing the clinic stuff?"

"I am. But it's different. Killing monsters is what we do to earn coins—what makes our fragments grow. I need that."

His face hardened. "I'm not comfortable with that. It's very dangerous in the field."

"I know. I've been there, remember?"

His face brightened. "I got it. Here." After going to the living room and back, he handed her an old brown locket.

Curse: Annoying Whispers detected on object.

Annoying Whispers: Wearer of object will suffer from nightmares when they sleep. After a month of nightmares, wearer shall experience hallucinations in the morning. Curse is absorbed from object.

Transfer curse or absorb?

Hex absorbed. Earned 100 coins. Total 9510.

"It worked, right? You got coins?" said Wayne with a joyous face.

"Yeah..." she said, then thought, *Not a lot though.*

"I'll collect these on my runs with the Apes. Problem solved. Come on. Get dressed. I'll meet you in the car." He grabbed his jacket, put on his linko and left, leaving her hanging with more questions and concerns.

Chapter 41

Lake, Generator, Shoef

A circular machine more than fifteen meters tall stood silently under a dome-shaped warehouse. Large metallic discs fitted the inside of the machine riveted with large fist-sized capacitors at the circumference. On the exterior, multiple layers of titanium casings housed the machine as thick coils of wire branched out and connected to an array of cylindrical glass cages the size of one average human. Near the machine, a latched door hung open on the steel floors. Lake was welding machinery underground that was hooked onto the ward generator. Sparks flew from his fingertips through his newly improved S-Glove.

From a hastily put together contraption, the S-Glove 2.0 now enveloped his whole arm up to his shoulders as a grey, thick, skintight semi-liquid material. It offered flexibility, durability, protection and comfort, while also acting as a shield and as clothes. Most of its composition was produced from the carcass of a slime monster while the glowing violet lines and dot patterns resembling chipsets were from a new technology called mana circuits. Recently developed by Zurciks, mana circuits were a re-envisioning of beast cores—not just a source of energy, but to be the actual circuit board itself. The new tech paved the way for small and lightweight items perfect for closers. Currently, mana circuits were only available in shotgun-sized cannons and bomb-sized grenades. Lake took the idea further and constructed them as wearable material for both offense and defense.

"How's my favorite engineer?" asked Maxwell from the control room separated from the rest of the space, with glass windows and steel walls.

On his head, Lake wore a black visor that wrapped around and protected his head and eyes. Made from a tough beetle monster, he saw through the glowing violet line in the center. The S-Visor served as protection, visual display, scanner and his linko all at the same time. "Hey Maxwell, give me a sec," he said.

Maxwell gestured at a few assistants who entered from another entrance controlling hover carts with numerous crates stacked on it. "I brought you your request," he ordered them from the communications board inside the control room.

The S-Visor retracted to his ears as he ceased welding with his S-Glove. "Are those the monster cores?" After closing the latch on the floor, he inspected the cores in the crates.

"Is this enough?"

"More than enough. Did you send some to Zone Rumaf?"

"Of course, they got their refill already. Who do you think you're talking to?" He stood straight.

"Just asking."

"When will you be done?"

Lake opened a second latch on the floor and started transferring the cores into it. "I only need to fill it up and make some final adjustments." He ordered the assistants to empty the other crates as well.

A click-clack of heels echoed from the speakers as Vivian appeared next to Maxwell inside the room. "Sounds exciting," she said.

"Lake, I'd like you to meet Vivian. She's the chief of trade and finance of Amazing Discoveries," introduced Maxwell. "She's the reason we could get this plenty of cores."

He nodded at her. "I'm trying to focus on getting this done. Forgive me if I don't go over and shake your hand."

She flicked her hair. "I'm the one intruding on your work time. I should apologize. I do admit I am very excited for the new generator for Zone Shoef. I've seen and heard a lot of good things from Zone Untef —my expectations are high."

The last ward generators for Zone Untef were faulty to a degree. Apart from warding against the rift for only eight hours continuously due to overheating, it consumed a lot of cores to power it up. The new generator Lake had made addressed the timing issue and extended the run-time so it could be a twenty-four-seven operating device with minimal maintenance that only needed once a day in a week to power down. The core consumption was also cut in half.

"And Hairless Ape's best engineer won't let you down," Maxwell boasted. "This generator will keep our zone safe from rifts—no surprises at all throughout the week. Except for one day for maintenance—which Hairless Ape and the other guilds are already coordinating to handle the downtime for patrols and raids."

"Sounds promising," said Vivian, her voice echoing in the speakers with Maxwell. "There was a rumor I overheard that the new generator not only wards against rifts, but monsters as well. Is that true?"

He crossed his arms. "I can certainly see how that rumor started. I witnessed it myself."

Her brow raised. "Do tell."

He proceeded by telling her about an incident from a patrol he was working on near the borders of Untef and the lawless lands. A horde of centaurs wound up chasing his team and they assumed a tactical retreat back to their vehicles. But centaurs, being agile and swift, were able to catch up to them. Once the closer team neared the guard towers, the centaurs started turning back like a line was drawn that they could not cross. This same thing happened with other guilds and ordinary freemen who sought shelter in Zone Untef. From then on, the number of refugees seeking shelter at Untef exploded because of the rumors. "I wouldn't believe it if I wasn't there to see it myself," finished Maxwell.

"But was there any change to the actual generator to make them turn away?" asked Vivian.

"As far as I know, my team improved all the problems but didn't add any features," he said. "Otherwise, I would've charged the mayor more. Right, Lake?"

"Uh yeah." Lake glanced at the system open in his peripheral vision. The item Area Shielding floated on the screen. It had the power to protect a claimed area from unaffiliated beings—which meant monsters and probably people. He had been testing this item out coincidentally when he finished the ward generator, so it probably was the reason for monsters avoiding Untef since technically he, being the owner, was in constant conflict with them. But as to the details, it was still confusing. The system kept advising him that only allied entities could cross.

"That is indeed intriguing," said Vivian.

Lake closed the latch after filling up the hole with cores up to the brim. "That should do it." He entered the control room and observed multiple floating screens. "Status check," he ordered.

"Power from Core Nest 1 stable," stated an assistant. "2 stable. 3 is stable..." He went on to report each storage of cores as stable.

"All right. Start it up."

"Starting generator."

Light and electric waves flooded the cylindrical cages as the discs started up. A loud hum reverberated in the air with minute vibrations disturbing the metal floors. From 20 degrees, the temperature ascended to the thirties as the discs rotated in 330km/h, causing almost everyone to remove their jackets and second layers. When the sound of the machinery settled to a serene oscillation, the temperature fell to 27 degrees and the cages dimmed, a soft pink light exploded from the machine and pushed itself out all the way to the borders of Zone Shoef.

> Congratulations for Creating a Ward Generator to keep the people of Zone Shoef safe from outliers.
> You are rewarded with 50,000 coins.
> It is recommended to claim Zone Shoef to enjoy the full benefits of your achievements.

Lake read the notices carefully. Like before with Zone Untef, he had received a lot of coins for creating a ward generator. Though the last was around 10k less than what he had just received. He attributed this to the population difference of the zone with Untef being smaller than Shoef. But ever since rumors of the monsters staying away from Untef spread, the number of refugees had increased, resulting in larger coin rewards. He theorized that the system rewarded him when he saved people however the manner it may be, directly or indirectly. Therefore, continuing with the generator projects, though strenuous, was very fruitful.

> You have consumed Area Claim Crystal. Current Area: Zone Shoef has been claimed by Hero.
> Areas Claimed: Quisix, Zone Pugof, Zone Untef, Zone Shoef, Zone J-law

> Two refugees have settled in your territory. 200 coins for providing safety and security.

"Temperature has stabilized to 28 degrees to 29 degrees, RoR has decelerated to 302 km/h, Core 1 has reached 80..." the assistant reported on each part of the generator.

It seemed like getting more areas under his control was the best option for getting more coins. Lake checked his own status:

> CANDIDATE STATUS:
> Name: Lake Deskenn | Profile: Hero | Coins: 18,250
> Activated Fragments: Soul Weaving – A, Hero's Retreat – F (innate), Mind's Eye – C, Outlier Materials Expert – C, Bisenti Craftsman – A, Spatial Apprentice – D, Enduring Body – E
> Available Fragments Left: 1

A lot of his fragments had improved during his work with the generators, including Soul Weaving, Mind's Eye and the new ones he'd acquired: Craftsman and Materials Expert. He wondered how he would fair against monsters now that he had changed. It had been a while since he left to kill monsters, apart from that one time he'd travelled to Zone J-Law which was the closest lawless land from Untef and claimed the area for his experiments. One significant result from that experiment was that to increase his available fragments he could claim more areas without buying them with coins. Consequently, it increased his authority as well. What was authority? The system mentioned it's the influence he had on entities and areas. The explanation was pretty vague. He added it to the list of things to experiment with.

When the report finished, Lake said, "Good work, everyone. Keep monitoring the machinery for forty-eight hours. Report to me with any inconsistencies."

"Congratulations on your second working generator." Vivian shook his hand.

"Thanks."

"Amazing Discoveries has a lot of artifacts and 7s you could use to experiment with," said Maxwell. "I mentioned you being a sorcerer and ability user. Hairless

Ape's secrets and contracts extend to Amazing Discoveries, so you won't have to worry about anything."

"If you want me to sign a personal non-disclosure agreement, I'll sign one right now," she offered.

The fragment: Outlier Materials Expert grew by Lake touching and manipulating materials that were from the rift. He had used most of the stock from Ape and he had grown the rank from F to C. The difficulty of increasing his rank rose with every rank he had achieved. Therefore, exploring another stock of outliers was good news. "I'm simply a 14. Sorcery doesn't go well with my abilities. If Maxwell trusts you, I trust you. I also want to hire you to identify some of the 7s I got from a previous 2. Want to make sure nothing's useful before I deconstruct them." His Mind's Eye offered similar abilities to appraising, but he'd rather outsource the work than do it himself.

"We offer the best appraising in all the freezones. I'll schedule meetings and send it to your linko," said Vivian. "There's nothing simple about a 14. We look forward to working with you."

Lake shook hands with her. "Same here."

Chapter 42

Keri, Amazing Discoveries, Troef (Past)

Chatterbox, the young, adopted brother Keri remembered him as, turned to the twenty-year-old Keri with a troubled face. "I am not Charlie. I am not the Chatterbox you named. I am Silaw, the Will of this World. Do not try to force yourself to do anything. Your soul and body have been damaged greatly. I can only mend your body in my current state. It will take decades for you to fully heal—or you can heal it yourself once you form your fragments. But with your soul damaged, it will be difficult."

Keri relived the same scene she had remembered from her dreams. But this time, she was the observer rather than the person experiencing everything. She stared at her younger self and Silaw.

Silaw's sights focused outside the window of the orphanage. "Come. There are other matters we have to take care of." He touched young Keri and they both disappeared from sight.

The scenes blurred as the environment changed from the neighborhood in Kermoz to the control room of the media broadcasting tower in the same zone. Silaw and the younger Keri appeared in a large room, seemingly cloaked from everyone. Present Keri materialized next to them.

"Keri?" a familiar male voice sounded next to her.

Present Keri turned to her left and saw an attractive man in jeans and a shirt. "Lake? You're here." She hugged him.

"What's wrong? Where's here? Is this Kermoz?" He held her for a while before letting go and observing the room around him.

Zuobic soldiers manned the area as they stood guard at the entrances and in hallways while scientists scrambled from one computer panel to another. Panicked expressions hardened further whenever they checked their screens and smashed the keys of the computer. Some cursed while others cried out. With each command they typed, more and more sweat poured from their pores. Some of their shoulders drooped while others trembled. The monitors that floated around them showed all the mayhem that ensued in the streets of Zone Kermoz. Black human-like monsters with colorful capes summoned fireballs to destroy buildings and tornadoes to blow people away.

Lake looked at the screens and the soldiers. "Is this that day? The rift in Kermoz? I was at the Rainbow Amusement Park when it all went down. Remember?" he asked.

Keri nodded and pointed to her younger self and Charlie observing the soldiers. "This is the part where I was. A memory that I shut out." She told him of the circumstances that led to this point.

"Is that for real?" asked Lake. "This Silaw person made you a candidate?"

Before Keri could answer, a younger Cervantes with fewer lines on his face stormed the room. "You stupid imbeciles. Close the rift now," he commanded with a deep voice.

Lake gawked at the major. "Major Cervantes? What's happening?" He hovered over the screens, trying to read everything he could. After a few moments, a horrified expression replaced his confusion.

"What's wrong?" asked Keri. "What are they doing?"

He tried to speak, but it seemed like a lump was caught in his throat. "They-they opened a rift," he said in a low voice.

Keri shook her head. "How? What?"

"Sir, we've tried using the inverse frequency of the ray, but it still doesn't work," said one of the scientists. "I've tried it three times now."

"Try reversing the process with the same frequency and the inverse," ordered Cervantes.

"But sir, I've done that already," the scientist said.

Cervantes roared, "Imbeciles!"

An assistant rushed to his side. "Sir, we've tried everything we can think of. We are out of options."

"I am truly surrounded by idiots."

A soldier approached him and said, "Sir, your wife, I mean, Sergeant Cervantes is here to see you. Should I turn her away?"

"What is it now? I'm busy," he hounded, turning red. "Can't you see what's going on outside?"

The soldier paled as he was sprayed with saliva. "Sir, it's about the baby," he whispered.

"Incompetent woman." He stormed to the exit to meet his wife.

At the corner of the room, where the shadows cloaked the corners, Charlie was sitting next to twenties Keri, who was watching the scene. A golden mist covered them, shielding them from the sights of normal human eyes. While Charlie observed the events with a focused gaze, Keri leaned against the wall, clutching the video game her mom had given her. Present Keri could somehow feel and know what younger Keri was experiencing. And she knew her mind, body and soul were all shattered. It barely held together to make her function. She was surprised she was still alive at the time.

A golden wisp materialized next to them. "Great Silaw, I have returned. Apologies, I have died and failed to fulfill my tasks. How may I serve?"

Silaw pointed at the frazzled scientists. "You did what you could, Fynn. No one expected that our own people would betray us. Zuobic has reached a technological breakthrough—they have created a portal to the other worlds."

Fynn gasped as much as a wisp with no mouth could. "It was as the enemy Will had said. Without the protection of the outworlds—"

"Wills are free to invade, claim souls and areas and kill candidates," he finished. "If it was not for this unprepared vessel, I would not have been able to stop it."

At the doors, Cervantes had finished his conversation outside and returned. He read messages from his glassy. "Listen, new orders from the president and general, initiate main explosives," he shouted.

A soldier with a purple badge for captain stepped up. He had red hair and freckles on his nose. "The nuke, sir? Do you want me to evacuate the soldiers and the civilians?" he asked.

"Tony?" Lake said, looking at the captain.

"Do you know him?" asked Keri.

"I think he's Tony's dad. I think his name was Paulo Gallagher,' said Lake. "Tony was right about Cervantes."

Keri wanted to ask another question but stopped after seeing a sad look on Lake's face.

"Monster killing is our priority, but if we do that, we will wipe out innocent lives—children, women, men—healthy people and even the sick—everyone," explained Captain Gallagher. "Please let me issue an evacuation before we go through the worst."

"Target has been set to triangulate the rift," announced one of the scientists. "I've calibrated the trigger button to your linko, sir."

Cervantes nodded. "Everyone, evacuate immediately."

The captain reached for his supervisor's sleeve. "Sir, with all due respect, this is wrong. Please, let me evacuate ten people at least."

Cervantes set his deadpan gaze on his hand, then his face as he slowly let go. "Captain Gallagher, I order you to escort the scientists back to base this instant," ordered the major.

His head shifted down as his shoulders sagged. "Yes, sir," he answered with a tinge of sadness.

One by one, the people in the room set their computers to self-destruct, then they fetched their bags and other things before leaving for the exit. No one stopped to chat, exchanged opinions or expressed their dislike or approval of the situation—all Zuobic personnel—soldiers and scientists evacuated with haste.

The halls and room quickly emptied until Cervantes was the last one left. He moved towards the exit and closed the doors halfway. When only a small space was open, he reached for his linko and activated the explosions. A countdown commenced on the biggest screen. He glowered at it before leaving, closing the doors shut.

At the corner of the room, Fynn flew around and hovered at the screens where the people were being attacked by caped monsters. "Scientist, mages—they are all the same. I detest them," complained the wisp.

Silaw shrugged. "This is the nature of humans and souls who pursue answers to questions beyond them. Enough of this chatter, I must close the hole they have made." He came closer to the screens.

The wisp buzzed in the air. "Are you able to stop this bomb as well?"

"If I can, I will. But sadly, I'm afraid I'll have to give up this space to seal the hole they have made."

"What about Keri?" Fynn floated above twenties Keri.

He returned to her, glancing at her condition and the video game. His left hand touched the box while his right pressed on her chest. A golden mist floated from the game and entered into her body. The heftiness she felt in her chest lightened by a tad bit as the scenes in her head slowly made sense.

"What did you do, Great Silaw?"

"I've mended the damage to her soul with a clean soul fashioned from the game's characters. It will hold her sanity and keep her functioning until she can heal herself."

The golden wisp turned bright orange. "Won't that corrupt her'? Two souls cannot mix. Even if it's a clean and fresh one, her own would reject the other."

Silaw tucked away the stray hairs on her face. "I've bound it as a fragment. It should suffice, though I'm not sure what this will do when her abilities grow. See to her safety. You are not allowed to talk to her or influence her decisions in any way." He moved towards the windows, gazing at the bright rift.

"I understand. But what of you?"

A gentle smile crossed his face. "Helping her is the best way to help me. Maiden, please call me when you are able."

Fynn rested above Keri's head. "We shall leave now." They vanished in a flash.

***

In her room in a shared apartment with Wayne, Keri jolted awake back into her reality. Sweat dripped from her face and back as she panted heavily. Her hand gripped her chest and crumpled her shirt. The thing inside of her, what was it? Her head was clear of her memories of the past. Right after that incident in Kermoz, she was given financial support by the army to get herself back on track. But the whole time she thought she was an orphan, alone ever since she was a child—but that backstory was Princess Bolo's history. The princess was an orphan until the queen mother found her in her teens. She had been kidnapped when she was a baby due to a power struggle for the throne. Wait—this was not her memory. It was someone else's. She was a Richforth, the daughter of two soldiers who served as desk officers in the army. "What is wrong with me?" She breathed out, clutching her head.

"Keri, you awake?" said Wayne from the kitchen.

Her heart skipped a beat. In a split second, she was already inside the bathroom, locking the door. Footsteps resounded as Wayne seemed to pace at the other side of the door. "Is everything okay? You're up early," he said.

The feelings she had for Wayne overflowed from her—these disgusting, lusty desires overwhelmed her. Her aspirations did not end at being someone's love interest—that was fine for some people, but not for her. Her dream lied in helping refugees and the less fortunate, uplifting the lives that had been ruined by outliers. Getting married and being fucked by a lot of beautiful hot men were fantasies of Princess Bolo. "Who am I?" she murmured.

"What was that?" asked Wayne.

"I have diarrhea. It's really bad. Some went on the floor," she babbled in panic and thought, *What am I saying?*

"Uh—okay. Do you want me to get you something?"

She screamed on the inside for Wayne to go away. "No, I'm good. Go to work." She put her palms on her mouth and blew, mimicking farting and excreting sounds.

"That sounds bad. Ah, okay. Um, we're escorting a transport again. I'll be back tomorrow. If you need me, call me, I'll be here as soon as I can."

"Don't worry about me." She pretend-farted again.

"Take care. See you. Bye."

After five minutes, she opened the bathroom door and peaked outside. When she confirmed it was all clear, she made herself coco and sat at the dining table. As the chocolate warmed her insides, she frowned. She put the cup down. Morning cups of coco were the princess' go-to drink, not hers. "It looked like shit anyway."

After discarding the drink in the sink, she fixed herself a cup of tea instead—Keri Richforth's morning routine.

It started from there. Keri nitpicked at everything she did. At the table while eating, Richforth would usually have one leg on the chair while the other hung freely. When she found herself sitting daintily and with manners, like a princess, she'd revert back to Richforth comfort. At the clinic, in her five-minute breaks, she would normally search online in her glassy for news. But the sites she visited ended up being clothing stores with hot male models in it. The act was too much like what Bolo would do, so she ended up taking a quick walk around the block to clear her head. Even at home, though she found herself lusting after Wayne, she'd smile and talk her way out of situations when he would get close.

"I have a headache, sorry," she said when he'd almost kiss her.

When he hugged her from the back, she extricated herself from him. "My tummy hurts."

"Monthly period, sorry," she stated the next time.

When Wayne confronted her about all these ailments, stating his concern that it could be something more, she lied, "I'll see the doctor and let you know."

The next time he came home, she took it upon herself to cook for the night. When he questioned her about it, she said, "I know I haven't been the best these days, I'm trying to make it up to you. Besides aren't you sick of take-out?" Though she implied it was all for him, truthfully it was all for her. She'd make herself so busy in the kitchen cooking and cleaning up that she would not have any time for Wayne. By the time she finished everything, he was passed out on their bed waiting for her. When morning came, he'd be gone for another mission.

One morning, she woke up again from a successful night of evading her lover. Though a big part of her lusted after him, she couldn't bring herself to do what Bolo would do. After dressing in green workout clothes, she rode the elevator to the lobby. Her body leaned on the corner of the elevator as hopes of running around the border could suppress the weighing guilt in her heart. The lift stopped at a lower floor and slid open. A beautiful young man entered with a sullen expression. In his hand, he crumpled an intricately decorated leather eye mask. When the doors closed, he banged his head on it as tears burst out. He bawled. His shoulders hunched as his fists punched the door once, then twice. Tears kept flowing from his pretty face. He was far from an ugly crier—the saltwater droplets made him appear more angelic and heart-breaking. It was unfair that a man could be this attractive at such a painful moment.

When the elevator jingled, he wiped his face with his sleeves and shook his head. As the doors slid open, more light streamed from the outside and brightened his sunken face, making him more recognizable.

Keri was hesitant before, thinking it could not possibly be him. But now she was certain. "Lake?" she called to him as he stepped out.

Lake turned to her with a hint of shock, embarrassment, then shame.

Chapter 43

Lake, Cluster RSTU

Earlier in the day, in his apartment in Zone Untef, the doorbell jingled. Lake placed his coffee on the kitchen bench and opened the door.

Maxwell entered and looked around. "Woah, looks and smells like an antique store in here. You do know the guild has a storage unit. You could put these over there." He pointed at the spears, fangs and other assortments scattered in boxes in the apartment.

The engineer had earned all of this from his trips to Quisix and he had been trading them for large amounts of money and other resources with Amazing Discoveries.

"It's fine. I'm used to it. How can I help?" He opened the backpack and started taking out more items he had gotten from his trip.

He started testing the blades stacked on a corner. "There's a weird thing happening in Quisix."

"Like what?"

"My team tried to go back and check on the area, but there was an invisible barrier around it. They went around it and there was no way in. Above or below. Do you know anything about it?"

Lake had set the setting for Quisix to allow entry to only him. He explained the nuances of claiming a territory for candidates like him. "...and these all came from there."

Maxwell was quiet for a while before he responded, "Not that I'm not grateful for everything you've done, but this candidate thing, I can't shake the feeling that this could be something bigger."

"You're not wrong about that. What I told you is all from experimentation," he said. "There's more, but I don't want to say anything until I'm sure about them."

He pouted. "Makes me really jealous. Is there an application somewhere for it?"

His thoughts fled to Keri. He assumed she started the whole initiation at WalkBy from what Keri had told him in their dreams together. "I'll let you know once a spot opens up," he said.

"Not afraid of having competition? I might claim all the territory there is and leave you hanging." He crossed his arms.

Lake started to put some weapons and monster parts he didn't need inside his pack. "As long as monsters don't have it, I don't care who owns them."

"You sure about that?"

After grabbing a stack of capes, he looked up at him. "What do you mean?"

"Your army friends have publicized outlier 14. They've confirmed that ability users are indeed real, and they're asking if anyone who knows of any clues about them could come forward."

He shook his head as he dumped all the cape into the bag. "They've always been looking for sorcerers and item users—now it's 14 too."

"They've been turning all freezones and stray camps upside down for these people. It's more than recruiting. It's harassment—kidnapping."

"Thanks for letting me know. But I don't know if I can help with anything. I haven't been there in months. And I was in training, not a full-fledged soldier," he said. "And all these new powers? I'm still trying things out."

Maxwell showed a video from his glassy. The scuffle at the convenience store played out. "What about this?" he asked.

"Where'd you get that?" Lake felt like a bone was stuck in his throat.

"It's been circulating around the dark web. A lot of people are saying Zuobic is looking for these people. There is also a reward for anyone who finds them."

Why is Cervantes after us? Will he experiment on us too? Kermoz's last moments before destruction flashed in his head. "Is that true?" he asked.

Maxwell shrugged and pocketed the glassy. "You know what my theory is. This was the start of the candidate selection, and Zuobic knows that. Now they're looking for everyone in this video, figuring they might be some super powered people."

"I think so too. But I need to confirm that, and I think I need to talk to Keri about it." After removing a load of flasks from his pack, Lake smoothed his hair. He spotted the elixir he had gotten from the red mage and placed it in his pocket.

"She's been up and about already for a few days. Haven't you seen her?"

He shook his head. "Been busy." He had been busy, but after the last dream, he wasn't sure how to talk to her. Wouldn't she blame him for Kermoz? Not like he was one of the soldiers assigned to the mission, but he was part of the army. Or was he? *This is annoying and confusing.*

"If you ever know more about the army or this candidate thing, let me know. A lot of our members don't take kindly to federates or their army. There's been a lot of beef, not just with the Apes, but closers in general."

Lake recalled the endless competition between human resources between the empire, the federation and other big nations, leaving freezones mostly defenseless. Guilds were mostly stuck trying to help freezones, creating a living for themselves and helping free people. "Then why'd you trust me?" he asked.

"You saved us."

"Simple as that?"

Maxwell shrugged. "It is unless you make it complicated. Right now, I want to trust you—no, I do trust you. Tomorrow might be different."

"I'd never break—

He held a hand up. "What if your superior comes knocking on this door asking you to come back? What then?"

"That doesn't mean anything. It's not like I'll reveal any secrets if I went back to the army." He expressed himself with a gesture of his hands.

"Are you really saying that? Being here, knowing about us, and what Zuobic's goals are?"

An odd silence filled the space between them. He realized that all of the information such as who they were, what they do, what they were like, equipment they have and more could all be used against them. If Zuobic wanted to, with his intel, they could ambush them, steal their supplies, items and abduct special people. Not that they would—at least that's what he'd thought before. But now, he wasn't so sure.

"Anyway, I've been looking at your pack and that bag is not getting any fuller," said the guild leader. "What is that?"

Lake figured it would gain his attention, so he showed it off: the mana circuits that lined the cloth, the big hole inside and its sturdy, durable and colorful material. "I call it S-Pack." The simple yet fashionable bag was powered with monster cores and had a capacity equal to the size of a small room. The only caveat was that the item must fit through the hole of the bag or it could not enter.

He rubbed his chin with his hand. "How much for one?"

Lake turned down his advances for acquiring the product or producing it. Further, he explained that this was a testing phase. Anything to do with mass productions or custom orders tracked near the bottom of his to-do list. "Is that all? I have to go meet Riley. I'm running late." After putting on his S-Pack, he opened the door and gestured to him to follow.

Maxwell tailed after him with a blank face. "One more thing, the results from Tony's autopsy came back. Here it is. If you want to talk, I'm a good listener." He tapped on his glassy, sending the file.

His S-Visor hummed when a lens formed from the left ear and covered his left eye. The report opened inside the lens as he walked. Tony's legs and eye conditions were highlighted in yellow, detailing his state before he died. He scanned through them quickly and stopped at a paragraph at the end: 'T-30 mins before the subject's death...'

Lake sneered at the remark, like Tony was never alive, like he didn't have any feelings or relationships. His whole life was reduced to *subject* and that was it. He had not noticed Maxwell waving goodbye as he went on with his way.

He continued to read: '...the subject experienced mass clotting in the limbs due to ferric chloride poisoning and outlier venom. Strain and type mostly associated with R1X1 with 83% likelihood. Venom is a nonlethal substance if it comes into contact with the skin with 95% chances of survival. Venom poses no inherent effects or exacerbation when mixed with ferric chloride.'

Lake left the cable car on his way to Amazing Discoveries with a perturbed expression. *How did Tony die if there was a 95% chance of survival from the venom?* he thought to himself.

'The venom was lethal due to it entering several open wounds. In this state, the subject would have experienced mild paralysis, disorientation and shortness of breath due to arteries thinning and slowing of blood circulation. If treated quickly with anti-venom or detoxification spells as first aid, the subject would have had a higher chance of surviving. But the subject was treated with healing spells: Mending Touch and Blessed Rejuvenation. Mending Touch, a 1-rune healing spell, is a first-aid spell that regenerated tissues. At this level, it would have only had a mild effect. Any regeneration of tissues would only help to speed up blood circulation and oxygen transfer in the body to heal it. Without removing the poison, it would serve as a detriment. When Blessed Rejuvenation was cast, an 8-rune healing spell, the effects of the poison were increased several times, therefore hastening the subject's death."

"Are you okay?" asked Riley.

Lake sat on a desk-chair inside the appraiser's unruly storage room on a floor inside Amazing Discoveries. He waited for the woman to sort through the items he brought in his S-Pack while he read. "Huh—what?" He tore himself away from the lens of the S-Visor and focused on her.

"Are you reading a horror article? You look like you've been spooked." Riley was moving items from the bag into a pile on the floor.

"A random battle report," he answered with a straight face. "Did you say something?"

"I've stacked all the things I'm going to buy here, and these items are for auction, and these ones are my pending stuff. I'll send the price list later," she said. "Here are the things you ordered before."

Lake walked over to a pile of materials inside a crate and started filling his empty pack again. As each item entered his bag, he realized other things he could've done to save Tony. A bar of orichalcum went in as he thought of bandaging Tony's wounds instead of healing him. A monocle outlier artifact for ghostly entities in, while he thought about carrying Tony to a proper medic. A cloth cut from a death knight's cape in, and a thought of ordering Tony to stay out of the mage fight. A tuft of harpy feathers, this time wondering if he should have let Tony oversleep that day instead of waking him. As each item filled his bag, the weight stayed the same because of the outlier technology he had installed. He wished for the same upgrade for the increasing burden on his heart.

"Lake, yooohoo, anyone there?" Riley waved her hand in the air from across the room.

Lake broke away from his own thoughts. "Huh? What?"

"Ya sure about selling this one?" She held up an intricately designed leather mask without holes. It was the useable and undamaged mask he had salvaged from the three red lizard mages in Quisix.

"Is there anything different with that?"

Goggles materialized over her face as she inspected the face mask up close. "It isn't that great, but I think 17s can use it. It allows the user to see source and energy. Basically, kind of like X-ray or thermal vision. I don't think a lot of people can use it anyway if they aren't sorcerers. It's one of those picky 7s for 8s."

Some items and artefacts (outlier #7) were selective of who could wield them; it made the pool for owners (item users, closers or outlier #8s) even smaller. Lake had a way around this rule through his Soul Weaving. He'd bind the source and user's soul together to make them compatible. He'd only recently learned how to do it through Maxwell's requests. "Do you...do you think, if someone blind could use it, they could see?" he asked.

The goggles Riley wore extended like binoculars, zooming in on the mask further. "It shuts the user's normal vision so they can definitely feel the source around him. A blind person can use this surely. But again, the chances of finding a person compatible this is slim. Much less for blind people. Ya sure ya don't want this?"

He cleared all the things he needed and closed his bag. "No, you can keep it." He slipped his bag on his back.

"Okay. Easy-peasy." She placed the mask on top of a half-filled crate.

Lake left the storeroom and went to the elevator. His palms pressed against the scanner. Then he chose the ground floor when floor options surfaced in the panel of the scanner. He waited. He thought of things he could've said to Tony; 'You're blind—you won't be able to help. You're crippled—you'll hold me back. You're a nuisance—you'll be in the way.' Cruel things, but necessary things to keep him alive. He'd rather have him hate and disregard him if it meant he could have lived.

But he didn't, and it was all because of him. He died because of him. Tony died because he killed him.

With a hard expression, he turned and stomped back into the storeroom. His sights focused on the leather mask lying atop the crate close to Riley. "I'm taking it back," he said.

"Uh, okay," said Riley with mild surprise.

Lake swiped it from the crate and stormed out of the storeroom. The elevator chimed when he was meters from it. The moment it opened, he slipped in, turned about. The doors closed shut. He slammed his head on the door, crumpled the mask in his hands; tears burst from his eyes. *I killed him,* he said in a never-ending rhyme in his head. He punched the door; tears streamed down his face. His fingers rubbed against the leather mask, like it was his most precious thing. *If only...* The strings of what-ifs haunted his thoughts. Then, he yanked it on both sides, like it was the most hideous thing. When he realized he was about to destroy it, he let go and pocketed the damn thing. He punched the wall this time when the elevator stopped at the ground floor. The bell jingled and the doors slid aside. He snorted the bawling back and wiped his face with his sleeve.

Upon stepping out, someone called out for him, someone he distinctly knew the voice of. For a millisecond, he thought the voice was coming from his right or left. Then he realized it was from behind—unable to stop himself from turning back—unable to change his shocked face. After confirming his guess about the voice, to whom it belonged to, a tinge of familiarity and positivity rocked his heart. Shame tore at his insides. How could he feel happy just by looking at her, knowing he had killed his friend?

Chapter 44

Keri, Roads of Troef

Traffic signal warnings from cable cars and cranes; commuters bustling to reach their destinations; colleagues chatting about work; kids playing ball in the side-streets; floating billboards hovering on air with their propellers; cars honking, demanding their way—all of those noises filled the vast space of the valley. But no matter how loud they were, no matter how people talked, how motors sounded or devices blared, nothing could pierce the silence between Keri and Lake as they walked to no place, to no destination whatsoever. After both of them had left the elevator, it was simply one leg over the other to wherever they'd end up.

Keri Bolo would have intruded—asked him what was wrong. She would even insert her own opinions. Her lips would not have held back. In contrast, Keri Richforth would sit down with him, spend time with him and give him space until he was ready to talk. But the Keri with Lake now was not a Bolo, nor was she entirely certain she was a Richforth.

A passing ice cream store caught her eye. With quick feet, she went to the store, bought two vanilla and chocolate cones and rushed back to Lake. She slowed to his pace and gestured for him to choose. He looked at it like it was an alien sort of thing—something he had never seen before. Keri sighed and forced the vanilla one into his hand. Lake, again, stared at the white thing like it was some sort of puzzle in need of a solution. Keri licked her chocolate ice cream and smiled at its sweetness. Like a clueless child, he copied her and licked the ice cream. Once, then twice, then again and again. Keri smiled again, from the ice cream and the company whose grim state she had broken through.

Keri spoke, "When I was little, I always had this fantasy that I'd become a princess, and a prince would come for me and swear eternal love to me. But growing up, I found that boys weren't really interested in me. They preferred someone who was thinner, bigger boobs, bigger ass, prettier—not this hair, or these clothes, or this face—someone different. So I found other boys that were interested in me. Boys in a game.

"It's always nice when they asked how my day was going, or if I had seen the show and would like to go out, or if I wanted to try the new dessert—they'd always smile at me, ask me questions, really wait for me to answer, like really wait. They don't just butt into the conversation trying to get past you, like you're some kind of obstacle in a relay race. And at the end of the date, they'd kiss me, or they'd ask me in or they'd wait for me to ask them in—they actually wanted to touch me, make love to me, be with me." Tears built up in her eyes.

Lake opened his mouth to speak. But Keri cut him off and continued, "I know they weren't real. I know they're just fantasies, I'm not crazy. But sometimes I wish I was. I've met a lot of guys in my life, but nothing comes close to when a boy in a game looks into your eyes, tells you you're the most beautiful girl he has ever seen and makes love to you with his eyes open." Tears fell freely from her face, and she let them. There was something about Lake that brought out her truths and not make her feel any awkwardness nor shame.

He rubbed her back. "I'm sorry you felt like that," he said.

She forced herself to finish her ice cream, then wiped her face with tissues from her pockets. "There's no need to feel sorry for me. I don't even know if that one was true. I hate crying." She snorted.

"What do you mean?"

"I'm an ugly crier, can't you see?"

He shook his head. "Not that—what you said—is it not real?"

"Oh, I don't know. That is what I remember. But I don't know if that was true or not," she reminded him of the details of her last dream, where Silaw merged a new soul and the game with her.

Lake's gaze hardened. "Did you ask Charlie about that?"

"I tried to ask him more. But he was being really dodgy about it," Keri complained. "No, you're still healing—you can't have all the answers. Like that makes a difference."

"I see. If that's the case, I think we should wait until you're better. We can't push you to know this if there's consequences."

Keri pouted. "I thought you'd be on my side. Like charge him and demand he answer our questions. We need answers."

"Yeah, but would you really do that, Charlie? I mean, he's still a kid, and there's a super-being living inside him. That must be difficult." He made a crestfallen expression.

She sighed. "But it's unfair. I want the answers now. I need help. These things in my head are driving me insane. I'm not good with thinking too much."

"Well, how about we concentrate on things you do know first. Maybe stick to that then sort out the other things you remember?" he asked. "And for the record, you're not an ugly crier."

She blushed. "Sure. Whatever."

"Okay. What do you know to be true?"

As she recounted the facts, they ate the ice cream, and then they were atop the landscape, next to a guard tower, overlooking the vast valley. They both sat on a bench near the edge. It went as followed:

- Keri grew up and lived with her real parents, Portia and Xander Richforth, until the Kermoz incident.

- After, she was in a mental institution for recovery, then got a job at Padala Services. While she was there, she believed she was an orphan from when she was eight.

- She vaguely remembered Fynn telling her about Silaw and his candidates both as a child and as an adult.

"It gets confusing, if I remember anything about Silaw and the system," Keri grumbled. "It's like, which one is which?"

Lake stretched his neck. "Let's talk about that then. What do you know of the system?"

Fynn would open the story with a faraway kingdom that is invaded by monsters from the skies. The people of the land prayed to the Will of the World to help them survive. The Will answered their call and gifted special powers to people who had special souls.

"That doesn't really give you or me any facts," Lake said in exasperation. "Is there anything more substantial than that?"

"Fynn always told it like a story," she answered. "Removing all the fluffy stuff, I think:

1. Silaw selects candidates who have special souls through a test.

2. Candidates are supposed to increase their authority.

3. Candidates are divided into active and passive types.

4. To become a true candidate, they have to gain followers."

"Wait. Silaw wasn't there in WalkBy, was he?" asked Lake.

Keri thought about this, and strangely, she had the answers for it. "What happened in WalkBy, that's a test. Whatever happens in that dimension are like simulations that don't affect real life.

"And I think I triggered that test, that reality warp to happen. My fragment, Prima, aside from keeping my souls stable and suppressing all these memories in my head, it gave me the authority to call for help when the Will of the World cannot."

"That's likely. I assume Silaw's indisposed because he plugged the hole in the outworlds? I think the outworlds were these dimensions, the worlds inside the rifts. They always appear like a number in the system. They're there to hold off the invaders for a while until people on our side can get rid of the monsters, judging by the rifts only being a 1-way portal at the start." Lake crossed his arms and leaned back on the bench.

"Oh, I get that too. Like A2DX-something," she added. "So they're like the waiting area for monsters to come over?"

"In a way, yes. Rifts and the outworlds give us time to fight back. What's authority then?"

"From what I understand, it's like the results of our duties," said Keri, biting her lip. "Closing rifts, claiming areas, preventing more rifts, invaders and a Will from crossing over and taking our world. Basically, claiming a lot of areas and protecting them equals more authority."

He nods. "Okay. Easy enough. We've been doing that. What's the active and passive type?"

She scratched her head. "I'm not too sure. I know that a Maiden, like me, is passive, and another one called the Ferry is. Everyone else is active. I think."

"Useless..." Lake frowned.

"Oh, I'm sorry. I just don't really know."

He shook his head. "Oh, not you, the system. I asked it what active and passive is. It said I need to raise my authority for details.'"

Keri shrugged. "Yeah, it isn't that reliable sometimes."

"And the followers?" asked Lake. "I'm guessing you don't know anything about that?"

She shook her head. "I feel like I should, but I don't, at least not now. What I'm sure of is if we don't protect Silaw, there won't be a world for us in the present or in the future," she said with a grave tone.

After a while, he asked, "Do you feel better now?"

Keri went over her memories and it felt like she had a handle on what's real, what's not and what she was uncertain of. "I do, actually. Thanks, Lake."

"Did you tell Wayne any of this?" He set his sights at a distance.

She exhaled with a tired look and decided to let out what she had been thinking, "What am I supposed to say? Hey, I said I like you before but that was the old me. Now I have all these new memories, from before we ever met, and I'm not sure I feel that way now. But can you wait? Cause I'm trying to figure out all these things in my head, once I figure out who I am, maybe this thing between us can work."

"That's the way to go. Really good. I'm sure he'll definitely understand." Lake nodded with enthusiasm.

She looked at him with a dead stare. "You're kidding, right?"

"Sorry." He made a half-apologetic, half-smiling face.

She pulled her legs up to the bench, hugged them and rested her head over it. "He won't even let me go fight. How am I supposed to earn coins if I don't fight? He just gives me cursed items—that's not enough."

"Cursed items?"

She explained another way for her to earn coins was by absorbing the effects of outlier artefacts. And in turn, he told her about how saving people earns him coins. "There's something else for me. You know how it seems like a game? For me, it's like a sim-dating game, and I'm the main character," she said in a slow, unsure way.

His brows perked. "What does that mean?"

Keri slowly explained the features of a sim-dating game and her system. That for every interaction with the target lovers, she gets coins. "So, yeah, like whoever I'm like attracted to. If I pursue them, I get coins."

"Targets? That means you have more than one person you're attracted to. That's normal," he said clinically. "I assume Wayne was one of them. Who are the others?"

"Maxwell," she admitted, not meeting his eyes.

He nodded. "Yeah, yeah, I can definitely see that. The guy's a born leader, you know? He could probably run for mayor or president. That all?"

Her breath stopped at the question. She couldn't bring herself to say the words, so instead she pointed at him and looked in the other direction.

Lake scrutinized her finger with a cloudy expression. "Me?"

She covered her face. "With pseudo-dreams and the kissing, I don't know. Please forget about it. I just wanted to let you know that I've got other ways of getting it."

"Right. Sorry. I-um-you-know, it's a pseudo-dream. I think it happens a lot in, ah, there. So, what else is on your mind?" His face reddened.

Hastily trying to change the subject, Keri rambled on various things, including how she ran and sparred with Vivian to be more prepared for fights. But it had its limits, and she was ready for a real-life battle experience. But Wayne blocked her from doing that, and she was so damn ready for something more.

Lake searched his backpack. "It should be here somewhere."

She stopped her rant, curious about what he was looking for.

"Got it." He pulled out a big black board with violet lines and dots—mana circuits.

"Is that a ski board?"

Lake stood up and wore his backpack. "It's my hoverboard, I made it for long distance travel. My boots can't take us that far that fast." The mana circuits on the board brightened as it floated a meter above ground.

Keri rose to her feet. "I'm not getting it. Hey, what are you—"

In a swift motion, Lake swept her off her feet into a princess carry. "Relax, I've got you." The violet lines on his boots glowed as he floated on air and mounted the board. Black-violet attachments surfaced from the board and hooked onto his boots. "Careful." He slowly placed her in the front while keeping a firm arm around her waist. "I didn't design this with a passenger in mind, so I'm going to have to hold you. Hope that's okay," he said.

"I still don't get what's happening," she said, but thought, *I don't mind either. You smell really good.*

"You said you needed to fight monsters, so we're going to where the monsters are."

"Now? But I don't have my battle suit."

"I've got some extras here," he said. "Did you bring a weapon?"

She still had her Trainee Sword around her neck and the Soulsword from the Dragon Knight was bound to her in a magical way, so she could summon it anytime. "I do. But I—ahhhh!" The board sped forward. The air hitting them was tolerable at first at forty km/h, but as it increased, Keri's eyes started to dry out and her body shivered.

"This should make things better." His S-Glove glowed violet as a dome of light encased the two, shielding them from air and dirt.

"Uh, thanks." She smiled at him, and then he looked at her. Their eyes locked for a moment, but then she felt hot and embarrassed and looked away. For some reason, he did too. The ride was quiet and awkward; she could feel his breathing and warmth behind her, and she spaced out on any conversation starters—instead, she indulged in his light citrusy fragrance.

The landscape slowly changed from rocks and dirt to bushes, grass fields and spots of soil. Not long after, beetles the size of children buzzed in the air. They had red horns and brilliant ruby eyes. The hoverboard halted ways away from a group that floated around a pile of shit.

"It's called rubitles. They're a bit slow, but they can overwhelm you in numbers." Lake levelled the board close to the ground as he hopped off.

Keri dismounted the board with a helping hand from him. "Where'd you find this place? If there's a monster here, then is there a rift here?"

"Apes closed it weeks ago; these are what's left."

"They look deadly—and disgusting."

"They're slow though, and despite the big shiny eyes, they have limited vision." He took out a small circular device that covered his whole palm from his pockets. After clicking a small button on it, it enlarged to a wide disc with sharp, glowing violet blades that cracked with electricity. It floated right above his hand. "Lock on target." As his S-Visor covered his eyes, he flung the disc like a boomerang. It swung in a wide arc and hit one, killing it instantly. The disc rounded back to him and he caught it afloat over his hand.

The other rubitles buzzed with commotion after witnessing their comrade die. But after searching frantically in their vicinity, they could not find the source of the attack and they calmed again. "See, nothing to it," said Lake.

"What's that? I've never seen a weapon like that," said Keri.

He held out the disc. "This? I made it. I call it the S-Disc. Short for source disc. I needed a ranged weapon that wasn't a gun. Feels useless if I run out of bullets—not a fan of it."

"Let me guess, the thing on your face is called an S-Mask."

He smirked. "Close, S-Visor."

She pointed at his feet. "S-Boots?"

"Yeah. How'd you know?"

She gave him a knowing look. "You've got a bad naming sense."

"Hey, it's simple and easy to remember," he defended. "Enough about my tools—you wanted monsters, have at it."

A clock made of light materialized and fast-forwarded an hour on the ground where Keri stood as her necklace blinked from her neck to her hands and turned into a sword. In a flash, she appeared next to one of the rubitles, cut it in half, then escaped. She was right back to where she started. Again, the beetles buzzed about their friend dying.

"That was good," commented Lake.

"They're easy," she said with surprise.

"Because they are. They're one of the easiest monsters to kill. How much did that give you?"

Monster slain. Earned 50 coins. Total 11050

"50?" reported Keri. "Is that good?"

"It's a normal monster. Harder ones give you more."

A smile crept on her face. "Lend me the battle suit," she said. After putting the suit over her leggings and shirt, she started hunting for the rubitles one by one. She'd go in, attack, and back out. At most, she'd execute three swings before the monsters died. Three hours flew as she cleared the whole area of rubitles. Sweat glistened off her skin as she huffed in satisfaction. "That was awesome. Are there more?" she asked.

Lake levitated nearby, watching over her. "There are, further out. But it takes a while to get to. How about we go there tomorrow?"

"Don't you have work?" She walked back towards him.

He shrugged. "I can do work in the morning, then we can come here in the afternoon."

"And that's okay?"

"I've got assistants, should be fine."

"Okay. It's a date," she blurted out. "I mean, not a date, cause we're not together. I have a boyfriend. And you have a girlfriend. Like a friend-thing. Hanging out thing. I mean—yeah. It's a hang out."

"It's a hang-out," he repeated with a nod.

As she sensed a slight disappointment in his tone, she added, "You have someone, right? That lady from the store."

"Jella? We broke up." He made a downcast expression.

"Oh, I'm sorry," said Keri with a consoling face, though it was far from what she actually felt. Ecstatic and giddy were more appropriate descriptions.

He shook his head. "Forget it. I'm starting to think people I'm close to leave me in one way or another. But when I'm with you, I don't think about that as much."

"Then let's hang out more." She wanted to ask more about it, but a part of her, the Richforth side, told her not to. So she let it go and let him take her home.

Chapter 45

Keri, Lawless Lands

The wind blasted against Lake's face as he surfed above the soil on his hoverboard. He maneuvered left and right, away from boulders and trees in passing. When he'd run into a pit or gap, he'd jump over them as mini thrusters pushed him to glide before falling closer to the ground. As he looked back, his S-Visor locked onto each rubitle as targets that chased after him, counting twenty-five flyers. "This should be enough. Are you ready?" he asked over his linko.

Up ahead, Keri was in her battle stance, holding her blade upright. "Bring it," she said.

As Lake approached her, the hoverboard propelled smoke from its rear, blinding the rubitles. Then a clock illuminated below Keri's feet. As he passed her, she disappeared in a flash. She appeared next to the nearest monster and cut it in half in one second. The next second, she flashed to the one behind it and sliced it apart. Then the next after another. Twenty-six seconds later, Keri landed a few meters away with twenty-five beetles falling apart behind her all at the same time. Blood and guts sprayed on the ground.

The hero braked and swiveled back around. "How much was that?"

...monster slain. Earned 20 coins. Total 12030

"Lousy twenty each. Why is it giving me less?" whined Keri. Lately, she had been going out with Lake almost daily to gain more coins.

Lake started picking up the useful remains and putting it in his bag. "They're probably too easy for you. I think we should go further out. Maybe kill something harder."

She helped collect monster parts as well and handed it all to him to keep. "I'm good with that. Are you sure you don't want to fight with me? I feel bad going on a bus."

"Bus?"

"It's a game term. Means a higher-level person helps the newbie get experience."

"I told you I earn coins by creating ward-generators. I got a lot recently for the third one. So I don't mind helping you out," he said. "Before we leave, I think you should claim this area."

"I've been meaning to do that, but I don't know how."

He explained the ways to go about buying and using the claim crystal. After a few minutes, Keri had a red and blue crystal in her hand. She consumed one after the other.

You have consumed Area Claim Crystal. Current Area: Zone E-law has been claimed by Maiden. Areas Claimed: E-law, A2. Connecting outer dimension to home dimension. E-law & A2 now connected.

Lake stared at her closely and spoke, "You feel it, don't you? Like the whole space is yours and what you want—"

"—the area will obey," she finished. By her will, she knew that the area would move around her. The rifts that Lake mentioned were at her beck and call, and then she felt something was missing in this place, but she could not pinpoint exactly what.

Lake continued to explain what the other crystals were for and the rifts she could summon. With a part of her memory recovering, Keri refreshed their conversation about the outworlds. The dimensions in the rifts (outlier #3) were the first defense for their world, barring the horde of monsters from all coming in at once. The color of the rift signified how new the rifts were. The fresher it was, the more time people had a chance to close them.

Whenever the humanoid monsters invaded with their hordes, they carried with them a part of their home-world dimension, which was the building block of the outworlds. If the enemies succeeded in claiming an area in Silaw, they'd bridge their world together. But if they lost, the outworlds would transfer ownership to the candidates who defeated them, increasing the space and land of Silaw.

"Champions," said Keri while she clung to Lake's waist aboard his hoverboard.

"What?" asked Lake, who sped along grasslands.

"The humanoid monsters are called champions, I remember. They are given a day to reclaim the areas they have lost to us. Just as the rift is our warning that they are coming to invade," she explained in a somber tone. "But in Kermoz, there were no rifts with colors to warn us, nor outworlds to hold them back. We let them in."

Lake made a stern expression. "I still can't believe they could do something like that."

It was late for her to realize he was part of the army. "I'm sorry, I didn't mean to—"

"It's not your fault," he cut her off. "I've been hearing bad things about them. I was hoping it was all rumors, or at least only a few bad apples. I didn't expect it was the whole lot of them."

"I want to believe in them. My parents didn't know, and they were part of the army. There might be a good reason for that."

"There's a good reason for nuking a whole zone? For killing everyone we loved? My family died in that accident, I don't know why I was defending the army." The volume of his voice raised.

She gulped. "Is that why you're still here?"

Lake glanced back. "What?"

"You know, because you can't decide if going back to the army is the right thing for you, with all the wrong things they're doing."

"That, and I guess, you." He looked far ahead and slowed to a cruise.

Her heart skipped a beat. "Me?"

"I've lost people in my life." He continued to explain the circumstances surrounding his family's death. "If it wasn't for me, if my dad had prioritized saving my mom and brother, they'd still be alive."

"That's no one's fault—especially not yours," argued Keri. "I don't know them, but I think your mom and brother would've been happy your dad saved you."

He shook his head and told her about the death of his squad at Kermoz, blaming himself for not helping them right and not doing more. Then he added Tony's death, how he died by his hands. Keri insisted that was not the truth. "The test said I killed him. My spell literally ended his life," he shouted back at her.

She wanted to argue, but would he listen? He was so far into his own guilt that she was not sure if whatever she said could help.

"Sorry. Anyway, before I left for my mission to Kermoz, my superior knew about you. He's the same guy we saw in the pseudo-dream. The one who gave the order to kill everyone in Kermoz."

"What?"

"He saw the footage of us disappearing from WalkBy. He knew, for some reason, that we were somehow the outliers—especially you."

The snide face of the army-man in her dreams popped in her head and sent chills down her spine. The cruel, disgusting man was Lake's superior? "Will the army experiment on me?" she asked.

"Probably. He's definitely capable of doing that," he sounded defeated. "But don't worry, I won't let anyone do that to you."

She was worried but she blushed and kept quiet for most of the ride.

The hoverboard cruised to a stop and descended to the ground. As he helped her off, he said, "We're here. I'm sorry I didn't mean to unload all that—"

Keri turned around and hugged him. Lake opened his mouth to speak but just stood there instead. Then the next moment, he embraced her and rested his head next to hers. They stood there wrapped in each other's arms, in a field of grass and flowers leading up to the mountains, for several minutes.

Silence hung over the two as they trekked through the mountains, but it was unlike the time they met at Amazing Discoveries. Though their eyes were peeled for any monsters, Keri was more conscious and aware of Lake walking beside her. His dreamy eyes, dimples, cleft chin and great smile—all of it was so much like the elven prince in *Love Me, Princess*. But after observing him closely, she found there were some obvious differences: the ears, of course, obviously not pointed but round, his eyes, though the shape was the same, his were a richer brown, and instead of an arch, his brows ran straight above his eyes. The more she saw him, the more she was convinced that he was real, not like the prince in her games.

He was missing the air of royalty and tinge of arrogance, only his curiosity and mellow confidence lingered.

Wait. What was she thinking? Why was she taking note of all these details? She knew the elven prince was not real, and only in her fantasies, but to put those feeling onto Lake? And being very aware that he was real, and still pining after him. *Do I really like him more than as a friend? That is not going to work. He just broke up with Jella, and love is the last thing he's worrying about.* She shook her head.

Lake glanced at her, as if he knew she was thinking about him. He flashed his killer smile, blushed, then looked away.

Congratulations! You have advanced your relationship with Target Love #1.
Your feelings for each other have grown.
2000 coins earned. Total 14030.

Does he—could he possibly—is there any chance—that maybe—he has feelings for me? That sounds ridiculous. But does he, really?

"I think I'm falling for you," she heard him say.

She froze. "What? Can you repeat that?" said Keri, knowing fully well this could be one of her delusions.

"Go slow, you might fall. There might be some flyers around," said Lake. "You never know what rifts spit out."

"A rift?" she asked. *So, do you? Or do you not like me?*

He pointed atop the mountain; a blue rift shimmered. "Looks new. Seems like no one knows about this one yet." No poles or warning signs stood around the vicinity to warn travelers. Discovered dangers or rifts had at least one sign to warn people—or if that was not possible, they'd send out the coordinates to their linkos and the device would warn them if they were near one.

"Why is there a rift here? Didn't I claim the zone already?" asked Keri. "I even used the shielding crystal. No new ones should pop up."

"That area must be outside Zone E-law."

As the two moved closer to the rift with care over their surroundings, Keri felt her control over the area decrease. By the time they reached the rift, she understood it was new territory. "It is a different area," she confirmed.

Lake had a claim crystal floating in his hand. "I can't use reds. The system says we have to purge all active rifts before continuing. We can try and close it, or we can call the guild." Safety protocols for civilians were to call their local zone authorities of any rift or monster sightings if they had no contact with any affiliated guild. In their case, they both were tied to the Apes.

She inspected the shimmering blue gate before them while a stray, enigmatic memory flared in her mind. "Did you know that only one of the candidates can sense the areas that are claimed in their world," she blurted out, almost not thinking of her words.

"Sense? What do you mean?" Lake recorded their coordinates.

"There would always be a Hero when the Will of the World calls for its candidates. It's a standard. And if he fails, there's another candidate who is supposed to save everyone else, but differently."

He stopped fiddling with his S-Glove and looked up. "That's the Maiden?"

"The Maiden is a fallback for the Will. She isn't always present if the Will can fulfill its duties," she denied his statement. "There's a third. That candidate can sense the areas that have been claimed by champions and candidates. They know where the rifts are, and where its most dangerous."

"Like the Slayer?"

"Maybe the Slayer or the Ferry. Must be one of them."

"You mentioned that one before. Can you add another candidate?"

"No. I think that one time at the WalkBy was all I can do," stated Keri. "Maybe if someone dies? Or Silaw comes back and makes another one?"

"Any idea on how the types are? Like active or passive?"

Keri frowned and thought for a moment before saying, "It has something to do with followers, I think. Still not sure."

"It's strange how it all comes to you." He narrowed his eyes at her.

She shrugged. "Another thing you should know is that you shouldn't be using spells at all."

"What?"

Keri let her hand glide over the rift, feeling its energies. "In Fynn's stories, there was like this group of mages who used rune magic. One of the candidates tried to use it but discovered it was a crutch for people who couldn't wield the purest version of source. The candidate discovered he was closer to using the purest source than any of the mages."

"It does sound like a children's story, but at the same time, I feel like it's a story from inside the rifts," he said in a low tone. "You're creeping me out."

She walked away from the rifts and clutched her head. "I'm creeping myself out. These stupid things in my head, it's honestly destroying me," she cried.

Lake came up to her and put a hand over her shoulders. "Keri, look at me." After a hesitating pause, she stared at his dark brown eyes. "I see you as Keri. Keri who is awkward, weird, unapologetic—"

"—this is not making me feel better," inserted Keri.

"—also, the Keri who is wild, different and kind. The Keri who stands up for what she believes in and doesn't care what other people think about her."

"Okay that's starting to sound nice."

He gripped her shoulders. "I admire the Keri that I see and know. A few jumbled memories and a game in your head won't change that. You are you. Simple as that."

Keri felt like she was drowning in those eyes that gazed at her. This gorgeous man saw right through her in ways she could never see for herself. His heart weighed more than his looks ever could. As he moved his face closer to hers, she felt her body stiffen as her neck stretched to meet his head. When their lips were mere centimeters from each other, she whispered, "I should go home."

"Are you sure?" he asked gently.

She paused for a while before she nodded.

"I'll...take you home." A hint of disappointment laced his tone.

"And the rift?"

"I'll report it to the guild."

Chapter 46

Keri, Residence Floor, Amazing Discoveries

At Amazing Discoveries, Keri carefully stepped off the elevator and into their residence floor. Darkness cloaked the living space, blending with the ten o'clock night sky. She moved to the glassy attached to the wall and flicked a button. As the blinds descended on the windows and the lights illuminated the dark room, Wayne appeared sitting on the sofa with a brooding face.

Keri half-jumped. "Oh, it's you. You scared me. I thought you weren't coming home 'til tomorrow?" She leaned against the wall.

"Mission ended fast. Where'd you get that suit?" His eyes narrowed.

She gulped. Whenever she got home, she would always have the time to undress and store Lake's battle suit. "I bought it." She sat on the couch and took off her shoes.

"Why did you need another one? You have the old ones that you haven't been using."

Her mind blanked. "To practice. Like I said, Vivian and I were sparring."

"Vivian? You were sparring with Vivian?"

"I know you don't like it, but I'm really happy that—"

"Vivian? The same woman who told me an hour ago that you were out exploring the lawless lands?"

A slight annoyance aroused in her. "She wasn't supposed to—"

"I've known Vivian longer than you have. I know when she's lying," his voice deepened. "And I know right now, you're lying to me too Keri."

Keri rose from the couch and placed her shoes on the rack. "What do you want me to say? I've been killing rubitles? And I'm actually good at killing monsters that kill humans?" She changed into comfortable slip-ons.

"Rubitles? That's far out in the lawless lands. How'd you get there? How'd you know about them?"

She looked at the wall for a moment, trying to figure out what to say. "Internet. It's easy to search things like that. And if you've paid any attention to what I've been saying, I'm actually a fast runner." She turned to him. "A very fast runner."

Wayne averted his gaze and asked under his breath, "It's that pretty boy from the army, isn't it?"

"Lake has nothing to do with this. I am a candidate—the Maiden candidate. I need to be stronger," defended Keri. "People are dying, and I'm supposed to be the one that saves them—all of them—the whole world. Do you know what that means? Because I can't even wrap my head around it."

He rose from his seat, towered over her and shouted, "Don't lie to me, Keri. You've been sleeping with that nerd this whole time. The zone guards saw you—Apes saw you—I saw you leaving with that sissy sorcerer."

She took a step back, feeling the wall behind her. Instead of backing down, she pushed herself forward and reasoned, "Of all the people, Wayne, I thought you would understand. You're a candidate—"

"It's in the cameras, Keri," he shouted over her. "Everyone—the whole zone—the whole cluster—saw you coming and going with that nerdy fed-fag."

Her nose flared. "Lake has done nothing but be kind to me. He helped me fight and gave me confidence in myself. I don't have to be afraid of monsters, the rift or any alien that comes through those rifts. He helped me to be strong. Do you understand that? We are not together. But if you keep being like this, I might as well be with him—"

As fast as sound, Wayne grabbed her by the neck and pushed her against the wall—cracks cratered around her. "You are mine. Do you hear me? No one can ever have you," he growled.

"Wayne—I—" She struggled to loosen his hold, but he overpowered her with his strength.

"No one can touch you. We are destined to be together. You are mine." Blue flames flickered around his silhouette.

"Can't—bre—uhk." She felt stifled and asphyxiated.

Fire blazed in his irises. "You are mine."

Her arms flailed; her vision blurred, "Way—"

Wayne's face shifted with different emotions, from raw anger to stoic to shock. He immediately let go of Keri as she slid on the floor. "Keri, I'm sorry. I didn't mean it." He shook her by the shoulders.

Air returned to her lungs as she coughed, trying to breathe rapidly. "Ugghh…"

He embraced her. "Thank goodness, you're okay. I'm sorry. I didn't mean to do that. You know I love you, right? I got emotional. I wasn't thinking." He pushed the strands of hair off her face.

"Urg—ter."

"I'm sorry, baby. I'm really, really sorry. You don't look like you're okay."

She coughed, trying to ingest more air.

"Stay right here. I'll go get you some water." He kissed her forehead then went to the kitchen.

On the floor where she sat, a clock of light emerged. Its hands wound backwards as the fractures on her back mended themselves. The restrictive pressure in her lungs and throat ceased to exist. The marks vanished like it had never been there. "Haaaa…" She exhaled freely as the clock disappeared.

Wayne came back with a glass of water. "Here."

She took the cup and drank from it; her guzzling echoed through the silence between them. When she emptied the cup, she returned it.

"You finished that fast, want another one?" When she nodded, he got up and went back to the kitchen. "You know, they say you should drink eight glasses of water every day to be healthy."

"Yea? Who said that?" asked Keri in a tone as nonchalant as she could produce. Grabbing her outdoor shoes and coat from the hanger, she lightly hurried to the elevator and pressed the button. As Wayne babbled about some more water trivia, she switched her footwear to outdoor ones; and when the doors slid open, she fumbled inside and pressed the close and ground button at the same time.

Tears fell from her face as the elevator moved. Her hands wiped them as they fell. She snorted them back and tapped her cheeks. When she arrived on the ground floor, she marched out and wore her coat. Halfway across the lobby, a familiar voice sounded from her right, "Are you heading out? Isn't it a bit late?"

Keri blinked back the tears then turned around with a slight grin. "Hey Viv, need some air. I'll see you tomorrow." She continued up until she reached the door.

"You're seeing him again, aren't you?" said Vivian aloud.

"Like I said, fresh air."

She walked up to her. "Stop doing this, Keri. You're in a relationship—you should honor that and stop seeing another man."

She tried to calm her shaking hands. "We're just friends, Vivian." She exited the building.

Vivian followed after her. "You might not have done anything with him. But talking to him, laughing with him, being around him—it's emotional cheating."

Keri zipped her coat and increased her strides. "You don't know anything."

"Keri, you're better than this. Don't throw away a good man for someone you barely know. What do you know about Lake? Zuobic soldiers are never the good guys," she hounded her from behind. "They treat you badly, they're too ambitious they don't pay attention to you, they only have power in mind."

Keri stopped and faced her. "He hit me, is that what you want to hear?"

"Lake hit you? I knew it—"

"Wayne hit me," she interjected. "Not Lake. Wayne. Wayne hit me."

The wrinkles on the sides of her eyes creased. "I've known Wayne for a long time. He would never hurt someone he loves."

"Clearly he has never loved you." As she turned, Vivian pulled her arm back.

"Don't play the victim, Keri. Strong women like us—no good comes from playing the victim. People will look down on you—and that robs us of our power," she stated in a deeper tone. "Besides, even if he did hit you, don't tell me all your abilities vanished? You're fast. You could have avoided that easily."

"I wasn't prepared." Her nostrils flared.

Vivian tilted her head. "Like I said, don't play the victim."

She snatched her arm back. "You know what? Instead of focusing your attention on me, why don't you focus on your family."

"Don't change the subject."

"Charlie isn't your son." Her heart pounded.

Vivian shook her head. "Pick on the same-sex couple who can't make their own child, is that it? That's low. Even for you."

"That's obvious, duh. I'm not talking about that," Keri quipped. "Charlie isn't Charlie. He is the Will of the World. He is the culmination and personification of all the souls in this world—ooh mysterious. But get this: he's damaged and not doing a good job of protecting people." She pointed at the refugees camped outside the gates and begging for entry and food.

She rolled her eyes. "Now you're making stuff up."

"Am I? Charlie is Silaw. Why do you think he disappears? And where does he go? He has a day job that's consuming him. His work is to protect people—protect everyone—protect me. Why do you think he has that strange protection power? Huh? Also, he sucks at it. He fucked up his only job and now I have freaking migraines, and my memories are all fucked up. Then I find out I'm the reason for new candidates being chosen, fall in love to be strong, then save the world? All because he's on sick leave? Fuck that."

"Don't put my child into this," she said in a firm voice.

"Why don't you ask him? Oh, I forgot, you can't. I'm the only one who can talk to him," she boasted. "You know why? Because he dumped his responsibilities on me. Surprise. I'm the substitute here to clean up your son's mess."

She slapped her. "Enough."

Keri rubbed her cheek. "Yea, it's enough." She turned and left.

Chapter 47

Lake, Untef

At his apartment, Lake thought over solutions for locating and sorting claimed areas. Day after day, this whole hero-thing had been consuming him. The construction of generators and area reclamation fed not only his pocket with system coins, but his heart. He felt good knowing that people could sleep safe and sound in their homes and in this zone. They wouldn't have to worry about monster disturbances or a rift suddenly appearing and killing them, or taking their loved ones away. This new thing opened dreams and goals in his head that he had not thought possible when he was in Zuobic. This was a good thing, and he couldn't wait to do more.

Now, he racked his brains for a way to catalogue all the zones and categorize them from claimed to invaded. But how was he going to do that? He didn't even know where to start. If he were Major Cervantes, he'd know what to do. He probably would survey the missing areas and kept a record somewhere already—even had drones on standby. The army definitely would have a close watch on those.

Or he could simply ask the Slayer? He'd rather not get tangled up with that guy. Besides, he wasn't sure he had the fragment for searching areas. Maybe the Ferry? *I don't even know where the Ferry is or who they are,* he thought.

As he finished his easy-cook pasta for dinner, a square lens covered his left eye and displayed a message:

On his S-Glove, a glass panel surfaced above the equipment. He replied to ask what Maxwell needed in his glove before he went to his bedroom. He stripped off all his gear and clothes before hopping into the shower.

As water ran over his body, he went through the system shop, trying to find an item to search for claimed areas. He went through the list but found nothing. A lot had upgrades to his areas, but nothing that could search for areas out of his control. Did he really have to talk to Wayne? An annoying feeling crept into his heart when he thought about the big man. He concluded that he should discuss options with Keri about creating a list rather than wasting a brain cell thinking about the oversized idiot.

His mind then veered to what Keri had said about his abilities when he hopped out of the shower, wrapped a towel around his waist and started brushing his teeth. Was runic sorcery really a crutch for his growth? He did have to admit that soul weaving was easier than casting spells. Though sorcery offered more for offense, it was not like he was defenseless without them. More so, he felt more useful with creating tech and weaving than he had ever felt being a sorcerer. Maybe he should concentrate on that and give up sorcery?

After leaving the bathroom, he picked up his glassy from the kitchen counter and connected it to his S-Visor and S-Glove. Notifications of missed calls from Maxwell surfaced. Just as he was about to call back, a new message interrupted him:

Keri: *Are you awake?*

Lake: *Yes, you ok?*

He waited for a few minutes for the reply, but it never came. As he placed his glassy on his bed side table, the doorbell rang. Thoughts of who the mysterious guest was ran in his head, but none came to him that would visit past midnight. He checked the cameras at the entrance on the ground floor with his glassy: Keri waited, hunched and shivering in her coat. After buzzing her in, it took a couple of minutes before she chimed at his door. When he opened it, he said, "Keri, are you okay? What's going—"

Keri lunged and hugged Lake as soon as she got in. Tears poured from her eyes.

"What happened?" asked Lake, slightly taken aback.

"Wayne, he came home—and then—hic—said I'm seeing—hic—push wall—warkghed faporemf," she cried, talked and hiccupped all at the same time.

"Huh?"

"He—come—hic—and then—boom—to the wall—ahhhhh." She planted her face on his bare chest and whaled.

He patted her and brought her in. "Okay, okay, let's go inside." After helping her settle on the couch, he noticed the splat of snot and tears on him. "I'm gonna be right back."

As he turned to leave, she grabbed the towel and almost pulled it off, but Lake was quick to clamp it in with his hands. "Don't go..." cried Keri. She sniffled and blew on his towel.

He inspected his towel and his chest, now covered with snot. "You need tissues. I don't think my towel can handle all this." He escaped into the bathroom to clean up and dressed into a plain shirt and shorts. "Here," he said after placing a box of tissues on the coffee table.

Keri pulled one tissue after the other. When she'd grabbed ten, she smacked her face on it and blew hard. She wiped the snot off her face and blew her nose again. When it was filled, she grabbed fresh tissues and did it again. "Sorry—I didn't know where to—go," she stammered.

"Do you want something to drink?"

She nodded. As he turned to get it, she said, "Wait. Don't want—a mess." When he looked back, she handed the used tissues to him.

With a wary look to his hands, he went to the kitchen and made tea after throwing the tissues away and washing his hands. Was he disgusted by all this? Sure, but more than that, he felt sorry for Keri. He didn't know what had happened, but he wanted to be here for her. Whatever she needed, he wanted to give it to her. But also, was it weird that he had a slight hard-on? "Careful, it's hot." He placed a pot of tea and a cup on the coffee table.

After pouring herself a cup, she slowly sipped it and placed it down. "Am I a bad—person?"

"Why would you say that?"

"I told—Vivian Charlie isn't—her son." In a hiccupping and half-crying manner, she retold what had happened with Vivian. How she was hurtful and not at all empathetic about the truth. And the whole time, she blamed Charlie—Silaw—whoever he was. "I'm a bad—person," she finished.

"Do you really blame Charlie?"

"No. Yes. I don't know," she sniffed. "He's supposed to be like family. But he's also Silaw—he made me like this. I didn't ask for this—maybe it's their fault—the army's fault. If they hadn't—I don't know."

Lake was reminded that the army had experimented with the rifts—Kermoz's destruction was their fault. He wondered which division it was that did it. A part of him wanted to deny it was true, but he knew Keri would not lie about this. "You know what I don't get? The Spider-Woman in Kermoz," he said.

"What about—it?"

"When Kermoz was invaded, it wasn't spiders, it was those black things with capes."

"Mhhmm, svartal is what they're called, I think. But Silaw got rid of them," she said after blowing her nose. "We lost that area in the process. So maybe the spiders got to it after that?"

"That's what I don't get. If the spiders kept Kermoz, who brought it back to us? Which candidate claimed it?"

Keri dabbed her tears with the used tissue. "Didn't you do that?" She sipped her tea.

He shook his head. "It was already there when I got to it. I think the champion was claiming it back. That was why it got there so fast. Do you think, maybe it was Wayne?" he broached the subject carefully.

After placing the cup down, she sobbed softly for a few seconds before it turned to a wail. "I came—rewerammi—aaaahhh," she cried incomprehensible words, trying to vocalize what had happened. Lake sat next to her and rubbed her back, to which she responded with more incomprehensible statements. After a few minutes, she had calmed down and drank more of her tea. Then she told him of what had happened from the moment she got home.

The first few words she spoke of had Lake sympathetically listening out of care for her. But the story went to the conversation of doubt with Wayne—doubt about her choices and her company. A tinge of delight lingered in Lake's heart. He found the bad events happening to Wayne amusing. Then the entertainment stopped and things became difficult. He stopped rubbing her back when he heard of her grasping for air, grasping for life. The image of her fighting for her life ran wild in his head. His other hand, the hand on his lap, turned to a fist as source, the invisible power, flooded into his balled-up hand. Her story finished with her healing herself and getting out of the apartment—then she connected it with what happened with Vivian. But throughout that time, source kept building inside him, madly circulating in his soul, screaming for a way out. Then, all of it stopped. Keri had placed a hand on his leg and tried to smile.

"Thank you," said Keri

The cloud of anger manifesting in source vanished like a puff of smoke. "Huh?"

"Thank you for listening. It's hard, people not believing you."

"I believe you." He held her hand and their eyes locked onto each other. Moments passed while they sat in silence looking into each other's eyes—save for the beating of his heart that tremored in his head. He gulped. Maybe now's the time to pick up where they left off? He chanced a kiss.

Inches from his face, Keri tilted her head aside. "Do you have something to eat?" she asked.

"Hmm?"

"Haven't had anything for dinner." She avoided his gaze.

From fighting with her boyfriend and friend, to kissing a new man—he assumed it was too fast for her. *Way to go, Lake. Real smooth,* he thought. "Is pasta okay?" he asked, pulling away.

"Pasta's nice."

He cleared the coffee table and went back to the kitchen with a sigh. Blame and embarrassment lingered within him as he prepared another plate of pasta and waited for the microwave to do its magic. After drinking a glass of water to quench his thirst and douse his fantasies of kissing the woman he liked, he sighed again. The chime of the microwave cut through his downtrodden mood. "Here's your dinner—" As he delivered the plate, he stopped midway. Keri was asleep on the couch. He shook his head. *What am I doing? She had her heart broken—and all I'm thinking about is getting some.*

After setting the plate on the coffee table, Lake carefully placed her arms beneath her to try and carry her. Once he did, she stirred. He thought he had woken her, but then she snored softly on his bicep. A grin plastered his face. In a swift move, he lifted her into his arms in a princess-carry, walked her over to the spare bedroom and laid her on the bed. After he removed her shoes, he placed a blanket over her and gazed at her.

"Do you know that time when we met again? Inside the rift. Tony had just—I thought I was walking with a warning sign: Careful, Death Imminent," he whispered and grinned darkly. "It was my mom and brother first—I can barely remember what they were like. Then you, my squad, Tony. I killed Tony—did you know that? I think I told you that. I helped the poison kill him faster, according to the autopsy report. The only thought that kept me going that time was that I had to leave this place, because Tony would want to leave this place. I have to get him out of that lizard-infested nightmare.

"I moved, walked, and there you were. Alive. I thought I was dreaming again, but it was real. I couldn't believe it. More than thankful for you breathing and living. I said: Yeah, maybe I don't really have a sign on my head. Maybe I can save people. Maybe." He pushed her colorful hair away from her face.

"I like you, Keri—I think maybe I'm falling for you, too. Not just because of that, but because you're fun, crazy, weird. A candidate, who is supposed to save the world, the Maiden, and you're every bit as strong and cool, as anyone else."

Keri turned over to the other side. "Kiss me," she murmured in her sleep.

Lake smiled, kissed her cheek and left the room. "Good night, Keri."

Chapter 48

Keri, Untef

Five in the morning, Keri awoke with a pounding headache. Arguments from last night came to her in a flash, and it made her even more weary and queasy, adding to her already sore body. She sat up on bed upon realizing she didn't know where she was—then it all came back—how she plastered Lake with all her spit, tears and snot, coupled with her complaints, woes and worries. She hid under the sheets, hoping her embarrassment could be covered by it. Then she threw it altogether when she remembered how he had leaned in for a kiss. Her hands covered her mouth and she exhaled. A scent of day-old protein bars mixed with chicken soup wafted back. "Nobody wants to kiss this mouth." She coughed.

Raising her armpit, she sniffed it. It smelled like rotting onions and garlic. She gagged. "I need a shower," she said, silently appreciating that she avoided that kiss from Lake. If he did and they did it, what would he think about her stinking self? She couldn't imagine him going down on her smelling like this.

After being disoriented for a few minutes, she found the bathroom. She immediately stripped off her funky clothes and jumped in the shower, using all the products Lake had that she could. Thirty minutes flew by before she came out with a towel wrapped around her body, smelling and looking clean and fresh. Now, the only problem was, what should she wear?

In the dark of Lake's room, she tiptoed in. Lake was fast asleep under the covers with the bedsheet covering him up to his neck. When she spotted the closet, she made a careful but quick beeline to it. But then she hit her knee on the bed frame. She jumped up and down on one leg as she held on to her knee. Then she stepped on his boots that made her trip over and fall on the bed.

In a swift motion, Lake got up, grabbed her by the arm and pinned her on the bed. He pressed hard on her back. "Who are you—and Keri?" His face changed from a startled outburst to a muddled look.

"Oh, hey Lake, morning, how are you?" she said, struggling from his grip.

"What are you doing?"

"Can you let go? Cause I can't." Her face was pressed against the sheets.

"Uh yeah, sorry." He immediately let go.

She massaged her neck and slowly turned to him. "I was trying to find clothes—" Her jaw dropped. "You're naked."

"I sleep in the nude." His face reddened as he snatched a pillow to cover himself.

Her eyes kept focused on his exposed areas. "Nice. I mean—I should find clothes."

"I left clothes for you outside—you should go," he said with a quivering tone.

Her mind screamed that she should leave and get dressed while she was at it. But instead, her hand seemed like it had a mind of its own as it slowly unwrapped herself, exposing herself fully. She gulped and hesitatingly met his gaze. His gaze burned through her; it was as if he was hungry for her? Was he lusting over her? No, this couldn't be it. There was no way he'd think that. As doubt bloomed in her head, she reached for the towel to cover herself, but then he said, "Nice." She froze.

Lake reached out a hand. His fingertips touched her waist, then traced up her body and caressed her boob. Once he held her face, they stared at each other for minutes as if both were waiting for permission. She copied him, tracing her hand up his abs, his chest and then his neck. Slowly, he brought his head down to hers and their lips touched. Fire burned in Keri as their lips and tongues intertwined in a wet, searing kiss. The motions of their mouths drowned out for minutes and then continued further as their hands explored each other's bodies. When they took a second to breathe, they took in each other's faces, then their bodies, both panting. Then they knew, they were not going back to sleep.

Chapter 49

Lake, Cafe, Untef

As the noon sun began to flow into the window, Lake was busy staring at Keri's sleeping face—both of them still in bed. He had been staring at her for an hour ever since he woke up. His fingers dangled around her colorful hair and ran up and down her smooth skin. The growls of his stomach pulled him away from her as he kissed her goodbye and got dressed. Before he left, he placed a note on the bedside table: *Getting food. Brb. –Lake.*

Silent footfalls echoed around his apartment as he dressed in jeans and a jumper. After fitting his gloves and visor, he checked on her again and then left. When he arrived at the café next door, the smell of coffee, pancakes and bread enveloped the entire space. His stomach grumbled some more.

"The usual for takeaway?" the café owner asked.

"Add a croissant sandwich and another coffee to it," replied Lake.

He grinned. "Having brunch with a lady, perhaps? Or a fella?"

Lake shrugged. "Lady. Definitely lady. And yeah, something like that."

The owner high-fived him. "Nice. Happy for you, man. I'll make it extra special today."

"You don't have to."

"When one of my regulars has a special day, I'm gonna make it even more special. I'll take care of it, be with you in a minute."

Lake waited. On a typical day, he'd be quickly getting his breakfast and then rush off to work. But today was different. Though he did have to go to work, he decided to stay in for the day. What could he do? No—what could *they* do? Maybe shop? Women love shopping, don't they? Or they could sightsee over at the other zones? He had been there to work, but not to stroll or take a good look.

"Here you go. Good luck with your lady." The store owner passed him a bag filled with food and a tray of coffee.

He waved as he left the café. "Thanks, man. Appreciate it." When he checked the inside of the bag, a sedan braked in front of him.

The tinted windows rolled down. "Where have you been? I've been looking everywhere for you. Don't you answer your calls?" Maxwell barked successively.

"What?" asked Lake, barely understanding the barrage of questions.

"Get in." He motioned his hand.

"It's the morning. Can't this—"

"People are in danger. We need your help," he said in a firm tone.

Lake glanced at his building entrance, then at Maxwell's urgent stare. Sighing, he opened the car door and settled inside. Before he could even fasten his seatbelt, the car vroomed over to the highway bridges.

He enabled his S-Visor from sleep and mute. Messages and missed calls from Maxwell buzzed and clouded the lens. All of it demanding where he was and saying he had to see something important. "Sorry. I came home late last night, and some things came up," said Lake.

The two were silent for a while with a permanent scowl on Maxwell's face. As he drove, he tapped on the glassy installed on the car's dashboard. A translucent map of the whole valley appeared over the window on the passenger's side. It displayed the Cluster RSTU and the zones around it. A few villages were highlighted blue, but mostly, the surrounding areas were all part of the lawless lands. Small pins blinked on the areas beyond them. It formed an irregular perimeter encasing the whole cluster.

The pins seemed like rifts were appearing around them. "Is that what I think it is?" asked Lake, zooming the image on the window with his fingertips.

"It started two days ago. Usually, we only get two, at most four new rifts. Not like this."

"I don't get it. I was just here the other day. There weren't any of these."

"You were there?"

He nodded. "Before I came to a rift, I was here with Keri. We were training, killing monsters." Mentally, he asked the system about the weird phenomena.

Normally, it wouldn't reply with anything useful or tell him he needed to increase his authority. But he thought he might as well try.

> Champions of other worlds have noticed the growing authority and presence of the hero candidate. They seek to claim resources surrounding the hero's domain before the candidate grows stronger. This is a common tactic executed by invaders when defenders have acquired and consolidated their first five areas.
>
> System upgraded. Due to incoming invasion, alerts about your territories will now appear. Please adjust your area settings.

Another screen popped to the side where his areas were listed with options under them. There were settings to change entrances and exits to his claimed areas by invaders and local inhabitants. It also showed the time left for the shielding around them before it expired. After a few toggles, he set them to disallow entry to monsters, champions and invaders and allow unaligned humans. When he asked about alignment, the system responded:

> When humans and other entities select a candidate to align themselves with, they become the candidate's followers.

So, followers are people? And they can actually choose which candidate they follow? How? And why? Lake thought.

He wanted to play around with it more, but they had already arrived at the Ape's building. After parking the car underground, the two went up to the war room of the Hairless Apes. Glass panels and floating screens populated the 1,000 square-meter room. Rows of desks and computers filled the center area with a lot of Apes typing and collecting data. As the two walked to the center platform, Lake saw the screens showing various areas around them where closers were preparing to enter a rift. This included the sites for the generators he worked at in each zone of the Cluster. One particular screen showed the actual journey inside the rift—it was a space where rocks and land floated in the sky.

"You have tech that allows you to broadcast from another dimension?" asked Lake. "When did you invent that?"

"Oh, that thing? It's Deeg's superpower," said Ivo, who was typing at one of the desks near the elevated platform.

"Is he a 14 too?"

"Oh sorry, I'm confusing you. It's an artefact, a princess tiara. Deeg only wears it when he needs to—he says it reduces his masculinity. I honestly think it's cute."

"Shut up, Ivo," Deeg ordered through the speakers. He was talking through the broadcast.

"We can talk directly to him?" gasped Lake. His inner geek salivated over the item.

Maxwell glanced at him. "I know what you're thinking, but we have bigger things to discuss. Are you okay with me telling them?"

Lake nodded. He had discussed the whole candidate issue with the guild leader before. He figured since he was dealing with three, he ought to know the whole story. Since it would probably affect the whole world, it was best to let someone else know about it. When he had unloaded it to him, whenever he visited his place of work, he felt lighter. He realized unloading to him was not only for the sake of humanity but also helped him keep his sanity intact. He felt like this guild that put its trust in him, and those who worked for him, deserved to know the truth.

"Apes, listen up, can I have your attention? What I'm about to say is not to leave this room," announced Maxwell. "Every bit of information here can be discussed amongst ourselves—but it's only for our ears. This goes for all of the teams, combat and non-combat, listening to this broadcast. Keep this to yourselves."

Ivo and the rest of the people in the war room made a serious face and answered, "Yes sir."

Deeg and the team leaders all reported in. "Copy, sir. All information is confidential."

Maxwell explained the circumstances around the rifts, claiming areas and champions. He entertained questions as they came up with Lake chiming in for clarity. A few doubted the new information was real, but after pointing out Lake's work with their weapons and Ivo's and Maxwell's experiences with the hero, they stopped.

Lake moved to one of the screens showing a map of the clusters and lawless lands. He highlighted the zones he controlled in violet while Keri's were green.

"This is happening a lot because of me. The invaders have started to take notice. I'm sorry," he said after telling them that he had claimed a lot of areas.

For a moment, the apes were quiet. Then, Ivo pointed at the unhighlighted zones in the Cluster. "How about Troef and Rumaf?" he asked.

"They're not mine."

"That means rifts are going to open there, right? Monsters are going to attack?" A slight panic escaped his voice. "My wife's parents live there. Are they going to be all right?"

"My boyfriend lives there. Should he evacuate?" asked another Ape. Then more voices surfaced over the discussion, requesting guidance and expressing concerns.

"Settle down. I said, settle down!" Maxwell asked softly at first, but shouted when more spoke up. "We've got new ward generators, so rifts won't be a problem. Troef's the only one that hasn't been upgraded, but its gonna get installed soon, right? And the ward generators are going to keep them away, like the other monsters, right?"

Lake caught his glance and felt a knot in his stomach. "Actually, the reason monsters don't attack the zones are because of these." A blue gem with silver rings manifested in his grasp. He then explained how they worked.

"Just use it on Troef," urged Ivo. "I don't want to go all the way there just for my in-laws. They're a mess to evacuate."

Lake shook his head. "It doesn't work like that. If more than two candidates are present, they have to give up their rights to me. Keri owns it. I'll talk to her on the way there," he said to Maxwell.

After nodding to him, the Guild Leader addressed everyone. "You heard Lake. We have ways to protect ourselves from monsters. Everyone is safe as long as they're in the zones. Ivo, contact the zone officials, coordinate with them on evacuating to Zone Shoef and Untef, also figure out quarantine. It doesn't look like a good idea to be roaming about," he ordered.

"Rightio, Guild Leader," answered Ivo. "What should I say about Rumaf and Troef?"

"Tell them there's a potential monster invasion but keep it to the authorities. Ask them to move provisions from RT to SU," he said. "Deeg, continue closing the rest of the rifts. Your priority is red. Take breaks in between."

"Got it," replied Deeg.

When Maxwell turned to the engineer, Lake rattled off his tasks. "Get the generators running. Claim Rumaf and Troef. We also have the Zone Defense Project the mayor requested. I've managed to finish it with my team, but I haven't tested it yet. Hopefully, we don't have to use it."

Maxwell rested a hand on his shoulder. "I agree, that should be a last resort. For the candidate stuff, I don't care about the rules or feelings you three have about this. I don't care who owns Rumaf and Troef—just make it so that it's safe for everyone. Don't risk people's lives because of your ego." He squeezed Lake's shoulder.

Lake nodded and left for his apartment, catching a cab. He thought about experimenting more with what these areas and crystals were about. But right now, he had to reach Keri. When he arrived at his apartment in Untef, he started talking about what had happened, expecting Keri to be listening. But after walking into his living room, kitchen and his bedroom, the maiden was nowhere to be seen. He called her linko. After a few rings, it went to voicemail. He hung up, grabbed his glassy instead and texted:

> Lake: *I need to talk to you. I'm at the apartment.*

> Keri: *I'm at the restaurant next to Amazing Discoveries.*

> Lake: *Stay there. I'm coming to you.*

He quickly changed into his battle suit and added a long coat over it. After putting on his equipment and devices, he exited the apartment with his bag strapped to his back. The lens of his S-Visor covered his eyes and displayed the map of the Cluster RSTU. Looking at the paths, it'd be faster to go to Rumaf first before Troef. Outside the building, he took out his hoverboard and mounted it. After locking his destination on the map, the S-Board ascended a story in height and flew.

After less than half an hour, he arrived at the tallest building in Rumaf—an auction house and museum. From a large base, the slender tower sprawled high up in the air with irregular, rectangular and curved sections. Its twinkling green lights, reflective glasses and bronze-like steel structure stood unique amongst other structures. He hopped off his board and landed on the rooftop. With a mental command, the gold rings of the red claim crystal materialized in his left hand while the shining blue shielding crystal appeared in his right. As quickly as they appeared, they vanished.

> You have consumed Area Claim Crystal. Current Area: Zone Rumaf has been claimed by Hero.
> Areas Claimed: Quisix, Zone Pugof, Zone Untef, Zone Shoef, Zone J-law, Zone Rumaf
> You have consumed Shielding Crystal. Zone Rumaf is now protected for 730 hours.

He took out a few more blue crystals and placed protections on the other areas under his control. With a mental command, he pulled out the area settings from his system. More than a week ticked away for the shielding crystals in all of his controlled areas. On the monsters and people settings, he left them as it was—any person could come in, but no invaders could. Once that was done, he felt like he'd somehow accomplished something.

A call jingled from his S-Visor. "Something wrong?" asked Lake.

Maxwell's face appeared inside his lens display. "I don't know if I should trust you, but it doesn't look like you're a liar, and everything else that you did seems trustworthy."

"What? I'm not following. I told you all I know about the rifts."

His face hardened. "And all of these rifts and them coming now is all coincidence? When our guild is thinned out? I find that hard to believe."

"What? Who are you talking about?"

The lines of his jaw sharpened when he said, "Zuobic is here. The army is here."

At that statement, Lake's heart skipped a beat. He was very careful to cover his tracks online and offline. He made certain no clues about him and what he was doing in the freezones would leak out. It would not do well for the apes or the zone mayors to reveal his identity. "They must've gotten a tip somewhere. I never called them or reached out to them," he defended.

"Too late for that. They're at the gates in Rumaf. Authorities are trying to stall them. They're here on official business—they're here to collect a soldier."

"I need to meet with Keri. I'll call you soon."

He leaped off the building, mounted his S-Board and surfed towards Troef, gliding from rooftop to rooftop. Reaching for his S-Visor, he tried calling Keri but after a few rings, all he got was her voicemail. After leaving a few messages for her, he increased his speed further and hovered above the main cable of the cable cars. After ten minutes, he entered the borders of Zone Troef skidding at the end of a pole and landing on another building.

The Amazing Discoveries building was in sight, along with the restaurant next to it. After zooming in with his visor, he could see Keri chatting with some-one—through which he could only make out a large silhouette. A smile crept on Lake's face. She was safe. Looking to where the zone gate was, Lake saw two armed trucks waiting with four mech escorts. Painted on their bodies was the Zuobic national flag—a cog, fist and anemone interwoven in an arabesque design. The door of the leading truck opened as Cervantes climbed out of the passenger seat. He started speaking with the zone mayor.

All manners of scenarios popped into his head: *Are they here for me? Keri? Or both of us? Am I the next lab rat? If they find about the system, will they treat me as a traitor, a deserter? Am I scared? I've done nothing wrong. If anyone should be accused of wrongdoings, it should be them.*

"Damn it." He hopped off the building and descended to the ground with his S-Boots. As he ran towards Amazing Discoveries, a few bystanders looked at him and were wary of his display of advanced tech.

At the dumpling restaurant, Keri stormed out of the exit and into the back streets. Wayne was close behind with a panicked face. Smelling trouble, Lake sped over to where they were. Once he reached them, they were both arguing at each other:

"It was me," shouted Wayne. "I was the one at the store."

"What are you talking about?" asked Keri.

"I robbed the store in Zuobic. The federate doctors and healers turned me away—they didn't like free people. They said I have to be registered as a closer or a federate should sponsor me before I could get treatment. So I—"

"So you stole from the pharmacy in Walkby?" Keri breathed out. "What do you think that will do? It wouldn't have removed the curse from you."

His shoulders slumped. "I thought it would at least help my family and friends who forgot about me. They have meds for memory stuff, you know? I didn't mean to hurt anyone. Sure, the cash was pretty good too, who doesn't like money? Zuobic is rich enough—they won't care about a few drugs and some money."

She tried to speak, but no words formed. Then, her eyes widened. "The man in the rabbit mask—that was you?" she finally said.

"Keri, I wasn't myself that day. I didn't mean to shoot that lady. I wanted to—" A thunderbolt struck his back, causing him to fall on his knees. Smoke sizzled around his torn shirt, with no wounds visible except for a mild dark spot.

Lake stepped into the street with sparks emanating from his glove. "You killed Jella," he hissed.

Keri gasped. "Lake."

Chapter 50

Keri, Lake's Apartment, Early Morning

Sunlight peeking through the windows stirred Keri awake. The sheets wrapped her naked body as she turned over in the bed and noticed a note on the bedside table. The memories of last night flashed in her mind as she read the note—a smile snuck up on her face. Placing the note away, she only now noticed a new notification lingering at the edge of her vision, ignored the night before.

Congratulations! You have advanced your relationship with Target Love #1
through deep, consensual lovemaking.
Your feelings for each other have grown.
5000 coins earned. Total 19030.

With a giddy beat, she leaped to her feet and started something she had never had fun doing in her life—cleaning. She fumbled for loose clothes in Lake's closet and found a matching shirt and track pants. After dressing and making the bed, she found a closet full of cleaning supplies. Her first order of business was cleaning the floors. After switching to music on her linko, selecting an upbeat song, she tied her hair into a ponytail and started vacuuming. Four songs later, she proceeded to mop until Lake's floors were squeaky clean. As she got ready to dust, an audio message jingled in her linko.

"Please see me at the dumpling place next to our building," Wayne said in the recording. "I really need to talk to you."

She quickly grabbed a glassy and typed her reply: a straightforward *go screw yourself* message. But as her thumb almost pressed the send button, worry echoed in her head: *Does Wayne have the fragment to track claimed areas? Maybe he knows something about the Kermoz accident?* She grumbled, took a second and then sighed. Her fingers and nails clacked away on the glass device, confirming she'd meet him there.

With a heavy heart, she returned the cleaning materials to the closet. After a quick trip to the bathroom to refresh herself and a glass of water later, she was on her way to meet Wayne. Her hand clutched the handrail inside the public cable car as she rode together with other commuters, most likely heading to work. The days of her life in Zuobic, slaving away at the package counter, crept in her mind. She asked herself if she'd want to ever go back to Zuobic. Was there a life waiting for her back home? Padala Services was just an avenue to earn money. And as for the orphanage, it was just another ruin in Kermoz. "Do I stay here for good?" she whispered to herself as she got off the cable car and headed to the dumpling restaurant.

At the entrance, she quickly found Wayne. With his large frame and bearish aura, he was easy to spot sitting at a corner table away from prying eyes. Though far, some women still careened in their seats for lustful stares and men, intimidating ones. Wayne waved as she nodded and their eyes met.

"Hi," she said, settling on the seat in front of him.

"Thanks for seeing me," he said in a gruff voice. "Have you had breakfast? Want wanton noodle soup with beef?"

"I don't care." She wanted to get this over as soon as possible. She focused on her goal to get answers and not let her emotions take hold of her.

After instructing a waiter for their order, Wayne smiled at her, then pouted, "Whose clothes are those? Are those men's clothes?"

She gulped. The situation reminded her of *Love Me, Princess*. There was a scene where the princess was returning from her late-night stroll with the elven prince and the first knight caught her. Due to some circumstances, she was wearing commoner clothes, and he had asked her the same thing. The options for answers were:

1. I was attacked by monsters, (the elven prince saved me) but my

clothes were destroyed. This was the best thing I could find.

2. I was afraid people would notice me in my dress. I borrowed some clothing lying around.

3. At this odd circumstance, you question my clothes?

Keri chose option 3. "You asked me to come to ask about my clothes? After I escaped from you last night?"

His eyes narrowed. "Escape? Is that what you did? You left last night, after I was being nice to you."

"Nice? Is that what you call last night? After you—" She stopped herself from continuing and exhaled a large breath. "Do you have a fragment that lets you find claimed areas?" She focused on the reason why she was here.

"What?"

She breathed deeply. "At least one of the candidates should have a searching ability to find claimed areas. Do you have that?"

After a second of looking at her oddly, he said, "No. My fragments are all looking for monsters and busting them up. Nothing boring like that."

"Do you know about a fourth candidate? Have your heard of the title Ferry? Someone who could be like us?"

"Just you and that nerdy wuss."

She ignored the slur. "Do you know anything about Zone Kermoz? What happened there before?"

Wayne squirmed in his seat. "Why would I know anything about that? I was born in the freezones. I've never been there."

"Except for that time you asked for help with your curse?" suggested Keri.

"Uh yeah, there was that time. They turned me away faster than a hybrid cheetah and horse. What is this about?"

She explained the candidate's roles to him: how they should be claiming areas, the dangers of leaving it unclaimed for rifts and champions; and how it was their job to save and protect people.

Wayne's hands changed into fists for a moment before a movement distracted him. "Oh look, our order is here." He thanked the waiter for bringing them their bowls and immediately started eating.

She stared at him for quite some time, not touching her soup.

"Is there a problem with your food?" he asked with noodles halfway in his mouth. "Don't you like it? Is it too hot?"

"Wayne, what are you not telling me?" she asked in a cold voice.

He placed his chopsticks down. "I'm trying to have a meal here, Keri. What's with all of these questions? Aren't we trying to work things out? Why do I feel like I've done something wrong? You're the one who's been sleeping with that dorky twig."

She shook her head. "I-I-I can't do this." She rose to her feet and stormed out of the restaurant.

"Keri, wait," Wayne shouted from behind.

At the back streets, she snapped at him, "Go away, Wayne. I'm done talking to you." She continued on her way.

"So you're going to just leave me? For that faggy nerd?"

A line of flickering flames as tall as her knees blocked her way. "Wayne, let me go," ordered Keri.

Tiny embers dotted his irises. "I robbed that store in Zuobic. The federate doctors and healers turned me away—they didn't like free people. They said I have to be registered as a closer or a federate should sponsor me before I can get treatment. So, I—"

"So you stole from the pharmacy in WalkBy?" Keri breathed out. "What did you think that will do? It wouldn't have removed the curse from you."

His shoulders slumped. "I thought it would at least help my family and friends who forgot about me. They have meds for memory stuff, you know? I didn't mean to hurt anyone. Sure, cash was pretty good too, who doesn't like money? Zuobic is rich enough—they won't care about a few drugs and money."

The memory of that day came flooding back, the first time she had ever felt that horrified in her life. "The rabbit mask—that was you?" she finally said.

His face pleaded. "Keri, I wasn't myself that day. I didn't mean to shoot that lady. I wanted to—" A thunderbolt struck his back, causing him to fall on his knees. Smoke sizzled around his torn shirt, with no wounds visible except for a mild dark spot.

Lake stepped into the street with sparks emanating from his glove. "You killed Jella," he hissed.

"Lake," gasped Keri.

"You're going to pay for—" A blue pillar of flame engulfed Lake.

Wayne rose to his feet with his right hand balled into a fist covered in flames. "Shut your dirty mouth, cocksucker."

"Lake." As Keri ran to him, the line of blue fire changed into a circle, trapping her within. *Please be all right. Please be all right. I can heal you as long as you're alive,* she chanted in her head. As she reached out her hands to reverse time, the flames collapsed around her and burned her legs. She cried out and fell on her butt.

Wayne stared at her with a blank face—disappointment followed by anger and jealousy. "You really did sleep with him, huh? Why? He's nothing but a sissy sorcerer. He's not one of us. He's only trying to ruin our destiny as lovers, like the ones in your games." He knelt in front of her and held her cheeks. "I'm your knight in shining armor, not him. You gave me, my family and my friends back, and I saved you. I love you. We're both candidates—we're meant to be together. Don't you see? Why ruin that?" He hugged her tight and pressed his lips on hers.

No matter how she flexed and struggled, his grip was solid. She thought of summoning her sword, but he locked her arms tight. A tear fell on her face as he pressed himself more on her. She hated the feeling of being trapped. But what could she do? She was fast but not strong enough to break away from his inhuman grip. Then she found herself floating?

The two candidates gently rose and left the ground. Surprised, Wayne detached himself from her. "What's going on?" he barked as the two drifted away from each other. "Keri." He tried to reach for her, but they moved even further apart.

"She doesn't love you." The blue pillar of fire vanished, revealing Lake protected in a dome of light. His S-glove glowed in a soft white light.

Blue fire roared to life in Wayne's arms. "You. This is all your—" An invisible force slammed him to the ground, face first.

The display lights on Lake's glove changed from white to violet. "Like it? I call this magic 'the weight of your sins.'" A heavier force pressed the Slayer further into the ground, forming cracks and turning rocks into gravel.

Keri was gently placed down on the ground. "Lake, you're all right. I thought you were—look out!" A huge, blue-armored knight blazed into being and towered behind the hero.

As Lake turned back, the knight struck him with a heavy axe. At the last second, he shielded himself with his S-Glove before he smashed against a wall, creating a large new entrance. Just as Keri leapt to his rescue, Wayne caught her ankle, causing her to fall on her knees and arm, scraping them against gravel and concrete. She summoned her sword into her hand and slashed at his arm, instantly freeing herself from his grasp. After staggering up to a run, a wall of fire blocked her path. She gritted her teeth. She turned around and attacked Wayne. He caught the sword with his blazing hands and broke it into pieces. With his steel-like arms, he wrestled her into a tight hug from the back. "Don't leave me, Keri. I love you. Can't you see that? We're meant to be," Wayne pleaded.

"I don't love you," she spat at him. "You and I were a mistake. I was horny and I screwed around with you. I didn't know that back then, but I do now. There is no us."

"It's him, isn't it? As long as he is alive, there is no us. He is the problem."

"What? What are you talking about? Wayne, you're insane. Let me go." Her limbs felt like they were encased under cement with how he held her.

"Watch this, babe. You're going to love it." A cruel glint sparked in his eye as the knight marched over to Lake.

"No. Lake, get up," screamed Keri.

The knight held the axe up as Lake roused to consciousness. At the sight of the blade arcing toward his face, lightning erupted from his hand and shot through the knight, pushing it back. He gathered his bearings as he produced his S-Disc. Source flooded from his glove to the floating disc as it rotated at breakneck speeds. Electricity crackled around it as the spinning force increased by the dozens. Just as the knight was about to stand, he hurled the weapon like a frisbee. A smooth cut divided the knight's body in half as the S-Disc sliced through and exploded. The knight was destroyed.

"Lake." Keri smiled.

"As the saying goes, if ya want to do something right, ya gotta do it yourself." Wayne pushed Keri to the ground, grabbed her ankle by his palms and pressed it. Her bones cracked.

As she cried out in pain, Lake staggered to reach her. "Stop." He shot a lightning bolt at Wayne. The bolt hit his back, but Wayne did not stop.

Tears fell from Keri's face as her breathing labored. The pain in her leg begged for her attention. "Don't—no, no, don't aaaahhh." She cried out as he grabbed her other foot and broke it.

A smile cracked on Wayne's face. "There. Now you'll be a good girl and won't run away."

Rocks, bins, trash and debris floated around Lake as his deteriorating S-Glove glowed violet and red. "You. You. You monster." They zoomed across the air and all hit Wayne.

Flames covered his whole body as he shielded the assault with his arms. Wayne slowly started walking toward Lake as the attacks kept coming at him. When the sorcerer was within reach, the Slayer unfolded his arms and fire exploded around him, pushing Lake back.

"Is that all you've got?" guffawed Wayne.

The walls and streets around them were enveloped in fire. Lamp posts, doors, signs and ads were charred and destroyed. People had already fled at the first sign of danger—all panicked and were crying for help.

"Try this," Lake shouted as he threw a grenade. It exploded into a compressed nitrogen gas that instantly enveloped Wayne in a chamber of ice.

But it only held the man for a few seconds as fire blazed around him. The ice melted at a visible speed and instantaneously transformed into steam. "Is that a parlor trick? You a clown or something? Let me show you real power," he boasted.

Balls of concentrated fire formed behind him. Once they grew to the size of basketballs, they shot into the air. The path they traveled on melted and disintegrated. Each one bombarded Lake's Light Dome. No explosions appeared, but instead, they melted the barrier. At the last ball, the dome of light only covered Lake's legs and head. His whole body was burnt beyond recognition. He fell to his knees, sizzling.

In a flash, Keri appeared beside him with an immovable leg and a limping one. She caught him as they both fell to the ground. Clocks made of light surrounded them both as their wounds healed, slowly but surely.

Sirens resounded across the zone. "We are the Zuobic army. Please don't be alarmed. We are searching for a fugitive," a soldier broadcasted.

"Run," coughed Lake. "Leave me. The army is here for me."

"No. We're both getting out of here." Keri strengthened her power as their wounds healed faster.

"Get away from him," shouted Wayne as he began summoning balls of blue fire.

Despite being battered and torn, Lake's S-Glove lit up again. A hefty force slammed down on Wayne yet again. "Major, I'm here," he announced to his S-Visor as a dot blinked continuously under it.

Keri's eyes widened. "Did you just call the army?"

"They were already here. I only made things faster."

"What are you saying? We can escape." Panic roused on her face.

Lake looked at her as if he was saying goodbye. "I'm sorry, Keri." A hand reached out to her, and she expected he would hug or hold her—something that would be romantic and perfect for a scene in a game or movie. But the hand never held or caressed her; it instead shoved her back, hard. The next thing Keri knew, a rift had opened up behind her, and she fell in.

Chapter 51

Lake, Milz

Pain was the only thing that Lake could understand as he crouched on the ground. The heat of the balls had penetrated his Light Dome fully, leaving only his head and part of his legs protected. His exposed body suffered from third-degree burns. The battle suit that was supposed to protect his body was torn in shreds and flapped against the breeze and his minute movements. If it had not been for Enduring Body, he would have been sprawled on the floor screaming. His new fragment had protected him from critical damage. Despite that, his whole body pressed in on itself, wanting to collapse. Pain ravaged him—at least the parts that could still feel.

A comforting light surrounded him. The weight and pain was lesser. The screams in his thoughts diminished, giving way to his other sensibilities. He began to feel his limbs and move his muscles yet again. Warm, gentle hands caught him as he fell forward. Keri, with her tearing eyes, looked at him with an expression of apology and care wrapped it up in admiration and adoration. A small space in his mind opened up to a thought—and that thought was to save the woman he loved.

Sirens resounded across the zone. "We are the Zuobic army. Please don't be alarmed. We are searching for a fugitive," a soldier announced.

He didn't care if the army found him. But they would not get Keri. He wouldn't forgive himself if she ended up like Tony's father, a lab rat. "Run. Leave me. The army is here for me," he said as clearly as he could.

"No. We're both getting out of here." The light surrounding her flared brighter as their wounds healed faster.

Lake protested in his mind. She should leave. Why was she so stubborn? He thought of reprimanding her, but those last words had exhausted his breath. Any more arguments would not get through to her. He had to act.

Bombs were stashed in his bag. But before he could reach for it, he noticed a child peeking out from an apartment above him. The young child's curious face was stuck onto the window, watching the incident Lake had started. An old woman was on the next floor with a worried look as she observed the chaos brewing. All around, there were families with curious and frightened faces. The ice grenades had been the right choice earlier. Though it was useless against Wayne, it kept the surroundings safe.

But what about now? How could he save Keri? Firebombs were out of the question. His devices were running low on batteries, and some were battered, reaching the limits of their durability. He could, maybe, execute the Zone Defense Project? It was the mayor's request for the Cluster. He knew for a fact that Wayne would be decimated if he activated it—even the army right now would not stand a chance. But what of the free people? They would be caught up as collateral damage. He was supposed to be a hero that saved people—not someone who killed them, even by accident.

Thousands of lives were at risk to perish for his desires—for the love he felt. With a heavy sigh and troubled heart, he commanded his system to help—the same one he had asked it before.

> Escape unavailable. Previous rift has been used in Zone Kermoz and pathway is still open.
>
> Please re-enter Kermoz and claim the zone to re-enable Hero's Retreat.
>
> Do you want to open the rift?

Should I run away with her? thought Lake. All he wanted to do now was stay safe with her. But then the Apes came to mind and the people of this zone—he had no guarantees that Cervantes was not going to turn this place upside down looking for him. He couldn't count on Wayne keeping his former instructor's interest for long.

"Get away from him," shouted Wayne as he began summoning balls of blue fire.

Lake confirmed his choice in the system and checked his S-glove. The core had enough energy for one more use before it ran out and died from the damage. He activated the glove as a hefty force slammed down on Wayne again. His S-Visor connected to the channel the army used. "Major, I'm here," he said while sending his geo-location.

Keri's eyes widened. "Did you just call the army?"

"They were already here. I only made things faster."

"What are you saying? We can escape." Her nostrils flared.

He turned to her, willing the rift to open right behind her. "I'm sorry, Keri." He reached out a hand, wanting so much to hold her and kiss her one last time. But her life was more important than a kiss. He pushed her back. She fell through the rift, crossed dimensions, and vanished.

His S-Glove purred to its death, causing Wayne to break away from the artificial gravity. The balls of fire left his side and flew directly towards Lake. As it approached him, Lake closed his eyes and shielded himself with his arms. Thirty seconds passed when the balls should have melted him. But the impact never came. He opened his eyes. Several layers of Light Domes floated and protected him.

At the end of the street, four sorcerers in Zuobic uniform had their hands held up, maintaining the spells. Major Cervantes stood behind them, standing in a straight posture and with his hands behind his back. "Student Lake, helpless as ever. Here I was hoping you've improved. It seems that surviving like a cockroach is what you'll ever amount to."

"Sir." Lake nodded and avoided staring directly at him.

"Don't get in the way, Feds," Wayne yelled, stepping forward. But before he could get near his target, a bullet shot from above and hit his leg. The bullet bounced off of him like it had hit steel. He stopped and looked up. On the rooftops, several soldiers with guns revealed themselves. Silence ensued for a second before he fled the other direction. But a mech swerved in and blocked his path. He tried running down a street on the left, but another mech blocked it as well. A third mech blocked his last exit.

"What do we have here?" asked Cervantes from where he stood.

"A criminal, sir," answered Lake. "The thief at WalkBy wearing the rabbit mask."

His face relaxed. "Ah. That criminal. So he is like you? A 14 and 17?"

"I beg to differ, sir. He is nothing like me," he replied in a deep voice. "The only similarity we share is that we are both 14s. Nothing more."

Cervantes' expression went rigid. "Arrest him," he ordered.

The mechs advanced in on Wayne—two nets shot at him. Fire blazed around his body as he burned through the nets and launched himself at one giant robot. Landing on its shoulder, he jabbed and burned its head and chest until he got through to the pilot. As he grabbed the pilot by the neck, singeing her skin, a large glowing bullet knocked him off the mech, letting his hostage go. The second mech had fired a source-injected bullet meant for large-sized monsters. A large open wound sizzled with smoke on Wayne's right shoulder and arm. When he snapped his head towards his new attacker, his eyes glowed. The second mech stopped abruptly as the cockpit opened. Smoke rushed out as the pilot burned under blue flames, screaming in agony.

"Interesting," said Cervantes. "Gas him."

The soldiers scattered on the rooftops threw canisters below. It exploded and a cloud of sleeping gas erupted around Wayne. Undeterred by the smoke, he kept forward, but his movements were slower. Fire blazed around him again as he kept advancing. He reached for Lake again and beat the Light Dome around him.

"Very good. But it's time to go to sleep." Cervantes scribbled his fingers, drawing runes on top of each other with one hand. Once his hands balled into fists, a gale swept through the sleeping gas and swirled it around Wayne in a dense cloud. Then it invaded his nostrils and mouth, leaving none in the open air. At the last puff, Wayne's eyes rolled back in his head and he fell flat on the ground unconscious. "Capture him," he ordered.

Soldiers from above scrambled down from the fire exits as the Light Domes around Lake vanished. He, in turn, fell on his butt and released the breath he had been holding. The pain and exhaustion in his body was now more pronounced as the excitement abated.

Cervantes gazed at his student and scoffed. "You look absolutely hideous."

"Thank you for coming, sir," Lake huffed. Dizziness lurked within him.

"Of course, how can I not save my most prized student?"

He was about to ask him what he meant, but his body took over and shut his senses. The last thing he heard were murmurs from his former superior before he lost consciousness.

Lake opened his eyes as he found himself in what seemed like a hospital room. Out the window, he recognized the familiar concrete jungle, the crowded streets and the buzz of advertisements on billboards and drones. He was back in Zuobic. If he had to guess, he was probably in Milz—the closest zone to the border of the lawless lands and the freezones. Relief swept over him; it seemed, at least, that he'd survived and Keri was not here.

"You look fine for someone who's been asleep for a week," said Maggie as she entered the room in a doctor's coat.

"Maggie? Why are you—you're my doctor?" His brows met.

"I know, right? What a waste of my talent—tending to a burn victim. It's beneath me," she replied. "Anyway, you've saved me before, now it's only fair I do the same."

"Is that a thank you?"

"That's all you're ever going to get." She pulled out a glassy from her pockets and reviewed the chart on it as well the floating displays around the room.

"Am I going to leave here soon?" He scratched his right thigh.

"If you're asking about the hospital, about two more days at most, then you can leave. But if the question is where you'll go after..." She gestured over at the open door where two armed soldiers stood guard.

Lake peeked and nodded. "It's all right. I'm sure there's an investigation about me. Did they take anyone besides me?"

She raised a brow. "If you mean the muscle-head with anger issues, sure, we took him into custody. We're now running experiments on him. Major Cervantes will debrief you on that. I'm not allowed to say more."

That reassured him—it meant Keri really was safe. He checked his body; there were no signs of wounds or scars—just lingering pain. "Was this because of healing spells?" he asked.

"That, and a new drug Dr. Badez and I developed. It's called H1-Potion. It's going to revolutionize the war against monsters." She flicked her hair.

"That's great. Looks like you're going to help a lot of people."

Maggie raised a brow and then cleared her throat. "Uh, thanks. I don't see any problem with your recovery, so you should be good to leave tomorrow."

"Thanks, Maggie." He scratched his thigh again.

She went for the door and stopped at the frame. "I'm leaving today for the base. The nurses should be fine taking care of you. Whatever happened last time, I'm glad you're alive."

As soon as Maggie left, Lake crawled over to the med trolley left in his room. He searched each drawer and found a large X-ray tablet at the bottom. Booting it up, he undid his hospital gown and scanned his whole body. After a few zooms and angle changes, he found a microchip inserted between a layer of fat in his thigh. The design looked like a tracker to Lake. He itched to rip it out of him, but without knowing how it worked, it would be dangerous to do so. His equipment and bag were nowhere in sight. He figured they would have confiscated it. That didn't worry him too much since both items were weaved into his soul—no other person could use them. So unless they had a way to undo them, they'd be useless to them.

Slowing his breath and closing his eyes, he tugged on the faint strings that connected his soul with his items. He could barely feel them due to the distance, but he knew the general direction of where they were. So he had a way of finding them again. A plan slowly formed in his head.

Chapter 52

Keri, Family Home, Kermoz

"Hello, is anybody there?" shouted Keri. She had been walking around for hours in the empty streets of Kermoz, and she had yet to find a soul or a monster. The dilapidated buildings, the crumbling roads and the abandoned cars and shops all looked familiar to her. At the corner street was an ice cream shop she used to go to with her dad, and just down at the end was the salon where her mom went for mani-pedis and hair dyes. Memories of growing up slowly fixed themselves in her head. The images she had of herself as a child being an orphan were actually all the times she had spent with the kids in the youth center. She was projecting herself as the orphans she had taken care of. They were slowly unraveling, one by one. While deep in thought, her steps had taken her back to the youth center, her second home.

A golden wisp appeared and transformed into Fynn. He stood tall and lanky as he was before, not a day older. "Hi Keri." A misty yellow aura surrounded him.

"Fynn, you're here," said Keri, finally fully remembering her old boss.

A smiled crept on his face. "I've always been here. I just wasn't allowed to talk to you until you reached this point."

"This point?"

"Come, we should talk." As he led her back inside the center, he retold the stories he had told Keri and the kids. But this time, there were no dramas, just the facts:

The universe had a vast number of worlds existing in different dimensions. Some worlds flourished and were rich in resources, souls and source. Silaw was one such world, so for dying worlds, the only option was to steal them. That was the reason invaders, called champions, were coming to Silaw. But the worlds were protected by multiversal laws. One law was that to declare an invasion, a bridging dimension must be created—the outworlds. There, people of both worlds would battle. Winners earned rewards and the contested area. The bridging dimensions gave each side time to prepare, and it disallowed strong entities from crossing through immediately.

"The experiment in the broadcast station, the army made a hole without the outworld," Keri recalled the black human-like monsters with bright capes.

"Yes, they did. The Will of Svartals crossed through and possessed your dad. The red wisp."

"And the golden one that talked to Silaw was you?"

"Yes. Souls usually go through a cleansing phase for all their experiences, removing their memories. Silaw prevented that from happening and made sure I could help immediately after my death. I was banned from talking directly to you until your soul was ready and healthy." Fynn led her to the living room where it all happened.

Bloodstained floors covered in accumulated dust creaked from their footsteps as Fynn walked through and Keri followed. The walls and furniture had decayed from neglect. Unrecognizable bodies wearing army uniforms laid there next to smaller corpses. She looked away. The gunshot, the red mist, the panic, the fear, her brush with death—everything flooded back. She stormed straight to an empty bedroom and slammed the door shut.

Fynn reappeared next to her bed. "I'm sorry you have to be here."

Tears welled from her eyes. "Why? Why did I forget them? Why now?" she shouted.

"You know why," he said in a calming voice.

"Yes, I'm damaged. My soul's broken. I'm broken," she said out loud. "But why am I doing things differently? Why am I running after guys like they're some sort of validation for me? I used to want my career first. I wanted to help children. I don't want...

"My thoughts, my dreams, I don't know what is real anymore." She sat on the floor, wiping the tears from her eyes.

Fynn crossed the room and knelt, facing her. "Oh Keri. The confusing memories are working to right themselves piece by piece, you know that. And these different thoughts, they're not actually anyone else's. They're all yours."

"What are you saying? I feel like I was a different person back then to who I am now," she exclaimed. "None of what I do is the same. None of my priorities are the same. This new soul changed me."

"As it should," agreed Fynn. "The new soul within you suppressed the trauma so that you could continue to grow and become the person that you were meant to be. The game's main character served as a crutch for the missing you to build on—your personality and memories. It didn't change you into someone else. You grew as a person with it."

She looked up at him with tousled hair covering her bleary eyes. "But why am I thirsty? Like why do I like men so much? It's the same thing in the game."

He shrugged. "The new soul may have increased your desires for men heavily since your passion to help orphans needed to be sealed away. It just led you to a different goal instead. But at the end of the day, these feelings—happy, sad, weird, exciting, lusty—they are all yours, Keri. None of them were put into you. You changed because you changed with time, just like everyone else.

"You are still you, Keri. No matter how you move, what you like, what you dislike—these thoughts and actions are all still you." Fynn ran a ghostly hand across her cheek.

Her heart had calmed down a bit. "Is that all the game did to me?"

He nodded. "Silaw also used the game to make the system. To guide you and the other candidates, since he is indisposed."

Keri took a moment to just breathe and settle herself. Afterwards she asked, "What happened to him? And Charlie? Is he—are they okay?"

"Follow me." Fynn stood and went through the wall.

She exited the room and went to the next one. Inside, on the bed, rested Charlie sound asleep with Fynn hovering over him. "Silaw is the name of this world. All Wills inherit their name from their worlds because the Will is the personification of the World. They are the same being. Wills cannot appear and affect our lives directly without a vessel. Good vessels are young entities that are usually exposed to a lot of source. Either a sorcerer, or people trapped in the outworlds. Outlier 32s, humanoids, make good vessels," he explained.

Keri sat next to Charlie and caressed his hair. "So, Charlie and the kids, you were only using them. That's not fair."

"Believe me or not, they knew about it," said Fynn. "A vessel must be willing and must practice imbibing the Will's presence to get stronger. The stronger and more willing they are, the longer they live and last. Any other person would not last, or would die almost immediately, if they tried to host a Will."

"Like my dad," she spoke softly as she remembered Xander's deteriorating condition once he was possessed.

Fynn nodded, then told her the boy's story: Charlie had only known about Silaw for a few days when the Richforths brought him to the center. Being a vessel was new to him. The incident in Kermoz had pushed him to his limit. As Silaw, he had to remove the Svartal and slowly plug the hole the army created all by himself. He was successful over the many years that had passed, but it wasn't without a heavy cost. Both souls were weak and needed to rest. Silaw returned Charlie two years ago, hoping he could forget the trauma and mature as a person before becoming a vessel again.

But the incident at WalkBy happened and Keri's awakening triggered Charlie to revive as Silaw. Both souls were still weak, and therefore the process created an unstable Chatterbox. To make matters worse, the Slayer claimed and lost Kermoz, which reopened the rift the army had made. So Charlie and Silaw had to plug the hole again, leading to further instability for both souls. With some of the world's areas already claimed by champions, their abilities were limited, and their recoveries had stalled with the diminishing source.

"That is why he sleeps and recovers while he closes the rift here. Soon, Charlie will die and Silaw will return to the world, leaving a small hole for invaders to freely enter," finished Fynn.

"Die? He can't!" Panic rose in Keri's voice. "There must me something we can do."

"Claim this place. Put a shield around it, and establish it as your prime area," he urged. "That way, Silaw can freely remove himself from Charlie and the rift."

"Claim, shield, what? I don't get it. But if I can do it, I'll do it," she said with confidence.

"Follow me." Fynn transformed back into his wisp form and flew outside.

Chapter 53

Cervantes, Aberkyz

Sitting in his office, Cervantes observed two floating screens. The left showed Jella floating inside her tank—her head was wrapped in multiple devices that kept her alive. The experiments on her had been fruitful. Regarding the project for the H1 drug, they had begun piloting it on select soldiers—so far, the feedback had been positive. As a quick first aid, it was very successful. They were ready to start mass production. The second experiment, the soldier project, was successful as well.

"How is she?" he asked.

"Stable. Her body is very resilient," answered Badez, who stood behind him.

"And the new 14?"

"We're administering mind conditioning to him right now," answered Dr. Badez. "Seems to be working, but we'll have illusionary spells cast on him too."

The right screen showed Wayne in briefs. He had a hard-plastic helmet on that had several buttons and knobs. He stood at attention. Cervantes observed him closely at the screen as he read a glassy filled with notes from Badez's experiments. The document detailed Wayne's capacity to learn new abilities through things called fragments. How he could claim a space, and his insatiable desire to kill monsters—though there was a mild fear and anxiety against a thing called champions.

A third screen opened with the faces of people that were included in the WalkBy incident. A bunch of photos were crossed out, dead, excluding Lake and Jella. The man with a rabbit mask was replaced with Wayne's photo.

"Hmmm...does this mean...?" Cervantes' voice lingered.

"As the video suggests, he is the reason," answered Dr. Badez.

The doors to the office burst open as Vivian stormed in. The assistant came running behind her, insisting she turn back. She glanced at Cervantes with a pleading expression that he waved away. The assistant saluted and closed the doors behind her as she left.

"Your assistant is dramatic. Really, how could she not know me?" Vivian demanded.

"That was the idea, Viv," answered Cervantes. "To stop you from causing drama."

"Good day, Sergeant Cervantes," greeted Dr. Badez.

Vivian sneered at him, then smiled at her. "Former sergeant. I go by Vivian Chadstone now, or Mx. Chadstone. I see you're still here, Badez. You're working with him? Where has the pride of saving lives gone? Have you switched to murder instead of saving the dying? Is that your career goal now?"

She inhaled deeply and said, "Don't hate me, Vivian, you have no right to pass judgement on me. I wasn't the one who pushed you out. I'll leave you to the real monster." She gestured a farewell and left the room.

Cervantes rose from his seat and went to his drink bar at the side. "How is lesbian life going? Is it any different from real marriage? Oh, I forgot you still like penises, don't you? Does that go away? You know, my theory is that unlike real gay people, you like the companion of women, but lust after the hard body of men." A sexual rasp grated in his low voice.

"I think you settle with women because they are easier to control," he continued. "But behind all that bisexual drama, you're a plain woman who can't really get what she wants. Pity, you play the confused-lesbian-pretend-mother well."

"Fuck your opinions and your theory, Christopher," Vivian said dismissively. "Where is Keri?"

"We have thousands of staff and soldiers—you can't expect me to know all of them."

"Keri Bolo, she has a name, you stupid asshole. Not subject R-A-N-D-O-M-1," she spelled with spite.

He boiled water and prepared a cup of tea. "As usual, you are delusional, Vivian. I do not have anyone named Keri Bolo."

"Then why is she on this list?" She pointed at the third screen where Keri's photo was. She and another were greyed out.

"The crossed ones are dead. The grey ones are missing. I don't have her, as much as I want to. Do you want a cup? A medical doctor gave me a drink made from a monster plant. It's very refreshing." He sipped the warm blue liquid.

"Fine. If you don't have Keri, give me Wayne," demanded Vivian. "The deal was for search assistance and protection in exchange for Lake. I called you to Troef to get your soldier, not to abduct Wayne."

Cervantes went back to his desk and placed the cup of tea. "The deal was: you ask for my help to search for your fake son that keeps disappearing and coming back. Then he shows up, and you don't want the deal with me anymore? Next, you'll want to strike another deal for your family to become Zuosh, and for you to be exonerated? All that for a former student? Now you want me to help find your fake son, again? I'm terribly confused. It's hard to keep up with, Vivian. It's like our marriage all over again—you're always changing your mind," he said in a deep, condescending drawl.

She approached the desk closer. "It's not that hard. Protect my family and find my son and in exchange I get you your precious student back. Wayne is off the table."

"I don't make risky deals with unstable people. Besides, criminals are not off the table."

"He robbed a WalkBy, that's hardly a crime. I'll pay the fine."

He grinned as he sipped his tea. His linko chimed in as his assistant reported that his next appointment was already here. "Right on time. Send him in," he said back to the other line.

In civilian clothing, Lake entered and saluted. "Sir, I—Vivian?"

"Yes. I believe you've met my ex-wife."

"Ex-wife, that would mean..."

Cervantes watched as the cogs in his former student's head turned. When Lake's relaxed face turned serious, he smiled. Seeing the realization on his face, about being betrayed by people who he thought he could trust, was joyous to the major. Then, the next second, Lake had masked his emotions with a stoic look, waiting to hear his superior first before anything else. Another stroke of happiness tickled his heart. The boy had indeed grown.

"What are you playing at, Christopher? Are you shaming me?" asked Vivian.

He ignored the prattles of his ex-wife and activated a bigger floating screen. "Mr. Deskenn, this was taken some days after the incident in WalkBy." A video played on the screen. It showed a vast, deserted land with nothing but bushes, rocks and dirt. The next second, that changed. An old ruin of a city replaced the landscape.

"Zone Kermoz," Lake whispered.

The video continued as a rift opened in the middle of the street and a disoriented and ruffled Wayne exited. He dropped to the ground and puked while the rift closed. After a few minutes, he rose to his feet and started running. His head kept looking back like something was chasing after him, but nothing did. The video stopped.

"Wayne escaped a rift. That's good, isn't it?" asked Vivian. "He survived. That's more than most of us could do."

Cervantes smiled. "Yes. That is true. But he didn't finish the job. He left a level-2 monster undefeated in another dimension."

"Stop beating around the bush. Tell me what he did that was so incriminating."

"Care to explain, Civilian Lake? How a candidate is supposed to do their work?" asked Cervantes, staring deeply at his former student.

Sweat dotted on Lake's forehead. After a moment and a few deep breaths, he explained, "When monsters breakaway from rifts, the last one to appear before it closes are champions, what we call level-2, because of their human-like intelligence. Once they do, they claim a space in our world to bring into theirs, and it disappears from our dimension."

"That's what we call a 25, or a deleted space," added Cervantes. "Explain how to make them 24, the recovered space."

He licked his drying lips then said, "To bring them back, candidates must defeat the champion and claim their dimension. Wayne didn't kill the champion. He only brought Kermoz back for the Spider-Woman to reclaim it. He was the reason we got ambushed." The lines of his jaw stiffened.

"It wasn't his responsibility," defended Vivian. "He wasn't even a registered closer back then."

"You should say that to the president," said Cervantes.

She seethed. "You gave this to him?"

He moved closer to her head. "He knows everything. You know my orders have changed since the trouble eight years ago. I am very open to His Excellency now. You could say we're friends. When I sent him all these files, he immediately messaged me and said, 'Lock up the criminal.'

"If I were you, I'd be happy that my family is protected by the army. Whatever deal you think you can pull from our dead daughter, it will not work. Unless you want to exchange your deal for this gigolo," he whispered and slightly grinned.

Vivian's fierce stare was dowsed a few degrees cooler. "This is not over." She left the room with only the clack of her heels resounding.

A smile crept on Cervantes' face as she left. He moved to his desk, grabbed a small box and presented it to Lake. "Here you are."

Lake took the small box and opened it. "Sir? What is this for?" A golden medal with a violet tassel glinted against the light.

"For the hero who found the culprit of the Kermoz incident. The one who saved his squad. The one who tried to investigate the mysteries of missing spaces," said Cervantes with a grin. "Of course, it isn't only the medal. We are giving you your own permanent residence and a large number of credits."

He tried to give the box back. "Sir, I can't take this. I—"

His hands rose up in the air in a surrender. "I won't take it back. I've cleared it with the general and the president, it's all good."

"Major, this is not what I—"

He placed a hand on his shoulder. "I know, I know. You must've had your hesitations, troubles, being alone out there, death, monsters, strangers—out of touch with your teammates—your family. But you've accomplished something, Civilian Lake. Something to be proud of, even though you're still horrendous in combat. The tech you made—that glove and visor—extraordinary."

His ears reddened. "Tha—thank you, sir. About my stuff, do you think I can get them back?"

Cervantes handed him a violet star encircled by a steel ring—the badge of a captain. A cog, fist and anemone were engraved at the middle of the star. "We want you to come back. Start your enlistment as a captain, and you'll form your own division with a ten-man squad at the start. How about that?"

"I-I-I don't know what to say," he stuttered, speaking his mind. This was too much for him to process.

"Say yes, is there any other option?"

"I..."

"I know it's a shock. Let it all sink in. Rest at your new home—all of the details about that should be in your messages. Then after a few days, go to the admin center and show them this badge. They'll know it straight away, then they'll hand all your equipment back. How does that sound?"

"Yes sir," he said with a slight hesitation in his tone.

"Good. I expect you to be in good shape when you come back." He tapped his shoulder and went back to his desk.

Chapter 54

Lake, Chulz

Lake knew that Major Cervantes was a man of science and ambition. After reclaiming Zone Quisix and living in the freezones, he had the time to search for intelligence regarding past missions by the army. The Apes had access to the real reports that were from their perspective—the free people's perspective, who had no ties nor political agenda. More than one person, more than one report, cited that the army, led by Cervantes, had enslaved people and abducted closers and prioritized saving people last. Sure, at the end of the day, the rifts were closed, and the number of monsters dwindled to almost zero, but it was all at the expense of thousands of lives.

Staring out at his newly acquired wide two-story house with a blooming front garden, Lake couldn't help but be angry. This was the result of trampling on people's lives. A grandiose home for an officer in the army—was he one of them now?

Bags and boxes stuffed with his things from his dorm filled the entryway. After confirming that his escorts were staying outside his home, he quickly perused the boxes. Oddly, the other packed boxes came from his apartment in Zone Untef. Rummaging through them, he couldn't find any of the cores he saved or the weapons he'd collected from monsters. He guessed the army ransacked his home in Untef and collected anything they thought was valuable, leaving him with undesirable and inconsequential items. One thing that caught his attention though, was the red lizard's blindfold. The leathery fabric rubbed against his fingers as his failures echoed in his mind. Stashing it and his feelings, he gathered up the various items in the living room.

With a small drill here, a solder there and a few chip programmings later, he fashioned a small scanner embedded in a chocolate tin. From his spares, he grabbed an old linko model and connected them. Once connected, he went around his house and scanned every nook and cranny. Spy bugs were attached in a number of inconspicuous places: under a rug, in a vase, behind a bookshelf—they were everywhere. Though only a few were cubexes and the rest were audio ones, he felt uneasy and harassed.

Captain of a squad, more like a prisoner.

For a moment, he thought about disabling the bugs, but he figured they'd notice—he was careful enough to act like he was looking around the house while he inspected security devices.

After another round of walking, he settled into the master's bedroom, bringing some of his bags up. He pretended to put them in the walk-in closet, placing each one in. Casually, he removed his shirt and threw it over a lamp where a cubex was carefully hidden. He then turned the shower and music on, making sure it was loud enough before entering the walk-in closet and shutting it behind him. The space was one of the only places that wasn't bugged, aside from the kitchen pantry. He figured this was the best place for what he was about to do. On the floor, a med-gun, outlier knife, and some bandages and bottles of antiseptic spilled out from his bag—all pilfered from the hospital. Even the knife belonged to the security office in the ward. He stripped down to his underwear and breathed in deeply. It was going to be a long 'bath'.

Morning peeked behind the window shutters as Lake roused from his sleep. The pain around his leg made him scowl. He had passed out after successfully removing the tracker. His hands played around with the small chip from his nightstand. He had some ideas on where to keep it on him, but first, breakfast.

In the kitchen of his large new house, he cooked hashbrowns and sausages. The pantry was surprisingly well-stocked. But then again, stocking food was one way to keep him from going anywhere else. As he stood, munching on his breakfast, he looked outside the windows. His escorts had moved into a small house, the size of a garage, across from him. He had not noticed it yesterday with all of the things weighing on his mind. But it seemed to be they were here to stay. Once again, he felt the Major's proposal was for show. *It's a load of bullshit*, would be the words Keri would use in this situation. He wondered how she was, if she was fine and doing well. He could only hope she was safe and not mad at him for sending her away.

After putting his plate in the dishwasher, he set his mind to what he had to do: find a way to dispose of the tracker without alerting the army, find a way to protect himself, get his gear back—and then maybe escape? Definitely out of this place. He wanted—no, *needed*—to cut ties with the army completely. But where would he go? Back to the freezones?

Truth be told, what he was doing at Cluster RSTU was much more exciting for him. He didn't think he'd love being an engineer before since he wasn't saving lives or being on the frontlines fighting monsters. But whenever he set the generators running, or when new refugees settled nearby his protection, he'd get a notification. Like the one he received this morning:

> Four refugees have settled in your territory. 400 coins for providing safety and security.

For some reason, these notifications that he had originally put on silent made him feel fuzzy inside. It made him smile knowing he was actually doing what he longed for—what he'd dreamed of and worked toward his entire life. After transferring the boxes from the entryway into the house's study, he settled at the desk with tools on hand, parts on the desk and devices on the floor. He was ready to save lives in his own way. Lake knew he could be the person he longed to be without having to be a soldier. He could be the hero—no, he was ready to be the hero. Putting protective eyewear on over his head, he got to work.

Chapter 55

Keri, Underground Station, Kermoz

Under the ruins of Kermoz, through the tunnels dug by ghost-spiders, Keri stepped into a spacious cavern. The temperature was nearly freezing as ice blanketed the whole underground. Almost like statues, the carcasses of spider-ghosts lay trapped within ice pillars, unmoving. "It's just like what Lake said. How come the ice hasn't melted?" asked Keri.

Flynn floated next to her in his wisp form. "Ice produced from source always lasts longer and acts differently from normal ice. Keri, watch out!"

A red ray of disintegrating energy shot out, hit the wall and moved across. It almost sliced Keri in half if she had not used her speed to jump away from it and seek cover from a frozen rock. "What is that?" she huffed.

A large lump of ice stood out in the middle as the red light faded into it. The Spider-Woman's whole body was trapped in ice with part of its face missing. Six of its eyes danced with madness after seeing Keri—then one of the eyes darkened and stopped moving.

Keri tried to look. "Is that the champion?"

"Don't look," warned Fynn as Keri placed her firmly back on the rock. "It is the champion, the ruler of the ghost spider species. It is weakened from the ice."

"It almost killed me. That is not weak."

"Its eyes are still active. Be careful not to look into them and risk a curse befalling you."

Keri summoned the Soulsword as a blue-black long, light sword materialized in her grasp. It was the reward for killing the Dragon-Knight. Since her Trainee Sword was broken, this was her only weapon. Though she had used it once some time ago, she had not fully explored what the sword could do. "You forgot the freaking laser beams!" She picked up a rock on the ground, ready to throw it.

"Don't do that. It'll lock on this position and pierce the boulder with its laser," Fynn said. "I'll tell you when to move."

A clock made of light illuminated the ground where Keri stood and waited. The clock turned around a few times as her speed increased. Her heart thumped out of her chest from nervousness, but she kept reminding herself that it was just like she had trained with Lake. It's just another monster.

"Now!" shouted Fynn.

The next moment, Keri was heading for the enemy. She was halfway there while its eyes were looking away from her. When she was within arm's reach, the irises focused on her quickly and glowed bright red, but she leaped up in the air and spun behind its frozen, half-dead body. Her sword sliced across and the head of the Spider-Woman came flying off with shards of ice. It rolled across the frozen floor as its rage-filled eyes dimmed with its death.

Congratulations! You have defeated the champion of Ghost Spiders aka Spider-Woman.
You have increased available fragments to +1. You have earned 1800 coins.
Total coins: 20830.
You have earned the item: Shadowring.

"Quickly, now," urged Fynn.

Candidate Maiden has purchased 6 area crystals for 10050. Total coins 10780 coins.
You have consumed Area Claim and Shielding Crystal. Current Area: Zone Kermoz has been claimed by Maiden.
Areas Claimed: E-law, A2, Kermoz.
Please use another claim crystal for bridged dimension Kz-S1

"It's asking me to use another crystal for a bridged dimension?" inquired Keri. "What do I do?"

"Use another crystal," answered Fynn. "It's the dimension heading back to their world. champions must put one area of theirs at stake whenever they try to invade. It's a risk they have to take. Take it. It's your reward."

> You have consumed Area Claim and Shielding Crystal.
> Current Area: Kz-S1 has been claimed by Maiden.
> Areas Claimed: E-law, A2, Kermoz, Kz-S1.

She felt it. The area had reconnected back to Silaw. The other dimensions in her possession also established spatial pathways which she had access to. A rift opened before her at her mental command. After crossing through, she stepped onto the rooftop of the highest building in Kermoz. Somehow, she could see a dark hole covering the morning sky. She knew, partially, that the tear had been sealed. But it would take more source for it to be as good as before.

> The hole in Kermoz is sealed and restoration will begin. Source consumption has been calculated to 10 coins a day for restoration upkeep vs available coins.
> Please increase your coins to prevent dimensional overtake.
> Consumed 500 coins for initial re-sealing. Tomorrow's consumption will be reduced to 10 coins. Total 10280

Fynn reappeared before her as a human. "You did it, Keri," he said.

"Is that it? It's not going to open again, right?"

"If you prevent this place from falling into enemy hands, it should recover completely."

She placed her weight on one leg. "You don't make things easy, do you?"

"Our roles were never easy. I was tasked with gathering and guiding the vessels and you. And you, my dear, are here to save the world." He tried to touch her shoulder, but his hand only passed through.

Disappointment crossed her face, but she easily changed to expectation. "Is Charlie going to be okay? He's not gonna die, is he?"

He closed his eyes for a moment. "He's still asleep, but the shackles that tied him to this dimension are gone now, since we're back in Silaw. He's recovering slowly. The best thing for him is to gain full strength. To do that, you and the other candidates need to—"

"—gain authority. I know," finished Keri. "Is it okay to move Charlie? I was thinking he should at least be with his parents."

"It should be fine." Fynn's hand started to slowly fade.

"What's happening?"

He looked at his missing hand and vaporizing arm. "My time here is over. You have recovered. You're strong now, Keri. There's not much I can help you with at this point."

"Wait. No. We haven't even gossiped about the men in my life," she exclaimed. "I haven't told you I'm in love—or I think I am. You always talked about your sexcapades when you were younger, I now have input."

A snicker flashed on Fynn's translucent face. "I've been with you all this time, remember? I just wasn't allowed to interfere. And yes, I've seen you in your intimate moments. You need to work on your technique, especially your blowjobs."

She blushed. "Pervert! But seriously, Fynn, wait." She tried to grab him, but half of his body had already vanished.

"Don't worry, Keri. I think I'll be back. It's all up to Silaw." His whole figure was now barely visible.

"No..." Her voice was hoarse as tears welled up in the corner of her eyes.

"Goodbye, Keri," Fynn whispered. "Here's a little something."

Congratulations! Prima has upgraded to rank D.

Description: (1) The Maiden is the muse of the world. She has an affinity with Silaw, his blessings and the outworld artefacts. (2) Maiden can locate hidden candidates. (3) Maiden is supported by a soul fashioned from Princess Bolo.

Congratulations! Swordswoman Body has evolved to Bolo Sword Technique – C.

Description: The basics and intermediate techniques of the Bolo sword and the body that is one with the sword is imbued in the Maiden's body.

CANDIDATE STATUS:

Name: Keri Richforth | Profile: Maiden

Coins: 10280 | Remaining Fragments: 2

Activated Fragments: Prima – E (innate), Bolo Sword Technique – C, Pace of Time – B

Chapter 56

Jella, Lab Room, Aberkyz

Jella floated in her glass tank, unable to move, with a helmet that masked her whole head and tubes stuck into her naked body. The only part of her that moved were her eyes, which saw through the helmet. Weeks had floated by since the chatty doctor was replaced by the smug one. Or had it been months? Truthfully, Jella didn't know. Being stuck in a water tank like a fish without ever going outside or at least seeing a clock sucked the hope and life out of her. She inwardly snickered. At least the fish could swim about; she wasn't even allowed to move. Something in these tubes prevented her from recovering control over her motor skills. She felt it when they would remove her from the tank and place her on the operating table.

Her body rested flat on the table with the tubes removed and only the mask on her. In that instant, the nerves in her body started responding to her. She felt a slight tingle in her leg. The first time this had happened, she thought she was regaining feeling over her lower parts. When she saw a hover cart floating next to her, she tried to scream but produced muffled noises instead. A researcher carted her bloodied left leg. Her body convulsed and spasmed as if it wanted to run amok.

"Heart rate is 167," announced the smug doctor with the long black hair. "We should put her to sleep."

The older female doctor with short locks stared hard at her. "Cut the right toe off first. She can take it."

"Heart rate is still rising—are you sure, Dr. Badez?"

"Yes, Doctor Alkido. Cut the toe."

Alkido disappeared from Jella's vision as she felt the same twinge on her right. When she returned, the doctor held a bag with her toe inside. Her heart bubbled in fury. She imagined ripping the bitch's face apart and cutting her toes one by one. But none of that happened. Her body continued to spasm as she hyperventilated and passed out.

The next hour—or was it the next day? It was hard to tell. She only knew that her leg was gone as she mourned for it inside the glass tank. If the tanks were empty, her tears could've filled it instead.

"Subject has fully regrown her leg," announced Maggie, who was inspecting multiple screens. One showed a video of her in real time and the others displayed multiple scans of her body—one of which had no leg and the other with a leg.

Jella squinted as much as she could at the screens. From her position, she could actually see that her left leg was still with her. How was that possible?

"Time until full regeneration of the leg?" asked Dr. Badez.

"Thirty-six hours," answered Maggie.

Regeneration? She was regenerating? Was she a sorcerer? No, they used runes or sigils or whatever. So she was an ability user—the new outlier? A notification bleeped before her.

Congratulations! Molded Being has increased a rank. Molded Being – E. Description: (1) Candidate can mold her outer appearance according to her will. (2) No magic or physical damage can break nor change her appearance and physiology. Repairing mold will utilize candidate's source. (3) Mold is restricted to the likeness of humans. Cannot be molded into other beings.

"How long do you think her toe would take to regenerate?" asked Dr. Badez.

"One or two hours at most," answered Maggie.

Jella read the notification over and over again. For some reason, she accepted these things as a part of her new abilities. It wasn't like she could ignore them anyway, since she was stuck in this glass tube with nothing else to do. But the more she read, the more she understood that whatever they were doing to her body, this screen-system-thing was reacting to it, and it was changing her. For every cut and chop, for every harvest they made, they changed her. How dare they make changes to her body? To her own self. The dream of gutting these two burned bright inside her, distracting her from her grim reality.

The next day, the two bitches arrived. They pulled her out of the tank and onto the table. With a sharp bite instead of a slight twinge, her left leg was stolen from her yet again. She screamed inwardly, sweating like she had run a marathon and passed out after pushing herself for hours. This continued ten more times. Each time, the twinge changed from a soft pinch to actually feeling a knife slice through her skin. Though it was fast, the feeling had increased. She noticed the time she lost consciousness had decreased until she didn't anymore. According to the smug bitch, "The subject's regeneration time has decreased. Her body is learning and coping with the trauma faster."

"Those are good results," answered Dr. Badez.

Hearing the affirmative, Jella assumed it would be over now. They got what they needed. They'd let her sleep for a while. No more chopping. No more slicing her big toe off. After two days of rest, she still didn't know what the real time was. The clocks on the screens gave her reference to seconds and minutes as they ticked by, but the actual date was nowhere to be seen.

The lid of her tank opened again and the researchers pulled her out and put her back on the table. A knife sliced her left leg. *Are they doing it again?* she thought. But instead of the toe, she saw Maggie-smug-face move to her side and hold out a glowing knife. Alarm bells rang in her head as she saw the knife hover over her left arm. She convulsed and panicked again as the shining blade broke apart her skin and her blood dripped onto the table. In several practiced strokes, Maggie severed the nerves and flesh of her arm. When she got to the bone, the glowing knife was replaced by a shining hacksaw. Jella watched fervently as the insane doctor sawed through her bone. She gritted her teeth as she ordered her body to move and stop the bitch. But the operation continued until her arm was fully detached. The moment Maggie transferred the severed limb into a cold box, Jella passed out.

Days rolled into weeks as the same act was repeated. Ten more times for a set of arms. Ten more times for a set of two arms and one leg. Ten more times for her whole legs and fingers. Ten more times for her whole arms up to her shoulders and her two legs up to her pelvis. Then it switched to opening her chest cavity and harvesting her organs. First her stomach, then her lungs, then her intestines. Each time this happened, she raged, cried and boiled on the inside. The feeling was so clinical and repetitive that each time it happened, it became more bearable, until she understood true pain well enough to ignore it. She grew so used to it that she no longer passed out from the harvesting, nor cried on the inside. She just was. It happened so many times it pushed her fragment to its limit, to which her system responded:

> Congratulations! Molded Being has evolved to Forever Molded – A. Forever Molded – A. Description: (1) Candidate can mold her outer appearance according to her will and instructions. (2) No magic or physical damage can break nor change her appearance and physiology. Repairing breaks requires small source. (3) Mold may adapt to any material source but is restricted to the likeness and form of humans. Other beings cannot be molded into. (4) Fragment requires very minimal source to activate and none to deactivate.

Jella thought about the man named Lake that the smug-faced bitch had talked about a lot. She believed her memories had returned and knew in her heart that her memories were now intact, save for a few moments in the distant past, forgotten like any normal human would. But however much she thought about it, there was no such man called Lake in her life. Actually, there was no man in her life. Not before. Not ever.

She wondered what it was like if she went out with him—this man that they said she had dated. What was the feeling of having a man be with you, love you and stand beside you? Was it like in the movies and books? What would his hands feel like? What would his lips taste like? Would he be controlling or understanding? Would he be demanding but sweet? Would he have dreams for them? Would he rescue her from this place?

Insanity was slowly claiming her, wasn't it? No man in her life had ever looked at her like a lover would. Why would it change now? No man would ever rescue her. No one would.

Her daydreaming was cut short when the large, vault-like door to the laboratory opened and the two bitches came in. The smug-faced doctor had a tense gaze while the older one rubbed the sleepiness off her eyes. They looked exhausted. Was it late in the night or early in the day?

"What did the guard say?" Dr. Badez yawned, still in her night gown.

Maggie shook her head. "Not much. Only that we have to be alert for something. Someone tripped the alarm."

"The guards here are a bunch of idiots," she sighed. "Anyway, get the hover-gurney. We'll treat this as practice instead."

"Yes, Doctor." Maggie left the room.

Badez fiddled with the controls of the room. The tubes unhooked themselves from the subject while water slowly drained away from her tank. During that time, her heart rate increased. This would always happen. Badez had long ignored this change, saying it was how Jella coped with the procedures. But to Jella herself, it wasn't a coping mechanism; she was panicking. It was her will to fight back. The screams in her head begged and angrily shouted at her body to move—to react—to do anything. Numbness was a friend who had long introduced itself to her when this whole thing had become routine. Despite that, a fire of anger, hatred and retribution still blazed within her heart.

Maggie entered the room with a hoverchair. "There wasn't a gurney, use this one for now. I'll search the other rooms for one," she said and left again.

As the tank itself moved from an upright position to lying down, Jella's heart rate increased even more. *Move, move, move, fuck, fuck, move,* she repeated in her mind over and over again. *Not another leg. Not another arm or another liver. No fucking more.* She cried inwardly at her helplessness. Was this the price for having a good, healthy body? No. She refused to blame her perfect body for something done to her by other people. Her body was a gift to her. She was never religious, but she believed a higher power had given this special body to her. It was up to her to protect it, to fight for it. There were only people who sought to control her; people who wanted to use and abuse her, like her mom and dad. These scientists were no better off. If it were up to her, she'd take them over. Either snuff out the life in their hearts or control them. To her, they didn't deserve the lives they lived.

The tank's lid clicked open and Jella felt the cool air blanket her—it was far from the warm waters of the tank. But it was a feeling. Her senses came back faster than before. Previously, it would take until the procedure was done before they returned. It still wasn't fast enough. The madwoman readied her to be transported to the table again. *No. Not more knives. Not the saw again. No. No,* she repeated it over and over to herself. As Badez lifted her naked body onto the hoverchair, Jella's eyes rolled back and fluttered. Her body shook on the chair.

"She's seizing." Dr. Badez shoulders were struck as she raced to the table at the end of the room. Her hands were swift, filling a syringe with a green solution. As she tested a few drops in the air, she was back at her test subject's side, ready to prick her arm.

No more, thought Jella.

Suddenly, the seizures stopped and the hand that was about to stab her stopped as well. Jella's big brown eyes focused on Dr. Badez. The doctor stared at her subject blankly as she moved the syringe to the back of her own head. With no notice, she stabbed herself where the skull and the neck connected and drained the solution in. Badez fell to the ground. Unconscious or dead, Jella couldn't tell and didn't care.

Congratulations! You have learned another innate fragment: Out of Reach

– F.

Description: You can affect the thinking of entities within a limited distance from you. Effects are vastly limited to rank and candidate source capacity.

Chapter 57

Lake, R&D Building, Aberkyz

At the army's research and development building, staff had already left the premises, leaving very few for the night shift. The door to the basement's janitor closet opened silently. Lugging a duffel bag on his back, Lake crept up the empty halls toward the security room. He peeked at the window through the door while crouched, waiting for a chance to move in. There was only one guard in the room. The shifting schedules were still the same from when he'd come to this building for his side-jobs while he was a trainee. He knew he had about four hours to take his devices before another guard came.

He knelt down, opened his bag and pulled out a steel-fashioned electric crossbow he'd made. The handle was likened to a rifle trigger while the body had a rotating magazine, with large, thick charged needles the size of a forearm. Rising slowly, he knocked on the door and carefully opened it.

The soldier turned to him. "Did you forget something? I told you to—" A large needle shot through right on her shoulder then released an electric charge, shocking her entire body. She seized in her seat before slumping down unconscious.

Lake brought his bag in before closing the door behind him. He inspected the woman's wound. It was surface-level and hadn't punctured deep. His adjustments were right for humans. If he had increased the rotation force of his crossbow, he could deal critical damage, which he didn't want to, since he wasn't interested in killing them. After tying up and gagging the woman on the floor with ropes from his bag, he set to work on the security controls. He disabled all of the alarms, automatic drones and cut off any video feed relayed back to the army headquarters, sending them loops instead. Hopefully, that'd buy him more time.

For the real video feed, he had it routed to his new linko, so he had access to the camera in real time. Then he linked the other controls in his glassy.

When he was done, he left the door locked from the inside and proceeded to the upper floors in a stealthy approach.

Before coming here, he had given his escorts apple pies, secretly laced with sedatives. At first, they were against it, but after much persuasion, they gave in. Snores sounded around their separate lodgings after an hour. Packing his bags, he drove off in his escorts' car, left the tracker at home and made his way by instinct. When he found the R&D Building, it made sense that his equipment was there.

On his way, he lifted a lab coat from an office and put it on. Using the video feed in his linko, he avoided custodians, security guards and other late-night staff, opting to change directions or hide in empty rooms or behind bins and shelves.

After passing through a few more floors, he ended up in a room glittering with outlier treasures, gadgets, raw materials and prototype inventions stacked on large shelves. The researchers treated the place like a junkyard for failed experiments, pointless machinery experiments and rushed creations that could have benefited with more tinkering. Anything they required for their research, parts and materials passed through here. Everything they deemed useless was sent back there as well. A lot of the junk and creations caught Lake's eye. If he'd had the time, he would want to jump in and uncover the treasures. But sadly, he had to focus on finding his own gear first.

His hands grazed the lockers in the corner, inspecting them one by one. Each time he passed one, the connection he felt with his devices thrummed stronger. His tracks stopped at locker number eight. A keycard and a pin code were required to open the locks, which he had neither of. A quick connection to his glassy and a run of programs opened the lock in minutes.

The S-Visor, S-Glove and all of his other equipment rested inside. He immediately inspected each one and found that they were unusable—broken from the previous fight. Some, like his bag and visor, had been hacked and damaged, but nothing had been stolen from them. The internal systems had shut down before any data was copied. With a touch of his thumb and a tug at the source threads of his bag, it clicked open. A smile crept on his face. The contents remained intact.

A check on the clock and video feeds told him that he had time. Not a lot, but some time to make quick repairs.

After a slight tinkering and using the junk in the room, he had his S-Glove working again, powered by the extra cores in his bag. The display features were buggy, and the spells were on a lower setting, but it'd have to work for now. He bagged his devices and a few items in the room before leaving.

Using the video feed, he formed a pathway to the exit that didn't have people near it. Just as he turned a corner, he heard conversations at the far end. He immediately took cover behind a shelf. Moments later, Maggie left and disappeared into the elevator. Curiosity stirred within him about her reasons for being here. He could understand a doctor stopping by for clinical samples from research during the day, but at night?

With the movements of a stalking cat, he peered ever so slowly into the room Maggie had left. His mouth gaped.

A wide laboratory of naked men and women floated inside glass tanks filled with liquid. The treated water sloshed with bubbles as the subjects reflexively moved in their sleep. Strewn with leather, scales and other skin types, their bodies likened to abnormal cows full of patchwork as wires that looked like strings were attached to them. Some of the faces he didn't know, but he recognized some from video files. A few caught his attention. It was Osher Grace and some of his squad mates who went with him to Kermoz. These were good men who had protected Zuobic and its people. Tony was right. At this point, nothing surprised Lake anymore. The army was insane. Was there a way to free his squad mates?

A crash sounded at the end of the room where a large vault was open. It seemed to be an extension of the laboratory. Clutching his crossbow, he inched forward. As his heart rose and the distance closed, he had every intent of opening fire when he entered the vault, but all violent intent stopped abruptly.

Fully naked, Jella sat in the hoverchair with a blank stare.

The air in his lungs reduced as he held his breath. Her emotionless face, sunken eyes and thinned body presented itself in its unhealthy state. Though her beauty was still apparent, her figure was a far cry from what he remembered. For all this time, he thought she was fine running her own missions. After the breakup, he knew she'd be okay. She was a strong woman. But one quick look at her told him that what he'd thought was a lie. She was here, being experimented on by the very people she had trusted. The same ones he had trusted. But why? To make her a super-soldier?

He strapped his crossbow over his back with his bag. "Hey Jella. It's me, Lake. I'll get you out of here, okay?" He stared kindly into her eyes.

When she blinked, he smiled. The reward for the Dragon-Knight, the elixir, popped in his head. "I think this can help. I had it before, and it worked really great." From his bag, he drew out the last vial remaining and fed its contents to Jella.

Color returned to Jella. She managed to look up at him and nodded.

"See, it worked, right? Next is clothes..." He looked around and noticed Dr. Badez on the ground, dead. Shaking thoughts on the reason for her death, he stripped the doctor off her lab coat, clothes and ID cards. What was important was getting Jella and him out of here. Nothing else mattered. This place was sick.

"Good. I'll take you out of here. I'll probably have to go back for the rest, but you take priority," he said.

"Thank you," she breathed out.

After dressing Jella in Badez's clothes, he activated the hoverchair and connected it wirelessly with his linko. The hoverchair followed closely to Lake as they left the laboratory. Before they could even go further, Maggie had turned the hall with a gurney beside her and stopped. She saw Lake first, showing bewilderment, then surprise after noticing Jella with him.

"What are you doing here? You're not supposed to be here," she said.

His eyes narrowed at her. "Why are you here?"

"This place is off-limits to non-medical personnel. Leave." Maggie moved to grab the hover gurney, but Lake blocked her path.

"You know about this," declared Lake. "You know about the experiments they're doing to Jella, and our squad. And the rest of soldiers in here."

Her face grew dark. "This is for the greater good. Our ex-squad members were badly injured from the fight with that spider thing. This was the best choice they had to continue the good fight." She pushed him aside and stood next to Jella.

"Not if it meant they'd sacrifice themselves to be lab rats," he countered with a growl. "I know Jella, and she would never have agreed to this."

"A starless like you could never understand the vision the Major has for the army, for this country. This is the future of Zuobic: powerful super soldiers who can enter the rift, are unaffected by pain and strong enough to stand against the monsters. This will save us from the invasion, from the rifts and monsters. This is what Jella signed up for. This is what all of us signed up for—a way to help mankind survive."

"You can't do this to her." The volume of his voice increased.

"She is the key to all of this. Her body made this happen," said Maggie with an air of superiority. "Whatever happened that day in WalkBy, both you and her changed. But guess what? You still don't matter. Blood tests, brain checks—all of them have no conclusive evidence that you are better than before. The only thing that really changed is that you are worse. The uncontrollable condition for spell casting is a disability.

"Lake Deskenn, you are a disabled sorcerer. The story remains the same. Starless, disabled, useless. At the end of the day, Jella is still more than you'll ever be. She will change the world, give us better soldiers, lead us to victory. Not you." Her words leaked spite and contempt.

The words seeped deeply into Lake's being. All those words crushed him inside, but at the same time he wanted to crush those words back. For a long time, he'd believed those words, but deep inside, he knew they weren't true. He wanted—no, *needed*—to believe they weren't true. He raised his hand for a punch. "You—"

As Maggie reached for the handles of the hoverchair, Jella reached for her clothes and pulled her down. The doctor's face slammed against Jella's forehead. Maggie tried to pull away with a bloodied nose, but Jella yanked her again for the second time. Her brow burst and eyes sunk. Then she pulled her again for a third time, fourth and more until Lake lost count and he was able to focus again, recovering from surprise.

Lake tried to pull the bleeding and semi-conscious Maggie from Jella. After exerting more effort, he finally pried her away. "Stop. Stop. You'll kill her." He let the doctor lay on the ground.

He was about to say something to reprimand Jella, but the burning hate in Jella's eyes made him stop. Clearly, something happened between the two of them, something irreconcilable. It was not up to him to judge something he didn't understand and didn't know about. "Let's go," he said, activating the hoverchair to follow him again.

Guardsmen patrolled the spaces of the research building in twos and threes. Lake marched along the halls, peeked through the rooms and darted in and out of staircases—all the while Jella followed him. The two kept to the shadows and corners, hiding in closets and empty rooms when the guards came near them. There were moments when Lake acted to stop them from being alerted. Every time he did, the rest of the patrols were more alert, more discerning of their surroundings. Lake assumed the rest of the guards knew their comrades weren't replying, so the risk of an intruder gnawed at them. After a few more unconscious guards, they exited from the back entrance and into the car park.

Lake spotted a blue sedan in the corner. After a few moments of tinkering, he managed to get inside and start the engine. Then he went back for Jella. He tried to help her up, but she said, "I can do it."

Though a bit slow and wobbly, Jella walked up and got into the passenger's seat. Lake hopped on the driver's seat and the car sped off as soon as the doors shut. They passed through the automatic gates of the facility without any issues due to the car's registration. Whoever owned it, Lake was thankful and sorry, swearing to repay them someday. After a few miles on the road and a few stoplights, he exhaled a breath of relief. Were they safe? Lake wanted to ask the question but felt uneasy.

"Are we free?" asked Jella. Her focus darting behind her.

"I think so," he answered. "Are you doing okay?"

She nodded. "I can move now, thanks to that drink. What was that? It tasted horrible."

"Something I found in the rifts. Told you it'd work."

She smiled. "I'm glad you found me. Thank you."

That smile made him feel at ease, like she'd always used to. Something about her presence made him relax. Just as he was about to say more, the communication device installed in the car rang. Both of them froze and stared at the unknown number flashing on the glassy installed on the dashboard. The display had the option to do a video or audio call. Lake reached out to the display. "Don't answer it," said Jella.

"I think I know who's calling." Lake answered the call on audio only.

"Lake, you disappoint me," said Cervantes on the other line.

"Sir, I'm sorry, but I had to do this," Lake stated after calming his rising heartbeat.

"What are you going to do now? What's your next step?" asked Cervantes. When there was no response for a long moment, he continued, "I'll give you one last chance. Turn back around, return Jella to the hospital, and I promise that you will be safe. You will still have the promotion and the squad I promised you. Like nothing had ever happened. What do you say?" His voice was calm and deep, yet urging and forceful.

Lake looked outside the window, seeing the lights from the poles illuminate the dark road. The twinkling billboards and holographic ads tried to catch his attention. But he felt a hardness in his chest. When he was younger, he aspired to be a soldier to fight monsters because it was cool on television. Every chance he could get, he'd watch broadcasts about the fight against rift-monsters, outlier #1. But the crying and pleading faces of the survivors caught hold of a piece of his heart. He didn't understand what it was or how to approach it—only that it was uncomfortable. But instead of leaving or turning it off, he sat through it. Every day he'd watched it, until the incident at Zone Kermoz.

"I was so proud of myself when I got into the training program for sorcerers—I couldn't believe my luck. Me? A sorcerer? I thought, finally, something good is happening to me," stated Lake in somber tone. "Then people looked at me like I was some stupid kid because I can't cast a simple fireball. But one woman befriended me, told to me work hard, and I could achieve my dreams. I thought if my brother had gotten older, I would've wanted him to meet her."

Jella glanced at him.

"Apart from her, you were my goal. My idol. You're the soldier I aspired to be. Smart, strategic, powerful. When you gave me that mission, I gained more than hope."

"I see. As your superior and your idol, I wish for you to come back," said Cervantes with a softer tone. "How about I sweeten the deal? Be my apprentice.

I'll teach you the ropes of heading your own division. Impart my knowledge and secrets my competitors would die for. You'd be my righthand man, Lake. What do you say?"

"I'd say yes, a thousand times yes…if I hadn't been thrown into the rift," Lake's voice carried an ache to it. After a breather, he continued, "It was scary, and I honestly didn't know if I was going to survive. But I've gotten to know someone who came to feel like a brother, who was absolutely incorrigible. But really, really smart, confident, and most of all brave. He helped me stay focused."

Tony's memory flashed in his mind.

"And then there was a woman—who was odd and weird and sort of didn't really belong anywhere. She looked kinda off. But after knowing her, I discovered how honest she is. How true to herself she is and how strong of a woman she can be."

Keri's voice echoed in his head.

"And there's this group of people who look up to me, because of my talents and what I can do. These people saw me differently but accepted that fact easily. It wasn't a hindrance; they just embraced it. There were no tests, no questions.

"These people that I've met showed me that I can be of service to others. That I can save people even if I don't become a soldier. That I can be there to help."

After a moment, Cervantes responded, "Are you sure about this?"

Lake stared at the glassy on the dashboard. "With all due respect, sir, I can't turn back now. I won't. The army—no. You choose to hurt people for your own ends—people that I care about. I want to be the person that saves them. Helps them. Soldier or not, I choose to put their needs first, before the army or Zuobic's."

After a long pause, he inhaled deeply and finished, "Sir, I don't want to become you."

The other line was quiet for a while and then Cervantes asked, "Is that your final answer, Civilian Lake Deskenn?"

"Yes sir," he answered with a strong voice.

Another moment of silence came before the call ended with Cervantes saying, "Very well."

"What was that it?" asked Jella.

Lake shrugged, focusing on the road. Movement in the rear-view mirror caught his attention.

Four motorbikes vroomed closer to them, carrying men in grey battle suits and biker helmets. Two sat on his tail while the other two took positions on both sides of the car.

Jella whipped her head back and forth. "What do we do?"

"Check my bag. Grab two grenades."

At the side of the car, the biker was about to fire an automatic rifle at them. Jella fished out two grenades from the bag and tossed it outside. The grenades exploded into a pile of blue sticky muck that caught the two bikes and glued them together. They stumbled on the road before sticking to a parked car.

Jella searched through the bag. "Do you have a laser or something that's used on monsters?"

"Monsters?" asked Lake.

"These are super soldiers. The bodies you saw in the lab, this is what they become after all the experiments. Tough on the outside, and hollow inside."

"I don't like guns, but the crossbow is—" A flicker in the mirror distracted him as he looked up.

A rocket launcher zoomed right at them. Before they could do anything, Jella jumped on him and got between him and the rocket as it exploded. Fire covered the vehicle while the impact caused it to somersault in the air and land on its back. It skidded a few meters along the cement road before crashing into the front of an electronics shop. Debris and glass scattered everywhere and little embers decorated the destroyed vehicle.

CHAPTER 58

KERI, CHULZ

Kermoz had reconnected itself to Silaw, returning to Zuobic. Thus, getting around the area was easy for Keri once she called Riley to find out where she was. The Chadstones had moved to a penthouse apartment in Chulz. Charlie slept atop Keri, piggyback-style, when she buzzed on the doorbell.

The door immediately opened with Riley on the other side. "You're finally here. Thanks, Keri." Riley peeled Charlie off her back and carried him inside. She gestured Keri to follow her in.

"Honey, what's going on?" Vivian said from inside the apartment.

Riley moved over to the living room. "Looks who's here." She laid the boy on the couch.

Vivian gasped, placing her hands over her mouth. She looked from Charlie to Riley and then Keri. After a moment, she went on her knees and embraced her son. "Thank you," she said to Keri as tears rolled over her face.

After some crying and tears of gratitude went around, they all settled on the sofa. Charlie was asleep in Riley's embrace while Vivian was setting tea down on the coffee table. Keri took her time explaining the circumstances surrounding Charlie and her. The two mothers expressed themselves in wide eyes and gasps as they heard the full details of Keri and Charlie's two personas and responsibilities.

"Charlie will wake up?" asked Riley, emphasizing the word *will*.

Keri nodded. "He should soon, once I get more areas under control. But I'm not sure what happens after that—if Silaw will still use him as a vessel. Are you two okay with that?"

Riley exchanged glances with his wife then nodded. "We knew Charlie was different from the start. Not gonna lie, I didn't expect him to be this special, but we knew what we're getting ourselves into. If saving the world and the people is what he was put here to do, I'm not gonna be a mom that stops all that. It's just not gonna to be easy." She gave him a slight squeeze.

"We'll be here for him, whatever he needs," added Vivian.

Keri smiled at the two. She was happy Charlie ended up with such great parents.

"Still, that's some messed up shit they did," cursed Riley, referring to the army-made rift. "I can't help but think how Charlie and the other kids would have had better lives if that didn't happen."

Vivian placed her tea down. "I was there that day. My ex, Christopher, and I were pregnant. He was so focused on his work. We were always fighting, and I miscarried on that day. At the same time, people were dying, and I was escaping with him, bleeding. It was the most horrible day I've ever had."

Riley rubbed her thigh. "It was a tough day for everyone."

Vivian grabbed hold of her hand and said, "Keri, I owe you an apology. I gave into my own fears and trusted Wayne over you and our friendship. It was wrong of me to assume and not talk to you or try to understand you. I hope you can forgive me."

"I was really mad at you." Keri's voice was hoarse. "But what can I do, you're like my best friend, you know? It just hurt me when you didn't listen. You picked a stupid guy's word over me. That's just so unfair."

Vivian moved over to Keri and hugged her. "I know. When I moved to the freezones, people assumed the worst in me. They assumed a Zuosh who is above them, who belittles them. A different class of sorts. And I kind of projected those experiences into you. It isn't fair, you're right I really am sorry."

The two of them cried and hugged for a few more minutes before they got their bearings back. She pulled out a box of tissues out for both of them.

Riley laid Charlie down fully on the couch. "Where are you off to now?"

"I'm going to find Lake. I think the army has him." Keri wiped her face with a tissue.

She scratched her face. "Oh, they definitely have him all right."

"What happened?" Alarm brought her focus in.

Vivian cleared her throat and wiped away the tears. "Lake and the army..." She explained what had happened to Lake and Wayne as a result of her meddling. "Are you mad?" she asked after apologizing.

"A bit. But Lake always said the army would catch up to him eventually. He was only hiding out as long as he could until he was sure what to do. I'm still going after him." Keri summoned crystals in her hands. The first moment, they appeared, the next second, they vanished.

You have consumed Area Claim and Shielding Crystal. Current Area: Chulz has been claimed by Maiden. Areas Claimed: E-law, A2, Kermoz, Kz-S1, Chulz.

"Was that—do you own the zone now?" asked Vivian. "Is that how it works?"

"Yeah, I made it so the rifts won't open and monsters won't be able to come in," she replied. "This is the safest place in Zuobic now."

Vivian held her hand. "Thank you, Keri."

"It's fine. The people I love are here. It needs to be done." She glanced at Charlie sleeping. "Can you please contact Maxwell, and the guild? Tell them, I'm going after Lake, and that he doesn't have to worry."

Vivian shared a hesitant glance with Riley who crossed her arms. "About that, I think the guild has their hands full."

The lines on her forehead folded. "What's wrong?"

An unprecedented number of rifts had been opened around Cluster RSTU. Everyone was scrambling to evacuate to safer zones. The incident coincided with Vivian's plans to move and stay in Zuobic, and so she took that chance and left with her family. Vivian relayed this all to Keri with a despondent look in her eye.

"I still think we shouldn't have escaped like that," huffed Riley. "We could've helped them. Our employees, our friends, are there. They need us."

"We are not closers, nor fighters," argued Vivian. "We have a son to protect. A family that comes first."

She shook her head at her. "He's always been fine. My point is..."

As the couple argued, Keri tried her linko and called Maxwell herself. Since she was out of the rift, her call connected to the network. The pounding of her heart increased as the linko rang. She needed to know if the Apes were fine—if Maxwell was fine. But after a couple of rings, he didn't pick up. Then she tried Ivo. After a few rings, the call connected.

"Ivo, it's me, Keri. Are you doing okay? Is Maxwell all right?" asked Keri.

Screams and gunfire sounded in the background as Ivo replied, "I've had better days. I mean, I am fighting monsters now. Well, not fighting, more like escaping with civilians, which my wife doesn't like. But I rescued her parents at least, so she can't argue that I'm not needed, and she can't tell me to hide with them. Anyway, Keri, where are you? I think we really need your clock powers. No, I mean, not think, but really need it now. The Apes and the boss are spread thin. I mean the boss is tough, but I don't how long we will last."

"I'm so sorry, I'm in Zuobic. I'm trying to find Lake. But I'll help you now, I think Lake can—"

"Oh, did you say Lake?" he interrupted. "You know where he is?"

From the new upgrade of Prima, Keri could sense Lake's general direction. It was the same where she felt Wayne too. "He's with the army somewhere."

"Get him, Keri. We need him just as much as we need you," pleaded Ivo. "Boss said something about the Zone Defense Project he was working on. We really need to activate it. The tech team he left can't do anything without him."

She repeated it back to him, "Get Lake and tell him about Zone Defense—" The line was cut. She tried to reach him again, but it wouldn't connect.

"How are they?" asked Riley. She and Vivian had stopped bickering and waited for her reply.

She shook her head. "I have to find Lake. They need him. They need us. I have to go."

"Wait. Hold up." Riley left for a moment and came back with bags of gear.

"What do you think you're doing?" asked Vivian.

"I'm coming with her. If the Cluster needs Lake, I'm breaking him out," she declared. "You stay here and watch Charlie."

As Riley headed towards the door, Vivian reached out a hand. "No. You stay here. It's my fault Lake is there, I should be the one to help him out. We both know I'm the better fighter between the two of us." She stared into her eyes.

Riley deflated. "Fine. Please be nice to him. He's a good guy. And take care of yourself. Don't let anything happen to you."

"I will." The two kissed passionately—a kiss that wished for health and safety.

Keri looked at them with a bored face. "Can we go now, please? People are dying."

Vivian broke away first, a bit red. "Sorry. Let me just get my battle suit."

Chapter 59

Lake, Jaz

A ringing in his head and the screaming pain and exhaustion in his body blocked Lake from recovering his bearings. The rocket was surprising, but Jella blocking it was even more so. Why did she do that? He needed to know if she was okay, but the ringing and the pain stopped him from moving. His body hung upside on his seat with his arms hanging freely. Remembering the rune for healing, he cast it on himself, hoping his odd condition for sorcery would kick in. After a few tries, it did. The ringing and pain eased, and he felt lighter and more like himself.

"Jella?" Lake uttered as he fell on his shoulders after unbuckling himself.

Glass and debris scratched his arms as he crawled from his seat and out the window with his bag. A few coughs after and a quick look inside confirmed that no one was there. A slight dizziness came over him as he pulled himself up to stand. Looking ahead, he caught sight of a black charred body a few meters from the wreckage. He immediately hurried to it.

Lunging beside Jella, he tried to touch her, but pulled back after getting burnt. "Not this again. Not when I saved someone. Why does this keep happening?" He growled, angry at the people who caused this. Angry at the outliers. Angry at the rifts. As he tightened the grip on his clothes, he sensed something within her. Something weak, but strong at the same time.

Using his Mind's Vision, he saw her soul inside the body—vibrant and pulsing. From the other lifeforms he had observed, upon death, their souls floated away. But this one was different. It waited inside her like it had been a core, like monsters did. Strangely, it seemed to pull in source from around and distribute it around her body. She was healing?

"Is she a 14?" he breathed out. He recalled Maggie saying something that both he and she were changed after the WalkBy incident. So was this the change?

Now that he knew she was alive, his fingers traced a rune to heal. But they stopped mid-cast, trembling. *What if he made it worse again? What if she truly dies?* If she was healing already, he had to trust that. He had to trust Jella's abilities. She jumped in to save him knowing this. *I just have to protect her and give her time to recover,* he thought.

From his bag, he doused Jella with water from the bottles he kept on him, then put a jacket he had on her. With his bag in hand, he carried her over his back and marched away from the wreckage and onto the back alleyways.

After turning a corner, the train station came into view. Little to no passengers waited for the incoming train at this hour; it was only a few bystanders and late-night workers. As they headed up the platform, the remaining two bikers caught up to them and parked at the roadside.

Pulling his crossbow from his bag, he shot an electrified bolt at one of the soldiers. It stupefied him for a moment, but after a few seconds, he started fighting the electrocution. Lake didn't wait to find out more as the train stopped in front of him and opened its doors.

A broadcast started with an upbeat leitmotif as they entered the train. "Welcome to ECCENTRY—the only outlier core powered monorail system in the world. An outlier train for an outlier world. Sit back and relax. Have a safe journey." Chimes ended the broadcast with the doors sliding shut and the train resuming transport.

With a heave, he placed Jella in an empty seat. Lake pulled out a towel from his bag and covered her with it. Leaving her, he marched over to the next car, noticing the bikers had gotten onto the train as well and were now coming towards them. The moment the door opened, and a biker strolled in, two grenades left his pockets and exploded at the doors. Thick blue slime glued the whole door and the biker together, blocking the entrance and exit, leaving nothing to sneak through.

The few passengers on board fled from the car and onto the next one, screaming and trying to call for help on their linkos.

On the door, the goo expanded and reformed as the biker struggled to free himself. It lasted for a few minutes before it relaxed and took its resting shape.

The slime for the grenades he made could hold mammoth-type monsters down, so he doubted they could free themselves from it.

The second biker, unable to get through, left through the windows and climbed to the top of the traincar. Heavy footsteps thumped above them. Then consecutive blows banged from one spot on the roof.

Lake's S-Disc lit up as he took it out of the bag and into his grasp, preparing for the fight. A hole in the roof blew wide open as the biker jumped in. The flashing blades of the S-Disc met the biker head-on as Lake slashed and whirled, painting gashes on them. Though it wasn't deep, it somehow broke the soldier's skin. But that didn't last as the biker blocked with his arm, punched him in the gut and hit him with an uppercut that threw him into a seat.

Bile regurgitated from his mouth and pain coursed through his upper body. He was reminded of his fight with Wayne. Close-range fights were his weakness. He reminded himself to increase his body's strength with the system if he ever managed to get out of this alive. As he tried to get up, the biker was already in front of him. He swung his Disc across, but the biker dodged it and punched him again. This time, blood spat out from his mouth. As the biker pulled another fist back, Lake hoisted his S-Glove and activated the L-Dome spell. A small plate-like shield covered his upper body. The shield blocked a flurry of jabs before flickering and breaking entirely. The force of the blows pushed Lake back further into the seat and window behind him.

The biker pinned him down to the seat with his big hands, then smashed his head. The ringing in Lake's head came back. As his head lolled, he noticed another fist approach his face, but it stopped before it even connected. The biker let him go and stood straight, like he was waiting.

Lake gasped and coughed blood, questioning the interruption.

"I can't hold him long," whispered Jella, who was a few seats down. Half of her body remained charred while the rest was pink and bloody, slowly regenerating to full health.

Leaving the questions for later, Lake pushed the biker on the seats opposite him. He then grabbed a grenade and tossed it on to the biker. Goo exploded and bound the biker on the seats and holds.

Lake collapsed onto the seat next to Jella. "What was that?" His fingers doodled another rune for healing in the air.

"I don't know. It's something I can do," Jella said a bit louder than last time. Her throat was healing nicely, along with the rest of her body.

As the spell eased the ringing in his head, Lake tried another on his gut. "I think you're a 14," he croaked.

"An outlier?"

"Ability user is what they call us. We're rare."

"That's why they did those experiments on me." Her attention was focused at the super soldiers trying to get out of the slime.

He followed where she looked. "Don't worry. They won't get away with it."

The red burnt tissues on her face slowly faded, replaced by healthy, glowing skin. "What's your plan? I think they're still following us. I always felt weird when that big-forehead-guy looked at me. I doubt he'd call it quits after this," said Jella.

"Big-forehead-guy?" Creases appeared on his forehead.

"I mean, Major."

Lake let the oddity slide. "We go to a zone, that I own. They can't hurt us—or me at least, if I don't let them in."

"What does that mean?"

"Do you have a screen you see? Like in computers or games? That tells you a bunch of weird things?"

She responded with silence and wide eyes.

He nodded. "Sounds about right. We're candidates, us 14s. We're chosen to save people from rifts and the monsters inside. The screen-thing or system is our guide that makes us able to do what we do. It's the reason why you heal so fast, and I guess from what you did earlier, mind tricks?"

"O-okay..."

He gave a rough account of what the relationship between candidates, champions, rifts and deleted spaces were. "I'll explain it more later. Let me rest for a bit." He continued to cast healing spells on himself.

Silence eclipsed the train ride—both of them mulled over their thoughts. When they approached the destination, the broadcast chimed in with an upbeat leitmotif same as before. "You have arrived at Zone Jaz. Thank you for riding

ECCENTRY—the only outlier core powered monorail system in the world. An outlier train for an outlier world. Until next time," sounded the female voiceover. The train cruised to a stop and the slide-doors opened—except for the ones that had been broken or were already open.

"Can you stand?" asked Lake to Jella.

Jella showed off her perfectly healed legs. "Can you?"

Lake smiled. "Guess you're built stronger than me. Even as 14s, you still always come ahead of me." He rose to his feet with his bag in hand and headed for the door.

Jella followed suit, fiddling with what little clothes she had on. They got off the train and made their way to the exit but stopped before going further.

Armored vans and cars surrounded the whole parking lot facing the station. Soldiers left the vehicles, took out their guns and aimed all of it at them. From the back emerged Major Cervantes in a full battle suit with two sorcerers by his side. "You survived," he stated with mild interest.

Lake counted the soldiers to be around twenty and five sorcerers. He gulped, trying to figure out how to escape. "Let us leave. You don't own our lives," he declared.

He smirked. "Who wants to own you? The Starless Sorcerer. You mistake me for wanting to capture you—I want you dead. You are a disappointment, Lake Deskenn. A true disappointment as a sorcerer and a soldier. It was stupid on my part to actually trust and put my faith in you. What I want is her. She is the property of the military."

An emotional sting pierced Lake's heart. Not that he was expecting a gold star from the major, but hearing that from someone he idolized, hurt. But he'd get used to it. The important thing was, he was doing the right thing.

"I'm a person, not your pet," shouted Jella. "You don't get to decide for me. I decide for me."

"You belong to Zuobic. You swore as a soldier you would protect this nation in any way you can. This is the best way you can help your people," rebutted Cervantes. "Your blood, skin, everything—every part of you is what will make the future of Zuobic—the future to defeat the monsters and close the rifts forever.

Your preferences and ideals of individuality and as a person is of no consequence compared to the liberation of humanity."

Lake steeled his heart. "There is another way. We don't have to use her."

His brows perked up. "Oh, are you talking about the candidates and fragments?"

"H-h-how'd you know?" he stuttered.

"I heard about it from your friend, Wayne. I honestly think it's a good children's story," he mused. "A random bunch of people being given the power to close the rifts and save the world from invaders. Delusional idiots."

Lake thought about proving him wrong, explaining it to him, so he could discover how wrong he was. But he stopped himself. What good would come out doing so to a man who wanted to discard him? "Where's Wayne?" he asked.

"Oh, do you want that chance to fight?" He gestured with his chin towards a soldier. A moment later, a figure emerged from one of the armed trucks. Wayne stepped up towards the light of the vehicles, wearing a grey battle suit, the same as the bikers. His face was blank as he stared out into nothingness.

"Wayne?" Lake called out in an uncertain voice.

"He's not there," whispered Jella. "They've locked away his will—way deep in his mind. Like what they tried to do to me."

"Brain washing?" asked Lake.

"How do you like it?" boasted Cervantes. "I've made your former enemy into one of my greymen. Do you like the name of my new team? I like it. It has a nice ring to it. I was struggling with what to name them—and Project X8 does not roll off the tongue that easily. But enough of that, I strongly suggest you say a few words before I dispose of you."

Lake activated his barely functioning S-Glove and grasped a few of his grenades in his pockets. "Fuck you, Christopher," he said.

Cervantes placed a finger at his temple and sighed. "How crass. Idiots through and through. Squad leader, dispose of them," he said to a soldier to his left.

"What about the subject, sir?" the soldier asked.

He shrugged. "It doesn't matter if she is blown up. She will regenerate."

"Yes sir." All the soldiers around them aimed and fired.

A dome of light pulsed from Lake's S-Glove and surrounded them, shielding them both from fire. "We need to get out of here. This won't last long." The shield drained its power core relative to the impact it suffered. Lake knew as the assault went on, they would not be able to last.

"I'll cover you," volunteered Jella. "Use me as a shield to get out."

"Those are high speed bullets used for monsters. They'll go right through you."

"Explosions, bullets, they're all the same."

Next to Cervantes, the sorcerers cast spells, grabbing their attention. Two fireballs materialized and whooshed towards them. Jella stepped in front of Lake, putting her body right in between the shield and his, blocking his view.

After a breathless moment, the impact they expected didn't come. And to Lake's failing defense, he felt the barrage had lightened—no stopped? "What's happening?" Jella exclaimed.

Lake peeked around the side and gasped. The gunfire brightened the area in suspension. The bullets that left them cruised leisurely; the air they cut through made pathways visible to the eye. Inch by inch, they went at the speed of a turtle. The fireballs hung in the air with anticipation, taking almost forever to plummet. Like a scene in a movie, everything was trapped in slow motion.

Their face plastered in disbelief, gawking at their attackers.

A minivan drove right next to them with its wheels screeching from the sudden brake. From the passenger side, Keri shouted, "Get in!"

Chapter 60

Keri, Jaz

"Get in," Keri's repeated yells snapped the two's shocked stupor and made them rush into the minivan. They hobbled into the back seats. Before they could even close the doors, Vivian stepped on the gas pedal hard, making the minivan cry.

"Hey, thanks for saving us," Lake breathed out with a stupid grin.

"Anytime." She looked back at him with a bright smile. An urge to grab him and suck his face welled up within her, but she noticed something odd when a hand grabbed Lake by his arms.

"Are we safe with them?" whispered a gorgeous woman who seemed to be with Lake. Keri narrowed her eyes, by instinct, feeling very disturbed about the touch on his skin. Why was she clinging like that? What's with the pout? Obviously, she's just trying to get his attention. But what the fuck?

Lake smiled at the gorgeous woman. "Definitely. They're from Troef, a free-zone. Keri, this is Jella. Jella, this is Keri," he said like it was the most normal thing in the world introducing a hot lady to the woman you just slept with.

"Hi, I'm Keri, and this is Vivian." She gestured to the driver's seat as she thought, *What is she wearing? A jacket and a towel? Well, with boobs and a body like that I get why you're showing off. Is Lake looking?*

As Vivian drove, she smiled curtly at the rear-view mirror. "There're some clothes at the back if you want to change, Jella. It's in the bag. I think we're the same size, not sure about the shoes," she said.

Hearing the name again, Keri then only realized who she was and what it meant. Jella was Lake's ex. She caught glances of her dressing into mustard trousers and a black tank top. Her skin was flawless; and her boobs, tummy and hip ratio was proportioned really well—like it had been carved or molded or something.

As Jella put on a mustard-colored jacket and black rubber shoes, she asked, "How do you know each other?"

"I work for a guild, the Hairless Apes. Vivian owns an outlier shop called Amazing Discoveries which has deals with the Apes," answered Lake.

"Are you two business partners?"

"Yes, something akin to a friendly relationship as well," answered Vivian.

Once done dressing, Jella cozied over next to Lake. "And you work there too? Like someone in the storehouse?" she asked Keri. Somehow, Keri felt a belittling energy coming off of the statement. Was there shade in her question?

Before Keri could speak, Lake declared, "She's a 14 like us. She's also an Ape, and my girlfriend."

All thoughts about Jella were abandoned as Keri locked eyes with him. "I'm your girlfriend?" she asked.

"I would've asked the morning after, but things happened," said Lake. "I know it's not the best timing, but what do you say? Do you want to be my girlfriend?"

Keri was stunned for a second but got her bearings after Vivian elbowed her. "Yes. Yes, I want to be your girlfriend," she almost shouted.

Lake brightened as he moved closer to her for a quick kiss before returning to the seat.

Congratulations! You have earned the title: Girlfriend from Target Lover #1.

5000 coins earned. Total 15,280.

"Not to ruin the romantic vibe, but we're still being chased by my ex and his army. With guns, mechs and magic if you've forgotten," Keri interrupted. "Are you sure about going this way?"

"That's right. Keep heading that way." Keri pointed ahead.

The car left the populated sites of Jaz and entered the secured areas. Years ago, this place had been attacked, along with Kermoz, and was closed off as a result. Crushed buildings, old vehicles and cracked roads greeted them as they cruised to a stop over a pile of wreckage blocking the road. "We're going there." Keri gestured to the deteriorating bridge. She then hopped out of the car and popped the back open.

"That leads to Kermoz. Isn't that off limits?" Jella looked ahead. "I heard some of the nurses say it's a deleted space."

"Is it back? I wasn't able to claim it last time. The spider champion might still be there." Lake's voice was slightly on edge.

"Kermoz is safe now, I have control over it," Keri declared.

Vivian got down from the driver's seat and armed herself with a vest full of ammo, guns and grenades. "If you're looking for guns, blades or items, there's some over there." She pointed at another bag as she equipped herself with tessens. They were bladed fans that could conjure strong gales.

After a quick scan of the contents, Lake pulled out a few grenades and put in his bag. He then handed Jella a vest and guns. "I don't think the items here are compatible to you or me, but—"

"What's this for?" asked Jella, gesturing to the guns.

Lake raised a brow. "Sorry I can't bring a whole mech here for you. I know it doesn't make up for it, but at least you've got guns."

Jella paused for a second before wearing the vest and holstering the guns. "Cause I'm a mech pilot, and I like machines and guns," she stated very explicitly.

"Yeah. Are you okay?" He frowned at her.

"Nothing's wrong. I'm really good." She grinned.

He rummaged the bag further and pulled out outlier items: a glove and a princess tiara. Keri noticed the jewels on the royal accessory and a strong part of her wanted it. It reminded her heavily of *Love Me, Princess*. But as her hand reached out, Jella snatched it first and asked, "What's this for?"

Lake's eyes glowed as he inspected the tiara. "It's an outlier that can put any item the way it was before. But only small things and non-outlier stuff, I think. Like if you have a sword and it breaks, it can return it like it had never been broken before."

Jella put it on her head. "This is perfect for me. I don't have to worry about my clothes getting ruined. What do you think?" She posed in front of him.

"Looks good and useful for you." He nodded.

"Wait, doesn't she have to be compatible with the item for it to work?" asked Keri.

His eyes glowed again. "She is. Strangely, its attracted to royalty or someone of noble blood. That's funny, you said your family was the furthest from anything to do with the Empire," he inquired.

Jella shrugged. "Maybe a distant cousin I don't know about?"

"Is there anything there for me?" Keri asked, hoping for a crown as well. Or a comb, maybe? Or a mirror? Something princess-like?

Lake handed her the glove. "Here. It's good for managing source in your body. It helps prevent hypoetheria."

"Uh thanks." She wore the brown, simple, smelly glove.

"Yeah, that looks perfect on you. Simple," agreed Jella. "Very minimalistic."

Vivian grabbed another bag from the front and came back to them. "Are we good? We should go before they get to us."

Keri wanted another item, but Vivian's warnings took precedence, especially when she sensed the same energy that made her gravitate towards Lake and Jella. It was another candidate like them. The only person he knew who was like them was her ex. "We have to go. They're close." She started moving, traversing around the debris and up the bridge.

"Are you aware of them?" asked Lake, following behind.

She nodded. "Yeah, it's a Maiden thing. Feeling other candidates. That's how I found you two."

"It's Wayne, isn't it? He's after us."

"We need to get you two to the Cluster, fast," stated Vivian, following behind.

"The rifts," gasped Lake. "I totally forgot."

Their conversation cut short as the ground shook and the air reverberated with engine sounds. "What was that?" asked Jella, bringing up the rear.

Lake's jaw stiffened. "Mechs. It's the army's mech squad." His pace increased.

"Can't you use your hoverboard and get everyone there?" asked Keri. "I can match your speed."

He shook his head. "I haven't repaired it completely. I'm still lacking other functions. What's your plan?" he asked.

The mechs vroomed forward. They blasted the debris on the road and passed through. In mere seconds, they entered the bridge.

"My plan is for us to get to Kermoz and be safe," she shouted over the increased rumbling sound. "And then I'll open a rift from there."

Four mechs charged at them with guns at the ready. They pointed at them and fired. Keri immediately pulled on the source within her and released it. Various tiny clocks brightened under everyone's feet. The bullets that approached them slowed down and everyone was able to evade their trajectories. Their faces changed with bewilderment and excitement as they continued to dodge the rain of fire.

Jella twisted to the side to avoid bullets as she kept running. "What's going on?"

Keri skipped from one side to the other, evading the attacking mech behind her. "I slowed time down around you. I don't know how long it'll last."

As one mech zoomed over to them, Vivian intercepted it by pulling a rocket launcher from her bag. She put it on her shoulder and fired. The mech tried to evade it but the rocket released mini rockets that exploded in random directions. A few caught the mech and damaged it enough to make it unusable.

"Get back," shouted Jella as she rushed next to Vivian. Bullets sprayed at her from a different direction. She firmly rooted herself in place as holes decorated her body and tore through her new dress. Her injuries didn't last long as she regenerated at a visible rate. The tiara shimmered, mending her damaged outfit in similar fashion, covering the rips and bullet holes like they had never been there in the first place.

"Keri, slow them down," Lake shouted as he activated his old S-Boots. The boots launched him back toward the start of the bridge, crossing the distance in a single bound and landing him right next to one of the three remaining mechs. As Keri's powers slowed the giant robots to a glacial pace, Lake leaped onto one's back. His arms and fingers danced in the air as his eyes glowed. The mech stopped moving and the cockpit opened. Lake hopped inside, kicking the pilot in the face and knocking her out, then he threw her out. The cockpit closed as the mech turned to the remaining two and fired. "I've got this. Take the others and go," Lake broadcast from his hijacked robot.

"What? I'm not going to leave you!" protested Keri.

"Take them to the bridge, then come back for me," he repeated. When she didn't move, he shouted, "Go!"

Keri rushed over to the other two. "Who's first?"

"Take her and go," ordered Jella, who bled everywhere but kept her stance.

Keri quickly grabbed Vivian into a piggyback ride, shutting her up. "Hold tight." From a brisk walk to a jog, a few breaths left her, and her time abilities surged within. The distance grew short in seconds. When she broke a sweat, she had reached the end of the bridge and the start of Kermoz—her territory.

"I'll be right back," she said, running back.

"Your turn," Keri said to Jella, not waiting for confirmation. As she glanced at Lake's ex's figure in her regenerating outfit, she couldn't help but sigh. Fashion magazines and lingerie models came to mind. Despite the dirt and stains on her, she was sexy and hot. Why Lake would choose her over this hot number—she didn't know. Sure, she had lost a lot of weight due to running and the Swordswoman Body. But that was the thing; she had a swordswoman's body. Her body was made up of big, tough muscles and just a bit of fat. Also, her boobs weren't as bouncy, perky, or noticeable as Jella's. They even felt soft on her back. What was that about?

"Uh, thanks," said Jella as she knelt next to Vivian in Kermoz.

The words forced a smile on Keri's face as a reply. She didn't know how to respond to that. There was an awkward tension between the two of them. Should she clear the air or something? Like he's with her now and that there's no hard feelings whatsoever? *Ugh, this is confusing.* Wait. What was she supposed to do again? Right—Lake. As she turned to run back, she heard Vivian say, "He did it."

When the last of the mech's fell, Lake whipped at their direction and waved. The booster rockets on his mech's ankles flared as he accelerated to their location. But as he reached the end of the bridge, a meteor-like mass enveloped in blue flames zoomed the sky and crashed before them. As the dust cloud settled, Wayne blocked his path with a blank face. Lake instantly pointed his mech's rifle and fired. A knight made of metal and blue flame materialized and intercepted the bullets with its shield. It inched a step forward and grew to match the mech's size every second, even while it was under fire. It stopped when an arm's length away from Lake, then, the knight swung its lance at him. The mech dodged to the side and fired its gun again, but the knight defended itself with a shield.

"Watch out!" shouted Jella.

Stray blue fireballs hit Lake and toppled him back. Smoke sizzled from Wayne's hands. Keri had already appeared behind Wayne to stop him from casting another one. The soulsword glinted to life in her hands, swirling with black-green energy. The blade struck down, cutting a wide tear across his back. Blood spurted behind him. Without any sign of pain or even a reaction on his face, Wayne turned to her with a punch already in motion. A roar of blue flames launched her into the air and backward.

"Wayne, let us go or I'll fire," shouted Vivian. "Let us go. The Cluster is in trouble."

"He doesn't hear you," Jella told her, still healing. "The army has taken over his mind."

"Damn you, Christopher." Vivian fired her machine gun, but Wayne tanked the bullets.

A clock turned its hands backward as the burns around Keri vanished. She pulled upon the source within her again. A clock of light appeared on her ex's head and slowed him further, making it easier for Keri to fight him up close. "Wayne, just let us go." Continuous sword strikes landed on the former stripper, each carrying Keri's resolve to be free from him. Blood sprayed around the two former lovers, but Wayne kept blocking and spouting flames from his mouth and arms.

Throwing the emptied guns away, Vivian switched to her tessens. Her hands sliced downwards as sharp gales tore through the air and marked blood stripes on Wayne's flesh. "Wayne, this is not you. Fight it," she howled.

Keri followed up with speedy and evasive attacks. Whenever her ex swung his arms and created flames, she'd dodge to the side and deal damage with an opening, then she'd evade again for the next attack. She kept doing this to mitigate his strong blows, but some of the heat from his flames still scorched her. "Is there a way to reverse his condition?" she asked, feeling the flames burn her arms as she blocked with her sword.

"Not that I know of. From what I recall, healing them only further reinforces the brainwashing," said Vivian. "Unless you can turn back time, I don't think it will help."

"Luckily I can," Keri laughed, striking him with a big swing, then hopping back. Pulling the source around her once more, she unleashed it upon Wayne. A clock made of light rewound itself on his forehead.

Wayne stopped his advances, fell to his knees and clutched his head. "Aaahhhh," he growled.

"Come on, Wayne. Snap out of it. Don't let other people control you," shouted Keri.

The knight disappeared as it was about to strike its opponent. Getting a breather, Lake turned to the other scene and approached them. "Is he back?" he asked.

"I don't know. I'm trying the best I can." The Soulsword faded as she placed both of her hands over his head.

"He's in pain. His love for you is fighting with the compulsion the army placed on him," informed Jella.

"What? What did you just say?" asked Keri.

"Keep doing what you're doing," she insisted.

The sound of the air being ripped reverberated overhead. Two helicopters flew in view as spotlights shone on them. "That's enough, Lake. Surrender yourselves. You and your friends cannot win against the army," Cervantes announced, using speakers in the flying vehicle.

Vivian made a full pirouette with her tessens as gales of shredding wind ripped through the air and struck the helicopter while the second one steered clear from it. Fire burned from the back as the damaged helicopter whizzed down to an emergency landing. "Fuck off, Christopher!" she shouted.

Another gale fired at the second helicopter, but it hit a Light Dome that surrounded it instead. "I'm not surprised you're helping him, Vivian. You were always a thorn in my side. I'll be glad to be rid of you. Wayne, attack," broadcast Cervantes.

"The compulsion is winning, watch out," warned Jella.

A circle of blue fire whooshed out from Wayne and pushed everyone back. He howled at the top of his lungs as armor made of metal and fire formed over his body. A lance materialized in his right hand and a shield on his left. He charged at Keri without saying another word. Before he could hit her, Lake tackled him to the right with a battered robot. The mech towered over the candidate in size, but Wayne's strength and the heat pouring off of him melted the mech in seconds. It's rotors and thrusters turned to immovable slag as the whole vehicle was surrounded in dissolving air.

Jella pushed herself toward Wayne as a distraction. The heat melted her skin and competed with her body's regenerative power. Meanwhile, Keri dashed at the mech and carved a hole in its back. Lake was almost unconscious when she pulled him out. With all her strength, she heaved him onto her back and ran to the end of the bridge. She left him there and went back to the fight.

Pulling source around her again, she felt the familiar headache and shiver from hypoetheria. She was at her limit. But she pushed and cast a rewinding clock over at Wayne. The clock hands labored in the anti-clockwise direction while the flames around the Slayer brightened. "It's not working," she shouted as Wayne rose to his feet in complete normal, unhindered motion.

After throwing Jella away in a flaming ball, he marched onto their path with his weapons in hand. His arm cocked back, and he threw the lance forward. A blazing meteor-like object shot toward them. Keri tried to slow it down, but its trajectory stayed on course. The moment before it hit them, Vivian swung her tessen at it, managing to tweak its course. But its descent to the ground caused an explosion, catching them all in a wave of fire. Everyone suffered from burns and was knocked to the ground—conscious but struggling. Before they suffered more from their injuries, Keri immediately released another healing clock, reversing the damage that was dealt as much as she could. She could only do so much before the symptoms fought with her. She rested on debris, huffing, wheezing and shivering.

Wayne continued his march. Another lance was summoned in his grasp as he stopped a foot from where Keri had collapsed on the rubble. His face showed no compassion, nor the longing that Keri would have recognized. At least when he'd wanted to hurt her before, he did so with all of his love—if it could even be called that. Now, he was as cold as steel, despite the flames that licked his metal armor. "Go ahead. Do it. You're as much of a monster now as you were then. The difference back then was that I didn't see it. I was stupid," she coughed.

Her ex lifted the lance up to his head.

"No, stop," cried Lake, who was crawling forward.

But that didn't deter Wayne from bringing the weapon down on her. The second the lance was inches from her face, it stopped.

Keri's brows furrowed. She wondered why he was suspended. Then she noticed Jella was lying behind him with pure white eyes and a faint golden halo glowing around her head. Keri's mouth opened so she could ask what she was doing, but she felt the familiar mystical pull of a candidate was stronger than ever. She realized whenever Lake or Wayne used their abilities, the sense of Prima strengthened. She confirmed within her own ability that this was Jella's fragment—a mind-based fragment. "Do you have him? How long?" Keri asked instead.

The halo around her flickered. "I feel him slipping," Jella warned, rising to a sitting position.

As Vivian emerged from the rubble, battered and bruised, she said, "There are more coming."

From the distance, another helicopter joined Cervantes in the air. They flew right above the bridge, watching them. A dozen armored cars and mechs made the ground rumble with their heavy footsteps and treads; the vehicles running at max speed on their way to the candidates. They were not safe. Two hands carefully lifted Keri to stand and pulled her away from Wayne's aim. "What was the plan? We're here now," said Lake beside her.

At the mention of the plan, Keri snapped back into focus. Her head whipped from side to side, noting all of them were indeed in her zone. When she opened her mouth to speak, a blast erupted from their vicinity as Wayne launched himself against the oncoming vehicles and threw fire at the helicopters. Keri panicked in her head. Wayne was already here. She could have protected him—restored his memory. "What did you do?" she asked.

"I made him think that the army is trying to take you away from him," reasoned Jella. "They're all shitheads. Let them fight each other."

Lake pressed a hand on her shoulder. "Let him go. He'll be okay. He's strong." The hand stopped her from protesting. "I'm more worried about us—and Maxwell back at the cluster. They need us," he added.

As grenades, bullets, and blue fire shot in volleys on the other side of the bridge, Keri steeled her mind and calmed her heart. Her thoughts fled to Fynn's stories, trying to remember. "I, Keri Richforth, Maiden candidate and owner of this area, order this realm to disallow entry and exit from all entities and any harm that may come to it. To this, I offer 1000 soul coins," she announced.

> You have offered 1000 coins for the complete protection of Zone Kermoz.
> Shield Crystal is already in effect. Adjusting protection.
> Any harm, attempt to enter or exit, or break into or out of the area will be prohibited from any type of source, living or non-living, allied or non-allied entities for 72 hours.

The helicopter where Cervantes flew dodged the blue flames and headed their way instead. It broadcast his voice from the speakers of the chopper, "I applaud you, Lake, and your band of try-hards. But it will take more than turning my weapon against me to—" As the aerial vehicle flew towards them, it crashed into an invisible wall. Debris and flames illuminated the night air and flew away from Kermoz and into the river separating the two zones.

"Did he just crash to his death?" asked Jella, with a slightly joyous tone.

"I highly doubt he's dead," said Vivian. "But this should give us time."

A part of Keri rejoiced at the thought of him dying too—or at least because he'd be gone for now. He was the cause of Silaw and her family's demise. It would be nice if he wasn't around. But glancing at Lake's pained expression made her feel guilty. He was his superior after all. Lake might want something else for him, at least not his death.

"What now?" asked Vivian.

Keri willed a rift to open behind them, leading to Zone E-law. It was the closest area to Cluster RSTU she controlled. "To E-law?" asked Lake.

She nodded.

He looked around for a bit. "We should grab a car or something. We're not in the best shape to walk back to the cluster."

"What about them?" Jella pointed to the other mechs which had gone past Wayne's rampage and approached them.

"I wouldn't worry about them," Keri said with finality. The invisible wall blocked the mechs from proceeding further. Once the enemy understood it existed, a barrage of bullets and grenade explosions detonated against the wall. But no matter how strong or big the fireworks were, it remained unharmed and complete.

Lake turned from the scene. "Come on, let's go."

Chapter 61

Lake, E-law

Dawn broke as Lake and his party drove from Zone E-law to the RSTU Cluster in a van. No one said much during the trip. Mostly, everyone looked exhausted—or in shock from what had happened. A few minutes into the ride, Riley called Vivian, and the two exchanged updates. The damage and confusion the team had done at Kermoz and in the surrounding area had all of the soldiers scrambling to understand the situation. No one had seen Cervantes yet, and they were all trying to find him. Vivian talked with her wife while Keri slept beside her.

"So, you and Keri?" whispered Jella in the passenger seat.

"Yeah," repeated Lake. "I think I have you to thank for it."

"Me?"

"If you didn't break up with me, I wouldn't have gotten to experience new things. Try different things, or be open to anyone else."

Jella nodded. "That's good. Thanks again for rescuing me. Sorry I broke up with you over video—you still helped me even after that."

"Honestly, I haven't really thought about it," said Lake. "When I saw you, I thought I needed to save you. Just because we're not together doesn't mean we're not friends anymore."

She looked up at him. "What happened to you after that?" she asked with hesitation in her voice.

Lake told her an abridged version of what had happened, sticking to the system and finding his way to Keri in another dimension. "I've lost people, but I've gained new ones too," he finished, with his lips stretching to a smile. No joy emanated—instead, sadness was apparent.

"You forgot the important parts," grumbled Keri, waking from her loud sleep.

"Which is?" He glanced up at the mirror.

She explained the system, the circumstances that came with the power, Silaw's expectations and status. "You, me, Jella and Wayne. We've all been chosen to save the world and help Silaw recover his powers. The more areas we get under control, the stronger we get, and the safer everyone is," she finished.

"Me? Save the world?" squeaked Jella.

"Silaw chose us to prevent the invaders from winning. I was chosen as the Maiden, to help other candidates," stated Keri with strength in her voice. "You're the fourth candidate. You have a fragment that helps us know how many areas we have left to defend."

"How do I do that?" Her voice spotted a tone of curiosity.

Lake explained it to her like he had explained a thousand theories to her before. She'd listen intently with full attention and not say a word until he was done, like she did now. He instructed her on how to find the upgrades in her system. "Try purchasing it if you have any coins," he said.

"Congratulations, you unlocked a new fragment—territorial overview," she read from a screen only she could see. "Description: the candidate is able to discern the territories under her control. Then stuff about me and my status comes up. This fragment, it helps us?"

"Definitely, it'll keep our zones from being overrun."

"How do I get more coins?"

"We kill the invaders, or we get it from something else. I...get more from saving people." He tried his best to keep his eye on the road.

"Saving people? Is it because you're a Hero candidate?" Vivian asked after ending her call. "How obvious. Kinda self-absorbed."

Keri elbowed Vivian, to which she just shrugged. "What? It sounds like it," she replied.

"I didn't make the rules. This is how it is. Killing monsters gives us coins plus one other thing—and I'm anything but self-absorbed." Lake felt uncomfortable whenever people would single him out because of his looks or anything that made him look like a narcissist. He wanted to be more than just a pretty face.

"How about you, Keri? How do you get yours?" asked Jella.

Keri slightly jumped from the question, looking at Lake, then blushing. "Artefacts. She can absorb outlier 7s' powers into her own," Lake answered for her.

"And you are called what?" she prodded.

Keri appeared dejected; somehow, Lake sensed he had let her down somehow. "Maiden," she answered.

"It sounds so girly. Who came up with these names?" said Vivian. "I'm guessing Wayne's the hot rod, firefighter, or something?"

"Wayne is a Slayer. I think he gets more coins from killing monsters than us—that's all he ever did when we were together." There was a slight edge in Keri's tone.

"Does it have something to do with your title?" Jella guessed. "Hero for saving, Slayer for slaying and...Maiden for collecting items?"

"It seems like it reinforces the stereotype girls like collecting items and cute things," complained Vivian. "There is more to women than accessorizing, make-up and stuff. It's annoying."

Lake ignored the comment and asked Jella, "How about you? What was the other one called again?"

"She's the Ferry," Keri answered.

Keri finally remembered and told them of the passive and active candidates. All candidates can recruit people to their banner and cause. Once they swear their allegiance to a candidate, they become a follower. Once a certain number of followers are reached, active candidates can create outworlds and bring the fight to other dimensions. Passive candidates could gain followers but were not allowed to wage battles against other worlds. Passives were the defensive candidates: the Maiden and Ferry.

Jella gave her a quizzical expression. "I don't, I mean, I'm not—"

"—it's a lot," interrupted Keri. "I don't expect for you to save the world. But we've been given an opportunity to do something about it. I want to do something about it. At the very least, are you willing to work with us to help save our friends? And find captured areas?"

Jella smiled warmly at her, and Keri smiled back.

"Hero, Maiden, Slayer, Ferry—sounds awfully like a children's book—the bad kind," commented Vivian.

"Or a game," murmured Keri.

"Like *Love Me, Princess*," said Jella.

She brightened. "Oh, I forgot you played that too. I've got the new remake edition back at Zone Troef—we can play it together. Who's your favorite male target?"

Jella glanced at the side and said, "The prince." Keri opened her mouth to speak, but the Ferry continued on, "By the way, my new fragment lets me see a map. The whole E-law zone is colored green. Then it's all gray behind us." She pressed a finger in the air and then she cocked her head to the side.

"I own E-law, so am I green?" guessed Keri. "I like the color."

"Gray must not have owners," said Lake.

"There's also violet color up ahead. Zone Rumaf, Shoef and Untef," added Jella.

"Those are mine," said Lake. "I'm violet then."

"Who has red?" asked Jella with a pout.

"Red? Wayne's?" suggested Vivian.

"I don't think Wayne owns anything near the cluster," said Keri. "He did mention something about G-law."

"Hmmm, G-law, its colored blue. There's also a red cross icon moving from Troef and into Untef—along the borders. But I think it stopped there," Jella continued as she tapped the air. "Oh, there's a label: Champion Ursa. What does that mean?"

Keri gasped when Lake stepped on the accelerator. "It means we have to hurry," he declared.

CHAPTER 62

LAKE, CLUSTER RSTU

At Cluster RSTU, fire raged on at one part of the large valley as screams of terror and cries for help echoed. Armored bears the size of houses chased people with their large, deadly claws and salivating, fanged mouths. Drivers abandoned their vehicles to run away, only to be devoured by the hungry beasts. Commuters in cable cars were trapped in the cars as bears jumped up and plucked them from above like fruits on a tree. They climbed buildings and poked their arms in the windows, fiddling with the insides, and when they pulled their paws out, men and women were treated as hors d'oeuvres with their blood suckled like nectar from a flower.

"This is a massacre," Vivian gasped with tears in her eyes.

Keri said, "I have to help them."

As she was about to leave, Lake reached out a hand and stopped her. "We don't know what's going on."

"Maxwell and the Apes are down there. My friends are fighting. I'm going to help them," she said furiously.

"We are going to help our friends," he corrected. "Let's make a plan first."

"They're dying. Look at—"

He tightened his grip. "Trust me."

She shut her mouth and then nodded.

The scene of carnage pierced through Lake as the people he'd tried to keep safe died on his watch. What had happened to the generators he'd made and the shielding crystals he'd used? From the top of the valley, he watched as the people fled to the other zones. When they crossed the streets from Troef to Rumaf, Shoef or Untef, an invisible barrier blocked the chasing beasts. They pounded and growled, but the barrier stood and the people stayed safe. So it seemed Troef was the only exposed zone without a barrier. No candidate owned it.

"We need to help the people get into the other zones. Evacuate them from Troef," ordered Lake. "Vivian, can you help with that?"

"You don't have to ask," said Vivian. "These are my people, they deserve my help."

"I've got your linko in a party chat. We can all talk there," shouted Lake as she hurried away, confirming with a thumbs up.

Jella spoke up, "I want to help."

"Are you sure? You just got out of the lab and—"

"I'm fine. Didn't you see? I can't be killed," she said casually, like it had been a fact all along. "Besides, it's not like you're in the best shape either."

Lake acquiesced, knowing he was feeling out of sorts from the battle with Wayne. But he was healed enough to save people. "Can you cast your time spell on me? I need to go to the generator site," he asked Keri once Jella disappeared after Vivian's trail.

"The nearest one is Untef—that's kinda far. It's not going to last when I'm not there," said Keri.

"Then can you run with me?"

"I still feel hypoetheric. Casting it twice is kinda difficult all the way there. But I can carry you like I did the others?" she suggested with a sheepish smile.

Lake double-checked their party's linko connection before hopping onto Keri's back. He apologized to her, saying she shouldn't have to carry a man on her back. It was supposed to be the other way around. She laughed and said, "So boys can freely carry and help, and girls can't?" Shimmering clocks appeared on her ankles as she ran ahead.

"I didn't mean it like that, I just said—"

"It's exactly what you meant. I'm your girlfriend, that means I can help." She blushed. "Vivian's crap is rubbing off on me."

Lake was about to apologize again when a bear and a car flew in their direction. "Look out!" he shouted.

Keri slowed the flying car for a couple of seconds and dodged out of the pavements and onto the road where the cars had stopped and were empty of passengers. People ran and panicked around them, heading the same way they were—away from Troef and into Untef. Once they got to an intersection, they found a bear howling and throwing cars left and right. The people who had run ahead either stopped or were smashed into an SUV or sedan. She was about to cast another time spell to slow the cars, but Lake said to her, "Keep running. I'll take care of it."

Two types of grenades flew from Lake's grasp and onto the bear. A blue-colored one exploded first, wrapping the beast with goo—the same slime he had used before. The green one then took off, expelling a green mist. It had no effect on the slime, but it was different for the bear. Its fur and hide visibly started melting at a rapid pace.

Keri ran around the dying bear and onto the other side of the road. "What was that?" she asked.

"It's a bomb for monsters and otherworld creatures, and disregards human DNA," he said proudly. "Not sure about the name yet. Acid bomb? Green grenades? G-Bomb?"

"Whatever it is, they're awesome."

With Keri's fast pace, Lake kept hurling grenades. Monsters close to masses of people were his priority. A grenade exploded on a bear trying to ransack a bakery's customers through the front door, sticking its paws in. Goo and mist enveloped another bear, shaking a cable car in its mouth, waiting for the passengers to fall in. Twinkles of an explosion and a fast-moving green mist surrounded an apartment building with bears poking their heads through the windows, trying to get at its inhabitants. He helped people as much as he could on their way. But when they neared the borders of Untef, a group of bears pounded and scratched on the invisible wall. Others howled and tried to bite through it, but the wall stood and protected the people behind it.

Keri's eyes widened at the scene. "What are we gonna—" A bear jumped at them from the side and she dodged. The bear's shoulder pushed her back, flinging them to the side. As the two departed separated in midair, Lake reached out to grab Keri and pulled her into an embrace. He then maneuvered himself so that his feet landed on the wall. When he did, he activated his S-Boots and pushed with all his might. He flung forward and up in the direction of the invisible wall. A bear noticed his presence, opened its saliva-dripping mouth and awaited his descent. As he plummeted toward the bear, he adjusted himself and landed on its snout instead. The bear instantly snapped its mouth shut, but not before he launched himself into the air again and into the safety of the zone. The wall shimmered as he and Keri passed through it.

Once he landed, he put Keri down and ran to the site where the ward generator was. He dragged Keri by the hand. Both of them were out of breath, yet kept pushing every step forward. Banging vibrations spread from the invisible walls as cries echoed from the crowded streets and zone officials barked orders from their megaphones trying to bring order to the chaos of people fraught with fear, panic, and loss. The sounds around them arrested their hearts at the urgency of the situation.

At the entrance to the site, guards blocked their paths. "Turn back now. Civilians are gathered at the zone hall for shelter. Please head there," ordered one of the men with a large rifle.

"I'm Lake Deskenn, I work here. Please let me through," reasoned Lake, trying to push himself in.

The two guards pushed him back. "Get back now," shouted the other guard as he raised his rifle at him.

Clocks of light brightened over their heads as they paused in place. "Assholes, don't they know we're trying to help them? What's wrong with them?" Keri dragged Lake away from the guards and onto the entrance.

"The zone mayor must've asked them to guard this place. Don't blame them. I told the mayor if there was an invasion—this place will keep them safe." Lake accessed the security panel for the door, punching codes and executing scans.

Keri made a face. "Didn't you use the crystals? The wall is up," she said matter-of-factly.

"They don't know that. All they know is the ward generator is doing all of this." The doors unlocked and slid aside as they headed in.

The ward generator buzzed in a low staccato rhythm. Everything was as Lake had left it, untouched and working at its optimum capacity. He rushed toward the control panel as keys appeared on the glassy and screens materialized over air.

With a few rushed taps of his fingers, the entrance doors shut tight and more bolts and locks slid in place. "That should keep them out for a while," he said.

Keri whistled, moving towards the middle of the dome where the generator was. Lights cascaded over the circular machinery in a clockwise fashion. "Wow, you made this? Can I touch it?" she asked.

"You can," he laughed. "All of the sensitive devices are underground."

As Keri inspected the machines inside the room, she said in a wary tone, "Did you really mean it?"

A large screen and more smaller screens popped before Lake. Untef was displayed on the large, while the smaller ones showed the freezones. The claimed zones fared well without the beasts, despite the injured and panicked people. In stark contrast, fires, battles and blood ensued over at Troef. Zone guards and closers fought the beasts. The civilians were left to themselves to escape. "Mean what?" He looked up at her.

She avoided his gaze. "Me being your girlfriend."

He instantly blushed. "I just—I mean, if you don't want to—I'll res—"

"—I want to," she cut him off. "I want to be your girlfriend."

"Good. Is that it?" His attention was all on her.

She approached him in a slow walk. "Can we kiss on it?"

"Didn't we already?"

"I wasn't prepared that time."

He crossed the distance and instantly planted his mouth on hers. His tongue explored the inside of her mouth as he pressed himself closer to her. Heat generated inside of him, feeling himself being hard. As he pulled away for fearing it may go further, she instead grabbed him and jumped onto his arms while wrapping her legs around him. They proceeded in making out even more.

A tiny floating circle screen appeared on their left. "Sir Lake, where have you—" The technician Lake worked with on the generators appeared on the other end. His face froze and eyes locked on the scene.

The two quickly broke apart from the sound and fell on the floor with a thud. Lake quickly stood up. "Yeah?" he said, rubbing his pained buttocks.

The technician pointed to his own chin, gesturing in the video.

Lake touched his face as he realized saliva was all over his face. *I should really teach Keri how to be less sloppy with her kisses.*

With a satisfied nod, the technician started, "Sir, um, the city is in panic. Monsters are attacking us from the rift." A label at the bottom screen mentioned him being on the other generator site at Shoef.

"Right, right," said Lake, refocusing on the situation at hand. "Why didn't you release the Defense Project? This is an emergency."

A second circle screen materialized under the first, with Zone Rumaf labelled at the bottom. "We tried, sir, but all the security has your credentials for the final lock." A few more technicians peeked in the video.

Lake stretched his neck. "Right. We did install that. Everyone, activate zone emergency security systems now." His fingers tapped quickly on the glassy keys.

A lone screen displayed multiple locks and a very large exclamation icon with the words: *Warning! Cluster Defense System Activating!*

"Troef and Shoef security system first gate unlocked," reported the technician. "All device systems at full power, diagnostics clear."

"Rumaf and Untef security system first gate unlocked," the other technician announced. "All device systems at full power, diagnostics clear."

"Second gates unlocked," Lake said. "Green light for all security systems."

One by one, the locks on the screen animatedly opened. "Initiating," all of them said together.

In the screens across all of the zones, buildings, statues and earth walls grumbled and slid aside to create an opening to let mechs elevate and move forward, carried by steel platforms. The machine's helmet lights and indicators flashed, and their thrusters activated as they propelled themselves forward. Small drones flew after the mechs from their storage bays.

"Initiating safety announcement," said the technician.

All across the zones, the mechs broadcast in a calm female voice, "This is RSTUs mech security system. Please evacuate and seek safety at Zones Shoef, Rumaf and Untef. Follow the green lights to safety." The warning repeated itself over and over as the drones formed a line in the air, snaking back to the safe zones and flashing green.

A map of the cluster showed itself on another screen. Violet dots indicated the mechs. Red dots were the beasts. Groups of three mechs ganged up on each bear. They shot them down with rifles and rocket launchers, targeting the bears' faces and chests with high accuracy. Once they were dead, they moved on to their next targets. They kept chipping away at the beasts one after the other in a very streamlined manner. The red dots disappeared one after another.

"Woah, awesome," Keri marveled. "You built all of this?

"Yeah, with my team," Lake said humbly. "This is actually its test phase. I hadn't had the time to do a proper one—the army arrived sooner than I expected."

"Why didn't you use this against them? Or against Wayne?" she asked. "You could easily defeat them with this."

He shook his head. "Mechs are powerful, but in a city, they risk hurting civilians. It's easier to minimize damage with closers."

"Sir, we've got a boss monster up ahead," said the technician as the screens focused on a 60-meter-tall bear with black fur and silver armor.

"Champion Ursa," breathed out Lake.

"Sir, your orders?" asked one of the technicians.

Once he had a good look at the screens, Lake quickly left the control panel and headed over to a large container on the side. After opening the lock, he rummaged inside. "Keep away from the champion. Kill only the beasts around him. Prioritize the civilians," he said.

"Look, it's Maxwell, Ivo and the Apes." Keri pointed at a group of closers struggling against the champion's howls, large swings and massive strength. "What about them?"

Lake took out his back-up gloves, visor, boots and other equipment. "We're going to help them."

Chapter 63

Maxwell, Cluster RSTU

A ringing sound echoed in Maxwell's head, blocking all other waves from entering. Flat on the ground, he pushed himself into a sitting position, but a rocking pain pulsed through his head and prevented his body from making casual movements. He was at his limit. The grey aura, his ability that had given him great strength, sharpness and reflexes was empty. No matter how much he asked himself to swing his blade, to get up, to dodge, to attack, to do anything—his body was done. He'd had enough.

If only he had been less stubborn and had asked the rest of the free to evacuate, maybe he wouldn't be in this position. When the rifts had increased in number, he assured the cluster mayor that they would be okay. He relied heavily on his team, and Lake's new ward generators. But that went south very quickly when rifts started appearing in Rumaf. He knew Rumaf's generators weren't completed yet, but he remembered Lake was going to repair it, but then the army came. Reports mentioned they had abducted him and Keri. He wanted to investigate that, to lend assistance however he could, but the cluster needed him more. There was no time for them.

Still, when the mayor had asked him again, if it was best to evacuate, he said, "No. My Apes can handle it." That was true for the most part. The Hairless Apes did their job and closed the rifts while the other guilds took care of the rifts outside—near the clusters that increased in number. But then, the orange rift came—the largest one Maxwell had ever seen in his life. It was as tall as a ten-story building, five times larger than the beasts he had fought in the past. His A-team went in first, but came out with only one survivor, the lookout Ivo. Deeg and the rest of them were dead. Maxwell was broken by the news, but he couldn't allow himself to feel it. The supposed mourning, weeping, guilt, sadness and other emotions went in a box in his heart together with the other boxes of his life and family disputes and disappointments. Instead, he had asked his B-team, together with the other guilds, to investigate the orange rift. The manpower was more than triple what it was before.

Two days passed. Four people came back with news of failure. After, there wasn't much they could do. The guilds and zone officials debated on the next course of action: would they send another team, reinforce the zones, evacuate the zones, or call for the army, etc. The politics and arguments took their time. No resolution passed when the orange rift shifted to red and opened in two directions, letting the monsters invaded.

Before he came to the freezones, Maxwell swore to himself that he would have his own family. He would trust them completely. It would be better than his blood relatives who lied, stabbed others in the back and used people for their own benefit. He'd be wiser, richer, more powerful, but a better leader, a better person, and a better man. He'd be more than them in all aspects. He and his new family would grow to have a bigger influence, with stronger foundations.

As he finally sat on his butt, he had a good look at his surroundings. The buildings, shops and earthen walls in the valley had all collapsed, crushed into pieces. Demolished cars and other abandoned vehicles flooded the broken roads. Stray power lines and cables protruded in random spots along the traffic zones. Civilians lay lifeless on the ground with their eyes and faces in shock. Their bodies were painted in blood; their guts, innards and torsos were either mangled, chewed or missing. He knew who some of them were. Some were his previous clients, some were shop owners he frequented, and some were his Apes—his true family.

The ground shook as the bear, the size of a building, marched in his direction. With its black fur and silver armor, it exuded imposing strength, ferocity, and above all, danger. This was the annihilator of his family and his city—one of the champions Lake had mentioned. A monster so powerful that it had the capacity to think like they did. This was the monster that had wrought all of this damage and death. But as hatred and vengeance pulsed in his veins, ready to be used in a battle of blood and blades that would define his moment as a man and a leader, there was nothing he could do. He did not move. After he had sat down, the other muscles he thought he had control of simply rested. His muscle control was missing, shrugs, twists, and turning—even speaking escaped him. The involuntary jitters from his fingers were all that remained.

The large bear stopped before him. Huffs of air puffed out of its salivating mouth. Its crazed eyes hungered for him. He wanted to swear. He wanted to flip the beast a finger. But none of that happened. *At least, let me fuck up this bastard one last time,* he thought as the humongous bear lifted its paw for a strike. With no way to even insult it, Maxwell just stared it down in defiance—all 60 meters of it. If death awaited him, then he'd look it straight in the face and meet it head-on. If his gaze could cut, his clear gray eyes would have sliced the horizon.

The paw went down and hit the ground. Dust clouds and dirt filled the air. As the bear hoisted its limb to check on its kill, it groaned. Blood stains and guts were missing.

Maxwell's thoughts were blank. He was so focused on that single moment of life and death that he did not notice when a strong force had whisked him away, carrying him a safe distance from the champion. When his thoughts finally worked again, a strong woman filled his view.

"Are you okay?" asked Keri.

He did not know how long it was, but he gawked at her as if it was his first time seeing her. She always had the most beautiful eyes hidden under the glasses she used to wear but didn't anymore. Pity, now most men would see her as he saw her—beautiful.

"Maxwell, is it not working? Are you not feeling better?" she said with alarm in her voice.

It was a beat later that he noticed the clock of light shining beneath him. Control over his muscles slowly returned him, like they had been dried in the desert for days and days—and now water and nourishment sated them. Life and strength returned to him gradually. "You're here." He found he could speak again, though his voice was gruff.

The bear howled at the top of its lungs before Keri could reply, snatching their attentions. It pounded toward them, ready for a massacre, but it was cut short as a flying truck hit it on its right, causing it to tumble and roll to the side. Before it could get back up, brick walls, chunks of cement roads and other debris fell on it from above, burying it in a mountain of rubble.

High above in the sky, Lake rode his hoverboard and levitated a few cars around him, like a telekinetic juggler. "It's knocked out for now. It'll get back up soon." His voice was slightly audible on Keri's linko.

Disbelief filled Maxwell's mind. A few moments ago, he was under death's door, now he was saved? Maxwell grabbed Keri's hand and linked his linko into their conversation. "Lake, you ass, where have you been?" he shouted.

"Sorry about that, Guild Leader," said Lake. "Had to rescue a friend back home. I'm here now."

"Weren't you the one who needed rescuing?" Keri joined in.

Lake snickered. "Maybe we can talk details later…"

Maxwell laughed at the two of them. A tiny break in his heart went out for Keri, but he was okay with it. If someone could make her happy, Lake was a good choice. "My guild. Some of them are still underground," he said as reality set in.

"We got them out, Maxwell, no need to worry," replied Vivian in the party-link and waved at them from a few meters away. She was with a beautiful woman who gazed intently at nowhere in particular.

The woman pointed over at a rundown pizza place. "There's two of them there." Both of them ran to the spot and started digging. After a few moments, two closers were found. Vivian continued to dig them out while Jella focused on finding others.

"That's Jella, she can find people," answered Keri to Maxwell's confused look.

"You know, this is going to cost you," Vivian joked. "I don't charge low for my particular services."

Maxwell chuckled, "For the first time, I don't care how much it costs."

"Is that you, Guild Leader? Not caring about finances?" asked Lake. "I find that hard to believe."

The mound of dirt and debris where the champion was buried rumbled. Then it exploded as the bear howled and stomped forward in anger.

"There's more people in this area," reported Jella. "Keep the fight away from here."

"Care to be our frontman, Keri? Or frontwoman?" asked Lake.

"Me? Why me?" asked Keri.

"Because of your speed and sword skills?"

"And you heal yourself," added Vivian. "You're like a very sturdy shield? Is that what you call it in your games?"

Keri stood and summoned Soulsword as specks of green-black energy formed around her hand. "You mean a tank? Oh, okay, that makes sense. That is my build. Fine, I'll do it."

Maxwell held her arm. "Are you sure about this? Give me some time, I'll be ready—"

"I'm okay. Don't worry, I can handle this," she cut him off. "I'm part of the Apes too, right?" She marched over to the mountain-tall beast and clutched her sword by her side.

His hand still lingered in the air as she left him. Gone was the weird, demanding and clueless woman he had accidentally saved. She'd been transformed into a strong woman, one who knew herself and the world she lived in. Maxwell silently placed his hopes on her to save the zone, well, until he could heal himself good enough to join the fight again. But for now, she could have the spotlight. "You certainly are," he said, glad to have another member of his family.

"Ready on your call." Lake levitated more debris into the air around them.

A smile stretched on Keri's lips before she answered, "Let's do this."

Chapter 64

Keri, Lobby, Amazing Discoveries

It took the morning until early afternoon before Champion Ursa and its underlings were defeated. Keri's team and the other guilds killed every single monster in the cluster's vicinity.

On the ground floor of Amazing Discoveries, the Hairless Apes sat on the waiting benches and floors. The area had been designated as a rest stop for all closers as they took shifts guarding and patrolling while everyone else returned to their homes and tried to restore their shaken lives.

Lake was helping Jella purchase and use gems in the corner of the store, while Maxwell and Vivian talked business with some of the Apes and Keri went around the room asking who needed healing when the entrance opened. Riley rushed in with Charlie. They scanned the room. Once they found Vivian, they rushed over to where she was and hugged her. Riley peppered her with questions about how she was doing, or if she was hurt, to which she replied with no.

"I'm glad you're okay, Mom," said Charlie.

Vivian gasped. "You—you can talk?" She looked from him to Riley.

"He started doing that earlier when he woke up," responded Riley. "I can't believe it either."

She embraced Charlie tightly and started to cry. He tried to get his mom off of him, but she was locked around him tight. Keri smiled at the sight.

"I did it," Jella said, jumping up from her seat. "It says I'm the owner of Troef, and it's protected."

Keri was about to say congratulations when Charlie started glowing.

"Buddy, what's happening?" Riley asked.

Keri felt source convalesce around and in the child's body. "Silaw's descending. Step back," she warned.

Vivian released the hug and backed away with a confused face. Everyone in the room focused on the young boy as golden wisps encircled him. After a few seconds, the wisps rushed into his body as a golden aura emanated from him.

Charlie's confused and anxious expression changed into a calm demeanor. "Candidates, thank you for defeating the invaders and champions and reclaiming the areas for our world. Everyone else, thank you for helping." He bowed.

Murmurs started around amongst the guild with disbelieving expressions.

"Are you Silaw? Or Charlie?" asked Riley.

Charlie smiled. "Apologies for the late introductions. I am Silaw, I am inhabiting Charlie's body as my vessel. Do not worry for his safety or sanity. He is in control of himself and lends his body to me willingly, when needed. He has welcomed me since before the destruction of Kermoz."

"Are you here just to say thanks?" asked Lake.

"My time is limited. The areas you have claimed have restored some of the source and souls that I use to exist and guard our world. But the damage and exhaustion I suffered from repairing the hole and keeping the Wills from getting bigger took much from me," explained Silaw. "But you deserve your questions answered, so I will allow you to ask a few."

"Is there a way for Charlie not to be your vessel?" Vivian seized the moment and quickly asked.

He shook his head. "He will always be my vessel. So long as he lives, he and I are intertwined. But if you can find me other willing vessels, outlier 32s as you call them, I can reduce my time using his body. It does take a considerable amount of stress to maintain my Will." He hugged himself.

"What do you want from us?" asked Lake.

"Simply save your fellows. Stop the invaders. Gain more authority," answered Silaw. "Continue doing what you have been doing all this time, that is what I want. How you do this, what approaches you take, those are none of my concern. So long as the world survives, I am grateful."

Jella stepped closer. "What if we don't want to?" A few heads turned to her.

He shrugged. "I cannot control your actions. But do know that whatever you choose, invaders from other worlds will come. They will take our land, our source and our souls for their own benefit. Everyone here has the power to stop them. Candidates, even more so, as leaders of this war."

"Lands and source, I kinda understand what people use them for," Riley spoke up. "But souls?"

"Wills use souls as sustenance."

"What? You eat them?" she exclaimed.

"Wills can devour souls to grow, expand their abilities and develop the world. Wills who invade usually have an insatiable hunger. But do not worry about them for now. Unless they have conquered areas abundant in source and land, they will not be able to cross with their vessels."

Maxwell raised a hand. "How do I become a candidate?"

"Keri's selection has ended and she has chosen. No more candidates can be chosen by her."

"All right. When's the next selection? Sign me up on that one."

"The selection process only happens when the selector is in danger from multiple sources, including invaders, and there are not enough candidates present to help save the world," explained Silaw. "At this time, I believe we have enough candidates to stop the invaders. Followers would need to rally under the candidates, and having a lot of choices will limit the powers of each force. But just in case, if any of the candidates die, the Ferry can initiate a new round of selection."

Everyone turned to Jella whose face blanched from the attention.

Keri cleared her throat and questioned, "Why put a new soul and a video game in me? Couldn't you just heal me, without all of that?"

A weary expression shadowed Silaw for a second before he said, "A devoured soul usually has no way to recover. But yours was half-eaten, which made it possible for an added soul to help and restore you completely, but it was not without consequences."

The jumbled memories and weird dreams and hallucinations juggled in Keri's thoughts.

"When candidates are selected, a guide is usually created for them. This could be a spirit, a wisp or something similar," added Silaw. "This time, I made it into a game. I thought your love and familiarity with games would help you adapt more easily."

After a few moments, when everyone was deep in their thoughts, Lake said, "So these fragments, this power, it's up to us how to use it? No orders? No consequences? No catch?"

Silaw nodded. "Help the world. Extinguish the invaders. Or do something completely different. What you do with them is up to you, and your responsibility. This should help make your decision clearer."

Attention: Due to increased world stabilization and your increased authority level, a new update is now available.

System Update 2.0: Followers has been unlocked. Help Menu unlocked. Your profile will be shared to all non-allied souls belonging to this world. If they choose to ally themselves to you, they become your followers. Candidates gain benefits from the number of followers they have.

Please gather as many followers as you can.

For more details, visit the Help Menu.

"Followers..." read Keri from the screen.

"Hey, is the linko network broken or something?" asked one of the apes. "I got this weird update, and it isn't one of my games. Silaw System?"

Maxwell gaped. "Is this the same system you guys have been on the whole time?"

"This is pretty nifty. It looks simpler than I imagined it would be." Riley poked in the air as if something was there.

Silaw then addressed everyone on the floor. "I'm at my limit. I will rest until I am fully healed. Everyone, make good choices, your decisions will shape the future of this world. Until we meet again." The golden glow evaporated, leaving Charlie in a weakened, dizzy state. Vivian helped him to a couch.

After a beat and letting all that sink in, Keri asked, "Now what?"

Lake moved to her side. "For now, best we rest and rebuild. After that, we save the world."

She smiled. She knew Lake would always say the right thing for situations like these. Helping people came naturally to him.

"Would you like to help me, my dear Maiden?" He grinned and offered her his hand.

She grasped and held his hand tight. "Of course, my Hero. Any time."

Keri rubbed the callouses in his palm. "By the way, where are these from?" she asked just loud enough for the two of them to hear.

"Training, fixing mechs, sorcery—a bit of everything." Lake stared at his free hand fraught with callouses as well, while everyone else buzzed with their own chatter regarding Silaw and the system update.

I wonder how it feels like if he rubbed it on me. "How does it feel like when you mas—" She abruptly stopped herself, realizing what she was saying, turning beet red.

"What do you—oh." His ears reddened as well.

"Sorry. I was just thinking—no I wasn't really thinking right."

Lake shook his head. "No, don't apologize. Maybe, we could, try it on you?" he said hesitantly.

"Yes, please," Keri responded a second after she had heard him say.

"Coo-cool. Cool," he stuttered and looked away.

"Wanna do it now?"

THE END

ACKNOWLEDGEMENTS

To the one holding this book and having gone through it from cover to cover, I appreciate you picking this up and reading it all the way through. I hope I have entertained you and made your life just a bit better.

I dedicate this to my parents: to my dad, who has shown me hard work and determination; and to my mom, who patiently taught me words, tenses and how subjects and verbs need to agree, even though they sometimes don't.

I am thankful to my sister, Jennifer, for demonstrating that books and words aren't meant only for education, but for fun and entertainment.

I am grateful for Kyle, my love, who has been my steady rock through this entire journey. From supporting me on day one to loving me every day, I love and thank you.

To my loyal friends who have known and continuously supported me in this endeavor, I am forever grateful for your cheers and positivity. You know who you are.

To my draft readers: Isabelle Felix and Cielo Bellerose, for gushing and *lol-ing* in romantic and funny scenes, and being confused by illogical character dynamics, plot holes and inconsistencies, thank you.

To my editors: Tiffany Lee, Denver Murphy, Sam Sachs and Gabby D'Aloia, for your professionalism, honesty and care about the story and the characters within it, thank you.

To my cover designer Santiago Latorre, for your imagination and *mad skillz;* thank you.

And to YOU, I am beyond thankful for holding my hand through the ups, downs and everything in between. O.O

ABOUT THE AUTHOR

EmC Lorenzo lived his previous life as a mage, raining down fire on bandits and charming authority to do his bidding. Now in this life, he weaves enchanting tales and spells words for drama and comedy to conjure entertainment and delight from unsuspecting readers who like to read author bios.

To keep scientists, the government and creeps away, he cloaks himself as an Asian-Australian who loves to swim, lift weights and cooks feasts plenty enough for unwanted guests to glamour them into thinking he is a basic, normal person, just like anyone else.

*Discover his inner workings on emclorenzo.com

*Be enchanted and blindly follow him on socials: facebook.com/emclorenzo

AFTERWORD

I hope you enjoyed this novel. To ensure that you've received an authentic copy, I kindly ask that you make sure this book was purchased through Amazon [as the seller] or from authorized retail bookstores and platforms. Purchasing from third-party resellers may not guarantee the quality of the book you receive and doesn't contribute to my earnings. By choosing to buy through the recommended channels, you are supporting my ability to continue this series and create more new worlds and characters. I appreciate your understanding and support in fostering a thriving community of readers and writers.

For any feedback; or if you find any errors, including typos, spelling, inconsistencies and more, please email me(at)emclorenzo(dot)com. Please include the platform and device you're using, as well as the page and chapter. For physical copies printed via POD [print-on-demand], I do not have any influence over how the printers operate and print my books, but I can definitely reach out and send them your feedback.

As an indie novelist, I try to cover the gap and correct things as best as I can, but sometimes things fall through the cracks. By reaching out, this will help me in creating better works in the future.

Thank you!